"You're in the Shadowlands because I need your help."

"What if I don't want to help you? Why would I *ever* want to help you?"

"Because you don't really have a choice." He turned her around to face him then, apparently satisfied that she wouldn't take a swing until he gave her the word.

Solmir was handsome, a fact she hated twofold—hated that it was true and hated that she noticed.

And his eyes. They were blue. Blue in all this gray and black and white.

"I'm not going to attempt to justify myself to you." But the look in those blue eyes said he might want to. "I will simply tell you, with complete honesty, that everything I did on the surface was for a purpose."

"And that purpose was?"

A bladed smile without any warmth bent his mouth. "To kill the Kings."

Praise for
For the Wolf

"Whitten weaves a captivating tale in this debut...an un-put-down-able fairy tale that traces the boundaries of duty, love, and loss. A masterful debut from a must-read new voice in fantasy."

—*Kirkus* (starred review)

"This hauntingly beautiful, fractured retelling of Little Red Riding Hood is dark, emotional, and filled with tense action. Whitten's debut is epic and enthralling." —*Library Journal* (starred review)

"Whitten debuts with a dark, dazzling reimagining of 'Little Red Riding Hood.'...With clever, immersive prose and a subtle touch of horror, this is sure to enchant." —*Publishers Weekly* (starred review)

"Drenched in atmosphere, with sharp and biting prose, Whitten's *For the Wolf* is a glorious journey through woods deep and so very dark. A stunning debut."

—Erin A. Craig, *New York Times* bestselling author of *House of Salt and Sorrows*

"A brilliant dark-fantasy debut. I loved it! I was completely swept away by the worldbuilding, the characters, and the delicate gorgeousness of the writing."

—Jodi Picoult, *New York Times* bestselling author

"Atmospheric, folkloric, and half-familiar. If you ever wished 'Beauty and the Beast' had more eldritch forest monsters and political machinations, this is the romance for you."

—Alix E. Harrow, author of *The Ten Thousand Doors of January*

By Hannah Whitten

THE WILDERWOOD

For the Wolf
For the Throne

FOR
the
THRONE

Book Two of The Wilderwood

HANNAH
WHITTEN

orbit

orbitbooks.net

Copyright © 2022 by Hannah Whitten
Excerpt from *The Foxglove King* copyright © 2022 by Hannah Whitten
Excerpt from *One Dark Window* copyright © 2022 by Rachel Gillig

Cover design by Lisa Marie Pompilio
Cover illustrations by Arcangel and Shutterstock
Cover copyright © 2022 by Hachette Book Group, Inc.
Author photograph by Caleb Whitten

Orbit
Hachette Book Group
1290 Avenue of the Americas
New York, NY 10104
orbitbooks.net

First Edition: June 2022
Simultaneously published in Great Britain by Orbit

Orbit is an imprint of Hachette Book Group.
The Orbit name and logo are trademarks of Little, Brown Book Group Limited.

The publisher is not responsible for websites (or their content) that are not owned by the publisher.

The Hachette Speakers Bureau provides a wide range of authors for speaking events. To find out more, go to www.hachettespeakersbureau.com or call (866) 376-6591.

Library of Congress Cataloging-in-Publication Data
Names: Whitten, Hannah, author.
Title: For the throne / Hannah Whitten.
Description: First edition. | New York, NY : Orbit, 2022. | Series: The wilderwood ; book 2
Identifiers: LCCN 2021052029 | ISBN 9780316592819 (trade paperback) |
ISBN 9780316592826 (ebook) | ISBN 9780316592833 (ebook other)
Classification: LCC PS3623.H5864 F667 2021 | DDC 813/.6—dc23
LC record available at https://lccn.loc.gov/2021052029

ISBNs: 9780316592819 (trade paperback), 9780316592826 (ebook)

Printed in the United States of America

LSC-C

Printing 1, 2022

To anyone who grew thorns instead of flowers—
You had your reasons.

This thing of darkness I
Acknowledge mine.

—Shakespeare, *The Tempest* (5.1.275–276)

Add
a second light and you get a second darkness, it's only
fair.

—Richard Siken, "Portrait of Fryderyk
in Shifting Light"

mirror mirror

three years ago

S he couldn't sleep.

That wasn't so strange. Sleep had never come easily to Neve, not even in the cradle; apparently, it'd taken an elaborate bedtime ritual of stories and songs to get her infant self to slumber, the nursemaids taking turns in an endless cycle of walking and bouncing the tiny First Daughter before she was finally soothed to rest.

Not much had changed, really. Neve still had to wear her mind thin before it would accept respite, had to tie it up in knots until the threads wore out. It'd never really bothered her, as sleeping often seemed like a waste of time, hours that could be better spent working.

Like now.

Neve tapped her fingers on her comforter, filled with fine down from Ryltish geese and spun with soft fibers from Karseckan looms. Prayer-taxes put to use. She probably had one of the most comfortable beds in Valleyda, which seemed wasteful, with how little she used it lately.

Wasteful or not, sleep wasn't coming anytime soon. Muttering a curse, Neve pushed herself up.

The floor was cold, but she didn't bother finding slippers. There was a fireplace in the library that was never completely banked; she'd be warm enough.

A taper in a pewter stand and a book of matches waited on her bedside table. Neve struck the match, blooming sulfur-scent into the chilled air as she touched flame to wick. She nudged her door open quietly, careful to keep it from squeaking, and padded out into the corridor.

She passed a guard or two dozing at their posts, but if they saw her, they didn't speak. The First Daughter haunting the halls was nothing new. For a year now, she'd been sneaking out of her room at night, heading to the library. Finding every scrap of information she could about Wolves and woods and Second Daughters.

Her steps slowed the closer she got to Red's door, stalling a decision she didn't really have to make. Red used to join her on these nighttime excursions, as unable to sleep as Neve. But last year, after she turned sixteen, after...well, *after*, Red had stopped coming with Neve to the library. Stopped trying to find a way out of the awful bargain she'd been born into.

It made something that was almost anger burn in Neve's belly, Red's compliance. Her acceptance of the unacceptable. Maybe her twin really did think it was for the greater good, but in her darkest moments, Neve thought it was more like cowardice. If fate delivered you something awful, why would you decide you had to take it? What could ever make that decision fit comfortably in your mind?

So Neve kept going to the library, kept pulling from the shelves every book that so much as mentioned the Wolves or the Kings or prophecies or bargains and reading them cover to cover. Red might be willing to walk into the mouth of a monster, but Neve was going to find a way to make the monster choke.

She could fix this.

Despite knowing what the answer would be, she lingered a moment outside Red's door. Silence from within, silence in the hall, silence in the soft dark cut by moonlight through the window.

Neve sighed. She walked on.

The double doors to the library opened at her touch, the hinges well-oiled and gleaming. The Valleydan library was prized, something queens had added to over centuries, full of rare books and art—some

She hiccupped one sob, quiet against the shush of the fire, then pushed the emotions down. That, at least, she could control.

After a moment, she stood, leaning wearily against the table like an old woman, before heading to the door. She couldn't do this tonight, insomnia or no.

Neve was halfway to the door before a surge of rage eclipsed the gentler kind of anger that raised tears. She didn't think before she acted; she strode back to the table, grabbed the useless book, and threw it into the fire.

The leather popped and bubbled, filling the room with an acrid smell as the paper inside caught flame. The book flipped open, as if in a death throe, shrinking as the fire winnowed it away, turned it into so much smoke. The force of such rapid destruction made the pages flip. Neve caught the lines and arcs of half-eaten letters on the back cover—a *T*, an *N*, a *Y*.

She left before the book finished burning.

As she passed Red's room again, she looked to the window on the wall opposite and told herself it wasn't because she didn't want to see Red's closed door, didn't want to think about her sister sleeping behind it and how the clock was rapidly ticking down to a time when Red wouldn't be.

Most of the lights in the city were doused at such a late hour, and the sky spread above the streets in a swath of midnight blue, pocked with stars. It was clear enough to pick out constellations, and Neve stopped almost unconsciously, eyes tracing brilliant patterns.

The Sisters constellation was halfway over the horizon. One of the Sister shapes was visible, hand outstretched to the other still hidden behind the curve of the world.

The angle made it look as if she were reaching into the earth.

Chapter One

Neve

In the trees, something was moving.

Neve stopped running, slamming against a trunk hard enough to knock the breath from her lungs. She felt half mad and looked it, too—fleeing from a tower into a nightmare landscape, where trees grew upside down and everything was shades of black and white and gray.

Shadowlands. The prison of monsters, the prison of gods. An underworld, a half world, darkness anchored beneath the Wilderwood.

It made a twisting sort of sense. One had consumed Red, so the other consumed Neve.

Minutes ago, she'd woken in a glass coffin, woken with her veins inked black and her mind muddied. And *he'd* been there. And Neve hadn't thought, hadn't spared a second for niceties or explanations. She'd pushed up out of that coffin, and she'd run.

Now, of course, she was slightly regretting it.

She tried to calm her breathing, soften its rattle, panic closing in as she eyed the thing in the forest—*can you still call it a forest if the trees are upside down?*—ahead of her. It was too large to see in its entirety, shifts of gray against the white trunks, just enough to give the impression of slow, ponderous movement.

Her heartbeat was almost calming to a regular pace when a hand closed around her arm, heralding a harsh whisper in her ear.

"And where," Solmir murmured, "do you think you're going, Neverah?"

Instinct had her elbow shooting back, aiming for some soft part of him—assuming he had any; the body pressed against her was all slender hard angles and sharp planes, a man built like a knife. Still, her elbow elicited a quick grunt, though it was more of surprise than pain, and that was bolstering enough for her to kick out with her foot, trying to stomp on his heel.

"On every soulless Old One, you're *barefoot*." He sounded more exasperated than anything, still speaking in that close whisper right at the shell of her ear. "Do you really think you're going to—"

He cut himself off with another grunt as Neve's fist drove into his hip bone.

It hurt her as much as it sounded like it hurt him, and Neve's lips peeled back from her teeth with a hoarse, angry cry. It wasn't loud, but in the strange silence of this place, it echoed.

Solmir froze, eyes darting from her to the creature in the forest, still moving slow and sinuous through the trees. Then his hand clapped over her mouth.

Neve writhed against his hold—she'd rather take her chances with the thing in the inverted trees than be so close to him. He solved the issue of her clawing hands by wrapping another arm around her waist, trapping her elbows against her ribs and the small of her back flush to his hips. "Listen," he murmured in her ear, and damn him, it sounded like he was trying to be soothing. "I know you hate me. That's fine. But I promise you will hate what that thing does to you more."

Her lips moved vainly against his palm, and Neve had half a thought to bite him, to tell him that there was nothing in this world or the one she'd just left that she hated more than him at that moment. But then the thing in the trees turned, enough for her to see its face.

Face might not be the most accurate thing to call it. Really, it was just a mouth. A mouth with rings on rings of teeth, razor-sharp and as long as she was tall.

Neve made a small sound behind Solmir's hand. She stopped struggling.

The toothed thing in the trees breathed, and the stink of it washed over Neve like a wave, carrion-thick and fever-hot, heightened by the cold of the air. Solmir pulled her tighter against him, arm a vise around her middle. They stood still, and waited.

After what seemed like an age, the thing turned, that awful mouth facing away from them again. It resumed its slow meander through the inverted trees.

A heartbeat, then Solmir let her go.

Neve rounded on him, a snarl on her mouth and fingers curled into fists. She raised one of them, but he was faster. Solmir's hand closed around hers in midair, stopping it before it reached his jaw.

"Come now, Neverah," he said, the ghost of a hateful smile on his lips. "All those lessons in diplomacy, and you won't even hear me out?"

"Diplomacy is for honorable men." Their linked hands shook in the air, oppositional forces. "It doesn't apply here."

"Fair enough." A quick twist of his hand, and her arm was pinned behind her, between her body and the hard plane of his. "Then we'll do this the undiplomatic way. I think you secretly like that better, anyway. You seem to jump at any excuse for violence."

She jerked against him. He laughed, dark and humorless. "Tell you what, little queen. I say my piece, and then you're welcome to hit me. As hard as you want. Anywhere you want." There was an edge to his voice, something she couldn't quite identify. Rueful and angry, a low burn of ferocity like a banked fire. "Do we have a deal?"

It wasn't like she had many other options. "Fine," Neve said. "Talk."

He relaxed behind her, slightly, though his hold on her arm remained unyielding. He wore silver rings on almost all of his fingers, and they bit into her skin, spots of deeper cold in a cold world. "You're in the Shadowlands."

"I gathered," she replied, trying to let fierceness carve out any fear in her tone.

"Smart woman." He adjusted his hold, silver chilling the fragile length of her forearm. "You're in the Shadowlands," he continued, "because I need your help."

"What if I don't want to help you? Why would I *ever* want to help you?"

"Because you don't really have a choice." He turned her around to face him then, apparently satisfied that she wouldn't take a swing until he gave her the word.

Solmir was handsome, a fact she hated twofold—hated that it was true and hated that she noticed. Long, straight hair spilled over his shoulders, almost to his elbows. She didn't know its color, since the monotone of the Shadowlands washed it out, but it looked a middling gray, like it'd be somewhere between gold and brown in a place with color. Dark brows slashed like dagger strikes on a high forehead; his nose was straight and prominent over a thin mouth with a wicked curve. Considerably tall, so that when he peered down at her, he looked almost like a bird of prey eyeing something caught in a trap.

And his eyes. They were blue. Blue in all this gray and black and white.

"I'm not going to attempt to justify myself to you." But the look in those blue eyes said he might want to. "I will simply tell you, with complete honesty, that everything I did on the surface was for a purpose."

"And that purpose was?"

A bladed smile without any warmth bent his mouth. "To kill the Kings."

Neve was very good at keeping her emotions off her face and out of her limbs, playacting impassivity, so she stood statue-still as confusion and the stomach swoop of blasphemy churned in her mind, attempting to take this piece and fit it somewhere that made sense.

"You," she said finally, "are going to have to explain more than that."

"Come on, Neverah." He shook his head, all that hair swinging to brush her chest. "You didn't think they were something *good*, did you? I know you didn't. I saw how you never wanted to touch that branch shard. All of this was for your sister, never because of some misguided piety."

"Do *not* talk about my sister."

Queenly, an order, and his eyes briefly widened. "Understood, Your Majesty."

Inexplicably, the title brought heat to her face. Neve wrenched her arm from his hold, though she didn't try to hit him. Yet. "So you want to kill the Kings. Is that why you tried to bring them through?"

Solmir nodded, a solemnity that sat strangely against the mocking way he'd spoken to her.

A terrible, twisted grove, blood on white branches, darkness dripping. Her memories of what happened before she woke here were scattered, hard to gather, hard to meld into a whole picture. But she knew, deep in her bones where cold magic twined, that before she'd been pulled into the Shadowlands, Kiri and Solmir and the other priestesses had been making a doorway between the worlds. Using *her* to make a doorway. Anchoring her to the inverse of the forest that anchored Red, making them dark mirrors of each other.

Red. Shadows damn her, she couldn't think about Red right now.

Neve swallowed, banishing the itch of grief that hung in the back of her throat. "You're just going to try to kill the Kings here instead, then?"

"I'd love to. But I can't." That cold smile again, all angles. "Nothing can truly die in the Shadowlands, I'm afraid."

The fact itself might've been comforting were it not for the way he delivered it. As both a challenge and the winning card in a hand, eyes glittering and mouth a harsh line.

But Neve didn't have much of a chance to ponder it.

The inverted trees whipped from side to side, the spindly roots stretching into the cold sky and waving like skeletal fingers. A sound like tearing metal echoed through the gray, and with a crash, the long-bodied monster shot out from the forest, toothed mouth gnashing at the air and coming straight toward them.

"Dammit," Solmir muttered, and thrust Neve aside.

She stumbled over dry ground and tangling branches, landing on her knees and away from the careening teeth. She still wore a white nightgown, flimsy against the cold and the press of rough bark. Had she known she'd be journeying to the underworld, she would've chosen her attire with more care.

The ridiculous thought, something that belonged to her life as a First Daughter rather than a queen and a heretic, was enough to loose a horrible, barking laugh.

Before her, Solmir stood in the path of that huge mouth, his own teeth bared in the rictus of a smile. He'd been wearing a coat before, dark and almost military-like, but now he'd thrown it to the side, pushed up the sleeves of the thin white shirt beneath. Black lines ran down his arms, like ink cascading from his heart instead of blood. Darkness pooled in his hands, blackening his fingers, his wrists. A thin line of ice shone across his knuckles.

The gnashing mouth of the wormlike monster was so close Neve could feel its breath.

Then Solmir opened his outstretched fists.

The darkness in his hands shot into the air, growing jagged and thorny, like he'd woven a net of brambles in his bloodstream and now cast it out. It fell on the monster, cutting into its gore-caked flesh, contracting around its body, and making it bellow.

But still the thing kept coming.

Fear was an unnatural emotion to see on Solmir; the angles of his face couldn't carry it well. His blue eyes widened, and his cruel mouth opened, but he allowed himself only a heartbeat of shock before he thrust his hands out again, trying to call up more shadows. The ink that crawled slowly down his skin wasn't quite as dark as before, more gray than black.

Magic, growing thin, running out. Neve still wasn't exactly sure of its mechanics, the cold thing that her blood on a sentinel shard had called into her bones—only that it was tied to this place, the inverse of Red's green and growing power. But she knew it still lived in her, chilled and thorned, made even more potent by the doorway they'd tried to open, the way they'd anchored her to that awful grove.

And she knew she didn't want to be eaten by a monster with that many teeth.

Unthinking, Neve followed the same pattern Solmir had. Her hands thrust out, and without her trying, darkness flowed down her veins, her fingers bending into fists as it gathered in her palms. It felt like winter, like biting wind, making her center so cold it was almost burning.

The burning cold went down her arms, settled in her hands, and when it was too much to bear, her fists opened.

Her own net of spiny magic snared the worm-thing right as its jaws came close enough to touch.

The effect was immediate. Where Solmir's thorns had seemed only to slow the thing down, Neve's stopped it cold. It writhed, shrieking into the gray sky, growing smaller as it withered away from the places where Neve's magic touched it. Curls of shadow spilled off its body, clouding the air, making a sort of chittering noise that was a strange, smaller echo of the worm-monster's bellows. A crack, another burst of gibbering shadow, and the thing was gone.

The shadows that were left raced into the forest, and Solmir grimaced after them, raising a hand and then letting it fall. "Shit," he muttered. "Well. We can get them next time. The power of a few shadow-creatures won't make much of a difference."

Neve stared wide-eyed at the space where the monster had been, her chest heaving beneath her nightgown as the darkness slowly faded from her veins. She was cold, so cold all over, water dripping from one palm where a thin scrim of ice had covered it. "I thought you said nothing could die here?"

"Did you see all those shadows?" He arched a brow, cool and collected, as if they hadn't just thrown magic at a giant worm that apparently wanted to eat them. "Those were scraps of the lesser beast. Its energy transmuted. Anything that appears to die here isn't gone, it just changes form."

Her mouth opened to question him further, to make a snide remark about how maybe if she threw magic at *him*, he'd change into a form that would be less irritating. But the white-hot flash of pain in her head cleared her mouth of anything but a moan.

Knees in the dirt, hands at her temples. Neve felt simultaneously as if she were being compacted down and flying apart, her body both crushed and expanded. Pain flared in her head, her stomach, along her nerve endings, cold like she'd never felt before settling into her middle with a throbbing ache.

Distantly, she heard Solmir curse again, felt hands press into the sides of her face, not gently. Her vision was blurry, but she saw the flash of black in her veins, something sharp pressing against her skin with every pulse.

"Dammit, woman," Solmir snarled. "You can't fade on me yet."

He settled into a crouch before her. "Down here, magic has a price, Neverah." He said it so calmly, but his fingers were tight on her temples, like he was trying to anchor her, keep her from dissolving. "On the surface, the Shadowlands' hold was weak because its magic was weak. But when you use its power here, this place hooks in you. Becomes part of you. And you can't handle that. This was a prison made for gods and monsters, and you are neither."

Gods and monsters. Which one was he, then?

"I can fix it." There was no softness in his pronouncement. It was all claw and tooth. "I can give you another anchor, something to pull power from that isn't the Shadowlands themselves."

She looked up at him, lips peeling back, speaking through the muddle of pain. "You killed Arick. You almost killed my sister. You *used* me." A shudder, a rip of thorns in her veins. "I don't want anything you're offering."

His hand closed around her arm, fingers long and elegant, the silver rings on them burning as he pulled her up. His face was all sharpness, knife-slash brows over those infernally blue eyes and a snarl on his mouth to match hers.

"I'm not offering," Solmir said.

He sealed his lips to hers in a bruising kiss.

Shock made her still, but Neve was aware enough to realize that this wasn't an embrace like any she'd been in before. It was more battle than kiss—she could feel his teeth behind his lips, the press of his mouth as good as a sword.

And as he kissed her, cruelly, something within Neve... shifted.

The pain of thorns tearing through her veins receded, shrank to a prick, then merely a sting. The pounding in her head lessened by slow degrees, leaching away the longer her lips stayed on Solmir's, the contact pulling magic out of her like tugging on the end of a coiled string. The emptying was both welcome and devastating, pain and power receding in equal measure. Her body felt more grounded as it went, more *her*.

Fragile and human, controlling nothing.

Solmir broke their not-kiss, but his arms still encircled her, holding her up in case she collapsed. He smelled like pine needles and snow, far reaches and open sky.

The look in his eyes reminded her too much of those months when he'd pretended to be Arick. When he'd played at kindness, at—

She shoved away from him, the heel of her hand striking against his chest. "What did you do to me?"

"I gave you a new anchor. Tied your power to me instead of to the Shadowlands. From now on, you want magic, you get it from me first. I'm your *vessel*." He caught her flailing hands, his face impassive, holding her still. "Our deal was one hit, Neverah, and you've already landed two."

They froze like that, his hands shackled around her wrists, her face anger-warped and tear-streaked.

His expression could've been mistaken for impassive from far away. But there were scant inches between her and the fallen King, and Neve could see the burn of regret and fury and something like sorrow in his blue eyes. Slowly, he let go of her, bent to pick up his discarded coat and tug it over his well-muscled shoulders. "I did what I had to do."

We do what we have to do.

Neve wrapped her arms around her middle, thinking again of how he'd been back on the surface. He'd acted like he cared for her, and she'd been stupid enough to believe it. It had been a ploy—she knew that now. A way to gain her trust. She wanted to ask him about it, ask him why he hadn't just been content to wear Arick's face, why he'd had to make it something so wounding. The only people who'd cared for her then had been Raffe and Arick, and to know that Arick's caring hadn't been real—hadn't been *Arick*—bored a hole through her.

"You killed Arick," she growled. "You don't get to use his words."

"They were never his." Solmir's eyes glittered. "They were mine."

It was an opening. Almost an invitation to ask, to find out what he'd meant by his kindness, his care. Neve didn't take it. She didn't want to know.

She swallowed against a barbed throat. "Is my sister alive?" She had a vague memory of seeing Red through smoky glass, but it wasn't enough to trust, and she needed to hear it from his mouth. "If she's not, I will kill you—truly kill you, not make you fly apart into magic smoke. And if I have to drag your ass to the surface to do it, I will."

"She's alive." He gave her a tiny nod. "We'll need her, I think, if this is going to work."

Neve's brow furrowed. "If what is going to work?"

"Killing the Kings, of course." A jagged grin curved Solmir's mouth. He turned, ambling back through the trees in the direction she'd run from, as if confident she would follow. "Funnily enough, dragging asses to the surface is exactly what we're going to do."

⊱⊰⊱⊰⊱⊰⊱⊰

All in all, she hadn't run very far. The tower loomed just beyond a thin lacing of inverted trees, visible through their leafless branches.

Though *branch* wasn't exactly the right term. The trees grew upside down, the thick boughs cutting through gray, dry dirt, making ridges tall enough to knock shins. Above her head, roots spread in the colorless air, spindly and still, stretching up as far as she could see before disappearing into mist.

A forest in a mirror, the grove they'd grown in the Shrine expanded, magnified.

Beyond the trees, however, was a barren gray waste that stretched for miles, unbroken by any tree, upside down or otherwise. The tower she'd woken up in pointed skyward in the desolate expanse, weathered brick wreathed in climbing black thorns. Solmir headed toward the doorway, nonchalant, as if they'd taken a morning constitutional and were headed in for a leisurely breakfast.

"How exactly do you plan to drag asses to the surface, then?" Neve crossed her arms against a shiver, the cold of this place sinking into her skin. "You failed to bring the Kings through once, so now you're just going to try again? Are you dull-witted as well as evil?"

Not one of her better insults, granted, but she'd just awoken in the underwold and escaped a monster; one couldn't really expect cleverness right now.

Solmir gave her an arch look as he pushed the door open, standing to the side and gesturing grandly for her to enter. Her fingers worked into fists at her sides as she did, pressing close to the other end of the threshold. Her skin remembered his, and it made her want to claw it off.

"Extremely dull-witted," he said as she passed. "And extremely evil."

Neve held her spine as straight as she possibly could.

In the distance, something rumbled. The earth shook, the stone floor of the tower trembling beneath her feet. Neve's hand shot out to steady herself against the wall, miraculously avoiding the thorns that lined the stairs.

Solmir's hand closed around her arm again, hauling her backward before positioning her across from him in the doorway. Her nose almost notched into the gap of his collarbone.

"Safest place in an earthquake," he said through clenched teeth, blue eyes scanning the horizon instead of looking at her. "Doorways. Remember that—it might come in handy."

The ground rumbled once more, then settled, grew still. Neve clutched the doorframe behind her with white-knuckled hands. "Does that happen often?"

"More often now." He turned from her, started up the stairs. "The Shadowlands are shaking apart. Growing more unstable." He snorted. "At least there's not much to hold back, not anymore. There's barely any

lesser beasts left, and only four Old Ones." A pause. "Maybe three, actually. I need to ask the Seamstress."

"You realize I don't understand anything you just said."

He gave her a razor grin that didn't reach his eyes. "Who's dull-
witted now?"

A shiver kept her from giving a biting answer, the cold of the Shadowlands cutting through her nightgown. Neve tried her best to hide it,
but Solmir noticed, mouth softening to be almost pensive. He shrugged
out of his coat.

Her head was shaking before he had his arms completely free of it. "I
don't want—"

"Yes, I know, you don't want anything I'm offering. Too bad. Take
the damn coat."

After a moment's hesitation, she did. It was warm from where he'd
worn it. Neve tried not to cringe away from the fabric.

A pause, then Solmir sighed. "I'm not exactly thrilled that you're
here, either, Neverah. This wasn't what I wanted."

"No, what you wanted was the Kings on the surface and my sister
dead."

"Not quite." It came through clenched teeth, as if he was trying very
hard not to give her the fight she was trying to push him into. "I told you
want I wanted. The Kings destroyed."

To show emotion was to show her hand, and Neve had given him
too much vulnerability already. He didn't deserve it, and she didn't have
much to spare. So she drew herself up, fought the way her face wanted to
twist to anger. Donned the mask again, and if he could see through it, at
least she was trying. "You expect me to believe that?"

"Again, you don't have much of a choice. I might be a liar, and a
murderer, and a whole host of other unsavory things, but I am also the
only thing in this whole underworld that gives a fraction of a care about
you." His bared teeth gleamed. "We want the same things, you and I. I
know you hate that."

He stood too close. She wanted to back away from him, but it would be a capitulation, and Neve refused to let him think he'd won anything. She narrowed her eyes. "Presumptuous of you."

"You want an end. And there were only ever two ways for this to end. Either the Kings are destroyed, soul and what's left of body, or they escape the Shadowlands when it finally dissolves." There were scars scored across his forehead, the most painful-looking on both his temples, lessening in severity in the center. He lifted his hand, rubbed them absently. "Believe it or not, I *did* try to take the easiest route for all of us, when I went to the surface."

"When you manipulated Arick." Nothing in his frame seemed penitent, and she probably couldn't change that, but Neve wouldn't let him hide behind half confessions. "When you manipulated *me*."

"You didn't have to be manipulated all that much, Your Majesty." His blue eyes burned in the dim gray light. "You barely needed a nudge."

She swallowed the taste of her pulse. Refused to duck her chin, refused to avert her gaze.

Solmir was the first to break eye contact, though the casual way he did made it feel less like a victory than Neve wanted. Another rub at his forehead, then his hand dropped, resting on the hilt of a dagger at his side. "I could've accomplished what I needed, what we *all* needed— really, Neverah, you should thank me—but your sister had to go and complicate things." A pause. "I should've expected that, I suppose. Fate is a bitch."

Her mouth opened to once again tell him to keep mentions of Red out of his mouth, but another quake came before she could.

Neve pitched sideways, slamming her knees onto the stairs, though this quake was minor compared to the first. Solmir didn't make for the doorway, instead bracing in a crouch with practiced fluidity. How long had this world been shaking apart, for him to look nearly used to it?

When the earth was still again, Solmir straightened, turning to walk up the stairs toward the circular room where she'd awoken. "You've probably put together that time is short," he called over his shoulder. "So I'd suggest you keep up."

Chapter Two

Red

The forest gave her dreams sometimes.

It made sense. To house magic as fully as she did, one had to expect that it would leave marks inside as well as out, carve golden grooves into her thoughts as surely as it haloed her eyes green and threaded ivy through her hair. No less unsettling, but a fairly mild side effect, all things considered.

It'd started right after she became the Wilderwood. Right after Neve was dragged down into the earth. Dreams that left golden afterimages, dreams that felt more real than the firings of her weary thoughts before finally trailing into sleep. The dreams were fairly simple, didn't last long. A mirror with no reflection. Stars wheeling in the sky, coming together to almost make the shapes of words, then spangling apart before she could read them.

But this was the most solid dream the Wilderwood had given Red yet: a tree. A white-trunked sentinel in a sea of mist, mist that obscured whatever the rest of the landscape might be. It started as a sapling, then grew—slowly, in the way of dreams, then immediately. Shooting up, spreading branches above her head, veined in swirling lines of gold and black.

Then, an apple in her hand. Warm and golden, heavier than an apple should be. She raised it to her lips, bit down. The taste of blood, and a horrible pain in her chest, as if she'd somehow torn out and eaten a vital part of herself.

Red's eyes opened, her middle twisting, copper flooding her mouth. Her heart beat fast against the base of her throat, spiderwebbing her veins in verdant green, then ebbed to a slower rhythm as she remembered where she was.

The Black Keep. With the Wolf.

A slight breeze blew through the open windows of their bedroom, carrying with it the scent of leaves and dirt and cinnamon, wafting eternal autumn. Dim morning light filtered over the bed, burnishing Eammon's dark hair in gold, highlighting the scars on his bare shoulders, bare abdomen.

She smiled to see them, banishing vestiges of bloody dreams as she burrowed into his side and traced one of the three white lines on his stomach with her finger. They'd rattled the forest back into linear time and out of endless twilight, and never was she so thankful for it as in the mornings. The Wolf looked very good in gray, early light.

Her trailing hand brushed the scars, his hipbone. Lower. He shifted, chin tilting up with a low, contented sigh when her fingers closed around him, but didn't wake.

Red grinned wickedly, replaced her hand with her mouth.

That was enough to wake him up. Eammon's eyes opened, amber ringed with a corona of deep green, immediately molten. One scarred hand slid into her hair. "Good morning."

"Very good morning," Red murmured against him before rising up to straddle his hips.

After, when her thoughts were no longer hazed and blazing and she was dressing for the day, Red thought back to her dream. This one felt different. Weighty, somehow.

Everything felt weighty recently, though. A week since the shadow grove, since the earth opened, since they thwarted Solmir's plan to bring the rest of the Kings to the other side and she and Eammon had become the Wilderwood entire, held in two bodies, two souls.

A week with no sign of Neve.

A week with no idea where to even start *looking*. The mirror in the tower showed her nothing, hadn't since she looked in it that last time and seen the Shadowlands, before they went to the edge of the forest and found it shattered. The forest buried in her bones gave her no clues, quiet now that it had its anchors, no longer speaking through dearly bought words but settled alongside her mind like moss on a stone. The forest outside of her, empty now of sentinels and sentience but still magic-touched, was nothing but autumn and gold.

Red was the most powerful she'd ever been. And she felt helpless.

The rough familiarity of Eammon's hands on the nape of her neck brought her mind back to the present. Lost in thought, she'd paused in the braiding of her hair, and he gathered it in his palms, picking up where she left off. "Something new troubling you?" His voice was low and morning-graveled. "Or the same?"

"The same," she murmured.

A soft noise of affirmation. The braid he made was lumpy, but he tied it off tight, gave it a slight tug so her neck craned up to see him behind her. He dropped a kiss on her forehead. "Maybe Raffe will have something new to tell Fife."

She sighed, leaning farther so the back of her head rested against the plane of Eammon's stomach. "Maybe." This would be the second time Fife had gone to the Valleydan capital, no longer constrained by the boundaries of the Wilderwood, though still bound in different ways—by the bargain he'd made for Lyra's life, in those few minutes when Eammon wasn't really Eammon but eclipsed by magic and forest. He met with Raffe in a tavern, the latter wearing the most nondescript clothes he could find, and they tried to figure out ways they might use the things at Raffe's disposal to find Neve.

Well. At his disposal for now. Before anyone figured out that the Queen was not actually recuperating from illness in a Florish holding, that her betrothed was not visiting Alpera, and that the High Priestess was not attending him.

If and when those things came to light, Raffe's use of the palace library and close watch over the Shrine might not be so easy.

Thus far, Valleyda's isolation had worked in their favor. The very things that made them notable made them undesirable as a territory to conquer—the Wilderwood on the northern border, the Second Daughter tithe, the poor soil and climate that never let warmth last long. And though two of those things were no longer deterrents, news traveled slowly, especially as the weather turned colder and courtiers holed up at home or abroad in preparation for the coming winter.

If they moved quietly, quickly, there'd never be any reason for the nobles to know Neve was gone. Red was too busy trying to bring her sister back from the underworld to fight over her throne, too.

She had half a mind to let it go, if it came to that. What good had a throne done either of them? Red certainly didn't want it.

Her eyes fluttered closed as she leaned back against Eammon, breathing in his library smell. Still the same, though the scent of leaves was more prominent now. "I had a dream. One from the Wilderwood." She opened one eye to peer up at him. "Did you?"

His hand strayed to her hair, tucking flyaway pieces behind her ears as his brows drew down and he thought back over the sleep she'd interrupted. "Not that I can recall, no." A flicker of heat in his eyes. "Though I did wake up rather compromised, so my memory is not as sharp as it could be."

Her lips twisted as she poked him hard in the stomach. She'd told him about the forest dreams when they first started happening. They happened to him, too—the quick flashes of image and feeling, too brief to make much sense of. Usually, if Red had a forest dream, so did Eammon, the thread of magic that twined through them both igniting in sync.

But this one, apparently, had been only for her. Red frowned. "It was stranger than the others. Longer. There was a tree. A sentinel. And an apple. When I took a bite out of it, it was bloody."

Eammon's hand stilled. Mentions of blood still made him tense, even now that the forest didn't require it of him anymore. Lyra teasingly called him squeamish, but it was with a sympathetic light in her eyes. The Wolf had faced enough blood for several lifetimes.

The momentary stiffness passed, his thumb tracing her jaw before his hand fell away. "Do you think it means something? The dreams the Wilderwood gives us generally don't, at least for me, but if you think it did…"

"It could." Red sighed. "Or it could mean that the spices Lyra brought us last night did a number on my head."

He snorted. "I'll check the library. See if there's anything that sounds similar in the histories, just to make sure. Mentions of bloody apples should be few and fairly specific, I'd think."

"I'll help after I see Fife off. I have a letter for Raffe."

"Another one?"

She shrugged, picking at a loose thread on the hem of her tunic. "If I was in his position, I'd want to know absolutely everything we were trying. If it was you that was lost."

The Wolf gave a low rumble of assent.

Red's fingers tapped against her leg, apprehensive. "If Raffe doesn't have anything new," she said finally, "we should talk about what to do next."

She didn't look up, but she heard the hitch in Eammon's sigh. It skirted close to a not-quite-argument, one that had been hanging in the air around them for days. They were searching two libraries and had come up with nothing so far to help them find Neve. Red's patience, a worn-thin thing to begin with, was nearly frayed through. Who knew what Neve was enduring while they wasted time with old books and caution?

The atmosphere crackled, waiting. Finally, Eammon nodded. "We'll talk about it," he said. Then he dropped another kiss on her forehead and disappeared down the stairs.

Red stood, stretching her arms above her head to work out the last of her morning stiffness. Delicious smells already wafted up from the kitchen—Lyra had arrived the night before after a brief jaunt south, the first of many trips around the continent she planned to take now that she was no longer beholden to the Wilderwood. Fife had gone all out for dinner the night before, and apparently he'd done the same for breakfast this morning.

The letter to Raffe sat on the desk, just one page, folded small. Red looked at it with her bottom lip between her teeth. There was more in it than just a relating of their lack of progress. A few lines scribbled at the end. Arick's birthday was soon. Raffe would remember without her reminding him, but Red felt she should mention it anyway. Proof that she remembered, too.

Grief for Arick was a strange thing, probably the strangest she'd felt in all of her uncanny sadnesses. She wasn't sorry she killed him; of all the strange emotions he stirred up, guilt wasn't one. She would've done much worse to save Eammon, to save Neve. Arick had made his choice when he called up Solmir, gave him his shadow and his life.

But she was still sorry he was gone.

Her mouth pressed to a thin, hard line as she picked up the letter and slipped it into her pocket. The next time she saw Solmir, she was going to kill him. Much more slowly than she'd killed Arick.

She walked down the stairs, thoughts turning from Arick and Solmir to closer concerns as she listened to Fife's and Lyra's voices in the dining room. Eammon had told Fife he could go with Lyra on her treks around the continent if he wanted; now that he and Red were the Wilderwood, and there was no real border to bind him into, it stood to reason he could travel as far and wide as she did. But Fife hadn't tried, going only as far as the Valleydan capital to meet with Raffe. Red wasn't sure what held him back, and she didn't feel comfortable asking, not when everything was still new, still raw. Not when none of them quite understood what Fife had gotten himself into when he bargained with the god Eammon had briefly become.

The new bargain he'd made with the Wilderwood—with Eammon—was different. She could feel it in the forest she carried, though she wasn't certain how. The Wilderwood had needed something from Fife that wasn't blood, wasn't fealty. The Mark on his arm was larger and more intricate than it'd been before, a tangle of roots beneath the skin that spanned nearly from his elbow to the middle of his forearm. The forest asked nothing of him; there were no shadow-creatures or breaches to throw blood at, hoping it might seal them closed.

Even in that thread of congruent forest-thought that ran parallel to her own, so close she could barely differentiate it, Red could discern nothing of what Fife's new bargain was supposed to mean.

It made them nervous, all three of them. Made them move cautiously around each other. And if that was painful for Red, she couldn't imagine how it must be for Fife and Eammon, who'd spent so long together in a small world of their own.

When she arrived in the dining room, Lyra was already seated, a steaming cup of coffee in her hand and a smile on her elfin face. Time in the sun outside of the forest had lightened the tips of her tightly coiled black hair, giving it a coppery shimmer. She raised her chipped mug in salute as Red walked through the door. "Are you actually going to sit and eat, or will you go the way of your husband and steal a slice of toast with barely a hello?"

"I'll sit." Red slid into her chair and took the cup Lyra offered, giving her a thankful grin when she saw the other woman had already doused her coffee with cream. "This smells far better than usual."

"Did you know coffee doesn't have to taste like limp bean water? I learned this when I took a detour into Meducia. They know their way around a beverage, between the wine and the coffee."

"I'm choosing not to be offended." Fife emerged from the kitchen, carrying what looked like a whole ham and setting it down next to the toast. "I'm choosing not to comment on the fact that you called my coffee *limp bean water.*"

Lyra wrinkled her nose and patted his reddish hair. "The very best limp bean water."

Fife smiled at her. It was the first true smile Red had seen from him in a week. He wore his long sleeves pulled down, hiding his Bargainer's Mark, and when Lyra turned back to her breakfast, he fiddled with the cuff, making sure it was still at his wrist.

He must've felt her watching. Hazel eyes slid to Red's; Fife gave a slight, rueful shrug.

So he hadn't told Lyra about the new bargain, hadn't shown her the new Mark. He needed to, and soon—Lyra remembered enough of their battle with Solmir at the inverted grove to know she'd been badly hurt. Eventually, she'd figure out what it was that saved her.

The three of them ate in companionable silence, Fife next to Lyra and Red across from them. Meals were a much more intricate affair now that they weren't limited to supplies only from the Edge. The villagers beyond the forest were still preparing for their great migration south—delayed by the currently quiet chaos in Valleyda—but Valdrek and Lear had already gone to the capital to scope out the new world they'd be returning to.

If they could find Neve—*when we find Neve*, Red thought to herself almost savagely, fingers tightening around her mug—Red knew she would help with the villagers' resettlement. But for now, with Raffe secretly holding things together in Valleyda by willpower alone, it didn't seem wise to try to move a whole tiny country from behind the Wilderwood. Those at the Edge agreed, and many of them were content to stay where they were, anyway. Now that the way through the forest was open and they could feasibly trade with the rest of the world, the land beyond the Wilderwood no longer seemed like a prison.

"Do you care to give this to Raffe when you see him?" Red asked, fishing the letter from her pocket.

Fife took it, cocking a brow when he felt how thin it was. "Anything new to report?"

"No." She sighed. "But he'd want to know that. No news is bad news."

Lyra picked up another piece of toast. "I thought it was 'no news is good news.'"

"We'll just leave it at 'no news is going to make Raffe more nervous than he already is.'"

Other than the brief reminder of Arick's birthday, the letter truly wasn't much—just a reiteration that although Red offered to the mirror every day, it still showed her nothing of her sister. Telling him, again, that she and Eammon were looking for any possible way to open the Shadowlands and pull Neve out.

Well. Any *safe* possible way.

Before they'd become the Wilderwood, there'd been countless accidental doors into the Shadowlands. The breaches, the churned black dirt around falling sentinels that birthed shadow-creatures and the lesser beast they'd fought after the first time he took her to the Edge. And that, Red thought, could be the answer they were looking for.

What if there was a way to re-create a doorway to the Shadowlands? To somehow free a sentinel from within one of them, like a loose tooth, plant it back in the ground and let its distance from them rot it just enough to open a way between the worlds?

She'd mentioned the idea to Eammon only once. He'd responded poorly. *Furious* would be more accurate, really, Eammon fire-eyed and low-voiced, looming over her like something avenging, asking her what the *fuck* she thought she was doing.

She hadn't realized until right then that it was the same way his mother had died. Gaya had attempted to open the Shadowlands and pull Solmir out, and the Wilderwood had consumed her for it, desperate to stop its own wounding.

It had to be different, this time. They held all of the forest between them, none of it attached to the earth anymore. Surely that meant it wouldn't riot, that it would understand? But Eammon was adamant and clearly terrified, so Red dropped the subject.

But the idea wouldn't leave her alone.

And her letter to Raffe *was* thin.

· "Wait a minute, Fife." Red stood, searching in her pockets for a pen—she'd taken to carrying one all the time, since Eammon was always in need of something to write with. Usually, there was a pen behind his ear, but Red preferred to let him borrow one from her and then figure that out on his own. "I have something to add."

Maybe the dream would serve as a comfort to Raffe, somehow, since there was nothing else new to report. And the library in Valleyda was vast—if she and Eammon couldn't find anything significant, it was possible he could.

She scribbled out the bare bones of the dream at the end of the letter, blowing on the ink to quicken its drying, and handed it back to Fife. "Tell him to write back if he has questions."

Fife nodded, tucking the letter into his jacket pocket. "Want to come?" he asked Lyra, not quite able to make it nonchalant. "Raffe always buys and puts me up in one of the nicer inns for the night."

"Sure." One more bite of toast, and Lyra stood, stretching her arms over her head. She'd bought new clothes in Valleyda, a gown the color of ice that perfectly contrasted her golden-brown skin, but she still wore her *tor* across her back. The pairing made her look fierce and delicate at once. "Then maybe we can talk about where you want to go next."

We stay together, him and me. She'd said that before, long before any of them knew that the forest would let them go so soon, that Red and Eammon would finally heal what had been broken. Lyra had gone off on her own at first only because Fife refused; Red wondered if he could beg off a second time. Even though Red understood his apprehension—understood that his new tie to the Wilderwood made him nervous to leave it—she hoped the next time Lyra asked, he'd choose to go.

Though part of her thought Fife was more nervous about Lyra seeing his new Mark than anything else.

All of them were still trying to navigate the labyrinth they'd made, no one quite sure how to press at its parameters. She and Eammon weren't confined to their forest. They carried the Wilderwood within; it couldn't hold them within a border that no longer existed. But with Neve missing and their power so new, neither of them had broached the subject of leaving. Especially now that they wore their magic so physically, so clearly. Red still didn't want to run into anyone from Valleyda, anyone who remembered her as just the Second Daughter who'd visited once before disappearing again—right before her sister, the new queen, was reportedly stricken ill. The potential for questions she didn't want to answer was too high, things were too fragile.

And if she was this nervous about it, she couldn't imagine what Eammon was feeling. Eammon, who'd completely lost himself the one time he breached the southern border of the Wilderwood, who hadn't known the world outside of it for centuries.

Well. There'd be time for all that. Once they found Neve. Red had been thinking recently of how she'd like to see the ocean again.

She saw Fife and Lyra out the door, watching the two of them amble into the gold-and-ocher expanse of the healed Wilderwood. Eammon was waiting for her down in the library. She should bring him another cup of coffee; he'd undoubtedly finished his first.

But Red walked, instead, toward the tower.

Since healing the Wilderwood, the vines on the outside of the tower had grown riotous, full of lush leaves and white blooms as big as her head. It was a beautiful thing, a spot of spring in all this autumn. And her magic, the wildly blooming forest beneath her skin, was still stronger there.

Though not strong enough to make the mirror work.

One try. She'd give it one try today, one beseeching sacrifice to see if it would surrender a glimpse of her sister. Then she'd join Eammon, scouring tomes for things they might not yet know about themselves, the Wilderwood, the Shadowlands. Things that might let them free Neve from the darkness that held her fast.

One try.

As she walked over the moss, Red's gaze—the deep brown of her irises ringed with green now, just like Eammon's—strayed to the iron gate, to the trees beyond. Only yellows and oranges, only brown bark, with no white sentinels to interrupt them.

"There has to be a door," Red whispered in the autumn of her wood, the words spoken aloud but also directed inward, at the forest she carried beneath her skin. "There has to be *something*."

No answer. But a breeze picked up, spinning golden leaves, and she felt an answering rustle along her spine.

Red jogged up the tower steps, already pulling strands of dark-gold hair from the lumpy braid Eammon had tied. Thin tendrils of ivy tangled in the blond, growing from her head just as naturally; she plucked one of those, too. Then blood, just a tiny drop of it, drawn from digging her nail into the pad of her opposite thumb. It reminded her of those first days in the Wilderwood, what felt like lifetimes ago, working at a hangnail to try to avoid using her magic.

Strange, what she used to be afraid of.

The blood she smeared on the gilt frame; the hair and ivy she wound through its whorls. "Show me my sister," Red commanded, in a layered voice that held clattering branches and blooming petals and whistling wind.

Nothing. Again. With a deep, shaking sigh, Red pushed up from the floor.

But something caught her eye in that matte gray surface. A shift, two crossing kinds of darkness, like something moving in a black, unlit room. She leaned forward until her nose almost touched the glass, peering at it.

The darkness in the mirror looked, almost, like a tangle of roots.

Chapter Three

Raffe

When an assassin finally came, Raffe was ready.

He'd *been* ready. Ever since that night at the edge of the Wilderwood—the night Neve disappeared—he'd been waiting for the other shoe to drop. It was a miracle it'd taken this long, really.

A week ago, he'd trekked to the village with Kiri slung over his back. He'd expected to run into trouble there—villagers awakened by the cosmic showdown happening at the border of the Wilderwood, a forest made a man brawling with one wreathed in shadow, ready to lash out in fear. But everyone, mysteriously, was asleep. Maybe through magic, maybe because people who chose to live so close to the Wilderwood had trained themselves not to notice strangeness, but the god-battle at the edge of the trees had apparently come and gone without comment.

Thankfully, Valleyda's northernmost village also played fast and loose with the law. Raffe had managed to find someone who didn't think twice about helping him cross the Florish border with a clearly injured woman, who raised barely an eyebrow when he paid for her passage to the Rylt in solid gold coins. It wasn't cheap, despite its brevity. Sailing westward to the cluster of islands that made the Rylt was three days' journey, usually, but he'd found a sailor who said he could make it in two. Raffe had paid enough for Kiri to have food, but not much more than that, and given the captain a story about how she was his distant aunt, raving mad. He wondered if the captain had believed him. At any rate, he'd believed his gold.

Once he returned to the capital, it'd been fairly easy to make the rest of Kiri's Order follow their High Priestess across the sea. A letter to the Ryltish Temple accompanied the rest of the priestesses on their voyage, and though the price of such a thing made his stomach and his purse ache, it was worth it to have them gone. Easy, too, had been the lying, both to the Temple and the court—Queen Neverah was so impressed with the piety in the Rylt, she'd sent Valleyda's own Order so they could learn from each other.

Raffe just had to trust that all the Valleydan priestesses he'd sent away were smart enough to keep their mouths shut about everything that had happened, and that any raving on Kiri's part could be chalked up to her injuries. Thus far, luck had held. But he was canny enough not to trust that it would forever.

More than once, Raffe thought that he should've just killed them. Killed Kiri, killed the priestesses. But he wasn't that bloodthirsty. Not yet.

Though it's probably what Neve would've done.

Neve. Arick. He'd pushed away the grief and frustration and a whole host of other unpleasant emotions surrounding them, keeping his feelings at arm's length through force of will—and wine when that failed. He'd remembered yesterday that Arick's birthday was soon, his mind serving the information up seemingly at random, and though he'd drained an entire bottle afterward, he hadn't truly grieved. He had no time. No energy. When this was all resolved, when he finally had Neve back, then they could grieve together.

Though even the context of *together* was an odd one for him.

He loved Neve. He had since they were children. But the shape of that love was more difficult to pin down than its mere reality—its edges and contours, how exactly it was supposed to fit in his chest. He loved Neve, but did he know her? He'd thought so, before. Before Red and the forest, before the trees in the Shrine, before he'd seen her pull in darkness and sink into the earth.

After seeing what she was capable of, what she was willing to do, he wasn't so sure he knew her at all.

All of these myriad thoughts were far from his mind now, however, as the assassin he'd expected ever since he arrived back at the capital finally crept into his room.

Raffe lay shirtless in his bed, eyes slit against the dark as he watched a figure moving through the shadows. He'd been dreaming before the assassin broke his light sleep. An odd one: a huge, white tree, the trunk swirled in gold and black.

The dregs of the dream still clung to the corners of his mind as he tracked the assassin through the room, peering through his lashes from nearly closed eyes. Raffe kept his breaths long and even, his limbs loose. When he slipped his hand under the pillow, where he kept a short dagger, he made it look like he was just shifting in his sleep.

The assassin wasn't deterred by his movement. And they weren't dressed for the job—black, yes, but it looked like they were wearing a gown? Surely that was just a trick of the light.

The shadowed figure crept closer. No shine of a blade, but there were other ways to kill someone. Raffe tightened his grip on the dagger hilt beneath his pillow. He'd find out who sent them before he killed them. At this point, he thought of mostly everyone as a potential enemy, but it'd be useful to know which ones weren't cowards.

When the figure got close enough to see the slit of his eyes, Raffe closed them. A deep, grounding breath through his nose, recalling the few things he'd retained from his year training with his *tor*. Warm breath ghosted over his cheek as the figure bent close.

Raffe sat up with a snarl, slicing the dagger through the air to stop right at the base of their throat.

"Kings and shadows, Raffe!" A bell-like laugh. Familiar. "You're quicker than I thought!"

His eyes narrowed, adjusting to the dim, to the coyly smiling figure at the end of his dagger. *"Kayu?"*

Okada Kayu, Third Daughter of the Niohni Emperor. Moonlight

glinted off her teeth as she grinned, reaching up to pull back her hood. Long, pin-straight black hair cascaded down her shoulders, and Kayu gave it an impatient shake. "I'll be honest, I'm impressed." Exaggeratedly pushing away the edge of Raffe's blade with a finger, she sidestepped to his table, scavenged up a match, and lit the half-melted taper. The flare of light shadowed her eyes as she turned to him with crossed arms. "When I got within inches and you were still asleep, I figured you'd be a goner."

"So you *were* trying to kill me?"

"Of course not. I just wanted to know if I *could*."

"That isn't the comfort you think it is."

"I wanted to try something I read about today. The Krahls of Elkyrath used to train their guards to walk almost silently by using this technique where they put all their weight on their heels. You see, you'd think it was the toe, like how we tiptoe when we want to be quiet, but that mostly just makes you prone to falling over—"

"You weren't silent. I woke up."

"Well, the Krahl of Elkyrath didn't train *me*."

Raffe ran a hand down his face. Ostensibly, Kayu was in Valleyda in order to use the library, making her the latest in a string of bookish women who'd made themselves thorns in his ass. Both Valedren twins, and now an Okada. He attracted a type into his orbit, apparently.

Kayu had arrived three days ago with no retinue and very little in the way of possessions. The letter she held, signed by Isla—and wasn't *that* a swift punch to the sternum—said that the Niohni princess was welcome to come stay in Valleyda for as long as she liked, that the court would be thrilled to host her while she studied navigation.

It was very similar to the letter Raffe had received when he was fourteen and headed here to learn about trade routes.

Arriving at the beginning of fall meant Kayu couldn't take up a true course of study with any Valleydan tutors until the season passed, since nearly everyone went to their own holdings to prepare for the rapidly approaching cold. But she didn't seem to mind.

Across from him, Kayu licked the pad of her finger and passed it idly through the candle-flame. Despite her nonchalant manner, she held herself rigidly, like she was less comfortable being in a man's room in the middle of the night than she wanted him to believe.

Raffe's eyes narrowed against the flickering light. "Elkyrathan assassination tactics aren't what I would think a student of navigation would spend time reading about."

"I'm well-rounded."

"It's certainly something that might interest a person plotting to take over a throne, though."

Some of the tension in Kayu's frame seemed to ebb, almost like his honesty was refreshing. Her heart-shaped face gave nothing away, though, her dark eyes trained on the candle and her finger passing through it. "You still don't believe me, then."

"That your family sending you here to study while the Queen is ill has nothing to do with you being next in line for the Valleydan throne? No. I don't."

She stiffened a bit, but her voice was flippant. "Please. You think *Valleyda* is worth starting a war? I've been to funerals livelier than this court." A shrug as she began twisting a strand of hair around her finger. "And I didn't know the Queen was ill. Last I heard, she was meddling in the Order, changing things that hadn't been changed in centuries. Seemed fairly healthy, to be doing all that."

It'd been a mistake to mention Neve. It made his chest feel hollowed out and full of a simmering anger all at the same time.

"She'll recover soon, I'm sure," Kayu continued. "Then maybe there will be a ball. I love balls. It's been ages since I went dancing."

"Maybe you could go home and convince your father to throw one."

Her finger froze, wound in black hair to the knuckle. Any mention of Kayu's father went over like a bucket of ice on a winter morning. "My father is more likely to throw me in the ocean than throw me a ball." She released her hair, looked away. "And I don't know how many times I'll have to tell you that both of my older sisters are married, one to a noblewoman in Elkyrath and one to our father's treasurer, and thus unavailable for the position of Queen."

"*You* aren't married." Any Queen succeeding to the Valleydan throne had to be either unmarried or married to someone from within the Valleydan court. Kayu was a third cousin of Red and Neve, some complicated matter involving a great aunt who remarried and bore children late in life to a Niohni noble. The line of succession was a tangled one, but it ended with Kayu, unmarried, and therefore eligible to become the next Queen of Valleyda.

Her full lips pulled to the side, an expression he couldn't read. "No, I'm not married." A pause, then she flipped her hand dismissively. "But I'm also unavailable, believe me. And I *do not want it.*"

The undesirability of Valleydan queenship was really the only thing saving them, since no one knew that the Second Daughter tithe was now moot. Raffe thought it would behoove him to keep that secret as long as he could.

Still, the arrival of a candidate for the crown within days of Neve disappearing into the Shadowlands was enough to give him pause, undesirable queenship or no.

Raffe wondered, not for the first time, if it was too late to really show an interest in the wine-shipping business.

The barest hint of sunlight filtered into the sky beyond the window, night's fist opening into fingers of dawn. He was fully awake now; trying to sleep again would be pointless. Scowling, Raffe got up, bunching his sheet around his waist as he crossed to the wardrobe. "Is there a reason you're sneaking in here in the wee hours of the morning other than seeing if you could kill me? Which I'm still not happy about, by the way. I could've killed *you.*"

"Take it as a testament to your nobility that I knew you wouldn't." Kayu sat in the wooden chair against the wall and propped her chin on her fist. "You are *achingly* noble, Raffe. Right on the edge of where attractive becomes exasperating."

"Fortunately, I don't particularly care about being attractive." He opened the wardrobe so the wide doors hid him from her view.

"Not to anyone but the Queen, right?"

He froze, fingers clenched around a pair of trousers. Only a moment passed before he pulled them on, the movement as nonchalant as he could make it. "What makes you say that?"

"I have two eyes, for one thing. And you, Raffe, walk around like a man carrying the weight of the whole world. Who else would you carry it for?"

Raffe yanked on a shirt with more force than was needed, nearly loosening a seam.

When he closed the wardrobe, Kayu sat back in his chair like the princess she was, this time elegantly crossing her legs at the ankles. The candlelight gilded her long, straight hair, so black it was nearly blue. "I can't wait to see her, once she recovers," she said. "I desperately want to meet the distant cousin who has you so in her thrall."

The word *thrall* made his jaw set tight. "She's recuperating in Floriane, and I doubt she'll be back before you're gone. The sacrifice of her sister greatly impacted her health."

That, at least, wasn't a lie.

"Floriane?" A flash of white in the dim; Kayu pulled a tightly folded sheet of paper from a pocket hidden in her skirt. "Strange, then, that a letter for you concerning her would come from the Rylt."

The Rylt. Kiri.

Shit, she worked fast.

Not worth playing coy, not that he was good at it, anyway. Raffe stalked across the room, held his hand out imperiously. Kayu passed him the letter with a smile. "I can tell you what it says, if you want. It's very simple. I was almost disappointed; I'd been reading up on common ciphers yesterday and thought I might have a chance to try one out."

"You are exhausting." He scanned the letter quickly, gaze snagging on the signature at the bottom before he managed to actually read any of the body. It was Kiri, all right.

Shit shit *shit*. "How did you get this?"

It took her a moment to answer, and when he looked up, there was a quick flash of apprehension in her eyes. Then it was gone, ephemeral enough to have been his imagination.

"When I saw a messenger headed to your room with a letter, I let him know I could take it to you." Kayu flashed a smile. "I might have implied that our meeting so early was for carnal reasons."

"Wonderful," Raffe muttered, turning his attention to the letter.

So much for hoping the former High Priestess would be incapacitated, that her injuries might render her insensate. Kiri wrote politely enough, skirting just around the edge of a revelation without actually delving into one. She thanked him for safe passage, and for sending her sisters, *at great personal cost, I'm sure.* She said that their accommodations in the Rylt proved most fortunate, a choice of words that made gooseflesh rise along the back of his neck.

It's easier to hear, across the sea, away from the cursed forest's clatter, Kiri wrote. *And many a wayward sister has turned to the cause.*

Nonsense. He wanted to dismiss it as nonsense. But he couldn't, not quite.

The letter hinted that more money might be needed for the Valleydan priestesses to find peace, a transparent attempt at a bribe—so benign a threat within the scope of everything else that he nearly choked back a laugh.

And then, at the end—*the Queen is well, you'll be happy to hear. She must find her key, take the proper steps. The stars write stories with many paths, but the Heart Tree is at the end of all of them.*

So she was still mad. Excellent. Stupendous, even.

Raffe folded the letter and tucked it into his doublet, working hard to keep a scowl off his face. "The High Priestess and her Order have gone to the Rylt to pray for the Queen. Since prayers are better heard when made in larger groups." He pulled *that* out of his ass; Raffe had little use for religion and barely knew the basics. But he used the courtly voice he usually reserved for when his parents came to visit, which hopefully gave his bullshit some weight. "Clearly, the pressure is getting to the High Priestess."

"Clearly." There was something flat and hard in Kayu's voice. "But why is she writing to you?"

"The Queen has entrusted me with keeping things in order until she recovers."

Kayu's eyes narrowed. "She entrusted *you*, a Meducian, instead of any of the Valleydan nobles?"

"You don't know this court." Raffe shook his head. "No one here is clamoring for a cursed throne."

Kayu huffed a rueful laugh. "See? The rule of a cold, mostly poor country that might require one to sacrifice a child isn't a highly desired commodity. Not by me, or by anyone else."

Relief softened Raffe's rigid spine.

A moment of quiet, but one that felt heavy, weighted with the action of what might come next. Raffe turned back to the wardrobe, pulled a doublet from within its depths, threaded his arms through. Waiting to see what she would do now, this shadow-damned woman who seemed determined to muck everything up.

Still sitting primly on his chair, Kayu nodded, as if she'd come to some conclusion.

With the same grace she did everything, she rose, her black skirts sweeping over the floor as she walked toward him. Raffe was tall, and Kayu was short. Still, when she looked up at him, she did not look cowed.

"If you're going to pull this off," she said quietly, "you're going to need money."

It was so unexpected, his mouth gaped for a moment.

She went on, taking advantage of his surprise, her manner slipping from flippant, bookish princess to something steelier. "Passage to the Rylt is expensive, and it sounds like Kiri isn't satisfied with whatever amount you sent her off with. You'll need money for winter food shipments—I know Valleyda has to import most of it, and if any other countries think they can raise prices in the Queen's absence, it will be more expensive than it already is. Not to mention the recent reductions in prayer-taxes." She paused. "The Queen's physicians are expensive, too, I'm sure."

It was a test, and the split second of silence afterward said he'd failed it. Kayu nodded. "I didn't think so. Where is she, then?"

"Floriane."

"Come *on*, Raffe."

He pressed his lips flat.

Kayu rolled her eyes. "Fine, don't tell me." She gave that one up more easily than he expected. "She's alive, though."

"She's alive. And she's coming back."

It was meant to be defiant, but Kayu just nodded, like he'd confirmed something she already knew.

"Your silence." It came out a sneer. "I'm sure that's expensive, too."

Angular brows drew together over her eyes. "You don't have to buy that."

Confusion struck him speechless.

She shrugged, looked away. "I meant what I said, about you being achingly noble. Nobility gets people eaten alive, especially people in foreign kingdoms with missing queens. I truly want to help you, Raffe." The rueful flicker of a smile. "This isn't the kind of thing you can do on your own."

His mouth desperately wanted to gape again. He clenched his jaw to keep it from happening.

Kayu patted his chest where he'd slid Kiri's letter between linen shirt and doublet. "Think about it." She glided away toward the door and slipped out. It closed quietly behind her.

Raffe stared at it for a moment, rubbing a hand nervously over his close-shorn hair. "Five shadow-damned Kings on five shitting *horses*."

Chapter Four

Neve

The tower was beautiful. Brutal, and unnerving, but beautiful. Neve could admit that much.

Four open windows stood at compass points in the walls, their sills carved with sinuous lines reminiscent of shadows, twisting and curling over the wood. A nearly bare shelf was pushed against one wall, housing a collection of cracked ceramic pots. Next to it, a fireplace glowed with still-lit embers that hadn't been teased into a full blaze. It was strange, to see fire devoid of color. The flames were nearly indistinguishable from the smoke.

Other than the shelf, the only furnishings in the room were a table, a chair, a cot pushed against the far wall.

And her coffin.

Neve froze at the top of the stairs, widened eyes fixed on the place where she'd awakened. The lid to the coffin, glass smoked with tendrils of darkness, was still half off the plinth where she'd pushed it.

Hello, Neve. You're awake.

That was the first thing she'd heard here, and there'd been a moment—a scant one—when it'd been a comfort. Hearing the voice of another person in this alien landscape, knowing she wasn't alone.

It wasn't a comfort anymore.

Solmir went to the shelf, picking up one of the ceramic pots and scowling down into its contents. "Not much," he muttered to himself, "but it will have to do." A canvas bag hung on one of the shelf's posts; he slung it over one shoulder and shoved a handful of whatever was in the pot into the bag. "Something convenient about this place," he said as he worked. "You don't need to eat here. One of the benefits of not being, in the most technical sense, alive. You don't necessarily need to sleep, either, but I still do." His chin jerked to the cot against the wall. "Old habit, I guess. Not like there's much else to do."

But Neve wasn't listening. She was still transfixed by the coffin.

He noticed. Blue eyes tracked from where she stood to where she looked, and the slash of his mouth bent. "How much do you remember?"

"Enough." It was scraped-sounding. "I remember the grove. The sentinels. The..." Her hand raised; she flexed her fingers, now pale gray, remembering when they were shot through with shadow.

She didn't finish, but Solmir nodded. Something flickered in his gaze, hard and bright. "And you remember choosing this?"

A challenge, almost, like he expected her to deny it. But Neve shrugged. "Yes," she murmured. "I remember that, too."

Her eyes opening to smoke-fogged glass, a familiar face on the other side. Red. Tearful and tattered, dusted with dirt. Red slamming her fists against the glass, screaming for her. A small part of Neve had been meanly satisfied to see that, to see Red trying to get to her as desperately as Neve had been trying all those months. Back when it felt simple.

She remembered looking down at herself. The pulsing, external veins, pumping darkness, connecting her to the inverted grove of sentinel trees. Making her a doorway to the underworld.

There'd been another face on the other side of that glass, too. Raffe. Even now, it felt like a spear through her middle. Raffe yelling for her, Raffe trying to save her. Always trying to save her, even after she'd made her choice back in Valleyda, plunging headlong into the darkness of the Shrine and her blood on branches.

In search of her sister, yes. But in search of other things, too.

And when faced with another choice, there in the grove, she'd pulled all that shadow inside.

Neve lifted her hands again, finally tearing her eyes away from the coffin to look down at her palms instead. Still unblemished by dark veins, but if she tried to call up magic, like she had outside—

"It won't work."

Solmir had moved nearly silently; he stood directly in front of her, face unreadable. "You don't have the magic anymore."

Her eyes narrowed. "If you think you can control me by making me think I'm powerless, you'll have to try a different angle. I haven't been powerless a day in my life, and I won't start now."

His brow arched, a cruel smile curving his mouth. "I would never presume to call you powerless, Neverah."

And that shouldn't have felt like a victory, but it did.

"However," Solmir continued, "using that power is going to take a bit more planning on your part from now on. Because it lives in me."

Her hands still hovered in the air between them, open-palmed, like she was waiting for him to give her something. "What are you talking about?"

"You don't remember that kiss?" His eyes glittered. "I'm wounded."

That kiss, a kiss that wasn't for heat or romance, but something cutting and calculated, a well-timed move in an intricate battle. The rush she'd felt, like something drained out of her.

Solmir tapped the center of her palm with a pale, elegant finger. "Pulling power from the Shadowlands itself is a dangerous game. It changes you, tangles up in you, anchors you here. Better to pull it from a different vessel. Something that can take in power and give it to you when you need it."

"You." Her teeth clenched on the word. "You're the vessel."

A muscle feathered in his jaw, but Solmir's slash of a smile didn't waver. "Precisely."

Her hands closed. "So I have to *kiss you* anytime I want to use my magic?"

She didn't have to tell him how much she hated that; her tone, frost and fury at once, did it for her. She'd just as soon kiss whatever that toothy thing was outside.

"It's not *your* magic, Neverah. It doesn't belong to anyone or any-thing but itself." Solmir turned back to the shelf and shoved a few more handfuls of whatever was in the ceramic pot into his bag. "And it doesn't have to be a kiss, though that is the most efficient method of transfer, for reasons I cannot possibly fathom but assume have to do with the melodramatic nature of the Wilderwood and the Shadowlands and their making. Just a skin-to-skin touch will do."

That was *better*, but not by much.

One last handful from the pot, then Solmir slung the bag over his shoulder. "I've done you a tremendous favor, really. Believe me, you don't want to let the Shadowlands alter you any more than they have to."

"So you're going to let it alter you instead?"

"I know what I'm doing," he replied, which wasn't really an answer at all. "Why, are you worried about me?"

Neve crossed her arms, still uncomfortably aware that she was wear-ing his coat. It smelled like pine, like cold and snow. "More worried that you're going to start growing fangs."

"Not yet." He turned, disappearing into the dark of the stairs and leaving her no choice but to follow. "The marks the Shadowlands have left on me are harder to spot, I'm afraid."

If she trained her mind only to pay attention to the tree trunks, it was easy to pretend that this was a normal walk through a normal wood. Not that she'd spent much time in forests of any kind—not with the specter of the Wilderwood looming so large over her whole life—but it kept her thoughts mostly quiet, calmed the lurking panic just beneath her sternum.

Up ahead, Solmir made no efforts to keep to a pace she could match. Her bare feet scrambled over packed dust and slicing branches and the skeletons of dead plants, just keeping the whip of his long hair in view. Solmir moved like a soldier, controlled and steady, walking tall despite the uneven ground. Whatever he'd packed into the bag over his shoul-der crunched unpleasantly with his movement.

She should probably keep him within arm's reach. Just in case she needed to use magic.

Damn you, she thought at his back. *Kings and shadows damn you to the deepest belly of the earth.*

An ironic epithet. There was really no further damnation she could wish on Solmir than he'd already found himself.

Neve looked down at her hands, pale and cold and empty. Experimentally, she bent her fingers. The barest hint of a sting in her veins, but no darkness in her wrists, no frost on her palms. It was obscene, that the magic's absence would make her feel bereft.

She'd told Solmir she wasn't powerless, that she'd never been. That was true—she was a First Daughter, a Queen. And Valleyda, for all its innumerable faults, at least recognized that more than only those who were assigned men at birth and aligned themselves with the distinction deserved to chart their own course. Even now, with the magic she couldn't stop thinking of as *hers* housed in a man she hated, she wasn't powerless.

But having power wasn't quite the same as being in control of it, and that was what she wanted.

It could be for the best, as much as the thought galled her. What Solmir had told her made sense, about the magic of the Shadowlands and the Wilderwood changing you.

After all, it'd changed Red.

The thought was an ache in her chest, like her heart had grown too heavy for her ribs to hold in place. Red, crouched on the root-riddled floor of the Shrine, feral, more wild than woman. Green veins and green around her eyes, the promise of more change to come. They'd mired themselves in opposite sides of a magic forest, in trees and in shadows.

Red entangled with a monster, and Neve with a fallen god.

Her eyes narrowed on Solmir up ahead. She'd followed him on instinct, sticking close to the devil she knew in the presence of so many here she didn't, but the feeling in her chest was nothing like safety. "Where are we going?"

"To see a friend." Solmir didn't turn around. His lick of long hair was a smoke-colored beacon in the solid black of the trees.

"A *friend*." She tried to keep the fear from her voice, hoped that the edge sneaking in could be mistaken for contempt. "A monster, or something worse? Or maybe all your talk of killing the Kings was a lie, and you're taking me right to them."

"If you believe one thing I tell you," Solmir said, still not turning, "make it this: The Kings and I are not on the same side. Get that through your head, Your Majesty."

"Stop calling me that." She wanted it to be in the tone of an order, but it never quite hefted the weight. "Stop calling me that if you're going to say it like it's a joke."

"You're a queen, Neverah." The sound of her name was harsh in his throat as he finally turned to face her, stopping in the middle of the path. He'd hardly ever called her Neve, even when he wore Arick's face. "You have a crown and a throne, and call me old-fashioned, but that requires some deference on my part."

Something knotted in her stomach. "You're a king."

The line of his mouth flattened. "I was."

Neve wasn't sure how to respond to that.

Solmir shifted back, away from her. His arms hung stiff by his sides, his face implacable. A standoff, two rulers unwilling to give quarter.

He broke first. Solmir reached up, rubbed at the scar on his temple, then turned around and started forward, once again nearly nonchalant. "I realize this is a lot to take in," he said conversationally. "But all I have ever been trying to do—yes, even on the surface, pretending to be poor, hapless Arick—has been about killing the Kings. Neutralizing their threat before they regain power the likes of which your world is not equipped to face. Could never be equipped to face." He glanced back at her, quickly, like he was checking for her reaction and was irritated with himself for doing so. "All of it—Kiri and Arick, the grove—it was all a means to an end. The moment the others came through, I was going to destroy them."

Another shudder rippled over the ground, not as strong as the one they'd felt at the tower, but close. Neve put a hand on one of the inverted trunks next to her, locked her knees against the pitch. Solmir didn't balance himself on anything, but she could tell that every muscle in his body tightened, see it in the way his shirt stretched across his shoulders and his thighs strained against the nondescript fabric of the dark pants he wore.

Damn him for being handsome. Life would be so much simpler if all monsters looked the part.

He recovered first, once the ground stopped writhing. The line of his mouth actually looked worried now, instead of just mocking. "It's getting worse," he muttered, nearly to himself. "Must be only three left."

Neve straightened on shaky legs. "It seems like the Shadowlands might end themselves if we just wait long enough."

She'd been only half serious, but the look Solmir leveled at her was grave. "Even if the Shadowlands collapse with the Kings in it, they won't be ended. Not really." He turned on his heel, striding away over the branches cutting through the dusty ground. "It takes more than that to vanquish a god."

They walked in silence. Neve shivered against the cold, tugging Solmir's coat around herself before she thought through exactly what she was doing. Part of her wanted to cringe away, but a bigger part of her was just cold.

After a moment, Solmir sighed, as if her silence were something that weighed on him. "I *did* try to do this the easiest way possible," he said. "Before your sister and her Wolf got in the way."

If he kept bringing up Red, she was going to tear him limb from limb and relish the fact that he couldn't really die here. "I don't believe that you've ever done something for the benefit of someone else in your life."

"First time for everything," he replied.

"Is that why you took all my magic? To prove your *noble intentions*?"

He half turned, the gleam of his blue eyes bright as flame-hearts in all this gray. The corner of his mouth twisted up, not in a smile. "I'd never claim that my intentions were noble, Neverah. I know what I am."

Her lips pressed into a tight line.

"I took it because the magic here rots your soul, turns you into a monster." He started forward again, climbing with agile grace over the thatched branches hilling the unnatural forest floor. One of them sliced up from the ground; he stood on it, looked down at her. "I don't expect a *thank you*, don't worry."

Neve glared up at him. "At least you know better than that."

Another bend of that cruel mouth into a not-smile. Solmir inclined his head, almost courtly, then hopped down and continued weaving through the inverted trees. He didn't offer Neve a hand to help her over the branch; she nearly stumbled, stubbing her bare toe against pale bark.

"If you want my soul to stay free of rot," she said, glowering at his back and trying to ignore the pain in her foot, "what about yours? Assuming you have one."

"Oh, I do." He sounded almost angry about it. "Withered and sorry thing though it is. But I managed to disentangle it from magic some time ago." His voice slanted low. "It was quite a feat, if you want to know the truth. The magic here likes to seep into every available place, take you over. Much like the magic in the Wilderwood, I'm told. But if I'm careful, I can keep the two from melding together."

"Do you want a medal?"

Blue eyes flickered her way. "A moment of silence will suffice."

And because her mind was already awash with things she couldn't quite wrap meaning around, Neve gave it to him.

She craned her neck as they walked, peering at the snatches of sky she could see between the thready roots of the inverted trees. Something that looked almost like stratified clouds marked the gray, but when she squinted at them, she saw that they were just more roots, high enough to be obscured in shifting mist.

"I don't deserve your trust. I know that much." Solmir resolutely faced forward, his tone and his stance casual in a way that seemed almost forced, like he'd been thinking the words over long before they escaped his mouth. "But, unfortunately, you're going to have to give it to me."

"I did trust you." It came out almost wounded, and Neve hated that, but she couldn't swallow the jagged sound out of her voice. "It put me here."

His hand tightened on the strap of the bag over his shoulder.

Neve's eyes narrowed at his back, something thorny and poisonous rising in her chest, despite the fact that all her power was housed in him now. "Maybe it's unfair to claim I trusted *you*, since you were pretending to be someone else all along. You've lied to me since the beginning, Solmir. How can you ask me for trust?"

Solmir turned. He closed the distance between them, nimble as a dancer, striding over the irregular, branch-covered ground to loom over her, hands clasped behind his back like a general addressing a wayward soldier.

"And you swallowed the lies without question, didn't you?" His gaze pinned her in place, spots of cold as chilling as his rings on her skin had been. "Even when the deepest part of you knew there was something happening. Even when you knew I wasn't Arick."

"I didn't know that." But that falling feeling in her stomach said she did, she did, she did.

"Don't insult your own intelligence. You didn't know the whole of it, maybe, you didn't know exactly what had happened, but you suspected. You knew he'd changed, that he was being influenced by more than Kiri. And you said nothing." He paused. "Not even when you knew they killed your mother."

Another quake saved her from trying to defend herself, trying to pretend what he said was a lie. It shook through the ground beneath them, enough to knock her off-balance, to send her stumbling against Solmir's chest. His hands came up to steady her, his palm against the sliver of her wrist his coat sleeve left bare.

Neve didn't take a moment to think. She turned her hand and closed her fingers around his.

He realized what she was doing. She felt him jerk against her, try to pull away, but she pulled first, *tugged* at him like a planet to its moon.

And that dark, thorned power he housed spilled into her waiting veins.

It stung, ripping at her insides, carving familiar wounds. Her palm eclipsed, then her fingers, veins going inky and running up her shoulder, toward her heart, then down her other side to mark the hand that didn't hold his.

Solmir wrenched himself away, but she was faster still. Neve opened a frost-laced hand between them like she was offering him something, and her offering was a bramble, flecked with dagger-long thorns, wrapping around his neck, a collar he couldn't pull out of.

But Solmir didn't look afraid, not in the slightest. Instead, he looked almost pleased. "Oh, yes," he murmured. "It looks like this is going to work out just fine."

"You told me you had nothing to do with my mother's death." Neve's voice was so calm. That was a difference between her and Red, one of many—Red wore her emotions where everyone could see, making no attempt to hide them. Neve was skilled in burying them deep, far down and distant, something to be dealt with later if they were dealt with at all.

"I didn't." Solmir's voice was just as calm, despite the shadow-made thorns digging into his neck. "The killings were all Kiri. But that was the moment you knew. The moment you were sure that whatever was happening was bigger than what you'd planned for. And you did nothing to stop it."

"Neither did you." Neve's fingers twitched; the thorns around Solmir's throat tightened, enough that she saw the flicker of a grimace at his mouth. "You said you tried to do this in a way that didn't hurt me, but when you saw that it did, you did *nothing.*"

"Did you want me to?" His face was all harsh angles. "You never asked me to stop any of it."

Her lips lifted back from her teeth. "I can't be your conscience."

A spark in his eye, a snarl to match hers. "And I can't be your spine."

They stood there, locked together by magic, a Queen and a King and the darkness of an underworld.

"It was always going to come to this." Solmir shifted, his collar of thorns digging into his skin. One pushed in at his throat, enough to pucker, not quite enough to pierce. "It was always going to come down to you to stop them, to annihilate them so that they can't make a world in their image. It was always going to be you and Redarys."

"Not if she'd just run." Neve shook her head, a shiver working over her at the contrast of this familiar argument happening in such a wholly unfamiliar place. "If Red had listened to me and not gone to the Wolf, none of this would've happened."

"You know that isn't true. You made the choices that led you here, Neverah. They're yours as much as they are hers. You could've run from it, but the two of you are for the Wolf and for the throne, and such things have a way of finding you even if you hide."

Her choices. Letting Kiri convince her there was a way to save Red from a fate she'd greeted with open arms. Bleeding on the sentinel shards to grow their inverted grove. Pulling in all that shadowed magic as she lay there in a glass coffin.

All these things she'd done for a measure of control, and it all led to the same place. To her choosing to *go*, the same as Red had, both of them trying to save the other.

It kept coming back to two women and the woods.

Solmir stared down at her, somehow still imperious even when collared with her thorns. His eyes were a sky-colored glitter in a place with no real sky, his too-long hair brushing the puckered scars in his forehead. "Are you going to release me, Your Majesty?"

"Can't you release yourself?" If it came out mocking, so be it. Kings and shadows knew he'd mocked her enough today.

He shifted, the first real sign of discomfort he'd shown without attempting to hide it. "Not until I absorb a few more shadow-creatures," he answered. "Our magic supply is running low, since we're unable to pull from the Shadowlands themselves without rather dire consequences. Pain and unraveling for you, the further rending of an already tattered soul for me." He tapped a finger against a thorn. "This was shamefully wasteful."

She scowled, fought the urge to clasp his arm and pull out more of their limited supply of magic just so she could curve one of those thorns into his mouth. Instead, Neve stood pin-straight and queenly and let her hand fall away, releasing her hold on the magic in the same instinctual way she'd unspooled it from him in the first place—the moon releasing a comet from its orbit.

Slowly, the thorns around Solmir's neck withered, retracted into themselves. They curled into plumes of gray smoke before dissipating into the air. It reminded her of when they killed the worm-monster from before, but these shadows didn't make any noise. She'd drained the magic out, stripped it of use.

Solmir stood close until the last of it was gone, close enough for her to feel the skate of his breath across her cheek.

Then he turned sharply on his heel, striding forward again. "Come on. My friend is waiting."

"You still haven't told me who your *friend* is."

"I don't know what her name was, before. But here, she's called the Seamstress." A glance over his shoulder. "I think you'll like her."

The forest grew denser before it thinned, inverted trunks growing close as threads on a loom, waiting for a weaver. The branches on the ground dipped and wove around each other, hard to navigate. In some places, they stacked almost like a madcap staircase, canting up and then down, and she'd nearly tripped into Solmir's back more than once. He tensed every time she came close, like he expected her to grab his arm and siphon magic out of him again. Neve tried not to relish that too much.

Both of them kept one eye to the reaches of the forest as they moved, wary of noise. The memory of that toothy wormlike thing was still extremely fresh in Neve's mind, and she had no desire to come upon something similar. Or something worse.

But the inverted forest was silent. It seemed like they were the only two sentient things for miles.

Another rumble, reverberating through the ground. They paused, braced atop latticed branches until it passed. An uneasy, wordless look passed between them. It was close to companionable, and they both seemed to notice that at the same time—Neve scowled, and Solmir's lip lifted, and they turned away from each other and back toward the path without another glance.

Slowly, the inverted forest tapered away, the upside-down trees growing farther apart. They came to a clearing, open enough so that Neve could see what passed for a sky, see the cloud-like smudges of faraway roots in the gray horizon. The branches on the ground thinned, snaking over the dry dirt like roots might, weaving together and lying flat.

In the center of the clearing sat a cottage. It looked so normal that Neve had to stare at it a moment, to see if her mind was somehow playing tricks. A perfectly ordinary cottage, log-built, with a plume of smoke twisting from the chimney into the gray sky. There was even a damn *goat* in the yard.

Her brow furrowed as she stepped forward, passing Solmir, drawn by the sight of something nearly normal. "The Seamstress seems to have made a cozy home for herself, all things considered."

What was meant to be a throwaway comment seemed to strike Solmir more heavily than she meant. He nodded, lips contemplatively twisted. "She did, before."

In the yard, the goat turned to look at her. Only then did Neve notice it had three eyes. It bleated, and the sound was like a crying child.

Neve's heart jumped into her throat; she started backward, nearly colliding with Solmir, then reversed direction, her nightgown knotting around her legs.

Solmir looked at the goat, shrugged. "Another lesser beast. A rather useless one."

"Useless, maybe, but damn unsettling." Her heartbeat slowed; Neve straightened. "Five *Kings*."

"It's extremely disconcerting that you use that as a curse," Solmir muttered.

But Neve wasn't paying attention. Her eyes had gone to the cottage, to the slow creep of the opening door.

Pushed by something that was decidedly not a human hand.

Chapter Five

Neve

Instinct told her to back away, to run into the inverted trees they'd left behind. Instead, Neve planted her feet, pulled the edges of Solmir's coat around herself as if it could be armor.

Solmir looked at her with one knife-slash brow arched. "There's nothing to be afraid of."

"Who says I'm afraid?"

"Every single thing about you right now says you're afraid."

She didn't like that, didn't like the idea that he could read her easily. "Concerned and afraid are not the same thing."

"Whatever you need to tell yourself, Neverah."

The door continued to press implacably forward, pushed by something that looked almost like...like spider legs. Three of them at least, moving in tandem like a hand might. Spiky dark fur studded the legs' lengths, and though the gloom inside the cottage hid whatever torso they attached to, the legs alone looked nearly as long as Neve was tall.

"What *is* that?" Neve did her best to keep her voice even, though it was a challenge. She hated spiders. Always had. Of *course* there'd be a giant spider here.

"*She*," Solmir said, with emphasis on the pronoun, "is the Seamstress. And you have nothing to fear from her. She only eats insects."

It wasn't exactly comforting, seeing as Neve hadn't yet seen any insects in the Shadowlands.

The door stood fully open now, a rectangular maw in the cottage's side. The legs—the Seamstress—had disappeared back into the gloom of her hovel. Apparently, the opening of the door was as much welcome as they'd get. Undeterred, Solmir started toward the door, unslinging the bag from his shoulder as he went.

For a moment, Neve considered staying out here, waiting for Solmir to finish whatever business he had with the Seamstress alone. But that three-eyed goat looked at her again, letting out another strange bleat—it sounded like a ship's horn, as if the thing was running through a remembered list of noises every time it opened its mouth—and that was enough to send her hurrying to catch up.

Right before the threshold, Solmir stopped. He inclined his head toward the dark, not quite a bow but a show of deference. "Beloved of an Old One, I cede my power as I cross into your holding, and follow no law but your own as long as I abide by your hearth." He set the bag down before the door.

A low chuckle from inside the cottage, unexpectedly melodious. "It smells like you don't have much power to cede, once-King. Your well is near run dry. But I do appreciate the gesture." Another one of those spider legs curved out of the dark, hooked the bag, and pulled it inside. The sound of a deep sniff, then a pleased click, like teeth snapping together. "Your offering is accepted. Be welcome, you and your guest."

Solmir looked at Neve, smirked. "Last chance to stay out here. You could make friends with the goat."

Neve didn't give him the dignity of a response. She strode forward and crossed the threshold before he did, fighting down fear until it was nothing but a cold twinge in her middle. Her hand flexed as she passed him, itching to scratch his skin and steal another jolt of magic, but she closed it to a fist.

The inside of the cottage was just as disconcertingly normal as the outside, once her eyes adjusted to the gloom. Spiny things hung from the ceiling the way herbs might; a closer look revealed that they were insect legs, spike-haired and segmented. They looked exactly like whatever Solmir had stuffed into the bag back at the tower, what he'd given the Seamstress as an offering.

Her mouth pulled down. It seemed like most of the things in the Shadowlands were dead, but apparently that hadn't always been the case, and Solmir had a stockpile of insect carcasses to offer in exchange for information. It made a nervous laugh itch at the back of her throat. She'd received so much training on trade, but she'd never considered bargaining with insect parts. Always something new to learn, apparently.

The small space was warmed by a crackling, colorless fire in a small hearth. A large wooden block sat in the center of the room—a table, maybe, though there were no chairs. Dark stains marred the block's surface, studded with pieces of torn iridescence, like wing remnants. A plain cupboard was pushed against the wall.

And when her eyes couldn't focus on the slightly twisted normalcy anymore, they had to turn to the cottage's occupant.

A woman. Most of one, anyway. A torso clad in a simple white shift, a graceful neck, a beautiful face framed by cascading black hair. She looked normal enough, from the waist up. But where her legs should be, there were clusters of spider limbs, longer than the woman was tall. When she smiled, her teeth were sharp, and her eyes gleamed multifaceted in the firelight.

Neve's mouth dried, but she was a queen, and the formal way Solmir had greeted the creature at the door told her she should show the same deference to the Seamstress as she would to any other dignitary. So instead of screaming and running out the door, she inclined her head. "Thank you for your welcome."

The Seamstress's grin widened, amused. "The little Shadow Queen, at last." The whisper seemed layered, as if this creature had as many voices as she did limbs, all of them pressed together and tuned to one key. The Seamstress moved forward, so graceful on her spider's legs that it looked like she floated, the torso of a woman in a writhing sea of black. "We've heard of you. Yes, we've heard so much of you and all you've done. The doorway you made and then closed." She nodded, suddenly solemn. "As you should have. There are no shortcuts through this, no matter how Solmir would like there to be. Someone must be a vessel."

Shadow Queen. The title felt familiar, though Neve couldn't put her finger on how.

"Someone *is* a vessel." Solmir closed the door and held his arms behind his back, voice nonchalant despite the stiff line of his posture. "Didn't you say you smelled it? I'm holding all the magic for our little queen here. She doesn't want to end up a monster."

"Why not?" The Seamstress cocked her head at Neve, dark hair cascading over her shoulders. "You've gotten close already, up in your own world. It's not so different down here. Just harder to hide."

"She didn't like the pain," Solmir said. "Or the changes." He almost sounded amused. Neve didn't look back to see if he was wearing that cruel smile again, because if he was, she might not be able to resist clawing it off.

"Oh, that." The Seamstress waved her hand. "Well. Power is pain, Shadow Queen, and *monster* in the eye of the beholder. You'll learn."

A rumble shook through the floor, enough to make the insect remains on the ceiling sway and the cupboard rattle.

"Tremors," the Seamstress said softly. "Death throes of a dying place."

"They're getting worse." Solmir came to stand beside Neve, his arms crossed over his chest. "We felt two coming here from the tower."

The creature nodded. "This world frays at the seams with each Old One that dies, dissolving further, becoming more unstable. Magic shaking loose as the gods fall. Only three left now."

For the first time since Neve had seen him in his true form, Solmir looked almost uncomfortable. Almost sympathetic. "And I assume yours is not one of the three."

"No." The Seamstress's eyes closed, a shiver of grief working through her human shoulders and down her spider limbs. "No. My Weaver is gone."

Solmir sighed, rubbing at his eyes with thumb and forefinger. The silver on his hands glinted, and when his hair fell back, Neve noticed a ring glimmering in his earlobe, too. "My heart aches as yours does."

"My sorrow is lessened by the presence of yours." Archaic phrases, platitudes from out of time, keeping Neve on the outside of the conversation.

"Do you mind speaking in terms I can understand?" Neve's voice came out thin but regal. "I'm made to believe our time is limited, and I'd like to get back to my own world as soon as possible."

A pause. Then the Seamstress threw back her head and gave a full-throated laugh—a beautiful, musical sound wholly at odds with her frightful appearance. "You may not hold the magic, little queen, but I don't think that will slow you down at all. You walk through the world like it will rise to your feet and bend to your fist." The Seamstress opened the bag Solmir had given her and began sorting the contents with her spider legs, keeping her human arms casually crossed. "It was always going to come down to the Shadow Queen and the Golden-Veined, to a vessel and a door. I told Solmir that; I told him twice—first, when he tried to bring through a queen that was not his own, then when he found a way to the surface. This place changed me utterly, but I still have a talent for future-telling. The stars I once read haven't changed, and they aren't beholden to the desires of a King who never wanted what he was given."

Solmir's eyes narrowed, but it was Neve who spoke. "Why do you keep calling me that? Shadow Queen?"

The Seamstress shrugged. "Because that is what you are," she said simply. "Or, at least, what you will be."

Neve's eyes darted to Solmir. But if the King had more insight, he kept it to himself, face cold and handsome and unreadable.

"The Shadow Queen, for the throne," the spider-woman mused. Her segmented legs bent behind her, making a dark throne of her own to perch on. The insect parts she'd sorted stayed in neat piles on the table. "Though not the throne you thought. Wolves and woods and thrones and darkness, whole worlds trapped in mostly human hearts. You and your sister have been part of it since the beginning, sunk deeper than either of you realized."

Neve's heart jumped at the word *sister*; she couldn't tell if it was in hope or fear or something caught between the two. "What do you know about Red?"

The Seamstress cocked her head. "Only what the stars told me, long ago. That she would become all light, while you do the opposite."

Light and dark. That's what it always was with the two of them. A dance of inversions, reflections in a mirror. "Is she all right?"

"I know not of what is happening on the surface," the Seamstress answered. "But were something to happen to the Lady Wolf, you would know."

A reassurance Neve had given herself over and over. If Red was gone, Neve would know.

She wondered if it went both ways. If Red felt her absence now as acutely as Neve had felt hers when she left for the Wilderwood.

"Don't worry, Shadow Queen. You two will find your way home to each other. That much is certain, though the circumstances of such a thing are mutable." The Seamstress's faceted eyes turned away from Neve, looked instead to Solmir. "But you must find the Heart Tree first."

There was a sense of capitalization there, of the words being more important than the sound of them let on. There was no reason for them to pit Neve's stomach the way they did.

Next to her, Solmir's crossed arms tightened over his chest. It pulled the fabric of his thin shirt taut, revealing the blurred outline of a strange, spiking tattoo circling his upper arm. "I figured as much," he muttered. "It seems to be the only door between the worlds that will actually open."

Irritation in his voice, calling back to a failed plan—a door ripped into the earth, blood on branches, and Neve in the center.

"Other ways can be forced open, well enough." The Seamstress flipped a dismissive hand. "But the only one powerful enough to draw the Kings to it is the Heart Tree."

Neve stiffened. Beside her, Solmir said nothing, but the look in his eyes was banked fire.

"That is neither here nor there, not anymore," the Seamstress continued. "Now we focus on what we know will work."

"Where is it, then?" Solmir asked, low and cold. Trying to mask anxiety with imperiousness. Neve recognized that; she did it herself.

"Where it's always been." Her offering finally sorted, the Seamstress's segmented legs began lifting the insect pieces into the air, affixing them to her ceiling beams. "A castle upside down. Home made a dark reflection."

Solmir's teeth clenched, tight enough so that Neve could almost hear them.

"But things have deteriorated there, just as they have elsewhere." The Seamstress plucked a leg from the piles on the table and popped it into her mouth. "Each of you will need the power of an Old One to enter the Heart Tree's presence. Thankfully, three remain, so you have choices of which two you want to destroy."

Neve's hands felt numb, thinking of the worm-thing, all those teeth. How much worse would an Old One be?

"The Serpent, the Oracle, and the Leviathan." The Seamstress spoke around a full mouth, ticking the leftover gods off on her human fingers. "If I were you, I would go with the first two. The Serpent is near death anyway, holding out against the pull of the Sanctum, and the Oracle is easier to deal with than the Leviathan, ever since you chained it."

Solmir made a noise that was neither agreement nor dissent.

The Seamstress placed her hands on the table, her head tipping forward so her hair hid her face. "My Weaver would offer you its power, were it here," she said quietly. "It was noble like that, willing to accept death for the greater good. And it knew that things must end, that a world made of shadow could not last."

A pause, the Seamstress's grief hanging heavy in the dusty air. "You can pass us the story of your god's dissolving, if you like." Solmir shifted on his feet. "It can make things easier to bear."

Her brow furrowed; Neve shot him a surprised, surreptitious glance. The King sounded almost...kind.

Those strange, faceted eyes closed as the Seamstress sighed. "I would be honored to give you the tale, if you consent to hold it."

"I would be honored to hold the tale, if you consent to give it." Cadences of ceremony, out of Neve's depth. A mourning ritual she had no context for, Solmir offering the bereaved creature some kind of comfort.

It made her stomach twist.

The Seamstress picked up a strand of her dark hair, began absently braiding it. Neve did something similar when her thoughts were rampant and her hands needed a task.

"I wasn't there," the Seamstress began, with an undercurrent of guilt. "My Weaver didn't live with me; it remained a wild creature. It roamed the trees, but always returned. Until it didn't." A shuddering breath. "Hours and days have no meaning here, where everything stays the same, but once it had been gone for long enough that my heart ached with absence, I knew something was wrong."

Neve's eyes flicked to Solmir. The former King still stood with his jaw tight and his arms crossed, but there was something more than cold in his blue eyes. Pity, maybe. Or guilt.

"I am no god," the Seamstress continued. "Power pulls them, the gravity of it tugging them forward—no matter how they might resist—to the Sanctum, where so much magic lies, or to open doors between worlds. I couldn't feel the pull, but my Weaver did. And it grew too strong to resist. My Weaver went to the Kings, went to their Sanctum, unable to stop itself." Her breathing shuddered. "They cut my god with the bones of one of the others; the Dragon, maybe, or the Hawk, one of those that succumbed earliest. They drained its power into themselves. And now my Weaver is gone."

A monstrous story in a monstrous place; a woman twisted for the love of a bestial god. But still, an answering grief stirred in Neve's chest, human feelings for these inhuman things.

"I felt it happen," the Seamstress said. "We were tied together so, my Weaver and I. For its love, I gave up my humanity. Part of me thought I would die once it did." She paused. "I'm sorry I didn't."

She fell quiet; no one filled it. Strange, how the emotions felt by monstrous gods so echoed Neve's own. How they didn't seem so different at all.

The Seamstress thoughtfully curled a segmented leg against her teeth. "I cannot tell time anymore, but I know much has passed since they took my Weaver. Why do you only come now, once-King?"

"Trying out those other plans." Solmir's eyes glittered; the softness he'd shown her while she told the tale of her loss was gone, and now he was all chill and hard edges. "The ones you told me were pointless."

Sharp teeth dimpled her lip as the Seamstress grinned. "I won't say I told you so."

Solmir grunted. "It might've worked, but there were...complications."

Complications like Red, like her Wolf. Even now, Neve didn't know how to feel about that. All these things she'd done to save a sister who didn't want to be saved, who'd made a home of her sacrificial altar.

"It wouldn't have," the Seamstress said flatly. "Open ways between worlds draw gods toward them, yes, but only the Heart Tree can draw something as powerful as the Kings. They felt your doorway, and I'm sure they tried their best to get to it. But they could never have been fully pulled through. Not as they are now."

Solmir's eyes darted Neve's way, a flash of blue too quick for her to try to read.

The Seamstress selected another insect piece from the pile of her offerings. "How busy you've been, once-King. I felt the rupture—all of us did, here on the fringes, though it was too small to draw the Old Ones—but I didn't think it was you who went through. Only a shadow-creature, or some lesser beast. I should've sensed the passage of one with a soul."

"I'm only about as important as some lesser beast now," Solmir said. "And my soul is a small, mean thing."

"Still remarkable you have one." The Seamstress sat back, chewing thoughtfully. "Mine sank into this place long ago, melded with the dark and the muck and the rot as I pulled up magic and let it twist me. I don't even remember what color my eyes were."

"Yours was compromised long before you came here, I think, or you would never have fallen in love with the Weaver." Teasing, it seemed, looked entirely different on Solmir than *mocking* did. There was a light in his eyes that wasn't malice; he held himself more loosely.

"Pots and kettles." The Seamstress flicked the ends of her spider legs like fingers. "I meant no offense. Long friendship tends to make tatters of manners."

"I know it's made tatters of mine." In one smooth motion, like it was something he'd practiced, Solmir sank to one knee. His fist came up and hovered before his forehead, chin tilted to the Seamstress's dusty floor.

Surprise made Neve's brows climb; she looked to the Seamstress, expecting her confusion to be mirrored. But though the creature looked stricken, it seemed more as if she was touched, like Solmir kneeling was one more piece of a ritual between gods and monsters that Neve didn't know.

Faceted arachnid eyes widened, the Seamstress's legs twitching as she backed up a step, one hand coming to her chest. "Oh, once-King, no." It was half a laugh and half a sob. "I'm not a god. I am not one to be shown deference, not beyond the words of welcome."

"You were the Beloved of the Weaver." Again, a sense of capitalization, as if *Beloved* was just as much a title as Shadow Queen. "And the Weaver is gone. I show you the deference I would've shown it." Solmir looked up, face solemn, with none of the contempt Neve had grown to expect as his default. "Anyone who can make an Old One feel something like love is deserving of deference."

The Seamstress quirked her mouth in a sorrowful smile. "You think love is so difficult," she murmured. "Such a fraught thing. But sometimes, it can be simple, even when everything around it is not."

Solmir said nothing. But when he straightened, his mouth was that thin line again, his expression arrogant and cold. Neve watched through narrowed eyes, unsure how to add up all these disparate parts into the whole of him. There was more to Solmir than cruelty and ambition, apparently, but she couldn't trace the fractures in that armor to see what waited beyond it.

Shadow Queen.

Neve flinched. Her head turned, looking for a speaker, whoever had just whispered in her ear. But there was no one else in the cabin, and no one close enough—

The Seamstress. Her eyes were fixed on Neve, hypnotizing in their strangeness, and her mouth didn't move. But it was her. Speaking, somehow, into Neve's head.

I have learned the ways of this place, how sinking yourself into it allows you to speak mind to mind. She sounded bemused, as much as one could when their voice was disembodied. *Swallowing shadow is swallowing a piece of this world, little queen, and then the things of this world can speak to you through it. You pulled us in when you pulled in the magic in your grove. And though the once-King carries that magic now, it still left its marks in you. Magic scars.* Something like a sigh brushed through her head. *I grow so weary of it. All of it.*

Neve glanced at Solmir—all his attention was on the pieces of insects hanging from the rafters. The words of the Old One's lover were for Neve alone, spoken only into her skull.

I was like you once, the Seamstress continued. *A human girl, caught in webs beyond my imagining. The Weaver looked so different on the surface, but I loved it enough to follow it into exile. And by the time I saw its true form, it was beautiful to me, for I'd been changed, too.* She paused. *Monstrousness is a curious thing. In its barest form, its simplest definition, a monster is merely something different than you think it should be. And who gets to decide what should be, anyway?*

Neve thought of black veins and ice, of thorns where flowers should be. She thought of Red, skin traced in green. Solmir held the magic because he knew how to keep it from changing him—at least, that's the reason he claimed. But what if Neve took it back? Would she become something like the Seamstress?

Not one like me, the Seamstress answered. She chuckled. It was an extremely disconcerting thing to hear in one's mind. *And there will be time for taking magic, or taking something else. There is much to hold in this world. The two of you will have to decide who holds what, Shadow Queen.*

What does that mean? Neve wasn't versed in how one carried on a conversation in their head. *To be the Shadow Queen?*

A stretch of silence before the Seamstress answered. *That, ultimately, is up to you.*

"Neverah?"

Solmir's voice startled her out of whatever trance the Seamstress had put her in. Neve shook her head, dispelling the ghost of the spider-woman's giggle. "What?"

His eyes swung between her and the Seamstress, understanding in the arch of one brow. "Ah. So they can talk in your head, too."

"*Too?*" Neve's hand half rose to her forehead, like her thoughts were a physical thing she could shield. "So everyone here can read minds?"

By the hearth, the Seamstress crowed laughter. "Nothing so pedestrian," she reassured her. "It takes immense power to speak mind-to-mind. The Old Ones can do it, and the Kings, though only if you're in their physical presence. Some of those Beloved, like me, though I am the only one left now. Unless you count that awful puppet the Leviathan has made of his Beloved's corpse, and I certainly do not." She gave a delicate shrug. "Just because someone speaks into your mind does not mean they can read it. They can only do that if you allow them." The touch of a sharp-toothed smile on her mouth, just this side of wicked. "Concentrate on not letting them in, Shadow Queen. None of the others will be as kind as I. They'll take your thoughts like pilfered gold without giving you the courtesy of knowing."

Neve swung around to face Solmir, teeth bared. "If you try to read my mind, I swear to you, I will rip your brain right out of your skull."

He raised his hands as if in surrender, a hateful smirk on his mouth, though the emotion in his eyes seemed more complicated than the expression would imply. "I'm not a King anymore, Neverah. Not in the way that matters. I can't read your mind." The smirk hitched higher. "Whatever dirty thoughts you have about me are safe."

She didn't acknowledge *that* with a reply, though her teeth felt close to cracking with the force of keeping her mouth shut.

Another peal of musical laughter from the Seamstress. "However this all plays out, once-King, at least you won't be bored."

"Bored might be better," Solmir muttered, his hands still raised and his eyes still burning.

The air between them crackled like a thunderstorm; then Solmir's arms dropped. He turned away from her, a dismissal that made angry heat flush her cheeks. "If the Heart Tree is where it's always been, then are the other Kings there, too? Trying to force it open?"

The Seamstress gathered a mug from the cupboard behind her, poured in liquid from the kettle over the fire. "How long has it been since you've seen the others, Solmir? You broke with them so long ago. After the first time you went to the Heart Tree. The first time you tried for the surface."

Something shuttered in his eyes. "We're not talking about that."

Spider legs and human hand waved in tandem. "Fine. My point is that you haven't seen the other Kings in centuries. Why do you think they wait for the Old Ones to be pulled to the Sanctum, rather than hunting them down? It's not for sport. It's because they cannot leave. They've delved so deep into Shadowlands magic that they've anchored themselves, as surely as stone to earth." She took a sip of the thick, muddy liquid in her cup, staining her teeth. "The only way the Kings can leave the Sanctum is if the Heart Tree is opened. Only its power is enough to disentangle them and draw them out."

Surprise was another emotion that didn't live easily on Solmir's face.

His mouth hung open a moment before snapping closed, and when he reached up to rub at the puckered scars on his forehead, there was a slight tremor in his hand.

"Physically, the Kings are trapped, but do not let that lull you into false security. They can still send out their thoughts, send projections of themselves. And though the projections cannot touch you, the darkness they command can." The Seamstress licked the dark liquid from her sharp teeth. "There is nothing like safety here. Do not delude yourself into thinking this will be easy."

Solmir's mouth was flat, his eyes narrow. He looked like a man working out a complicated equation in his head, as if this information somehow altered a plan he'd been making and now he needed to amend it. "If they think we're just going to open the Tree," he said, "there's no reason for them to stop us. They'll think we're trying to let them come through."

"They are not stupid," the Seamstress said sharply. "The Kings know that anything you attempt is not in their best interest, Solmir. They will not believe you have accepted your fate so easily." She shrugged, setting down her mug and turning to the cupboard again, her segmented legs pulling something from within its depths too quickly for Neve to see what it was. "I do not know if they will try to stop you from reaching the Tree, but they will not sit idly by as you do it. You play a complicated game, and it is impossible to know what moves they will make."

"What fate?" Neve asked, turning to Solmir. She kept her tone cool and her face implacable. "What fate have you not accepted?"

Another flash of calculation in his eyes; to be expected when speaking with Solmir, apparently. Every word out of his mouth always seemed carefully calibrated, honed to cut. "Being one of them," he answered. "Never being anything else, because once I was a King."

She wanted to respond with something sharp, something that sliced. But a ghost of vulnerability hung around his sneer, and for reasons she couldn't quite name, that kept her silent.

The Seamstress turned back around from the cupboard, whatever she'd retrieved hidden in all her spider legs. "If I were you," she said, ignoring the conversation they'd had while her back was turned, "I'd start with the Serpent."

"You make it sound like the Serpent will welcome us," Solmir said.

"It will, for it knows what your coming will mean. Live long enough, once-King, and death becomes a kindness. You aren't there yet, I don't think." A pause. "I am."

It hung there, a casual death wish. Neve couldn't tell whether it surprised Solmir or not. If it did, he hid it this time. No emotion flickered on his face at all; he could've been marble-carved.

The Seamstress broke the silence. She waved a hand at the corner of the cabin. "You look the same size as I was back when I had need of boots, Shadow Queen. There might be some over there."

She was loathe to turn her back on these two, but Neve *did* need shoes. She went to the corner and brushed away cobwebs, finding a dusty pair that looked ancient but intact enough to be an improvement over bare feet. She shoved the boots on and laced them up, glad for something to cut the chill even if it was centuries old.

Behind her, Solmir and the Seamstress stood in silence. But it was a heavy kind, one that made her wonder if they were carrying on a mental conversation of their own, one she'd been dismissed for.

"Thank you," she said as she walked the short distance back across the cabin, both out of genuine thanks and as a way to signal her presence if they were deep in each other's thoughts.

The Seamstress didn't look at her but gave Solmir a sad, small smile. "One favor for another." Her legs turned, revealing what she'd taken from the cupboard.

A bone.

On first glance, it looked like a human femur. But the proportions were off—it was too short, the nodule at one end too small. The other end had been carved into a sharp point, making it about the size and shape of a dagger.

"The Weaver gave me this," she said, peering at the ivory as if she could see a future in it. Maybe she could. "So many eons ago, when I was just a human woman with no idea what awaited me. A bone from one of my Weaver's own legs, as a token of our devotion." Her eyes turned to Solmir. "You have been a good friend, once-King. At least, in the way of friends in this place. And you hold the magic for the Shadow Queen." She put the bone in Solmir's hand and, slowly, knelt before him. "You will need more. And I am so tired."

Understanding slipped into place like a hand to a glove; the death of the wormlike lesser beast, the way it broke into shadow—but the shadow had been magic, unmoored from the Shadowlands, free for the taking.

That's what the Seamstress offered. More magic, through her death.

"I grow weary, Solmir. This world dies all around us." She looked up, faceted eyes peaceful. "My power is small. But you will need every scrap of it you can get, to do what you must do."

The King's eyes blazed blue, a battle in them whose sides Neve couldn't make sense of. Then he nodded, one jerk of his chin.

"May the next world be kinder, Beloved," he said quietly.

The Seamstress closed her eyes, smiled. "It has to be."

Then Solmir plunged the sharpened bone into her neck.

No blood. Instead, shadows, spilling from the wound like smoke. Scraps of magic skittering away from a dead vessel.

Solmir raised his hand. The shadows flocked to him, inking his palm black, his forearm, seeping up to his heart. His teeth set on edge, but he made no sound.

Neve wondered if it hurt.

Thank you.

It was a bare breath of sound against the inside of her skull, and she somehow knew Solmir heard the same thing, a warped kind of intimacy.

Then the Seamstress was gone, the cottage empty but for Neve and Solmir. She didn't even leave a stain on the floor, no sign of her life but the pulsing shadow working through Solmir's veins. Slowly, it faded, packed down and shut away.

Solmir stared at the spot on the floor where the Seamstress's body should be. Then he turned and strode out the door.

With a ragged swallow, Neve followed.

The cold air of the Shadowlands seemed almost fresh after the close quarters of the cottage. The three-eyed goat bleated in the yard, this time with a sound like shattering glass.

Solmir didn't face her, but when she approached, he held out the bone. "You take this." His voice was flat, inflectionless. "Only the bone of a god can kill another, and they must be gods that were made in the same way."

It was smooth and heavy in her hand, but weighed less than Neve thought it should. "So it could kill you?"

"Don't sound too excited." Solmir started forward. "I'm not a god anymore."

The goat bleated again, the sound of two blades meeting, and Neve turned to look at it, balancing the bone in her hand.

She thought of power, of need.

Solmir's eyes tracked from her to the goat, to the bone twisting in her grip. "Not much power," he said softly, the answer to a question she hadn't the stomach to ask. "But some."

"She said we would need it," Neve whispered.

A nod.

"Will this thing kill it?"

"Lesser beasts aren't gods; they can be vanquished by any god-bone, not just one from a creature made in the same way," Solmir said. "It's only gods themselves that get particular."

She nodded, the pad of her finger absently rubbing at the smooth ivory. "Can you take more?"

His lips skinned back from his teeth. "I can always take more."

Cautiously, Neve stepped toward the goatlike lesser beast. It bleated when she slammed the bone into its throat, and it sounded like a woman's scream.

Chapter Six

Neve

Neither of them spoke as they pushed through the inverted trees again, growing so close together Neve could use them like handholds as she picked her way over the uneven ground. Walking was much easier in boots.

Up ahead, Solmir didn't move with the predator-like grace she'd grown to expect. He seemed shaky, almost, like someone fighting off the first throes of a fever. His veins flickered sporadic darkness, fingers flexing out and then in again, as if something was trying to work out of them.

She eyed him warily. He'd said he could always take more magic, but it looked like it wasn't as easy as he'd made it sound.

Something almost like concern rose in her chest. Neve hated that. Solmir didn't deserve her concern.

Still, he was the only thing that seemed even marginally safe in the entire Shadowlands. And her only source of magic, if she didn't want to twist into something monstrous.

Another quake moved through the ground, making her cling to the trunk of an inverted tree to keep from falling. Ahead, Solmir did the same, steadying himself with one black-flickering hand against pale bark. When the earth settled, he spared her a glance to make sure she was in one piece before heading off again.

But then he stumbled, just slightly, disrupting his precise speed. He stopped, turned to face her, jaw drawn tight and hand pressed against his middle. His eyes were cast downward, but when Neve advanced a step, they flickered up to hers. She froze.

The whites of Solmir's eyes had gone completely dark.

Neve wanted to back away, to hold up her hands between them as a paltry shield. Instead, she frowned, hoping it covered her fear. "Are you going to pass out?"

Sharp and prim; she kept her concern behind her teeth. It was practical to be concerned, really. The last thing Neve needed was to be left in the Shadowlands alone.

"No, Neverah, I'm not going to pass out." The flickers of shadow along his veins had lessened, but his eyes were still new-moon black around the blazing ocean of his irises. He turned on his heel, resting his back against the trunk of a tree, rubbing at the scars on his forehead. The movement made a flash of that strange tattoo show through his shirt again. "Magic is a slippery thing to hold. Especially when you have to keep it from subsuming your soul."

Her brow arched. "So you're in a battle for your soul as we speak? Rather melodramatic."

"Truly." He pushed off the tree with a slight grimace, rings glinting as he swept back his hair. Darkness still fluttered along his limbs, but it disappeared even as Neve watched, shadow going wherever he kept it. "I'll be just fine in a moment or two. Don't waste any worry on me. I know you have a very limited supply for anyone who isn't Redarys."

Her brows slashed down, but Neve didn't reply.

His long hair trailed, smoke-colored, as Solmir moved through the trees again, every step seeming stronger. Neve chewed her lip a moment before following. "Where are we going?"

"Somewhere we can rest."

"I expect my questions to be answered clearly." Vowels clipped, tone measured. Damn her if she wouldn't still sound like a Queen, even in ancient boots and a bedraggled nightgown and Solmir's old, too-large coat. "It's the least you can do."

For a moment, she didn't think he'd reply. Solmir's gait had eased, all that thorny magic he'd absorbed finding comfortable places to wait until they needed it, and he turned fully around to face her. He didn't like half looks when he could help it, she'd noticed; he wasn't one for coy glances over the shoulder. Solmir seemed to prefer facing her head-on.

He dipped his head. "Yes, Your Majesty."

Neve balled her fists.

The corner of his mouth turned up, wicked and sharp. "The Weaver wasn't the only Old One who had an adherent follow them into the Shadowlands, though she's the only one still alive." He paused, only for a second, something dimming in his gaze. "Well. She was."

He didn't sound sorrowful, not really. But there was a finality in his tone, and a sense of emptiness. The difference between knowing something was gone and feeling its absence when you reached for it.

A minuscule shake of Solmir's head, only visible because of the way it stirred his hair. "The Dragon had one, long ago. The Rat, too—to each their own when deciding who to go to bed with, but *that* I can't quite wrap my head around. And the Leviathan." His mouth flicked down in distaste. "The Leviathan kept its lover's body, apparently. As a testament to their devotion. Love devolves very quickly into horror when gods are involved."

"Love can devolve quickly into horror with anyone," Neve said quietly.

"Don't I know it," he muttered as he pivoted away from her, started forward again.

The inverted forest looked all the same, no variation to mark the passage of distance or time, but Neve estimated they walked another mile before they reached the cabin.

This one looked even more uncanny than the Seamstress's had. The cabin was up on stilts, tall enough so that its roof brushed the underside of the ever-present fog that floated in place of clouds here. A rope ladder dangled from the platform that held the cabin to the ground, twisting gently back and forth. For all that the roof sagged—and there was one ragged hole gaping in the side Neve could see—the stilts themselves looked solid enough.

Still, when Solmir grabbed the ladder, Neve shook her head. "Absolutely not. Why would we—"

"Are you tired, Neverah?"

The question took her aback, but there was a heaviness in her eyes, and her limbs did feel harder to hold up the longer they lingered here, as if standing still had allowed exhaustion to catch her. "Is that relevant?"

Solmir's arms flexed, making the ladder swing back and forth. His hair followed, waving in the gray air. Neve hoped the rope snapped. "You've been awake far longer than your body is used to. We both need to get some sleep." A flash of teeth. "It seems we have quite the journey ahead of us, and I, for one, would like to be well rested."

He started climbing the ladder, the muscles of his back working as he hauled himself up, that tattoo on his arm prominent again through the fabric of his shirt.

Neve scowled at him. "So we're both going to sleep in the same decrepit cabin?"

"You're welcome to stay down there and sleep on the ground if you want."

"Kings on shitting horses," Neve muttered.

A snort came faintly from above her.

Climbing the rope in borrowed boots and a nightgown proved difficult, and Neve was out of breath when she reached the platform at the top. It seemed mostly sturdy, though there were gaps between some of the wooden planks large enough to put a foot through.

The door slumped open on broken hinges. Neve stepped through cautiously; the pervasive cold of the Shadowlands was even more pronounced up here, and she instinctually tugged Solmir's coat tighter around her shoulders.

The inside of the cabin was just as run-down as the outside. The gaping hole to the right of the door took out most of the wall—Solmir was in the process of pushing what looked like an old wardrobe in front of it to block out the breeze, shoulders working in a way that Neve was irritated with herself for noticing.

When the wardrobe was situated in front of the hole, Solmir straightened, dusted off his hands. He caught Neve's narrowed eyes and shrugged. "Won't do much for the cold, but better than nothing."

Other than the wardrobe, the only furnishings left in the cabin were a broken table listing against the opposite wall and a threadbare rug in the center of the room. Something was stuck in the rug's weave, spiny shards flecked with odd fibers.

Neve bent down to lightly touch one of them. Feathers.

"This was the home of the Hawk's lover. He's been dead a long time, almost as long as the Hawk has been." Solmir sat down against the wall and began unlacing his boots. "The Old Ones' lovers don't seem to outlast them for long."

"That's the trouble with religion," Neve said. "Tying the reason for your existence to a god seems to naturally lead to your existence not mattering much."

Solmir cocked a brow, still working his laces. "For someone who ushered in a new spiritual order, you hold religion in great contempt."

"You knew that already." Neve didn't follow his example of making herself as comfortable as she could, instead standing stiffly next to the rug. She still had his coat clutched around her. "I might've tried to show piety in the true world, but I don't think I fooled you."

His hands stilled; Solmir looked up at her, blue eyes narrow and blazing in the gray-scale gloom. It made Neve want to call the words back, cage them in her throat.

The moment passed; he turned back to his boots. "You fooled everyone else well enough, if it's any consolation." He snorted. "Except Kiri, maybe."

It was the opposite of consolation, but Neve didn't tell him that. Didn't tell him that the two villains in her story being able to read her better than anyone else was a fact that clawed her gut and hollowed her chest.

"I didn't fool Raffe," she said quietly. Almost a weapon. Proof that someone else looked at her and saw truth.

Mostly.

The name made Solmir's mouth twist as he leaned his head back against the wall. "Raffe would believe whatever you told him." He snorted. "That's what *true love* does, isn't it? I wouldn't know."

Her hands closed to fists in the too-long sleeves of his coat. True love. Right.

She shook her head, banishing thoughts of Raffe and whatever lay between them and all the invariable ways she'd broken it. With a sigh, she settled on the rug, then lay back, head cradled on threadbare fabric and broken feathers.

"Comfortable?" Solmir asked.

"Better than a glass coffin."

Silence. She heard Solmir shift against the wall. "I would say I was sorry about that," he said, voice nearly as sharp as hers had been, "but it was to keep you safe, actually. I understand that you have a hard time believing I'm concerned with your safety, but it's true." Another pause, longer, heavier in the cold air. "I need you, Neverah. Unfortunately for us both."

"It wasn't worth it," Neve said, curling up on her side. She pillowed her head on her arms, the fabric of his coat scratchy against her cheek, smelling of pine and snow.

"What wasn't?"

"Keeping me safe," she replied.

Fog. Not just around her—it felt like the fog was *in* her, like she'd dissipated and become nothing but smoke herself. It was peaceful, almost.

Dreaming. She must be dreaming.

Neve wasn't one to dream deeply or often, wasn't one for ascribing some sort of richer meaning to whatever her brain spilled out in sleep. But something felt...different here. Heavy. *Aware.*

She couldn't feel the floor, but she knew she was lying on it; couldn't feel the weave of the coat pressed against her face, but knew it was there. The pinions of old feathers poked through her nightgown, and she felt them as if they were pressing through thick fabric instead, present but distant.

And she felt magic.

Not much, nothing like what she'd carried before Solmir took it with that bruising, terrible kiss, or even the cold slither that had been a constant on the surface, when she was stealing it daily with blood on a sentinel. But there was a breath of it deep within her, the prick of thorns in her very center, like something had been permanently altered in ways kisses couldn't fix.

Her soul, maybe.

Slowly, the fog around her dispersed. As it did, the feeling of being incorporeal faded, Neve's consciousness weighting back down into her limbs.

The shifting fog revealed a massive tree.

But only part of one, the lower half. A tower of roots, twisting in on each other, tall as three of her. If she craned her neck, she could almost see where the trunk began in the fog, what seemed like miles above her head. Looking down, she saw she stood on roots, too. The tree was the only solid thing she could see, the rest of the world made only of mist.

The roots were white, like the branches in the Shrine, like the trees in the inverted forest. Dark veins ran through them, streaks of shadow that were still somehow luminescent. But far above, where the roots ended and the trunk began, were faint glimmers of gold.

Neverah Valedren.

A voice, reverberating all around her, coming from every direction and none at all. The diffuse sound made it difficult to pick out characteristics, but it came across as vaguely masculine, confident. Half familiar.

She took a step forward, toward the root tower. The tree itself grew no closer, but every step seemed to ground her more in her body. Her nightgown was gone, and Solmir's coat and the Seamstress's boots, leaving her in nothing but a gauzy white covering that reminded her uncomfortably of a shroud.

Following some deep dream instinct, Neve began to climb up the roots toward the trunk.

Something glimmered in all that white wood. As she drew closer, she saw it was a mirror, one framed in golden gilt that looked vaguely shabby against the luminous glow of the tree bark. Rusty stains marred the frame, the color almost unbearably lurid, and blond hairs had been woven through the whorls like rays from a faded sun.

But the mirror wasn't nearly as unsettling as the reflection it held.

Neve's veins were black under white skin, every one of them, tracing her entire frame in a lacing of darkness. Tiny spikes grew down from her wrist, largest near her hand, tapering into smaller points as they grew nearer her elbow. More thorns stood out from her knuckles, a gauntlet. And her eyes were wholly, completely black.

Just like Solmir's had been when he took in all that magic from the Seamstress, the lesser beasts they'd killed. Except hers didn't have the slightest touch of color that signified the presence of a soul.

This must be the monstrousness he was saving her from.

Gently, Neve lifted one thorn-laced hand and touched the mirror's silvery surface, her skin gray against the red and gold.

Something shifted in the glass. A momentary distortion of her reflection, her gauntness filled out and given color. Dark-gold hair, fierce brown eyes, a face with fuller lips and plumper cheeks than her own.

Red.

There and then gone, and Neve all but clawed at the mirror, her spiked hands arching on the glass as if she could smash it. "Red! Can you hear me? Come back!"

But her reflection was merely her own again, and even that was momentary. The mirror stopped picking up her image and instead showed only a thick tangle of tree roots touched with darkness.

Neve slapped her hand against the glass. "*Red!*"

Nothing.

She slid to her knees, pressing the heels of her hands against her eyes, mindless of her bracelets of thorns.

You almost have it.

That voice again, the one that had said her name, full and soft and somehow familiar, like a memory from childhood she couldn't quite hold together. Sorrow welled in it, one deep enough to make answering pain echo in her chest. She took her hands from her eyes—no blood, as if her thorns were incapable of harming their wielder—and peered into the fog. "What?"

You aren't ready to be the mirror yet. Not until you find the Tree, find the key.

Neve shook her head. Nonsense words in a nonsense place, but the voice had mentioned the Tree, and that made her think this was something she should pay attention to. "Who are you? An Old One? One of their adherents?"

A pause. Behind the mirror, in the gaps between the tree roots, Neve almost saw a figure. It was gone too quickly to make out anything distinct.

I don't know what I am. Not really. Faint, with a note of longing. *But I don't think I ever did.*

Frustration faded to something more complicated. Neve swallowed, gnawing on her bottom lip. "Why should I trust you, then?"

You probably shouldn't. Almost joking. *But you've made lots of questionable decisions when it comes to whom to trust.*

Damn her if she was going to be lectured by a disembodied voice in a shadowy not-quite-dream—she'd rather just get to the point. "Do you know something about the Tree?"

I think I do. Maybe. But memories... they're like fog. A billow of mist rolled across Neve's feet. *When I see you, it's easier. But I'm caught in between.*

"Between what?"

The two worlds. The two of you. Life and death, too, I think.

Neve wrapped her arms around herself, cold seeping through the gauzy dream-dress. "Tell me what you know."

The Tree waits for you, in the place it's always been. But just reaching it is not enough—there must be a mirrored journey, a matched love. And a key, if you're to return.

"So where do I get a key?" That seemed like the best place to start. Mirrored journeys, matching love… that, she could deal with later.

Once you need it, it will be there.

Neve frowned into the mist. "Are you sure you can't tell me who you are?"

A pause. *When I remember, I'll let you know.*

Fog slithered over Neve's skin. She shivered—it felt almost invasive, as if it were looking for something.

The voice went stern. *You're an empty vessel.*

She shifted on her feet. "Solmir is holding the magic. So I don't…" She trailed off, looked down at her thorny hands. "So I don't end up like this."

The voice fell quiet. More fog slid over her, considering.

That will change, it said finally. *The past and the present and the future all twine together here, and all paths look as solid as the one that will be. But he'll do what's right, in the end. That is solid and sure.*

He. Solmir? Neve didn't ask for clarification, but it made her mouth pull down. The idea of Solmir doing what was right, of it being *solid and sure,* seemed nearly as likely as her wanting to kiss him for any reason other than magic.

Another flash of a shape in the roots beyond the mirror, concrete enough for her to pick out broad shoulders and a narrow waist before it faded again. *Look up.*

She did. Slowly, a branch descended through the fog. Bare of leaves, and in addition to being crossed with dark veins, the white wood held glimmers of gold. Duality trapped in bark. It stopped right above her head, close enough for her to reach out and touch what grew there.

Apples. One black, one gold, one crimson.

Her hand nearly moved of its own accord, reaching up through the mist to touch the black apple. It was warm. Smelled somehow of copper. The points of tiny thorns studded the dark flesh, like they were growing outward from the apple's center.

Don't pick it.

An urgency in the voice. Neve dropped her hand. "What is this?" She breathed. "This is more than a dream."

Everything here is more than what it seems. The apples swayed gently above her head. *Having two worlds means having a place between them, and you belong to neither one nor the other. Things appear as you can conceive of them.* Amusement colored the voice. *That is no more an apple than you are, but your eyes need something to see.*

"Is this a place between worlds, then?"

In a way. A place between life and death. A place to lock things in. A pause. *We are too skilled at making prisons.*

Many words that gave few answers. Neve frowned, anxiously worked her nails into the meat of her palm. "Should I tell him?" she asked quietly. "About everything you've said?"

Do what you want, the voice said. *Everyone has to decide how best to tell the story of their own villain.*

Her nails bit deeper.

I have nothing else for you. She couldn't imagine how a disembodied voice managed to sound so weary. It pricked at that familiarity again, made her lips twist in an effort to recall where exactly she'd heard that same shade of tired, of run-down and heartsick. *Go back to him.*

And her eyes flew open at the command.

Neve stayed curled on her side for a moment, with a feeling like falling back into herself. Awareness came piecemeal, to her legs and then her arms, her heart. Physically, she hadn't moved, but it still felt like she'd traveled miles.

A place between worlds. Between life and death. Things too large and heavy to understand, things her thoughts couldn't wrap around.

But she didn't spend much time trying, distracted by something else. Because here, in this ruined cabin in the Shadowlands, someone was singing.

A language she didn't recognize, a low and droning melody that lilted up and down like a lullaby. She heard the scrape of metal across wood; then the song was interrupted with a curse.

Solmir sat with one knee bent and the other stretched out, leaning back against the wall of the cabin. His thumb was in his mouth, a dagger in his hand and a small piece of whittled wood lying on the floor, in a shape that looked deliberate.

His eyes flicked her way when she moved. "Good morning, sleeping beauty," he muttered around his thumb.

"Except there's no *morning* here." Neve sat up slowly, muscles protesting. "What were you singing?"

His thumb dropped from his mouth. A gray spot marred it, blood leached of color. "Was I singing?"

He looked so different, for that small moment. Sprawled out and vulnerable, human. Someone who might be capable of doing the right thing, whatever that was.

"Yes," Neve said, waspish. "Loudly."

The snap of her tone wasn't lost on him. Solmir straightened, wiped his thumb on his shirt, picked up the carved wood, and stuck it in his pocket. "Forgive me, Your Majesty. One whiles away the hours as they can."

"By singing and...whittling?"

"It *would* be drinking and bedsport, but the Shadowlands are woefully empty of wine and I'll wait for you to ask me for the other."

An angry flush ran from her forehead to her chest. "I'd sooner ask you to throw me into the mouth of the next lesser beast we come across."

"Don't threaten me with a good time." He stood, swept a hand toward the lolling door. "Now that we're both well rested, let's go destroy a god."

Chapter Seven

Red

"It *changed*, Eammon. I showed you yesterday, and you said to wait and see if it stayed." She waved her hand. "It *did*. It has to mean something."

Red stood next to the mirror, still fringed with strands of her split-ended hair and spotted with her blood, still with a pile of fingernail clippings as a macabre centerpiece before it. The sight of all her sacrifices discomfited Eammon, she could tell, but he didn't comment on them. He stood next to her, arms crossed, staring into the mirror with its reflected tangle of roots. His heavy brows drew together, his mouth pressed to a thin line.

The ghost of the argument that had dogged them for days hung close. She'd been understanding yesterday, had given it time to see if he was right and the change in the mirror was a fluke. Now she was ready for action. Ready to do something. Anything.

"It might," Eammon hedged, still reluctant. "Or it could mean the mirror just doesn't work anymore. Now that we're the Wilderwood, the magic has changed, the ties that made it show First Daughters altered in ways we don't understand yet."

"Yes, I'm aware, thank you. But your mother made the mirror to see her sister. *That* is its function, and that is what I am trying to do." Red's hand cut toward the mirror. "If it worked before, why wouldn't it now, when the Wilderwood is the strongest it's been in centuries?"

"Because before, Neve wasn't in the Shadowlands."

"But if it's supposed to help me see her—"

"Red, the Shadowlands are *wrong*." The last word was almost a growl. "It's an upside-down world filled with monsters that are terrible and gods that are worse. Even if we knew how to open it now that the Wilderwood has changed form, you can't just make a way into something like that, not without dire consequences. It's dark, and it's twisted, and it twists everything within it."

Everything within it. Like Neve.

Eammon kept his arms crossed tight over his broad chest, his pushed-up sleeves revealing the runnels of long-healed scars, the bark-like vambraces on his forearms. "It could be a clue," he said finally. "It could be nothing. I just don't want you to get your hopes up, Red. I don't want..." He trailed off, rubbed at his eyes with thumb and forefinger.

The quiet thickened around them, something that could suffocate. They'd circled this for days, and finally it was here.

Red swallowed. "You don't want what, Eammon?"

His hand dropped, finally, green-ringed eyes turning her way. "I don't want you to hurt yourself trying to save her," he said, each word spoken quiet and clear.

"But that's what she did for me."

"And did you want her to?"

"It's not the same. I didn't need saving. We *know* Neve does."

Eammon didn't respond to that. But his expression remained implacable.

Red's mouth felt like a vise from how tight she held it, as if her whole body were a bow and it the arrow. "You think we can't bring her back."

"I didn't say that."

"You didn't have to."

"I think there is a good chance we can bring her back." She knew every tone in Eammon's voice, knew when he was lying and when he told the truth and when he lingered somewhere in between. This was truth, but a thin one. "But it's not going to be easy, Red. She's in a prison that's meant to be impenetrable. It's going to take more than…than *hunches* and mirrors to pull her out of that, and we need to make sure we know what we're doing before we try anything."

Anger made her veins blaze bright green. "So you just want to read some more," she hissed, "while my sister is trapped with the monsters? With the Kings? I've seen what's down there, Eammon, and I'm not going to leave her."

"Of course we aren't going to leave her. But we need to take the time—"

"She doesn't *have time!*"

Red didn't mean to scream it; her voice was hoarse, and it made the words almost a half sob. Eammon's hands reached out, an instinct to comfort, but she backed away. His hands fell.

She held up her arm, traced in green veins, delicately braceleted in bark. "We have all the time in the world," she whispered. "But Neve doesn't. Neve is still human."

Eammon stood stiffly, eyes unreadable. "And do you regret no longer being human, Redarys?"

He still used her full name sometimes—in bed or in jest. But this was formal. Distant.

Her stomach bottomed out.

"Of course not," she breathed, but she couldn't quite make herself reach out and touch him. "You know that."

He didn't respond, just kept looking at her with that level amber-and-green gaze.

Finally, Eammon sighed. "I'll be in the library." He turned toward the staircase. "Come when you can." His footsteps echoed down the stairs, the door creaking at the bottom as he pushed it open.

Red crossed from the mirror over to one of the vine-carved windows, watching him trek across the courtyard to the Keep. Part of her wanted to call out to him, to reel him back, to let him take her on the floor of the tower until both of them forgot their argument.

She didn't.

Instead, she thought of all the trees within her, the Wilderwood she carried beneath her skin. The sentinels she and Eammon had absorbed, the sentinels whose rotting had opened doors into the Shadowlands.

Eammon wanted to wait. Wanted to find a way to Neve that was perfectly safe, one that didn't carry any risk. Red knew that wasn't possible. She understood his fear—the thought of losing him twisted everything in her middle into barbed knots—but Eammon didn't have a sibling. A twin. He couldn't understand this, the unique pain of it.

Red couldn't leave Neve in the Shadowlands any longer. She couldn't wait for Eammon to find his mythical perfect plan that didn't risk anything.

And she couldn't let him keep her from trying something that might work.

A rustle in her head, like wind through trees. A warning? A benediction? She didn't care. Her plan was loose and ill formed, but it was the only thing Red could think of that had a chance of working, and desperation covered a multitude of holes.

Down in the courtyard, Eammon paused at the door of the Keep. He turned, looked back up at her, eyes shadowed by noonday sun. Then he disappeared inside.

If she told him, he would stop her—might go so far as to lock her in the damn library. If Red was going to do this, it had to be now, and it had to be alone.

So as the door of the Keep closed behind Eammon, Red made her way to the stairs.

<hr />

There was no threat to her in the Wilderwood now, but going beyond the gate still made her heart kick up against her throat. Red closed it quietly behind her, though she knew no one was listening. Eammon would be nose-deep in a book by now, as much to forget about their argument as to find anything useful, and Fife and Lyra would still be on their way back from meeting Raffe after spending last night in the capital.

Still, she watched the trees warily as she slipped between them. Old habits were hard to break.

Moving quickly was a challenge with the mirror clutched to her chest. Red tilted it away from her abdomen, frowning into the surface. Still clogged with that strange and layered root-darkness, nearly impossible to make out if you didn't squint.

Surely, the roots meant she needed a sentinel. Needed to tug one from within herself, make a doorway to pull Neve through. What else could it mean?

Another rustle against her thoughts, the golden thread running alongside them vibrating like a plucked harp string. The Wilderwood communicating *something*, but she wasn't sure what.

There was so little Red understood about what she'd become. Woman on the outside—mostly—forest within. She remembered thinking of Eammon like a scale, tipping back and forth from bone to branch, the balance hard to hold. Since they'd become the Wilderwood, it was like they'd put a brace on those scales, kept them in perfect equilibrium.

So what might happen if she tipped them again? If she let what was inside back *out*?

Red shook her head, dispelling the doubt that wanted to collect in her thoughts and make itself something to stumble on. This was for Neve. She'd accept the consequences.

It was the least she could do.

Her route wasn't planned. But when Red arrived at the clearing where she'd laid the other Second Daughters' bones to rest—where she'd found Eammon half subsumed in forest, what felt like lifetimes ago—it seemed right. Gold and ocher leaves carpeted the ground, their sharp almost-cinnamon scent thick in the air. No more sentinels lined the circular edge, but the place still felt closer to holy than anywhere else she'd ever been.

One place in particular. There was no trace of the sentinel with the scar on its bark anymore—the sentinel where the words that mandated the Second Daughter sacrifice had appeared, where Tiernan Niryea Andraline, Gaya's older sister, had hacked them off and brought them back to Valleyda—but something in Red recognized the ground where it had been. She carried the map of the Wilderwood inside her, and this spot was marked.

After a moment of consideration, she sat the mirror on the ground where the tree had grown, faceup. The gold of her hair woven into the frame nearly matched the leaves. Red sank onto her knees beside it and pulled a short dagger from her belt.

Maybe this was foolish. Maybe it would do nothing—none of her other sacrifices to the mirror had. Or maybe this was finally the thing that would save Neve, here in the clearing where she'd saved Eammon, where magic and blood ran so closely together.

The only thing Red knew for sure was that she couldn't leave Neve in the dark. Couldn't leave her with the monsters.

It was what Neve would do for her.

The Wilderwood within Red was quiet. No rustling, not in her mind, not beneath her skin—usually, the run of her blood was a breeze that sent leaves stirring, the beat of her heart made branches sway. Now the forest rooted in her bones stayed frozen, waiting to see what she would do. To see how she might strike the scale.

Red took a deep breath. The dagger hovered over her palm, unsteady, and the golden line of the Wilderwood against her thoughts was still and silent.

She dropped the dagger. Blood had always been a stopgap, never a real solution—when Eammon had given her half the Wilderwood, at the edge of the forest when he was all magic, all he'd done was lay his hand on her heart.

A moment, then Red settled her hand on the autumn leaves, felt them crunch beneath her skin as she pressed her fingers toward the earth.

"I want to let one go," she said, after a beat of silence. "One of the sentinels. I need one outside of myself, so I can get to my sister." A noise that wasn't a laugh and wasn't a sob, something that lived in the wild, raw space between. "So I can open a locked door."

She felt slightly ridiculous, stating her intentions to the ground. But she remembered the moment she took the roots, in that dank prison beneath the Valleydan palace, and how she'd had to let the forest know exactly what she wanted. Let it know that everything she did was her own choice.

At first, nothing.

Then a roar.

It took her a moment to realize that it came from her own mouth, a flare of feeling licking up from her hand, down her arm, blazing around her heart. Red's back arched, not in pain, but something beyond it, so surpassing the binary of hurt and pleasure that it seemed of a different world than she knew.

A tearing within her, a wrenching of her spine, some vital thing ripped from her deepest places. Both more solid and more ephemeral than one of the sentinels she carried, as if her soul was detaching itself from her body.

Red was the forest inside, she was the world outside—she felt part of herself splitting off, rooting into the ground, spreading her awareness out from her own mind and into the earth and everything it touched.

Infinite. Omniscient.

She hadn't just tipped the scale—she'd knocked it over, upended the entire thing. Her blood and intention turned her inside out, made the human recede and the forest surge forward, unraveling her into light and unfettered magic. It was beautiful, it was intoxicating.

It was going to drive her mad.

Every single one of her veins ran verdant, then blazed to gold. Roots grew out of her hands, but they didn't split off—her skin paled, hardened, bark spreading up her arms and toward her heart.

She wasn't just freeing a sentinel. She was *becoming* one. Her and this tree, one and the same, her body made a doorway.

Red felt more than saw Eammon skid into the clearing, taking in her and the mirror lying by her side, knowing in a split second what she'd done. He cursed, loud and long. "Redarys!"

A *boom* rattled through the forest. It vibrated in Red's bones, through the parts of her that were sentinel and the parts that were still woman, almost like a call.

In her fingers—what had been her fingers, what were now roots, stretching through the earth—Red felt a heartbeat. Not her own, but a counterpoint, as if she'd reached for someone and grasped only part of them.

As the shock wave shot through the trees, Eammon...shifted. All the changes the Wilderwood had wrought in him blazed, obscuring his shape for a moment. Where he'd stood there was a hole, a man's shape in the atmosphere that held nothing but golden light and tall white trees, like someone had used his body as a canvas and painted the Wilderwood over it.

The golden thread of the forest running alongside her thoughts twinged, sending a melodious sound reverberating through her head, beautiful and terrible at once. The arm that bore her Mark—now half bark—burned and ached, as if she'd caged sunlight beneath her skin.

"Call yourself back, Redarys," Eammon snarled at her, in a voice layered in leaves and barely human at all. "Call yourself back to me."

It seemed too simple, the thought that she could simply *stop*. And did she really want to? If this was what saving Neve required of her? How far was too far, when you loved someone this much?

Eammon's eyes. Amber haloed in deepest green, aching and damp. "Please, Red." His voice, unfettered by leaves, hoarse and low. "Don't leave."

Don't you dare leave me here alone. She'd said it to him once, in this same clearing. A promise between them, before they'd admitted anything else. A promise she wouldn't break now.

Gritting teeth that felt like bark and tasted like sap, Red tugged at the Wilderwood, spearing her intention back into the ground just as she'd done when she began.

Not like this, she thought, sending the words like arrows. *Give me another way.*

And the Wilderwood sighed, as if it'd been wanting that all along.

Her consciousness collapsed back into a humanlike shape as Red pulled herself from the earth. At first, her fingers were still roots, white and thin, but slowly they retracted into the form of a hand, skin instead of bark. It hurt, and she shuddered.

A shape lay in her palm. Too clumped in dirt to make it out, as if she'd tugged something from within the earth. She didn't have time to puzzle over what it was—the ground rumbled beneath her, lurching like the back of a waking beast. It was enough to toss her off-balance; Red shoved the shape into the pocket of her tunic and braced her hands on the ground.

As soon as it had begun, the rumbling stopped.

And in the mirror, there was still nothing but dark tree roots.

The bitter tang of dirt in her mouth tasted like failure.

Across the clearing, Eammon's eyes blazed, brown and green, the veins above his bark-armored forearms standing stark against scarred skin. He looked more like a forest god than a man. They stared at each other, the air between them crackling.

"What are you doing?" It gritted through his teeth like a curse. "What are you *doing*, Red?"

"This made the most sense." She stood on shaking legs. "It's how the Shadowlands have always been opened before. I knew you would stop me if I told you."

"Damn right I would." He stepped forward, moving like a predator. "Damn right I would stop you from coming apart for no reason. From doing the absolute most dangerous thing you could, when you don't even know it will work."

"She's my sister, Eammon."

"And you're my *wife*." Almost a snarl, and his hands curled into claws. "You expect me to just sit by while you unravel?"

"It's what you expected of me, wasn't it?"

His mouth snapped shut.

Red closed her eyes, took a deep, shuddering breath. "I couldn't just not try."

Eammon shook his head. "You should've told—"

"*What* do you want?" A new voice, pierced through with so much vitriol it distracted both of them from their fury. Two pairs of forest-altered eyes turned to the edge of the clearing.

Fife, teeth bared and face stormy. One sleeve pushed up, his opposite hand clasped around his forearm. Beneath his fingers, the Bargainer's Mark blazed like a beacon.

The noise in her head, the burn in her arm. Fife must've felt it, too, Eammon's desperation making the Wilderwood send out its call.

Lyra stood behind Fife, expression unreadable, fawn-brown eyes wide. She looked at Red and Eammon, pressed her lips together, and turned away.

"Fife?" Confusion laced Eammon's voice. His hand wasn't on his Mark; he didn't look like he'd felt the call, though it'd struck through Fife and Red like an arrow.

She'd never seen Fife look quite so angry. Freckles stood out on his pale face, and his chest heaved as if he'd run miles.

"You *called*." A snarl through his clenched teeth, like the word was something he could bite in two. "We were almost to the Keep, but *you* called, and I had to come. So here I am." His hand slashed toward the surrounding forest. "What the *fuck* do you want, Eammon?"

Red swallowed. "It's my fault," she said quietly, moving to stand between Fife and Eammon. "I did something foolish, and it...Eammon panicked."

Lyra still faced away from them. But at the word *panic*, her shoulders stiffened, and Red heard her let out a single, rattling sigh.

"It was an accident," Eammon rumbled behind her. Red looked over her shoulder—his mouth was held that particular way that meant he was angry, but at himself, and his eyes were shaded in the sunlight. "That's not an excuse, but I promise, Fife, it wasn't intentional. You know—I hope you know I would never command you that way."

"And yet you did." Fife let go of his arm; the throbbing of the Mark seemed to have subsided, though pain still lived in the line of his jaw. "You, the Wilderwood, whatever you and it have become reeled me in. And it *hurts*, Eammon. Kings and shadows, it—"

"He knows it hurts." Red's voice cut across his, jagged and angry, at herself, at Fife, at Eammon, at everything. "No one knows how much the Wilderwood hurts better than Eammon does, Fife. He told you he didn't mean to."

"Did you feel it, too?" Fife's hazel eyes swung to Red. "Or are you exempt? Is it just those of us that aren't magic who get the pain?"

"I felt it," Red said, and in the corner of her eye, she saw Eammon's shoulders slump.

Still, he stepped forward. "We're all trying to figure out how this works now—"

"How it seems to work is that the Wilderwood hasn't gotten any better at communication, and *you* haven't gotten any better at listening."

Lyra's hand landed on Fife's arm, cutting him off before things could devolve further. "We're going back to the Keep." She glanced over her shoulder at Red and Eammon. "I don't think you should follow. Not for a while, at least."

Her voice was steady, but there was steel in it. She was upset, Red could tell, rattled and barely held together. There was a faraway look in her eyes, like she was turning over something new in her mind, some piece of information she hadn't yet had time to square with.

Understanding came quick. Fife still hadn't told Lyra about his bargain. It seemed that Fife's being called by his new Mark was the first Lyra had heard of it. The two of them needed a minute alone. And from the venomous looks Fife and Eammon kept shooting each other, they needed some space, too.

"We'll talk later," Red said quietly. Lyra would need someone to talk to. Red knew what it was like, to have someone you loved make difficult decisions on your behalf.

She knew it twice over.

With one last burning look, Fife followed Lyra into the forest. Before they disappeared into the shadows, Red saw Lyra take his hand.

Sighing, she turned to face her Wolf.

Eammon loomed over her, eyes sparking, the veins in his neck blazing green. His voice was all leaf-layered resonance now, one she felt as well as heard, and she knew he did it on purpose. "That was exceedingly stupid, Redarys."

"I couldn't just leave it, not knowing whether it might work." She couldn't loom like he could, but she matched his glare, and felt the brush of leaves over her scalp as the ivy threading through her hair unfurled. "I can't leave a path untaken just because it might be too hard, not like you can."

"That's not fair."

"No, it's not. But she's my *twin*." She shook her head, voice climbing. "You don't understand what that kind of loss is like, losing someone who's a part of you!"

"Don't I?" One hand hooked on her hip, pulling her closer as the other cupped her face. His thumb dragged roughly over her cheek, pulling down her bottom lip. "I lost my parents. I almost lost *you*." A tremor went through his scarred fingers. "I know what that fear is like, and you will not make me feel it again."

Heat flared in her middle, stoked higher by anger. "So you're ordering me around now?"

"I certainly am." And his lips crashed into hers, and she dug her nails into his shoulders hard enough to hurt, and it was exactly what both of them wanted. A release. A reprieve. Anger and lust and lostness tangled together, and this was an outlet for it, a way to fight and heal in equal measure. His teeth sank into her bottom lip, and Red gasped, tangling her hands in his hair.

He pulled back just enough to look at her, one hand on the back of her neck, the other running up her side as he dragged her tunic off. Burning mouth moving down her throat, over her collarbone, closing over her breast until her back arched and her gasp became a moan.

Eammon licked her, hard and rough, then moved down. He kissed her hipbone, pulled at the waist of her leggings, mouth on every inch of skin he revealed. When he'd pulled them off, Red anchoring her hands on his shoulders to kick them into the underbrush, he looked up at her, kneeling on the golden leaves like a penitent, his eyes bright and his dark hair mussed.

"You never let me lose myself, Red." His voice came out hoarse, his hands moving over her even as he spoke, as if she were something he couldn't quite believe he could hold. "You dragged me back every time, even when I wanted to kill you for it. So I won't let you lose yourself, either."

"I won't." She tugged at his shirt, pulled it over his head, threw it into the trees. Went to her knees, too, because that way she could touch more of his skin, press herself into his chest until his scars traced themselves onto her. "I won't lose myself."

"No, you fucking won't." His mouth pressed open against hers. "You don't get to make me need you this much and then go kill yourself trying to tear open a door. Understand?"

She didn't say it, but the way she moved against him, the way she pressed him down onto the earth and settled over his hips showed it instead.

He didn't let her stay there. She rode long enough to feel that familiar coiling in her middle, for sweat to sheen both their brows despite the chill of eternal fall, before Eammon gripped her waist and rolled her over, her back against the dirt and him above.

"Too quick," he said, bending down for a kiss as he pulled out of her. His mouth dragged against her hip, the tender skin where her thighs ended. "It'll be over too quick like that, and I want you to remember this."

She was going to tell him she always remembered, but then his mouth was on her and coherent speech was impossible.

When Eammon did this, he didn't stop until she saw stars, until the coiling heat within her exploded more than once. And only then did he rise over her, into her, arms braced on either side of her head and shoulders blocking out the sun.

They didn't speak. No need. And when they both peaked, he kissed her through it.

Later, they lay naked in the forest, pillowed on her cloak. Red rested her cheek against Eammon's chest, listening to the forest-chased thud of his heart. Her thoughts stretched, languid, nearing the syrup-slow of sleep.

And she saw fog.

She'd been lying down with Eammon, and now she stood, but she could still feel his skin against hers, still feel the weave of her cloak pressing into her side. A glance around revealed Eammon wasn't there, though—Red was alone, just her and the mist. A half dream, then, somewhere between awake and asleep.

She wasn't naked anymore, either. Instead, she wore something long and pale and gauzy, similar to the gown she'd worn when she was blessed as a sacrifice to the Wolf. Her mouth twisted wryly as she plucked at the fabric. Another dream-thing, taking pieces of life and desire and memory and stitching them together in odd ways.

But the fog sliding over her felt...palpable, almost. And Red knew, with crystal clarity, that she was being watched.

That's the kind of love you needed. Feral and fierce and capable of drawing blood.

She whipped around—as much as one can in a dream—peering narrow-eyed through the mist. No shapes appeared, nothing to give her a clue as to what might be speaking, though the voice sounded masculine and nearly familiar.

This was a dream, she was sure, but it was a damn strange one.

Unease prickled along her shoulder blades. She crossed her arms. "Who are you?"

A long-enough pause that she didn't think she'd get an answer. Then: *I don't know, really.*

The fog parted slowly, drifting away like breaths on cold air. Its leaving revealed where she was.

A tree. But Red was in the branches of it, perched on a bough as wide as she was tall with thin golden veins winding through the white bark.

Below her, endless mist, a trunk stretching downward for what looked like miles. If she squinted, she could see tangles of roots down there at the base of the impossibly tall trunk, touched with darkness.

Almost like what she'd seen in the mirror.

Red fell to her knees, leaning as far over the side of the branch as she dared, screaming down into the dark, "Neve!"

Not yet.

The voice sounded weary but firm, like a tired parent admonishing a rambunctious child. *You have your key. Your half of the Tree was within yourself, but she has to journey to her half and find her key there. You must be patient.*

She frowned. The voice came from everywhere at once, like the fog itself was whispering. Still, that sense of familiarity, a memory that wouldn't quite lock into place but might if she just saw who was speaking. Slowly, Red stood, tentatively walked forward along the branch.

Something caught her eye on another branch, a glimmer of incongruously bright color. Red frowned.

Apples. A cluster of three, one gold, one black, and one bloodred.

The Tree is the key is the mirror, came the voice, reverberating in the fog. *The Tree exists and doesn't exist. It is you, and it is the piece you carry.*

"I don't understand," Red murmured, eyes still on the apples.

Mirrored power and mirrored love, the voice answered. *That's what opens the Shadowlands. Opens the Heart Tree. Opens you.*

"That cleared up exactly nothing," Red muttered, but the rest of a salty retort died in her throat when her eyes slid sideways.

When she saw the mirror growing from the trunk of the tree.

The same mirror she'd brought with her, the mirror she'd been trying so hard to force to show her Neve. She saw her own reflection in it, half forest and half woman, wild-eyed and kiss-bruised. But then there was a shimmer, a gray-scale world reflected for half a moment. A woman both like her and not, with long black hair and black-welled eyes and thorns along her wrists.

Neve.

But as Red tried to run forward, heedless of the branch she stood on and the endless drop below, the dream slipped, became more like something her tired mind would form and less like its own reality. Her steps stretched too long and too slow, her grasping fingers couldn't touch the mirror's frame. It fell back, disappeared, and she followed it into the dark.

"Red?"

Eammon had rolled on his side, bracing one hand on the other side of her head and caging her in his arms, worry in his eyes. "You cried out."

She reached up and smoothed the line between his brows. "Sorry," she said. "Strange dream."

He frowned. "Again?"

Red nodded, pushing to sit up, hair mussed from sleep and sex. "It felt different this time." She searched for her hastily discarded tunic, stricken with the sudden need to find the thing she'd pulled from the earth. "Does the term *Heart Tree* mean anything to you?"

Eammon's frown deepened. "Not off the top of my head, no."

Her tunic was a few yards away—*damn, he really threw the thing*—tangled in a bush's low brambles. Red didn't bother disentangling it before reaching into the pocket, pulling out the mystery object that had been left in her hand when she almost became a sentinel. She knocked it against her knee to clear the dirt.

A key. Made of white wood and threaded with veins of gold, but unmistakably a key. And when she closed her hand tight around it, she felt the faint rhythm of a heartbeat, as if the key were a living thing, or at least connected to one.

She turned back to a still-confused Eammon, holding it aloft. "Whatever it is," she said, "it apparently has a lock."

Chapter Eight

Neve

Because Neve's most well-honed talent was torturing herself, she thought of Raffe as they walked.

The ever-present cold of the Shadowlands made his warmth easy to call to mind. Warm brown eyes, warm smile, warm mouth on hers for the one kiss they'd shared, there in her room with her mother dead and her hands iced from magic and Red still gone.

He'd kissed her like he wanted to pull her back from a cliff's edge.

But there'd been more to it than that, hadn't there? More than just wanting to save her and defaulting to what he thought might work?

Neve's lips pressed together, trying to remember, to replay that kiss in her mind. At the time, she hadn't thought of much beyond the feel of him, the purely physical rush of having something you thought was unattainable, even if only for a moment. That was the crux of what had always lived between them, potent and heady: the knowledge that it could never happen. But then it did, and what even was it?

A rescuing. Raffe throwing her a lifeline, something to cling to, as what she kept grabbing for slipped out of her hands.

It made her frown, to think of it in such stark terms. To try to recall emotion, when desperation was the only one she could name.

Long before she and Raffe had started orbiting each other like stars that might collide, he'd been her friend. And in the end, that's what she'd felt in that kiss, as heat-filled and thorough as it was. The desperation of a friend, faced with the possibility of losing someone to a darkness they didn't understand.

There is nothing you could do to make me stop loving you.

That was the way he told her he loved her. A confession, maybe, but not a surprise—of course they loved each other, that was never in question. But the specifications of it, the parameters and ways the corners fit...that was more complicated.

She hadn't said it back. She'd thought of that more than once since it happened. She hadn't said it back, and should she feel bad for that? It wouldn't have been a lie, but it would've been a truth without context, and was that worse than no response at all?

Neve wondered what he was doing. She wondered what they'd say to each other, if she saw him again. She wondered what she *wanted* him to say.

Thinking of Raffe made her think of Arick, and thinking of Arick made her think of Solmir—Solmir-as-Arick, wearing her betrothed's face, bending them all to his plans like they were nothing but tools.

She glowered at him, moving straight-backed and precise through the trees. All the weakness that absorbing magic had wrought in him was gone now, dark power packed down. A vessel, that's what he'd called himself. It tugged at her mind, that word, like it should hold more weight, like it was a piece of something larger. But Neve couldn't remember what.

"Watch your head."

His voice came quiet, startling her from her thoughts. Ahead of her, Solmir had turned to face her, gesturing up at the lowest branches—roots—on the upside-down trees.

Webbing. It was strung fine as silk, nearly invisible, but still thick, clouding the air. Neve grimaced. "I hate spiders," she muttered, low enough to be speaking to herself.

"Me too," Solmir said, turning back around and ducking to avoid the webs.

Her mouth twisted. Other than a shared goal of sending her back to her own world—and, hopefully, killing the other Kings—common ground with Solmir was not something she wanted to find.

The strange moments of tenderness he'd shown back when she thought he was Arick still haunted her. The way he'd moved, careful and caring at once. She wasn't sure how much of it had been his trying to make a convincing mask of Arick, to fill in the blanks of his being her betrothed. But not all of it felt like a mask.

Now that he was here, in his own body, that carefulness around her had stayed. Not as obvious, but there in glimmers, both in the way he treated her and the way he moved through this world. Giving her his coat. Humming a lullaby.

She couldn't quite categorize him, and Neve hated things she couldn't quantify. She'd always had a quick mind, able to decipher people within moments, know what they wanted and how she could use it. But Solmir eluded her, and that made her uneasy.

He needed her. And, for now, she needed him—she couldn't navigate the Old Ones' underworld on her own. Right now, Solmir was a necessary evil.

But if there ever came a moment when he wasn't . . . well. Then other choices might be made.

The trees thinned, eventually, revealing an open vista of gray. It might've been a field once—in some places, the dried husks of dead grasses still clung to the earth, stubbornly rooted into the cracked ground. Now it was nothing but a flat expanse, stretching ever forward, vast and featureless but for the figure of Solmir walking up ahead.

The rumbling started slow, crawling through the ground, making her borrowed boots shake. She looked up, found Solmir staring at her, blue eyes wide.

"Get on your knees," he said, and though the words were something she certainly would've given him an earful for in any other circumstance, Neve obeyed.

Just in time.

The ground shuddered like it was trying to break apart, raising a roar into the still air, making her teeth clatter together. Then it *did* break apart—fractures split the dry, dusty ground, shuddering open, yawning chasms of deep darkness.

A hairline crack appeared next to Neve's hand, widening rapidly into a fissure. She tried to scramble away, but the shuddering earth made directing movement nearly impossible, and more cracks ruptured around her, making an island of rapidly deteriorating safety where she crouched.

"Neverah!"

Solmir lurched toward her, bounced over the ground like a coin in a tin cup. He skidded around the opening chasms, kicking up clouds of gray dust. The whole not-quite-sky filled with the sound of breaking earth, collapsing dirt. A world shuddering itself apart.

He launched across the ground, landed next to her in a crouch. "Forgive me for the impropriety, Your Majesty," he hissed, then scooped her up and jumped across the growing fissure to a larger piece of solid earth. The landing made him stumble, and they sprawled onto the dirt, his arms braced next to her temples. The back of Neve's head slammed against the earth, hard enough to make her vision blur and pain spangle through her skull.

Wafts of black smoke billowed from the chasms like smoke from yawning mouths, curling up toward the gray mist that made the false sky. The chittering sound of it cut through the groan of the shattering ground—loose magic, untethered from the world by its breaking.

Solmir sprang up, standing over her like a predator defending its kill. His hands arched in the air, and with a roar, he called all that rogue magic in.

It was like watching someone be attacked by a swarm of wasps. The senseless, formless chittering sounds grew to a crescendo as the magic swooped toward Solmir, flowing into his open palms and shadowing him from fingertip to elbow, then higher. It came and kept coming, a seemingly endless wave billowing up from the ground and into his waiting hands.

He screamed as it happened, a harsh sound that could've been pain or anger or both, and it scared Neve more than anything else she'd heard in this underworld, anything else she'd seen. It was the sound of someone unraveling, and she closed her hands over her ears to drown it out.

Through it all, the ground kept shaking. The solid island where they were stayed intact, but the edges crumbled slowly, safety sloughing away as Solmir stood there and screamed and absorbed more darkness than anyone should be able to hold.

And then, finally, the rush of shadows stopped. Solmir crumpled, knees and hands hitting the dust, back heaving as inky darkness slithered over his skin, flickered like inverse fireflies. Thorns, finger-long, pricked through his arms, ripping up the fabric of his shirt. Claws curved where his nails should be.

A fallen god made a monster.

Neve scuttled backward, away from him, away from the twisted shape he was saving her from becoming. She thought of that strange dream she'd had in the cabin, the reflection of herself in the mirror.

Slowly, Solmir looked up. Fangs dug into his bottom lip, his teeth grown long and sharp. Black had swallowed the whites of his eyes, but his irises were still a burning, terrible blue. The signifier of his soul, still within him, still fighting.

But as he looked at her, the blue flickered.

He lurched to stand on unsteady feet, legs grown longer than they should be, strangely jointed. Even so, Solmir retained his stately grace as he stalked across the broken earth toward her, expressionless except for the involuntary sneer his too-long teeth pulled his mouth into.

Desperate to put space between them, Neve slid over the dusty ground, hands behind her. But one hand fell into empty space, almost making her lose her balance—nowhere to go, nowhere to run.

So she made herself stand, pulled to her full height, hiding the tremble in her jaw as the monster came closer.

Bare inches away from her, Solmir stopped. Shadows writhed in his eyes, but the blue held on, though she could see from the shudder of his muscles that it was a physical effort.

One clawed hand stretched toward her face, frosted with thin ice, stopping just before it touched her skin. Neve refused to flinch, refused to look away from Solmir's eyes, blue flickering to black and back again. She didn't know what he would do, swallowed up in darkness, the barest threads of humanity he'd held on to fraying under the strain. She didn't know, but she wouldn't show him fear.

Calculation in his eyes, a familiar emotion in his changed face. Solmir's claws fell away from her, as if a decision had been made. In the same moment, he turned, hands thrusting out into the gray air, and a shower of brambles pulsed from him, as thick and fast as blood from a sliced artery.

The flow of it lessened gradually, thorns dissolving into gray smoke as they left his hands. Solmir crumpled, knees hitting the cracked earth, back heaving as magic-made brambles poured from his fingers. The claws retracted, the darkness of his veins faded away. She didn't have to see his face to know the black eyes were blue again, his teeth blunted.

He'd become a monster, then bled the monster out. Humanity was such a transient thing here.

"Why did you do that?" Neve asked, a whisper that carried in the empty plain. "Why did you absorb all that magic if you knew it was going to do...to do that?"

There was worry in her voice. She didn't have the energy to try to hide it.

"Because if I didn't, it would've gone to the Kings." Solmir straightened slowly. He ran a hand over his hair, like he was afraid the minutes he'd spent as a monster had mussed it. "This way, even if we had to waste some of it, it would at least be used up so *they* couldn't have it."

He looked like himself again, a too-handsome man with too-cold eyes. "What were you doing?" Neve asked, still quiet, still worried. "When you came over to me..."

Solmir blinked. Turned his eyes away, just by a fraction, looking over her shoulder instead of at her face. "I was going to give you some of the magic," he said, clipped and emotionless, despite the slight tremor in his jaw. "It was too much, nearly to the point of overwhelming me, and I didn't know if I'd be able to let it go."

"Why didn't you?"

A pause before he answered, the column of his throat bobbing with a swallow. "Because you were terrified, Neverah," he said. "And the magic was such that I could only pass you enough to make any difference by kissing you. I wasn't going to do that. Not with the way you were looking at me."

Then he brushed past her, headed into the endless gray horizon. Neve frowned after him a moment before following.

Carefulness, consideration. Things he'd shown her on the surface, things that felt somehow dangerous here. She didn't want his care—it made things too complicated—but she was afraid of how this world would be for her if she didn't have it.

They walked in silence for a while before she spoke again, not quite sure how to phrase the question. "Your eyes..."

His pointer finger worked at the silver ring on his thumb as he walked, turning it in nervous revolutions. "What about them?"

"They almost went black, too."

A shrug. "Holding on to a soul and that much power at the same time is quite a feat. Souls and Shadowlands magic aren't things that can be held simultaneously—at least, not if you plan to keep them both." His head cocked toward the gray sky, the wispy impressions of faraway roots looking like smudged clouds. "Maybe I *do* want that medal."

The reference to an earlier jibe might've made her roll her eyes if she hadn't been so focused on the matter of magic and souls. "Is that what happened to Red?"

Solmir stopped then and turned to look at her. His arms crossed over his chest, the diffuse light of the Shadowlands limning his frame. "No," he said finally, almost soft, or at least as soft as his voice could get. "The magic of the Wilderwood is different. It...harmonizes with a soul, is the best way to put it. Amplifies it, instead of consuming it utterly. Redarys still has her soul." His brow climbed, a smirk playing at his mouth. "Just as stubborn and irritating as its always been."

Neve cracked a tiny smile despite herself. "Good," she murmured. "That's good."

He watched her a moment more, face unreadable, still twisting that ring around his thumb. The arms of his shirt were hopelessly torn from the thorns he'd grown, the tattoo circling his bicep visible. Three lines, the one at the top thickest, the one in the middle marked through with tiny vertical dashes, the one on the bottom simple.

Solmir turned on his heel, walking into the wasteland again. "I'm glad you think it's good," he said. "I'm sure Redarys has more use for hers than I do for mine."

Chapter Nine

Raffe

The Shrine gave him the shivers.

It always had, really. He'd never been much for religion—in most countries, day-to-day veneration was more for folk heroes and figures of local legend, faith on a smaller and more personal scale. If you weren't an Order priestess—or an unluckily fertile Valleydan queen—your dealings with the Kings were few. One might light a red candle a couple times a year, and you'd be married in white and buried in black, but the religion that had sprung up around the Five Kings wasn't one that required much of its penitents.

Raffe very much wished he could go back to that kind of distance.

He stood in the second room of the Shrine like one might stand at the edge of a cliff, hands held stiff by his sides, shoulders tense. The note from Red that Fife had delivered dangled from his fingers, so many words to tell him there was still no news, still no sign of Neve, still nothing. Another day passed with the Queen of Valleyda missing, and he was the only one who knew.

Well. Him and Kayu.

"Shit," he muttered, crumpling Red's letter in his hand.

The broken branches in the Shrine's second room looked a little worse for wear after Neve's campaign against them, but not by much. A little more crooked, a little more withered, but they stood strong in their stone bases, and though there were bloodstains on the floor, there were none on the bark.

Not that the Shrine was even necessary anymore, not really. Hardly anyone but the priestesses came to pray, and all of them were in the Rylt, either sent there by Neve or by him. He didn't know if it was the same in other Shrines in other kingdoms, but Valleyda had always been the most pious. Their religion was dying a slow death.

Now that Raffe knew what the Kings were, that the whole thing was built on lies and half-truths and power, being in the Shrine at all made him feel slightly ill.

Raffe didn't know why he was here, really. He'd searched the Shrine already, every inch of it, trying to see if there was some clue they'd missed, some leaving of Neve's strange experiments that might reveal the way to save her.

Despite everything, he'd reflexively reached for the table of red prayer candles when he entered. When he realized what he was doing, he shrank away like it was a basket full of snakes rather than wicks and wax. The Kings were the last people he wanted to hear from. He could revert to his childhood ways, he supposed, praying to some folktale figure, or the Plaguebreaker—but after meeting her in the flesh, that felt strange, too. The idea had occurred to him that maybe Red and Eammon were the thing to pray to now, but that felt even *more* strange, and useless besides. They didn't know what to do any more than he did.

His thoughts wandered to Kayu. He'd seen her this morning after breakfast, as he walked down to the Shrine—dressed in a sumptuous gown of purple silk with silver embroidery, her long black hair elaborately braided back from her face. She'd been strolling the gardens on the arm of Belvedere's valet—the master of trade kept quarters in the capital city, even as the seasons dipped toward cold, though he generally stayed away from the palace unless he had to come balance ledgers. Her eyes had flickered his way even as she laughed gaily at some quip the valet made, but other than an inclination of her head, she hadn't acknowledged Raffe at all. As if she hadn't been in his room playing at assassination in the small hours of yesterday morning. Reading his correspondence. Offering help.

Raffe rubbed a hand over his face. He would say he didn't trust Kayu as far as he could throw her, but she was a small woman, so he could probably throw her much farther than his trust would extend. Even still, he didn't see a way around taking her offer. She was right. He needed money.

And with everything else he had to deal with, trying to head off a curious Niohni princess was one task he just didn't have the mental capacity for. He'd let her help. And if things went awry...well, she'd played at assassin first.

Even as Raffe had the thought, his stomach went knotty. He wasn't nearly as bloodthirsty as one needed to be for this.

So when he turned and saw her standing behind him, eyes wide and a lit candle clutched in her hand, the string of profanity he let loose was truly impressive.

She cocked her head to the side. When he'd first seen her, he could've sworn the look in her eyes was somewhere near panic, but now she seemed cool and unruffled as ever. "Feeling pious, Raffe?"

Raffe gestured to the candle in her hand. "Not as pious as you, apparently."

Again, that flash of something wary across her heart-shaped face. But then Kayu shrugged. "Old habits." She passed him in a flutter of silk, going to fix her candle before one of the branch shards. She did it carefully, he noticed, with graceful movements that spoke of practice.

Candlelight shimmered over her gown as she turned to him, her back now on her prayer. Her ink-dark eyes narrowed at the branch shards lining the walls. "Not much for decoration."

"Is the Shrine in Nioh decorated?"

"It's austere, but better than this. Only having one branch to display means we can do more elsewhere; having so many really overwhelms the room."

"You could return to your stroll with what's-his-name, if the lack of decoration offends you so much."

"Don't be jealous. Aldous is quite spoken for; he and Belvedere have been together for years." She nodded at the note still held in Raffe's hand. "More news about the Queen?"

The word made his fingers flex; Raffe tucked the note into his pocket with a scowl. "Sorry, but the only way you're going to know the contents of my correspondence is if you steal it."

"Sounds like a challenge." But the words were softer than they should be; Kayu's face was pensive. She sighed, eyes swinging from him to the jagged shadows of the branches on the walls. "It's honestly remarkable that you've held everything together this long. I know the Valleydan court isn't necessarily one for intrigue—the cold saps it out of them, I guess. But your luck won't hold forever. Power is power, and eventually, someone will want it. The sooner you can find Neverah Valedren, the better."

Truer than Kayu could know. There was no way to tell what was happening to Neve in the Shadowlands, how she spent the days that ticked by as they got no closer to finding a way to save her. He played it over endlessly in his head—the glass coffin, the churning hurricane the grove became, the way she sank into the dirt with only a glimpse of that gray sky, that inverted forest, that endless dead land populated by undead things. It was a world totally unlike their own, and he had no frame of reference for how it worked, what it would do to her.

What it had *already* done, even before she disappeared into it. He hadn't forgotten that the last move of the night had been hers. How her eyes had opened, seeing Red—seeing him—and then closed as she pulled in all that darkness, let it overwhelm her. Became the shadows. Left him.

Which brought his thoughts around to Solmir.

In the months between Red leaving and the battle at the Wilderwood, Raffe hadn't known what to make of the relationship between Neve and Arick. It wasn't quite friendship, but wasn't quite something more, either. Still, he'd thought they were falling for each other at first, and it had made his middle feel empty, twisted. Jealousy, yes, but almost something like… relief? It was all so much to be caught up in, royalty and betrothals and the geometries of love. Maybe conceding defeat was better.

As time went on, his thinking had shifted—he no longer assumed Neve was falling for Arick, but it seemed Arick was falling for her. It flew in the face of everything Raffe thought he knew about the man. Arick had loved Red since they were old enough to know what that meant; she'd been his first everything. And though Arick's love wasn't the kind you could build a foundation on, it hadn't needed to be. They'd talked so much about trying to make Red run, but in the end, they'd all known she wouldn't. Raffe had known before Arick and Neve, but no matter how poorly they took it, it hadn't been a surprise.

So for Arick to suddenly decide he wanted Neve, his betrothed, even as they were attempting to bring Red home—it didn't make sense. And that should have been his first clue that Arick wasn't himself anymore.

Maybe *want* wasn't even the right way to put it. Solmir had been tender with Neve, careful. It was clear that he wanted her safe, even as things veered wildly out of control. But maybe that wasn't so much for want of her as it was for want of the *use* of her.

The thought made his fists clench even now.

By the time he'd figured it out, things had gone too far for him to halt them. He remembered running into the grove, seeing the coffin, flailing at it with his sword and his hands. Nothing.

Nothing.

And now Neve was trapped with Solmir in the underworld.

Next to him, Kayu was silent, watching the branch shards with her eyes narrowed and her full lips twisted to the side. Her manicured nails tapped on the silk sleeve of her dress, the picture of a princess.

He was too good at trusting people. Raffe wanted to believe everyone meant well, and he'd been burned by it more than once—though never scaled with these kinds of possible consequences, wars and successions and stolen thrones. Now it was an instinct he actively fought against.

But for reasons he didn't quite understand, he wanted to trust Kayu. Maybe it was loneliness—he was holding all of this together by way of tightly clenched threads and willpower. It would be nice to have someone here to help.

It would be nice to have someone he didn't have to hide from.

He could feel Red's note in the pocket of his doublet, shoved in next to Kiri's. He should've burned them both, but he kept rereading them instead, as if he could somehow wring sense from the words if he repeated them over and over in his head.

But if he knew nothing, and Red and Eammon knew nothing, who else was left to ask? Maybe Kiri would be more forthcoming with information in person.

"How much would it be for a passage to the Rylt?" he asked quietly.

Kayu, to her credit, didn't appear surprised at the question. She gave a graceful shrug. "Depends on how many people we're taking."

"Three. Wait, five." It might be a good idea to have Fife and Lyra there—he'd feel safer being around Kiri if he was surrounded by allies.

"Six," Kayu amended.

Too late, he recalled her phrasing when she answered his question, the use of *we*. "Kayu, you don't understand—"

"Do *not* say that to me." Since he'd known her—admittedly not long—Kayu had been nothing but calm, collected. Even when she was breaking into his room and pretending to be an assassin, she had the air of someone always in control, who knew exactly what the next three moves were and was amply prepared for them.

But now her dark eyes were fierce, her hands clenched into fists by her sides. She'd whirled around and glared up as if she really could kill him now if she had a weapon on her. Raffe's eyes widened, but he successfully fought the urge to step back, even when she advanced so close that her nose almost brushed his collarbone.

"Please don't act like I'm too dense to understand, Raffe." She was angry, obviously, but her voice stayed even. "If you want to go to the Rylt on my coin, I'm coming with you."

A moment, a breath. She was standing very close.

He couldn't afford to get them all to the Rylt on his own. And trying to bring Kiri back here would be both too visible and too dangerous— he didn't want that woman anywhere near Valleyda. Not to mention the complications of bringing Red and Eammon to the capital. It would be nigh impossible to hide what they were, now that they barely looked human. Maybe he could cook up some kind of explanation, give a half-truth, but it would be strained, and he couldn't stanch the gossip.

He didn't have any other options, and it almost felt like a relief.

"Fine," Raffe said, low and dark. "But if any of this gets out, I'll know exactly who is to blame. And I will not go easy."

"I would never expect you to," she said coolly.

And there they stood, too close and too heated, until the tension in the room was broken by the earth shaking.

The quake came out of nowhere. A pitch, a slide, a rumbling in the floor that sent them careening against each other and then to the ground. Instinctively, Raffe braced himself over Kayu, expecting falling rock and ruin.

But the rocks never came, as if the earthquake was centralized—focused on the pieces of sentinel trees. Around them, the stone walls groaned, but only the branch shards bent and twisted, like someone awakening from a long sleep. Shivers of color trembled over the white wood, gold and black, a dance of light and darkness that lasted only a blink.

Panicked, Raffe checked his palms, then grabbed Kayu's and checked them, too. No blood, no tiny cuts that might've accidentally awakened the shards. This was different, something new—

As soon as it began, it stopped. No more groaning, and the floor was once again level, unmoving. They crouched on the ground, both tense and ready for another round, but the Shrine was still and silent.

A heartbeat. The very ends of the branches twitched, once, like dying hands. Then, with a crack, they all changed their shape.

Keys. They all looked like keys.

A blink, and they were just branches again, so quickly Raffe wondered if he'd imagined it. But next to him, Kayu's eyes were wide, her mouth agape—she'd seen it, too.

"What in all the shadows was *that*?" she whispered.

"I don't know." Raffe sighed, shook his head. In for a sip, in for a pint. "But I know who will."

Chapter Ten

Neve

After two days of walking—she assumed, at least, since they'd stopped to sleep twice, taking turns watching the unchanging horizon while the other dozed fitfully far enough away for the comfort of the other—the landscape up ahead finally changed. Neve was embarrassed by the way her heart leapt to see something other than flat, cracked ground.

It looked like a mountain range, cragged and rough, a darker shade of charcoal against the ash-colored glow of the sky. The range stretched from side to side, like the curve of a bowl's edge, and seemed to grow larger as they walked closer, the only marker of time or distance she'd noticed since they left the inverted forest.

Solmir stayed a few yards ahead of her, but she didn't have to raise her voice to be heard. The silence of a dead world made sure her words carried. "How big are the Shadowlands?"

"Big enough," he answered, without turning around.

"And was it always like…this? Even before it started breaking apart?" The ground had stayed steady since the huge quake that shook magic from the depths of the earth, but Neve still stepped cautiously, prepared for the world to lurch at any moment.

"It's never been exactly vibrant," Solmir said drily, "but when the Old Ones first came here, with all their lesser-beast children, it wasn't quite so dead." His hand cut backward in the direction they'd come, then forward, toward the mountain range. "The whole of the Shadowlands is hemmed in by forest—the borders of the Wilderwood, though the exact measurements of the edges obviously don't match up—but the Old Ones shaped it as they wished. They each made their own territories here. The Serpent underground, the Weaver in the forests, the Dragon out past the Endless Sea, where the Leviathan lives. They fought against each other, took territories over, lost others. Treated it mostly like they treated the surface, just without humans getting in the way." He shrugged, dropped his hand. "It's never been pleasant. But it's been more than this."

She couldn't decide if the world he described sounded better or worse than the one they walked, but something else he'd said stuck out to her even more than the slapdash geography lesson. "The lesser beasts are the Old Ones' *children*?"

"That's as easy a way to put it as any." Solmir shrugged, making his hair ripple behind him. He still wore it down, though it had to get in the way. "The lesser beasts are weaker copies of the Old Ones they come from. The Old Ones are their only parent." He turned then, giving her an arch look and a wicked turn of his mouth. "Even the Old Ones that took lovers didn't manage to procreate with them."

Neve grimaced.

The only lesser beast they'd encountered so far was the three-eyed goat and that worm-thing with all the teeth. But Neve thought, unsettlingly, that what she'd been thinking of as *worm* could just as easily be *serpent*. "How long until we get there?"

"Patience, Your Majesty."

Neve could very patiently tear him limb from limb, but she fell silent, following him across the cracked not-desert.

Then, a rumble.

Solmir stopped and barely had time to cast out a hand in her direction before the pitching earth sent them careening into each other. The runnels in the dirt widened, spider-webbed. The quake wasn't as dire as the one before—no clouds of rogue magic bloomed from the chasms opening like hungry maws—but it still rattled Neve's teeth in her skull.

On the horizon before them, one of those mountainous smudges began to sink. A cloud of dust bloomed into the gray sky, the sound of its collapse made soft by distance.

The quake was over nearly as soon as it began, leaving her and Solmir canted together on the ground, pressing into each other for balance. The world shuddered once more and then was still.

He pushed up first, steadying before she did. Solmir stretched out a courtly hand.

Neve eyed it warily before lightly placing her fingers in his palm, nails clicking against all his silver rings. Solmir pulled her up, hand dropping as soon as she was safely upright. "Last time I helped you up, you siphoned off a sizable amount of magic."

"Don't tempt me," Neve muttered.

He cracked a sharp smile, then started out across the seemingly endless desert again. "We need to make haste."

She chewed her lip as she followed, a nervous tic she and Red shared. But where Red would pull her bottom lip between her teeth, almost flirtatious if you didn't know it was a mark of anxiety, Neve tended to gnaw hers bloody.

They walked on. Before long—minutes, hours, Neve didn't try to keep it straight anymore—something rose up in front of them, a small interruption against the endless horizon. A hill, maybe, but irregularly shaped, with strange humps and curves she couldn't quite make out.

It didn't seem like an entrance to a kingdom or a territory or anything else. Neve assumed they would pass it, a strange aberration in a stranger land, but Solmir curved his path toward the hill.

She frowned. "Is that where we're going, then?"

Solmir flipped his hand at the oddly shaped hill, the lazy imitation of a welcoming flourish. "Behold, the entrance to the Kingdom of the Serpent."

Neve's head canted to the side, trying to make this square with the image of the entrance she'd had in her head—something ornate, Temple-like, to mark the kingdom of a god. "Are all the territory entrances so… ordinary?"

"Depends on your definition." Solmir shaded his eyes from the pale glow of the sky to look toward the mountain range, then pointed with his chin. "That's the Oracle's domain, where we're going next. Does it seem ordinary to you?"

"Yes," she bit out, irritated. "They're just mountains."

"Look again."

With a sigh, Neve turned to the jagged line in the distance. This far away, the mountains were barely anything but looming shapes. She narrowed her eyes, squinting to bring them into focus.

The angles were strange. The edges of the mountains were pointed in odd directions, lumped up haphazardly. One bulge in particular looked uncannily familiar…

Her eyes widened. The bulge wasn't a rock. It was a giant skull.

"Bones," she murmured. "They're bones."

"Dead Old Ones." Solmir turned away from the graveyard range, eyes glittering. "A nightmarish territory for a nightmarish god."

"You don't seem to like the Oracle much."

"I don't like anything here much."

Fair enough, she guessed.

As they drew closer to the entrance, its features became easier to make out—the hill wasn't made of rock. Skulls, again. Rows of them, melted together as if by a torch, cobbled into lines like bricks. A few of them looked almost human, but most were from creatures Neve didn't recognize, the bones oddly shaped, the angles all wrong. "It's all damn bones here."

"One of the side effects of most things being dead," Solmir said.

In the center of the cairn was a hole, deep-earth dark. No stairs, but the floor of it seemed to slump downward, like an entrance to a purposefully formed cave. It brought easily to mind a huge, muscled serpent, working its way below ground over eons to make its own kingdom.

Neve shuddered.

Solmir noticed. "I suppose I'm going first, then?"

"You are *absolutely* going first."

He sighed, the breath of it stirring his hair. "Fine." Blue eyes turned to her, no humor in them. "I know the prospect of being near me is not one that appeals overmuch, but you'll want to stay close."

"I think I can overcome my distaste for an hour or two." Already, she stood closer to him than she ever had voluntarily, close enough to see a wink of silver through the strands of his loose hair—the ring punched in his earlobe. The man wore more jewelry than she ever had. "What will we find down there, other than the Serpent? More lesser beasts?"

"I doubt it. That thing you killed before we saw the Seamstress is the first child of the Serpent I've seen in years."

So that *was* one of the Serpent's children. Which meant that the Serpent must just be a larger, stronger version, probably with more teeth. Neve's pulse ticked in her wrists.

"But if we do..." Solmir stuck his hand in the pocket of his coat, the one she was still wearing. Neve lurched backward, a retort rising to her mouth, before Solmir pulled his hand away with something clutched in it.

The god-bone.

He flipped it around his finger, then offered it to her, blunt end first. "You use this."

Hesitantly, Neve held out her hand. He dropped the bone into it.

"I told you before that it won't work on me, but I feel the need to reiterate, since I'm sure it would hurt anyway." Solmir turned toward the dark. "You still need me, and I still need you."

Neve hefted the bone, tapped her thumbnail against the ivory. "Watch your tone, and I'll try to remember that."

He huffed half a laugh as he stepped into the maw of the cairn, shadow and light striping his hair. For the second time, he offered her his hand. "It'll be dark," he said, in explanation.

And for the second time, she put her hand in his. His skin was slightly warmer than the air, the chill of his silver rings like spots of ice against her palm.

He grinned at her. "Ready to commit high blasphemy?"

"Always."

Then Solmir plunged them into the dark.

Neve's vision adjusted quickly to the gloom—the equivalent of days spent in gray scale had already altered her sight. But there wasn't much to look at. The walls of the cavern were smooth stone, curving into a sloped ceiling. Flecks of mica glittered on the equally smooth stone floor, canted steeply downward. If she sat and pushed off, she could probably slide on it.

The thought made a nervous giggle rise in her throat; Neve clamped her teeth together to keep it in. Even though she could see, she kept one hand in Solmir's, the other gripping the bone.

A sound breathed up from the depths of the cave. Neve clasped Solmir's hand hard enough for his rings to dig into her skin; she pressed forward until the only thing separating their bodies was the bulky fabric of his coat.

"Jumpy?" he asked.

"I have reason to be."

"Not as much as I do. You're the one with the stabbing implement." Solmir took a step farther into the dark, pulling himself away from her, though their hands stayed clasped. Neve made herself keep the distance as she followed.

Her thoughts turned, inexplicably, to Raffe.

Neve shook her head, a tiny shudder, just enough to expel the memory of Raffe's kiss, his skin, his gentleness. Later, she admonished herself. She could think about him later, delve into that knot of feeling and pick it apart. Or she could leave it to freeze over, ossify, become something that would have to be cracked and broken rather than untangled. Keep shoving it down. She'd gotten so good at that.

An impatient tug on her hand—Solmir, tilting his head to the side to direct her gaze. A bloated, wormlike corpse lined the wall, as long as three grown men were tall. One of the Serpent's children, a lesser beast long dead. The thing's skin was a patchwork, like a snake in half molt, or meat left out too long.

And at one end, a gaping maw full of teeth.

Neve recoiled, fear making all the hair on her arms raise, before logic snapped in and told her the lesser beast was dead. She looked to Solmir. "Are you going to take its magic?"

"That thing has been dead for a while," Solmir answered. "Whatever magic it had is gone."

"To the Kings?"

"Unfortunately."

Neve kept her neck craned as they passed the corpse, unwilling to completely turn her back on it until the path curved and it was lost from sight. Even then, she couldn't shake the gooseflesh rippling over her shoulders.

What started as one tunnel into the earth expanded the deeper they went, more corridors bored into the stone walls at irregular intervals. Some of them were large enough to walk through, but others were so narrow that you'd have to crawl. Neve didn't let herself look at them for too long. Just thinking of inching through the earth like that made her palms clammy.

Finally, their path leveled off, terminating in a circular cavern. Tunnels branched in all directions, too dark to give a clue to what they held. Solmir stopped and dropped her hand, turning to glare at each tunnel in turn.

Neve crossed her arms. "Well? Where to now?"

"Give me a minute." For the first time she could remember, Solmir looked completely unsure. He shook out his shoulders, making his hair sway over his back. A moment, then he flexed his fingers, wiggling them as if he could coax some direction from the air. Trying to feel out the Serpent's power.

Trying, and apparently not getting very far. "Are you finding the right tunnel or calling a wayward dog?"

"Your Majesty, I beseech you for the gift of your silence."

She shifted back and forth, looking warily around the circular space while Solmir tried to figure out which tunnel to take. Her vision was somewhat hazier down here. Shadows curled around the stone walls, thick and dark and ominous, and she fought the urge to slink closer to Solmir again, just for the solid reassurance of not being alone.

For all her mocking, she understood the principle of what he was doing. Power attracted power, he'd said, and he was full to the brim. So was the Serpent. If he listened to the magic within him, all that power he held so she wouldn't have to, it should pull him toward the dying Old One.

Hopefully, before the dying Old One was pulled to the Five Kings, stuck in their Sanctum.

The Seamstress had told them that the Serpent was holding on, purposefully trying to avoid being absorbed by the Kings, increasing their magic with its own. But there was no way to know if it had been successful. No way to know until they went down one of these tunnels and found either a god or more empty darkness.

Both options made her wrap her arms tighter around herself, cocooning in Solmir's coat.

After what felt like an hour, Solmir's hands dropped. He turned to her, and Neve had been wrong—it wasn't surprise or even fear that looked most alien on his sharp-boned face. It was defeat.

"I don't know," he said, like it was as much a shock to him as it was to her.

For a moment, Neve stood in confused silence. Then she advanced a step, hands curling tight against her arms. "What do you mean, you don't know?"

"Exactly what it sounds like." Solmir reached up, nervously rubbed at the puckered scars on his forehead. His pointer finger turned the ring on his thumb round and round. "The magic isn't telling me where to go.

The power should call me, but it's...it's just not. Or, rather, it's trying to, but..." He shook his head. "I don't know. It's like the Serpent doesn't *want* me to find it."

She was right next to him now, glaring up as if she could use her eyes as daggers. "You mean you took us all the way down here, and you don't know—"

His palm over her mouth muffled the rest of her poison, and Neve had her hand half raised to try to twist from his grip before she saw why.

The shadows at the edges of the room were closer. Thicker, almost opaque. A small circle of unshadowed stone surrounded Neve and Solmir, but other than that, the whole room was covered in viscous darkness.

And emanating from it—a low, gibbering sound.

Shadow-creatures. Unfettered magic, like what had burst from the broken ground, like what had seeped out of the lesser beast as her thorns made it unravel. But there was something different about these. They were still, uniform, as if they were being controlled.

As if they'd already attached to something bigger, their magic directed by something stronger than they were.

Solmir turned slowly, dropping his hand from her mouth when it became clear she'd stay quiet. But his other hand found her wrist, squeezed so hard it hurt.

"Magic from the Serpent?" Her lips barely moved with the question, like sound would shatter the shadow-creatures' stasis. Even as she asked, though, she knew the answer was no. If the Serpent was dying, it wouldn't have the strength to hold all this raw power at attention.

"No." Barely sound, more a breath into her ear.

"Then can *you* take it?"

Slowly, Solmir shook his head. "It's already claimed."

Cold shot from Neve's sternum, down through her middle. A numbing kind of fear.

The wall of darkness stood, impenetrable, pressed close. Then, in the darkness, a glint of white.

Teeth.

Teeth in the shadows, sharp and elongated, a hundred maws filled with fangs. At first, they just hung there, but then they all dropped open and spoke.

"The prodigal."

A voice from everywhere and nowhere, layered and discordant. It took everything in Neve not to clap her hands over her ears. She tightened her grip on the god-bone in her other hand, wondering if it would work against something incorporeal.

All the teeth clicked together, a tandem fanged smile, before speaking in sync again. "Solmir, boy, we've been waiting for you. Welcome home."

"Calryes," Solmir breathed. Fear gleamed in his blue eyes, in his blanched face, and a terrified former god was the most terrifying thing Neve had ever seen.

But he recovered. Schooled his expression to cold, to haughtiness and impassivity. Almost casually, he turned, his death grip on her wrist his only tell.

Solmir shot a bladed grin into the shadows. "Hello, Father."

Chapter Eleven

Neve

A pause. Then a laugh, even louder and more horrible than the speaking of the hundreds of mouths had been, echoing and distorting in the dark.

Terror and incredulity warred in Neve's mind, her fingers tightening around the god-bone until her knuckles felt like they might crack. Calryes? *Father?* The legends said nothing of this, nothing of Solmir being one of the other Kings' sons, and though she couldn't quite make sense of why the revelation felt so world-bending, it was enough to make her stomach knot.

If Valchior was the leader of the Five Kings, then Calryes was his right hand.

Which meant they were in deep shit.

"Son." Calryes still spoke from hundreds of fanged shadow-mouths, but there was a denser space of darkness right in front of Solmir that appeared to be shifting, twisting into something new. "You've returned with a companion, I see. How interesting."

Solmir moved incrementally forward, placing himself between the swiftly coalescing shadows and Neve. Not protective, necessarily, more like he wanted to hide her from view, keep the King, swiftly coming into shape, from seeing the whole of her.

In every other circumstance, Neve refused to cower. But now, behind

Solmir, she let her head bow forward, let herself hide behind him. Some deep instinct told her this was not the time for queenly arrogance.

The darkness before Solmir slowly solidified. The essence of shadow remained, even as the darkness became a thin figure wearing a spiked crown. It shifted too much to settle on any one shape, was only the suggestion of a person.

The Kings couldn't leave the Sanctum, the Seamstress had said—they were trapped there, anchored down by all the magic they'd pulled in, becoming part of the Shadowlands. But they could send projections of themselves. This wasn't Calryes, it was merely a simulacrum.

That should have been more reassuring than it was.

"The little queen from the surface," the King continued, shadows seeping around his edges like mist on a moor. He didn't call her *Shadow Queen*, not like the Seamstress had, and for some reason that made relief run a cool finger down her spine. "And whatever for, Solmir?"

"Got lonely," Solmir said.

Neve glared at the back of his head.

"Here's hoping it works out better for you this time." The words were sly. The shadows around Calryes's vague shape shifted and coiled, vipers in a pit. "At least she came all the way through without dying. That's an improvement."

Solmir's hand clenched into a fist by his side, so tight it nearly trembled.

Behind him, Neve ran through quick calculations in her head, plans she knit together and then discarded. Calryes had known they were going to the Serpent's cairn, so it stood to reason he knew why: to harvest the dying god's power, take it before the Kings could. Was he here to try to take it himself?

No—no, that didn't make sense. If the Kings were trying to pull dying gods to the Sanctum, where they were physically trapped, that must mean they couldn't absorb magic unless they were truly present. Which meant he wasn't here to try to take the Serpent's power—he was here to try to keep Neve and Solmir from taking it.

And even though he couldn't physically touch them, the realization made her nerves spike.

Well, then. He'd just have to be distracted.

Neve stepped forward, striding around Solmir like he was furniture. He stood still and stupefied, the presence of the King—*his father*—stealing all his movement, replacing it with dread.

"You know why I'm here," Neve told the dark.

Silence. Then another roar of laughter, discordant and quick, from all those toothed mouths. "Do I?" A shimmer ran through Calryes's vaporous figure, the spiked crown that was the most solid part of him tipping back. "I can think of many reasons, little queen. None of them are kind."

"Neither am I."

"No," Calryes said contemplatively. "No, I don't think you are."

Thin tendrils of darkness curled around Neve's arms, almost like they were looking for something. A gasp caught in her teeth, but she didn't move, kept up her icy poise even though every part of her wanted to cringe away.

But the sight of the shadows on Neve ripped Solmir from his fearful stillness. He grabbed her wrist, tried to haul her back. She didn't let him, instead whipping her head to the side, eyes fierce and fixed on his.

She mouthed one word: *Go.*

He dropped his hand, but didn't follow her order, staring at her as if he were seeing her for the first time.

The shadows curling around her arms slithered away, like night insects chased off by light. "Hmm." Calryes's shape was too amorphous to reveal true movement, but Neve had the impression of him tapping thoughtfully on his chin. "No magic. At least, none that can really be used. But you've had it before, and recently. The scars are fresh."

Then the shadows shot toward Solmir.

If their twining around Neve was slow and sinuous, they went for Solmir with vicious intent, a striking attack rather than curious exploration. Darkness twisted around his throat, shackled his arms. Tendrils dove into his mouth, his nostrils, his eyes, delving deep and searching.

He screamed, raw and hoarse, worse than the scream he'd let out in the field when the world was shaking apart, when all its rogue magic rushed to him like rain to dry ground. The sound reverberated through the cavern, and it finally shattered Neve's queenly poise.

Part of her wanted to run for the surface. Part of her wanted to tear the shadows from Solmir and drag him with her. But she couldn't make herself do either, so she just slapped her hands over her ears, trying to drown out that terrible screaming.

"So he's become the vessel," Calryes mused casually, his son's pain having no effect on him at all. "Holding all that magic for you. It must seem noble, but don't let it fool you, little queen. Souls and magic are hard to hold all at once. Saving you from one just means he wants you for the other." A low chuckle. "Always trying to outrun fate."

Ropes made of darkness hauled Solmir from the ground, pulling him, writhing, into the air. He'd stopped screaming, finally, but his throat and eyes and nose were still full of those delving tendrils, and the tendons stood out in his neck, the veins stood out in his eyes. He looked at her, trying to communicate something, words in his gaze that he couldn't say with his mouth. The same order she'd tried to give him.

Go.

And as if that wordless order made it happen, something within Neve was calling.

A pull, a tug. Like a hook had been lodged in her sternum and reeled forward, gentle but demanding. She lurched a step before she had the thought to, then obeyed the instinct, breaking into a desperate run down the tunnel in front of them.

She expected Calryes to send shadows after her, try to trip her up, keep her captive. But the laugh that echoed in the cavern behind her was worse than any torment from the darkness would've been.

"Run fast, little queen!" Calyres called.

And Neve did.

All the tenuous vision she'd had before was gone now, siphoned away by the endless black of the underground. Still, Neve could mostly make out her surroundings, sparse as they were. Curved stone walls and a curved stone floor, sloping only ever downward. She passed a few more lesser-beast corpses, more mottled, tubelike bodies ending in teeth. One had died turned toward the tunnel instead of the wall, its mouth hanging open before her. Neve shuddered even as she ran on, careful to give it a wide berth.

She stopped running, eventually, the rasp of her breath the only sound. A few gasps, and then she made herself hold it, listening to see if she could hear anything, either from ahead of her or behind.

Nothing. She thought of Solmir, tortured by shadows—by his father—and squeezed her eyes shut. She'd left him there.

It was strange, to feel guilt for something done to Solmir. He was a King, a murderer who'd manipulated her with Arick's stolen face, and he undoubtedly deserved every awful thing that fell upon him.

But still, the guilt snaked around Neve's gut, knotting and uncomfortable.

She hefted the god-bone in her hand, holding it like a sword. Solmir would be fine. He'd gotten through worse than this.

And she had a god to stab.

Pulling in a deep, aching breath, Neve started running again.

The tug in her veins grew stronger the farther she went, drawing her downward, steady and inexorable. Neve had never liked caves—being underground made her feel jumpy and on edge; human beings were meant for sun and surface—but the beat of her pulse and the pull in her bones didn't give her time to consider her surroundings.

Not that she had time for fear, anyway. Neve was practiced at doing what she had to do, even when it scared her, even when it hurt.

She felt it when she was close. The tunnel, somewhat narrow up to this point, widened out into a vast, dark space. The air of it crept over her skin, a sense of cavernous emptiness that felt somehow lonely. The darkness here was thicker, too—not like the shadows anchored to

Calryes had been, not in a way that felt at all sentient, but just...dark. The deep darkness of something that had never been disturbed by light.

Tentatively, one hand held before her and the other clutching the god-bone, Neve stepped into it.

It swallowed her. No amount of eyes adjusting would make her see; here, there was nothing to brighten the gloom, and never had been. Only blackness, only shadows, sliding over her skin like dark velvet. Her breath seemed too loud, the cavern too silent.

So when she heard the moan, it came through bell-clear and ringing.

Neve froze, hands still before her. No words—what would they do? But she let her breath stay loud, a greeting any beast would understand.

There was no use in hiding, anyway. The Serpent knew she was here.

A fluttering against her temples, the touch of an alien consciousness scrabbling for purchase. It felt different than the Seamstress speaking into her mind, weightier, as if the thoughts trying to connect to hers had to translate themselves before they could be anything she'd understand. The Seamstress had been human once. The Serpent never had.

When the Serpent finally spoke, its words reverberated against her bones like they were woven into her marrow.

Shadow Queen.

"Yes." It was cold enough that her breath probably clouded, but Neve couldn't see it. Responding to the title felt natural, and hearing it from the Old One inspired no fear.

A sigh from a huge mouth, displacing the air. She felt her hair flutter. *You smell like stars and brimstone. I could tell you from the other, even miles away. You were the one I wanted.*

Neve's hands flexed by her sides. She thought of Solmir when they reached the tunnels, how he didn't know where to go. The Serpent had called her here instead. Wanted her to be the instrument of its destruction, the vessel of the power it gave up.

"Why?" she asked quietly.

A shift in the dark, ponderous and cataclysmic movement that she couldn't see but could feel. *There must be two vessels. A vessel for magic, a vessel for souls. They cannot be held simultaneously, not when there is more than one.* The Serpent paused, and Neve once again felt that scrabble against her skull, an inhuman mind translating itself for her. *Perhaps it is not my place to decide which you will be, Shadow Queen. But I find you worthier of my sympathies than the other.*

She didn't understand, not really, but Neve wasn't in the habit of admitting such things. She drew herself upright, bone clutched in her fist, and spoke the same words she'd said to Calryes. "You know why I'm here."

Yes. A huff, blowing the tatters of her nightgown against her legs. *I've lived this half-life much longer than I wanted to, holding out against the pretenders trying to draw me into their web, tangle my magic into theirs.* A pause. *But dying is hard business for one of my kind. We almost always need help. I'm glad it's you.*

The enormity of what she was about to do sat heavy on her shoulders. The memories of the pain she'd felt when she first used magic here, pulled from anything other than Solmir, made her want to turn around and run back through all that endless dark, run until she found some sort of light.

"Will it hurt?" she breathed. "Taking your magic?"

Important things often hurt, Shadow Queen. You know that.

She did.

But it will not be forever. Another sigh, stirring the air. *The magic in me is not tied into the foundations of this place. It is free. It will not weigh down your soul in the same way pulling it from the Shadowlands itself does.*

"So it's safe, then."

A laugh, echoing in her head. *Nothing here is. But it is necessary.*

Neve nodded, though she wasn't sure if the god could see. Still, her throat felt as if she'd swallowed a rock, as her fingers tightened around the shard of bone.

"Hesitation? I didn't expect that from you, Neverah."

A new voice, slicing through the shadows.

The darkness ahead of Neve coalesced, like Calryes's had above, shaping itself. Becoming a man, more solid than Calryes had been, as if he had a greater command of the magic here. Spikes growing from his head like a crown, strong shoulders under a rich purple robe, and a blaze of auburn hair, his handsomeness flickering to skeletal decay and back again.

She'd never seen him before. Still, she knew who he was.

Valchior.

The King smiled. "I expected you to stab our godly friend here the first chance you got. You like magic. You like *control*. And you'll have all of those things when you absorb its power."

Neve didn't respond, didn't move, faced with the greatest of the gods she'd been taught to worship and filled with a dread that was anything but holy. She could feel the Serpent's displeasure in her mind, sparking with inhuman fear, though that fear was a distant second to her own. She wondered if the King could sense it. If he liked it.

Valchior might be more solid than Calryes, but still his edges feathered, features shifting. Man, skull, shroud. In every form, though, a sharp smile hovered around his mouth, lips fuller and more sensual than a rotting god had any right to have.

"Aren't you lovely," he murmured, stepping forward as shadows boiled around his feet. "It's no surprise you turned our Solmir's head."

Even through the terror churning in her gut, Neve managed to twist her lips into a sneer. "We need each other. It's nothing more than that."

Valchior's head cocked to the side, face shifting skeletal as he chuckled. "Perhaps that's true. You did leave him at Calryes's mercy, and that's certainly not a pleasant family reunion."

Guilt, again, digging claws into her chest. Neve gritted her teeth against it.

"Did you figure out what he was doing, all his plans for you?" Valchior asked. "Did he make you ruthless, there on the surface?"

"He didn't make me anything." Neve tightened her grip on the bone.

Was it giving something away to say that? The spreading of the King's

lips into a cold smile said it was. "Interesting," he purred. "So the ruthless-
ness is all your own."

His voice slithered over her, calling down to deep fears she hadn't let
herself examine closely. Fears of what she'd become. What more she'd
do. She'd pressed all her lines until they gave way and hadn't yet had the
desire to redraw them.

"It's a liberating thing to realize, Neverah." Valchior wasn't quite
corporeal enough to pace around her. Instead, he appeared at different places in the shadows, drawn to cardinal points as the dark shifted
to accommodate him. "All that striving for goodness does nothing but
exhaust you. No one can even decide on what goodness really *is*. Such
an arbitrary thing, and we use it like a noose."

"Goodness is whatever you're not," she said, but it came out so small.

"Is it?" In front of her now, and close. Neve held every muscle frozen
to keep from flinching. "Because I think goodness is more about trying
to save those you love. Regardless of the cost."

She wanted to argue, but what could she say? Neve agreed, shadows
damn her. She agreed.

Valchior's smile widened. "We took similar paths, Neve. I tried to
save my daughter from the Wilderwood, from the Wolf. Tried to get
back the power that would keep us all safe from the gods this prison
world couldn't hold forever. Can you blame me for that, really?"

The King stopped his movement, standing still before her. The
flicker of his features from bone to beauty stopped, leaving him only
handsome, only regal. "This place wasn't made for us. You've seen how
it changes you. Are we to blame for what we've become?"

"You didn't have to." Sweat slicked the god-bone in her hand, made
it hard to grip. The cold air on her fear-clammy skin made her shiver.
"You didn't have to keep pulling power up from the Shadowlands, tying
your souls to its magic until you couldn't even leave your Sanctum. Solmir didn't."

"Solmir," Valchior hissed, "has not told you the entirety of his sorry
tale."

She knew that. Of course she did. He hadn't told her, and she hadn't asked, because there was too much to do and too much to worry about without shouldering the sob story of a fallen King who was both her captor and her way home.

She didn't need to know how much he'd lost, too.

"This world wasn't made to last." The air around her shifted as Valchior leaned forward. "And your world above isn't in the best shape either, is it? Murder and avarice, thieving and cruelty. Makes you wonder what good a soul is at all. But it wasn't like that before, when we all had common things to dread. Monsters make men band together. And when the monsters are the gods, are the *rulers*, even better—when men are given much to fear, they draw together even more tightly."

"Are you arguing that letting you and the others come back to the true world would be a *good* thing?"

"Merely making an observation, but yes, I think it could be." Valchior shrugged. "So much can be solved by fear. It's a most excellent tool. An excellent means of control."

"You can't rule through fear." It gritted through her teeth, forced out.

"A noble idea," Valchior conceded, "but empty. You never accomplished anything that wasn't through fear when you were queen on the surface, Neverah. And you know it. Everything you did, all the strides you made, were because everyone in your tiny court was afraid of you. Afraid of what you might do, unhinged and grieving." A warm laugh, incongruous in all this dark. "And you liked it."

Weren't villains supposed to lie? This would be easier if he were lying.

The thoughts of the Serpent still coiled around her own, tense but no longer fearful. Valchior had barely acknowledged the Old One. He couldn't do anything to the Serpent in this form, couldn't kill it to absorb its power.

Couldn't do anything to Neve, either, other than talk. Other than spill truths like blood and leave her desperately trying to stanch the wound.

"You can talk until you run out of air," Neve said, jaw set and fists clenched around her shard of bone. "But I will still do what I came down here to do."

The King stepped back, spread his arms wide. "I wouldn't dream of stopping you, Shadow Queen."

He said the title slowly, deliberately. Watched it make her flinch.

"We know who you are," Valchior murmured. "We know why you're here." He leaned forward to put his mouth close to her ear, and even though he was a shadow-made projection that couldn't touch her, Neve shrank away. "And we welcome it."

"Neverah?"

Solmir's voice, halfway to panic. It echoed down the corridor that led to the cairn, his boots sliding down the smooth rock of the tunnels above.

Valchior's dark-wreathed head turned toward the sound. Neve thought he'd fade away, but instead, his jovial smile widened. "Our errant King, back from his reunion. Calryes jumped at the chance to come see his son, you know. To keep him distracted, so you and I could talk. It was almost sweet."

Distractions. She'd known it had all been distractions, but hearing it confirmed—spun out in directions she hadn't anticipated—made anxiety curl through her middle.

"Neve, answer me!" It sounded like Solmir was sprinting now, rushing into the yawning dark.

Her shortened name. It still sounded strange to hear him say it.

"Quaint, that he comes for you," Valchior murmured. "That boy is a knot of contradictions." He chuckled. "Careful with that one, little queen. He might warm you in the cold, but he'll burn you in the end."

"*Neverah Valedren!*" Knife-edged with worry, her full name like a summons. The furthest thing from a knight in shining armor, coming to save her after she'd left him in shadow-shackles with a sadistic father.

In front of her, Valchior wavered. "And with that, I bid you farewell, Neverah." His edges spun, the facade of handsomeness fading to skeletal remains before drifting into mist. "Until we meet again."

Then Neve stood in the cavern, larger than she could fathom, alone except for the fallen King running toward her and the ancient god who wanted to die.

Shadow Queen. The Serpent's voice in her head was strained. *Please.*

Neve shook her head, steadied her hands. The weight of the bone was anchoring, smooth and cool. When she turned and headed toward the Serpent in the dark, she heard the god sigh.

Solmir still made his way down the corridor; she could hear him, cursing, sliding over stones and around the bloated corpses she'd run past.

She stretched out the hand not holding the shard of god-bone, stopping when warm scales met her palm, dry and rasping against her skin. Neve sensed a great bulk before her, a creature whose size would make her mind scramble, and was thankful for the darkness that hid it from view.

The Serpent sighed again, a massive sound that reverberated in the dark and in her mind. *I was not kind,* it said, in tones that recalled neither confession nor rebuttal. Just a statement of fact. *I crawled from the sea to the land with the intention of ending worlds. Sometimes, I did. A city is a world, to some. A village.* Something like a rueful laugh, stretched to strange in a god's mind. *I made waters undrinkable, land barren, poisoned whole stretches of earth.*

"What did they call you?" It seemed like the right question to ask. Neve felt strange taking the life of something without asking its name.

Many things. The Serpent settled, a rumble in the dark. *The World Serpent is the one that will come most easily to your tongue.*

"World Serpent," Neve repeated. She steadied the bone in her hand. "I hope you...I hope you rest well."

Anything will be an improvement, the god replied. Then, almost an afterthought: *None of your decisions will be easy, Shadow Queen, but I will tell you this: The Kings would be worse than we ever were. Humanity breeds cruelty in ways my kind does not understand.*

"We'll stop them," she murmured, not realizing until it left her mouth that she'd said *we.*

One way or another. One last sigh, wind rippling through the cavern. *Now make it quick.*

The beat of its massive heart thrummed through its scales. Neve's palms were cold against them. She closed her eyes.

Then Neve lifted the bone and plunged the sharp end into the Serpent's side.

It didn't take all that long, the dying of a god. The massive shape she couldn't see jerked, displacing cold air; she stepped backward to avoid being flung aside. Another heave, the movement sending skitters of rock across the toes of her boots, making the atmosphere shudder.

And as magic began to seep out of its body, first in a trickle, then a torrent, Neve lifted her hands.

Chapter Twelve

Red

R affe's here."
Red's head jerked up from the book she'd been reading, fast
enough to set a crick into her neck. *"Raffe?"*

Lyra leaned against the doorjamb of the library. Her arms crossed
over her gown, a deep green that set off the golden flecks in her dark
eyes. "He brought a guest, too."

That made Red's brow climb, her head swing to Eammon. He sat
beside her, slouched behind a stack of heretofore-useless books, face
tired and hair mussed. They'd been here for nearly the whole of the four
days since the clearing, searching volume by volume through everything in the library. So far, they'd found nothing.

Still, Eammon pored endlessly over his books until his eyes drooped,
and she often had to prod him awake to get him to come upstairs and
sleep in their bed instead of slumped over the table.

But most nights, she waited. And when he was asleep, Red picked up
the books he'd discarded as useless and kept looking for more mentions
of voices in dreams.

She'd told him most of her strange dream, of course. The fog, the
blood-warm apple, the Heart Tree, that there'd been a voice that spoke
in cryptic loops. But she kept it vague, didn't tell him everything about
the voice itself. Didn't tell him how familiar it felt, how personal.

That was part of it, somehow. She could tell, with the deep resonance of an unquestioned truth—whatever had to happen in order to save Neve *would* be personal, would reach into her in a way Eammon ultimately couldn't help with.

She knew he'd hate that, so she kept it to herself.

Red's hand stole into her pocket, to the key she kept there. Eammon didn't like looking at it, had only given it one cursory glance when she first showed it to him. But Red carried it everywhere, tracing her fingers over it like it was a worry stone, twisting it in her palm. It felt like a tangible link to Neve, the only thing she had to hold on to.

The Wolf closed his book, brows drawn low. His eyes flickered to Red's, a question—she shrugged. There hadn't been anything in her note that would've made Raffe think he needed to come here, at least not that she could figure. Especially when they all agreed it was best to try to keep the Wilderwood out of Valleyda's collective thoughts as much as possible right now.

Eammon stood, shoving a piece of scrap paper into the spine of his book to keep his place. "Won't do to keep them waiting." A weary hand rubbed over his mouth. "Why in all the *shadows* would he bring someone else into all this?"

"You'd know about letting others get caught up in messes they should steer clear of," Lyra murmured.

The three of them paused, animals once more aware of the traps set around them. Red couldn't find any anger in her, even though the wounded look on Eammon's face sliced her insides.

She and Eammon had talked of Fife and what happened in the clearing, deep in the night, pressed together, with their legs tangled and her cheek pillowed on his chest. What he remembered from the brief moment when he'd sent out the Wilderwood's call, everything else crowded out by panic. And what happened before, the day of the shadow grove, when he pulled in all of the forest to save her.

"I don't really remember any of it, either time," he'd whispered into the dark, the paneless maws of their windows letting in crisp autumn scent, crisp autumn air. "There was golden light. The feeling of being... being *vast*, taking up more space than should be possible. All of the parts of me scattered." Green-haloed eyes turned to hers, made luminous in moonlight, the worry in them stark. When Eammon spoke again, it was hushed. "How badly did it hurt, when you felt the call?"

"It wasn't that bad. Just...loud, in my head." She traced her hand over his chest, rested it on his heart. "You didn't hear anything at all?"

"Nothing. But the Wilderwood and I have coexisted for so long, it seems loud to me all the time." Eammon ran a hand through his tangled hair. "Fife said I hadn't gotten any better at listening to it. Seems like he's right."

"It's a hard thing to listen to," Red murmured. "Especially when it's been part of you for so many years."

"I just don't understand the rules anymore. Don't get me wrong, I vastly prefer this to what the Wilderwood and I were before, but part of me misses knowing exactly what the forest wanted from me." He shifted beneath her. "Maybe I shouldn't have let him bargain to save Lyra. She wasn't dying, just hurt, and he was panicked. But I didn't...I didn't know it'd be like *this*." He paused, idly twining a strand of golden hair and ivy around his finger. "It's different," he said finally. "This bargain is different than the one he made before, but I don't know how. It's like the Wilderwood knows something I don't."

"But you had to let him." Red looked up, flicked a lock of dark, overlong hair out of his eyes. The point of a tiny antler brushed her fingertip. "Lyra wasn't connected to the Wilderwood enough for you to heal her without a trade."

"I know. I couldn't leave her like that." A huff, his hand coming up to capture hers and cage it against his chest. "But now I've left Fife like *this*."

Red turned her head to press a kiss on his bare, scarred shoulder. "They'll come around."

"They shouldn't have to," he'd murmured. But it'd been low, sonorous, and soon his breathing had evened and he'd dropped into sleep.

Now, in the library, Eammon's eyes were still shadowed with guilt. He didn't respond to Lyra, bracing himself with knuckles against the table for one deep breath before pushing up and going to the door. She let him pass without a word.

Lips pressed together, Red moved to follow. When she reached Lyra, she paused, eyes still ahead. "He didn't mean to get Fife tangled up in this again," she said softly.

She thought Lyra might not respond, but after a moment, the other woman sighed, her shoulders dipping low. "I know." A corkscrew curl hung in her eye; Lyra knuckled it back. "Fife made the choice to bargain. And Eammon..." A shrug. "Well. He wasn't exactly in a position to refuse, I guess."

"He would have." Red knew her Wolf down to the bones, the way his mind worked and the things that sparked his guilt. "If he'd been himself, he would have tried to find another way. Something other than a bargain."

"There wasn't one," Lyra said wearily. "We all know that."

Red had no rebuttal.

Lyra's nails tapped against the sleeve of her gown, her eyes still fixed on the floor. "It was to save me," she said, so quiet it was nearly a whisper. "Fife bargained to save me, so I shouldn't be mad, right? But all those years, those centuries longer than we ever should have lived, all he wanted was to be free of this damn forest. And I—" She caught the words and swallowed them, heaved a quiet sigh. "I don't want to be the reason he's not. He doesn't resent me for it, not yet. But I can't imagine that he *won't*, eventually. And what do I do then?"

Red put out her hand. A heartbeat, and Lyra placed hers in it, allowing comfort. "Fife loves you," Red said, simple and plain and true. "Exactly like you need him to. And he has for so long now, it's stood up against so much more time than it ever should've had to. He won't regret anything that saved you."

"I know." Lyra shook her head. "I just... *Kings*, I wish he'd told me. I wish I hadn't had to find out like this."

"He should have." Red snorted, giving Lyra's hand a gentle pull as they left the library and went to the staircase. "Secrecy never serves them well, does it?"

"You'd think they'd learn."

Eammon stood at the top of the stairs already, holding himself stiff and unsure, eyes shadowed by lowered brows. He nodded once as Red and Lyra climbed up the steps but didn't look their way, all his attention on the man at the door. "Raffe."

"Wolf." Raffe stood in the center of the foyer just as uneasily as Eammon did, dressed for traveling and anonymity. Dark trousers, boots, dark doublet, no *tor* to be seen. His fingers flexed back and forth, like he wished he had something to hold in them, and his eyes reluctantly left Eammon to find Red, as if he thought the Wolf might jump the moment he wasn't making eye contact. "Lady Wolf."

The title shouldn't have stung. It did anyway. Careful distance, wrought by the replacing of her name. A sign that things between them were unutterably different than before, that easy friendship muddled. "Hello, Raffe."

He didn't respond to the greeting. Instead, he looked behind Red, a spark of reverence lighting his face. Lyra was the only thing that had ever brought Raffe close to piety. He raised his fist to his forehead. "Plaguebreaker."

The shift of her feet was Lyra's only outward sign of discomfort. She raised her own fist, quick, then let it fall. "Raffe." Then, eyes sliding pointedly to Raffe's left, "Raffe's friend."

Raffe's friend—Kings and shadows, it was so strange to see someone that wasn't the five of them in the Keep; what was he *thinking*?—was dressed similarly to him, in a dark gown and gray cloak. She was beautiful, shorter and smaller than Red, with a waterfall of straight black hair and dark-bright eyes in a heart-shaped face.

Ironically, she seemed far more at ease than Raffe did. No fear in her eyes, just something near to awe. Her mouth hung open, her gaze eating up the Keep with a mix of trepidation and delight.

"Who are you?" Red didn't quite mean for the question to sound so rude, but it came cracking out of her in shocked surprise. They'd all agreed this needed to stay secret—the way the Wilderwood had changed, the way Red was so much more than just a Second Daughter. Nothing good could come of involving too many people.

But Raffe's guest didn't seem taken aback. She grinned, dipping her head—not a bow, which according to the few courtly manners Red remembered, meant she was also royalty.

Fantastic.

"Okada Kayu," she said, in a low, sweet voice that sounded like that of a singer. "Third Daughter of the Niohni Emperor, long may he reign." The last was said with a wry twist of her mouth, a flash in her eyes. "Not that I care overmuch."

Nioh. A collection of islands to the east, beyond the edges of the continent, known for their advances in science, particularly botany. Red remembered that the gardeners at the Valleydan palace had tried to cultivate some Niohni flowers once, sky blue and delicate, large as dinner plates. The climate had been far too harsh for them, leaching their color and leaving them limp on their stalks.

For all her beauty, Kayu didn't remind Red of those flowers at all. She seemed like someone who thrived in conditions others thought she should wilt under.

Eammon's eyes swung to Raffe, crackling green and amber. "What is the meaning of this, Raffe? I thought we agreed not to tell—"

"If it's any consolation," Kayu said, "he didn't tell me." She drifted from her place at Raffe's side, going to the wall and peering up at the tapestry of Ciaran and Gaya. It still hung there, threadbare and muddied. Red and Eammon hadn't found much time for interior decorating. "I figured most of it out on my own. Your plan of just hoping everyone ignores the Wilderwood only works for those who would be inclined to ignore it anyway. Which, to be fair, is most people." She lifted a finger, lightly touched the tapestry with thoughtful reverence. "But anyone with a curious bone in their body is going to figure out something is off eventually. And anyone with a brain to go along with that curious bone is going to figure out it has something to do with the missing Valleydan queen."

Red put a warning hand on Eammon's tense arm. The shape of his anxiety was easy to map. Another thing they'd murmured of at night, when there was no space between them and words came easily—what might happen if those who'd lived for so long in fear of the Wolf in the Wilderwood realized he was vulnerable. Pitchforks and pyres, centuries of terror and anger breaking against the boundaries of a forest that would no longer keep them out.

"I know what's happening." Kayu dropped her hand, turned to face them. "I know Queen Neverah has gone to the Shadowlands. And I know you're looking for a way to bring her back."

Red turned incredulous eyes to Raffe. "What part of *we should keep this quiet* meant *bring Niohni royalty to the Keep* to you?"

Circles stood out under his dark eyes, like sleep had been a hard thing to come by. "She figured it out, Red. It seemed more prudent to keep her close. Where we can keep an eye on her." He rubbed a weary hand over his face. "I am cursed to be surrounded by the bookish and prying."

"To his credit, Raffe was doing an excellent job keeping things under wraps," Kayu said, gesturing gracefully to the man in question. "But I came to Valleyda to study, so study I did. It wasn't hard to see that something was off, once I started paying attention." She dropped her hand, shrugged. "And I had taken more than a passing interest in the whole Valleydan Second Daughter mess before I came. It's a fascinating custom, if you can get over how awful it is."

Red exchanged a quick look with Eammon. The Wolf's brows were low, his mouth a flat line. Clearly, the other woman's explanation didn't convince him.

But Red was inclined to believe her. It didn't seem odd that a neglected princess from a faraway land might find herself taken with the fairy tale that Valleyda became every time a Second Daughter was born.

Still, it wasn't ideal. With a sigh, Red pinched the bridge of her nose between thumb and forefinger, a nervous tic she'd picked up from Eammon. "What do you want, Kayu? We don't have money—"

"Everyone thinks I want money." Kayu sounded nearly disgusted, rolling dark eyes. She left the tapestry, going instead to the vine laced along the wall, studded in its flickerless, forest-magic-made flames. "I have quite enough of my own, thank you. And I'm planning on parting with a significant portion of it to help you find your sister."

Trepidation drew up every line of Eammon's form, but the dip of his head and the flicker of his eyes toward Red said this was her call. He'd go along with whatever she wanted.

Red blew out a deep breath. She didn't know how money would play into finding Neve, but nothing else they'd done had gotten them any closer. *Desperate* was a weak word for the emotions snared in her branch-laden chest.

And Kayu knew. Knew Neve was gone, knew Red and Eammon had become the Wilderwood, knew the sacrifice of Second Daughters was a thing of the past. Dangerous knowledge, all of it. Raffe was right, it'd be prudent to keep her close.

She nodded to Eammon. Kayu could stay.

Kayu studiously peered at the flames on the wall through the whole exchange, knowingly giving them time to decide. She must've sensed when an agreement was reached—a breath after Eammon's nod, she gestured to the vine. "This is interesting. Forest magic?" She looked over her shoulder, pointer finger wavering between Red and Eammon. "Raffe told me you two have...something...going on with the Wilderwood."

"That's one way to put it," Eammon muttered.

Raffe sighed. "If you have chairs in this ruin, you'd better find them," he said as he headed toward the sunken dining room to the right of the door. "I have a lot to tell you. You'll want to sit down."

"So Kiri knows what the Heart Tree is?"

Dregs of long-cold tea sat in chipped mugs before them. Red's arms were crossed on the table, her neck bent over to stare at the letter written in Kiri's swirling script. Eammon's hand rested on the back of her neck, a soothing weight. Lyra sat on Red's other side, and Fife, tense and silent, sat next to her—he'd come in from errands in the Edge before Raffe started talking.

Across from them, as if they'd arranged themselves like opposing armies, Raffe sat next to Kayu, staring into the leaves at the bottom of his cup. Throughout his whole tale—Kiri's letter, the ends of the branches twisting into keys in the Shrine, Kayu's offer of help—Kayu herself appeared to be barely listening, her attention captured more by the surrounding Keep, as if she was reading a fairy story for the first time.

"She mentioned it by name, but didn't give any specifics." Raffe shook his head, running a hand over his close-shorn hair. "And her letter mentions something about a key. What happened with the branches in the Shrine makes me think she knows more than she put in the letter."

"So Neve has to find a key, too." Red's own lay on the table. When Raffe mentioned the branches in the Shrine, she'd pulled it from her pocket, told him about how it came to her.

Eammon's eyes had flickered to the key briefly when she first brought it out before he looked away, as if it still unsettled him. But now he was peering at it with a line between his brows, almost studiously.

"How did you find yours?" Raffe asked. "I assume it came to you right when those branches changed shape, and that was four days ago, sometime in the afternoon. Do you remember what you were doing?"

The tips of Eammon's ears turned scarlet.

Red cleared her throat, shifted in her seat. "I was trying to get to Neve," she said, leaving out the specifics of both the attempt and what came after. "If Neve's key is supposed to come to her the same way, I suppose it will happen while she's trying to get to me."

That sent all of them into silence, what logically followed hanging over their heads: If Neve didn't have a key yet—and none of them had reason to think she did—did that mean she wasn't trying to get back?

Eammon broke the tense quiet. "I think I recognize your key, Red."

She swung around to look at him, brow furrowed. Eammon still stared at the key on the table, mouth twisted up like it did when he was thinking hard. "It could be nothing," he cautioned, "but there's something that looks like a grove of keys carved into the walls of the Edge. Valdrek might know something."

"It's worth a try," Raffe said. "I'll take any connection we can get at this point."

"There are lots of carvings on that wall." Lyra's voice came out gentle, like she didn't want anyone to get their hopes up. "It might be a connection, or it might just be a coincidence. And Kiri is mad, we can all agree there. Her talk of keys and trees could just be ravings."

At that, Kayu's expression darkened, just for a moment. Red couldn't tell if it was in agreement or distaste or something in between.

"She's undoubtedly mad, but the things in her letter correspond with Red's dream." Eammon sat forward, giving the back of Red's neck a squeeze and the key one more pointed look before he ran the hand over his face. "We shouldn't discount her fully."

"Mad or not, the best way to find out what Kiri means is to go ask her in person. All of us." It was the first time Kayu had spoken since Raffe ushered them into the dining room and began his strange account, and it came out with conviction. Her dark eyes went from the greenery-choked window to Red. "I can pay for passage to the Rylt."

"We can't." Eammon shook his head, quick and sharp. "What if Neve comes back while we're gone?"

"I don't think Neve coming back can happen without me," Red said gently.

He knew that. Red knew he did. She also knew his reluctance to leave the Wilderwood wasn't all about the possibility of missing Neve. Nerves tensed his shoulders—she settled her palm on his knee, squeezed.

Lyra shook her head. "The rest of us can pass as normal, but Red and Eammon can't." She gestured to the flourish of Red's Bargainer's Mark, the ivy in her hair. "How do you plan to explain all that to a ship's crew?"

"We'll wear cloaks." Now that there was some semblance of a plan coming together, some possibility that they could move forward with saving Neve, Red wasn't about to let it slip through her fingers. "Stay out of sight as much as possible. We can make it work."

"And I'll pay the crew very well," Kayu said. "Well enough that a story about my friends' strange illnesses won't be questioned."

Beside her, Eammon's lips twisted, his knee bouncing nervously beneath the table. But he said nothing.

Red slipped her hand into his, curled her fingers around his scarred ones. "Eammon?"

He'd conceded to her in the foyer, told her without words that the things having to do with Neve were hers to decide. But she didn't want to make this decision for him.

His hand tightened around hers. Eammon looked up at Kayu and nodded.

Kayu clapped her hands, dark eyes sparkling. "Wonderful! I'll make the arrangements. We should be able to leave within a few days. It's a three-day journey, so pack accordingly." She looked to Lyra and Fife, inclining her head. "Raffe assumed you two would want to go, as well. The whole gang."

The fact that she included herself in *the whole gang* went without saying.

Chagrin and resignation chased themselves over Raffe's face, but there was something else there, too. He looked almost grateful. When Kayu moved, his eyes followed, a mix of irritation and wariness and begrudging respect.

"If we're going to ask Valdrek about that carving, we should do it today," Eammon said. He pushed up from the table, eager to be headed toward something that might hold answers.

Red nodded. "But I ... I want to check the mirror again first."

Eammon froze. One hand spasmed by his side.

They hadn't looked at the mirror—hadn't spoken of it—since that day in the clearing. Eammon had brought it back to the tower, and there it had stayed. Red had made herself stay away from it, but now something in her felt pulled there.

She kept thinking about Neve, how she had to look for a key. What if she'd found it but couldn't communicate with Red until she looked in the mirror? What if something in the glass surface had changed, giving them another clue? She couldn't leave it to chance.

Red grabbed Eammon's hand, squeezed it. "I just want to make sure."

He looked at her with his lips pressed together. A laden moment, then he nodded.

"That damn mirror gives me the shivers," Raffe muttered.

Eammon snorted.

It was an awkward trek across the courtyard to the tower, the sky darkening steadily toward night and casting everything in dusky purple shadow. Kayu's eyes were round and wondering, trying to take in everything at once. Every time she reached out like she might touch something, moss on the wall or a flower woven into the rubble, Raffe would bat away her hand. The third time he did it, she batted back. "It's bad form to treat your moneylender like a child."

"It's dangerous here."

"Not anymore." Red glanced at them over her shoulder. "Eammon and I have the forest well in hand."

Eammon pushed open the tower door, and they caravanned up the stairs, into the circular room with its four windows and paper sun. Books spilled over the table, left from when Red and Eammon had desperately needed a change of scenery from the library.

The Wolf crouched, crooking his fingers at the fireplace—a moment, then flames caught along the logs, hovering right over the wood without actually burning it. Kayu's eyes widened.

The mirror was propped against the wall between two of the windows, covered with one of Eammon's old cloaks. He pulled it away, mouth a displeased line, and dropped the cloak onto the floor.

At first, it appeared as if nothing had changed from the last time Red looked. The surface of the mirror was still choked with tree roots, crowding against the glass, their shape barely visible as more than twisted darkness.

Cautiously, Red stepped forward, reaching up and pulling a strand of hair from her braid. She knelt, wrapped the hair into the whorls of the frame.

A moment. Then the roots pressed against the mirror glass began to slowly unfurl.

They unraveled like a thread from a hem, and Red stared until her vision went blurry, expecting something to be revealed behind their shift. But one by one, they fell back, revealing still nothing—just an endless expanse of featureless gray. No Neve, no Shadowlands. No clues.

Slowly, the matte gray peeled away, like a snake shedding its skin, leaving silver reflectiveness behind. Just a mirror.

Just a mirror, beaming her reflection back to her, a wild woman with ivy in her hair and a ring of green around her irises. Magic, power seeping through her skin to show itself.

Slowly, her reflection changed. Mist billowed in from the edges of the frame, covering her form, making it gray and amorphous. It reminded her of her dream, being somewhere in between.

When the voice came, it reminded her of the dream, too. The same voice, vaguely familiar. The golden thread of the Wilderwood running next to her thoughts vibrated with it, underscoring it like a harp, the two of them in harmony.

She's taken the first step in becoming your mirror. Taken the power of a dark god, taken shadow where you took light. The two of you are too strong for mere glass to connect you anymore.

Her brows knit. "I don't—"

And then the mirror shattered.

She screamed as it happened, the sound of her cry mingling with the ice-crack of breaking glass. The shards exploded out from the worn gilt frame in a storm of needles; Eammon lunged in front of her, throwing up a forearm in front of his eyes. Fife cursed, Kayu gasped. Red barely registered any of it, limbs gone limp, thoughts gone hazy.

She's taken the first step in becoming your mirror.

Red sat down on the worn wooden floor, gaze miles away, her body feeling as distant as Neve did. Eammon crouched next to her, cradled her hand. There was glass in it. He carefully picked the slivers out.

"I don't understand." Raffe shook his head, glass crunching beneath his boots as he stepped toward the now-empty frame. "It just...just shattered, after telling us nothing..."

"It told me something," Red murmured.

Eammon's eyes darted up to hers, worry darkening the green and amber.

"I heard the voice from my dream," Red said. Blood leaked slowly from her hand. "And it told me Neve had taken the first step in becoming my mirror."

"But what does that *mean*?" Raffe sounded somewhere between panicked and angry.

Red didn't get a chance to answer. Her vision grayed, her muscles slackening, every ounce of energy drained from her like water through a sieve. She was vaguely aware of her head slumping onto Eammon's shoulder, her hand trailing through the shards of mirror on the floor, and then she knew nothing.

Chapter Thirteen

Neve

She didn't remember the return to the surface, not really. There were snatches of lucidity—the crumble of rock against her boots, the way her bedraggled hem slid along the stone floor, the feel of cave wall beneath one palm and Solmir's skin against the other—but for the most part, Neve was drifting, caught in twists of shadows that coursed through her veins to join the knot of cold in her middle, spinning like a black sun.

A god's magic, made her own.

There were substances some courtiers indulged in, bought on dimly lit street corners at strange hours of night. Things with odd names and odder looks, powders to place under the tongue or liquids to be carefully plied with a needle into a vein. Neve had never tried any of them, not having them offered and not caring enough to seek them out—wine did well enough for forgetting. But Arick had tried once, and had told her that it felt like flying, like some huge hand had plucked you up and flung you into the places between stars, and all you felt was the rush with no fear of the fall.

This was better.

Forget being flung; Neve *was* the place between stars, a cosmos held beneath her skin, a galaxy in human shape. She'd held up her hands after killing the Serpent, and it didn't matter that she hadn't done this before, that she didn't know how to absorb power from another creature—it came to her anyway, slid beneath her skin like a dagger into a sheath. There was a bite of pain at first, but nothing like what she'd felt when she first woke up, when she pulled magic from the Shadowlands itself. It really *was* different, taking power as death freed it from an Old One or a lesser beast.

And though her veins blackened as if her blood had run to ink and thorns pressed through her wrists like brutal jewelry, Neve felt safe. She felt infinite.

When the initial rush of all that absorbed magic began to wear off, making her aware of her body as flesh and blood instead of a conduit of shadows, Neve could've cried at the loss. Darkness was so much easier than the intricacies of humanity.

She paused right at the cairn's entrance, the band of shadow where the lip of it blocked the thin gray light. Her palm pressed against her chest; she gasped, as if she'd forgotten to breathe up until this moment.

"Are you hurt?"

Solmir, worry hardening the edges of his voice, making the question a demand. He'd released her hand at some point, a fact she didn't realize until she saw him reaching back toward her, skin striped by light and dark as he stood on the outside of the cairn. His beard hadn't grown in the days they'd been traveling, she noticed. Still cut short, framing a strong chin. One more reminder that time didn't run as it should here. That life and its markers held little weight.

"I'm fine," Neve replied, and her voice sounded distant, airy. "More than fine."

His hand still stretched toward her, a slight tremor in his fingers. "It doesn't...it doesn't hurt?"

"Hurt is temporary."

A frown wrinkled his brow, twisted that blade-shaped mouth to the side. He grabbed her hand, a darting motion like a killing strike, and Neve knew he wanted her to let the magic go, to let it flow into him rather than live in her. But it wasn't something he could *make* her do.

He'd kissed her to take it once, the first time—but she'd been confused and afraid then, scattered. And that was just power from the Shadowlands, not a god.

Now Neve was focused. Controlled. He wouldn't have this magic until she decided to give it to him.

His brows drew down farther, but Solmir didn't say anything. After a moment, he dropped her hand.

"It feels so different," she murmured. Neve looked down at her wrists, twisted them gently back and forth to admire her thorns. There was a delicate beauty to them, for all their sharpness.

"It *is* different." An emotion she couldn't name wavered beneath the surface of his voice. "The Serpent let you kill it, but you still did the deed yourself. Power you gain through your own actions sits differently than power that's given."

Didn't she know it. How power conferred by nothing but name or title was never truly yours alone, always tugged at and picked apart by those who bestowed it. How power could be nothing but the strings that held you up; maybe it hiked you higher than others, but you were still a puppet.

All Solmir's vitriol against the other Kings made sense, given that framework. Especially now that she knew Calyres was his father, that he'd had less of a choice here than she'd always thought.

Odd, how much more she seemed to understand him with all this shadowed god-magic coursing through her.

Neve cocked her head. She felt loose and strung thin, the weave of her made threadbare by the magic she carried. "You didn't tell me Calryes is your father."

His expression shuttered, all that worry choking itself out, becoming hard angles and arrogance. "I wasn't under the impression you were interested in my family history."

"I am if your family history is going to interfere with me getting home."

"I've wanted to kill the Kings for longer than you've been alive, Neverah.

The fact that one happens to be my father is inconsequential." Solmir crossed his arms over his chest. "We have no warm feelings toward each other. As I'm sure was made clear earlier."

Earlier, when he'd been shackled by shadows, tortured by them. *Kept busy.*

She hadn't thought of Valchior as the Serpent's power settled into her veins, but now her conversation with the King's projection came to the forefront of her mind. He'd called her Shadow Queen. Said the Kings knew why she was here. Said they welcomed it.

None of it made sense to her. If the Kings knew she was here as part of Solmir's plan to bring them into the true world, where they could be killed, why would they welcome that?

The Kings were playing a different game than Solmir was. Same pieces, disparate moves. And Neve was caught in the middle.

It made her decision easy: She'd keep what Valchior said to herself.

"It was made perfectly clear that you and your father are estranged." She crossed her arms, too, mirroring Solmir's closed-off stance, still inside the lip of the cairn. "But you should've told me. If we're supposed to be working together, you should tell me everything."

Different games, different pieces, different rules. Just because she'd decided to keep secrets didn't mean she wouldn't try to tear Solmir's out.

Still, Neve had no expectations of sudden honesty. So when the former King slid his blue eyes away from hers, softened his crossed arms, and sighed, it was as much a surprise to her as it seemed to be to him. "I'm a bastard. Calryes slept with my mother when he visited the walled city that became Alpera. Didn't know I was a result until later."

So he was from Alpera. It made sense—he looked like ice and snow, smelled like pines.

"My mother was the third-born daughter of the king. But once Calryes found out he'd sired a son—one who could use magic—he had everyone in the way of me becoming the heir killed."

"Including your mother?"

His voice became slightly quieter. Still clipped, but roughened. "Including my mother. And my two half brothers."

It made something in her chest simultaneously numb and burning, that he'd lost his mother, too. That he'd lived through that grief, and then let it be inflicted on her.

"We weren't close," he said, almost like he could read her emotions in the air around them. "To phrase it more kindly than it deserves. She wanted to forget I existed. My older brothers were cruel, to me and to everyone else—they would've made terrible kings. So when I realized what Calryes was doing, I didn't try to stop him."

The numbness passed, became only burning—sympathy or anger or something in between. Neve didn't know if she was comforted or horrified to know that she and her villain had so much in common.

"The possibility of having a son ruling the land to Elkyrath's immediate north was valuable enough to him to employ his famed assassins," Solmir continued. "So yes, Calryes is my father, and the reason I'm one of the Five Kings. It wasn't exactly my idea."

The notion of Solmir being bullied into anything, even being a King, seemed utterly at odds with the man who stood before her now. But Neve knew about that, too. How family could crumble you, even when nothing else could.

So she wrenched her thoughts away from family. Refused to dwell on how the wounds in her and the wounds in him reflected each other, matching points of pain.

"It's still so strange to me, to think of people just...born able to do magic." Neve leaned against the cairn wall, tipped her head back to study the stone ceiling. It was almost comfortable to speak to Solmir like this, him in the light and her in the dark. "The world was so different."

"So much worse," Solmir muttered. He mimicked her, leaning his shoulder against the wall on the outside of the cairn. If the rock hadn't been between them, their shoulders would've touched. "No good came of magic being loose, uncontained. There was no moral test to determine who could wield it and who couldn't, and most people are terrible."

"That reveals a rather bleak view of humanity."

"I include myself in the assessment." He slanted those blue eyes her way. "Are you saying you disagree?"

"*That's* a trap."

"Such a clever little queen."

Neve worried her dry, chapped lip between her teeth. "Some people are good," she murmured quietly. She thought of Raffe, steady and sure and kind. Of Red, who would probably never think of herself in such a way, but who loved so fiercely, so intensely that she was willing to walk into the Wilderwood in order to keep everyone safe. "I'll admit that I haven't met many of them, but I have to believe that people—most people—are good."

Solmir was quiet for a moment. She couldn't see his face, but she saw the way his body shifted, as he looked away from the cairn and out at the gray landscape. "For someone who has seen all the lies behind belief, you have a great capacity for faith, Neverah."

Idly, Neve pressed the pad of her finger against one of her thorns. A prick, a warm well of blood, crimson leached to charcoal in the monotone of the underworld. Already, she could feel the magic settling in, trying to make a more permanent home of her. Trying to anchor her to the Shadowlands, make these changes permanent. Make her something that couldn't go home.

With a sigh, Neve pushed off the wall and stalked out into the flat gray light of a sunless land, thorn-wreathed hands rising before her. "Let's get this over with, then."

No kiss this time. Even a bruising, cruel kiss like the one they'd shared to transfer power before felt like too much closeness right now, with the strands of history strung between them, the ghosts of understanding hanging close.

He'd killed Arick. He'd hurt Red. He would've killed Red's Wolf, and though Neve certainly had no love lost for the monster who'd married her sister, one more grudge to stack up against Solmir was a good thing to have.

She couldn't forget who he was, no matter their similarities. No matter how the longer she spent with him, the less like a complete villain he seemed. He was a former King, a fallen god. A means to an end.

So Neve put her hands on either side of Solmir's face, pressed all those thorns against his sharp angles, and let the magic of the Serpent go.

It left as easily as it had come, sliding out of her and into Solmir, though it took longer than it would have if she'd kissed him. The thorns on her wrists shrank as his eyes blackened, the veins in her arms paled as his darkened. The changes flickered, not permanent, only flashes as Solmir took the magic and stored it away, a vessel for power. He shuddered between her palms.

When all the magic had been drained from her, Neve dropped her hands. Solmir stayed with his head bowed, shivering a little before opening his eyes to hers. "I half believed you were going to keep it."

He said it like he knew, like he'd mapped her thoughts on her face. Neve was less and less concerned with the changes this power wrought in her. Less and less concerned with what it might mean for her soul. It'd be so easy to keep the magic, keep the control it offered. To let herself become part of this dead world, mighty and untouchable, damn the consequences.

But Neve had a life waiting. People waiting, people the man before her had hurt. Who he'd hurt again, if he had to.

Neve turned, striding into the cracked desert. The world rumbled softly beneath her feet, as if it was past the point of ever being truly stable again.

"We only need one monster," she said. "And you're already so good at it."

<hr>

The mirror was gone.

Neve lay cradled in the tower of twisting tree roots, white bark threaded with veins of shadow. They'd shaped themselves around her—curled to her temple so she could rest her head, slithered around her back so she could lay on her side. The same long, white shroud shifted against her legs.

But the mirror was gone. At first, Neve thought maybe it was just too high for her to see, grown into a different portion of the trunk than last time. But in the lopsided logic of dreams, she knew it was gone. The only things here were Neve and the mist and the impossible tree she reclined against.

Was that supposed to make her panic? It didn't. All Neve felt was puzzlement. Her head cocked to the side; the root cradling it slid away, job done. The others slowly shrank back into the labyrinth of their tower as she stood.

Neve craned her neck, peered upward. A faint hint of gold, miles above her head. It seemed brighter.

What had the voice called this, before? A place between. Between life and death, between two worlds. Red on one side and her on the other.

You've taken the first step.

The voice. Stronger this time, less timid, still familiar in a way she couldn't quite name.

Even knowing she wouldn't see anyone, Neve still whipped around, staring, searching the endless fog. "What do you mean?"

Exactly what I said. She could practically hear the eye roll. Did the owner of the voice even have eyes? *You took in a god's power. Magic, the inverse of what Redarys holds. A dark reflection.*

"I didn't keep it." Neve flexed her fingers, surreptitiously checking for thorns.

But you could have. You just chose not to. So much of this will come down to choice, in the end. A rueful laugh echoed through the mist, from everywhere and nowhere. *A lesson learned isn't easily discarded.*

Neve frowned. "So that's why the mirror is gone? Because I took the Serpent's power?"

You don't need a compass when you are yourself a map.

Her frown deepened. Neve continued forward into the fog, though no matter how far she walked, the tower of tree roots behind her never seemed to get farther away. "And in your metaphor here, the mirror is the compass."

Well done.

"And I'm the map."

Not you alone.

Neve's feet stuttered. She paused a moment before picking up her ambling again. "Me and Red, then," she said quietly.

A first and a second and a third to take what is left. Something melancholy in the voice's tone now, like the mention of Red weighed as heavy on it as on Neve. *But you and Redarys only, for the Tree to open. Prophecies can come piecemeal.*

The cold knot in Neve's middle felt suddenly heavy, like she carried lead behind her ribs. That place where she pushed everything, guilt and shame and every other emotion she didn't feel like dealing with, the convenient cage where she held all her true feelings about everything that had happened since she and Red turned twenty. Her hand pressed against her stomach as if she somehow had to keep it from escaping, from ripping her open in its desperation to be known.

Such things can't be pushed away forever. Mournful, tired. *All truths must face the light, in order to have the power to get to the Tree. To get the key.*

"But we know where the Tree is," Neve said. Then, almost begrudgingly, "Or Solmir does, at least."

The location is not everything. You need the power of two gods, one for each of you. And then, when you find the Tree, you must make your choice. To become what the stars have promised, or to leave the burden to those who come after.

Neve shook her head. "What do you mean? Make what kind of choice?" But even as the words left her mouth, they grew thin, faded, the tree roots and the mist blanking out.

"Neverah?"

Vision gray, swimming up out of her head, out of sleep. Neve sat up, wincing—sleeping on the hard-packed desert dust wasn't doing her bones any favors. "What?"

Solmir sat a few feet away, back against a rock, legs stretched out in front of him as he whittled that piece of wood again. "You made a noise."

She rubbed at the back of her neck, tried to run her fingers through her tangled hair. "Did you sleep?" she asked, because she didn't want to ask what kind of noise she'd made, and she didn't want to think about him paying close enough attention to be concerned at whatever kind of noise it was. Didn't want to think about how she'd done the same, in those scant moments they stole for sleep, watching his face twist and his brows furrow when she should've been watching the empty landscape.

There was no *night* here. The not-sky was the same dim gray, no change in the monotonous horizon. But still, when Neve could barely keep her eyes open and grew unsteady on her feet, Solmir had insisted they stop at an outcropping of stones—real stone this time, not soldered-together bone. Neve had been asleep nearly as soon as she stopped walking, the fatigue of carrying a god's power and then releasing it so draining that such vulnerability didn't seem something to worry over. She knew Solmir would watch her back.

At some point, against all her better judgment, she'd started to trust him.

Valchior's words, whispered in the dark. *He'll burn you in the end.*

Not if I burn him first, Neve thought, a rebuttal to a memory. But it sounded hollow, even inside her own head.

Solmir's sleeves were pushed up to his elbows, revealing muscled forearms as he carved. The rips in his sleeves gaped around the band of the tattoo circling his bicep.

"What's that on your arm?" Neve drew her knees in toward her chest. She might be awake, but she wasn't ready to start walking again just yet. And she *was* curious.

"Clan tattoo," he said, clipped. "Old Alperan custom. They needled it into me when I became king." He gestured to his arm with the knife, pointing at each band in turn. "Thick one is for the people. The one with all the lines is for the king before me—some uncle, I suppose, I didn't really know the man before Elkyrathi assassins gutted him. And the thin one is for me. The least important part of the whole equation."

He went back to his whittling. Neve bit her lip.

Here was another spit of common ground between them, unwelcome and unable to be ignored. The mantle of rulership, how it gave you power while stripping you of personhood. Especially when it wasn't really something you wanted.

Neve had been raised knowing she would someday be Queen. The fact hadn't held any sort of emotional weight; it was just what would happen, her inevitable trajectory. And once she did become Queen, she didn't view the position as anything more than the means to an end. The circumstance of Red's birth had condemned her to be sacrificed to the woods, and Neve resolved to use the circumstance of her own to save her. Queendom was something that had happened to her, not something she'd sought out.

Solmir was the only person to talk to here, but he was also one of the few people who would understand that.

She tucked her chin against her knees. "When my mother betrothed me to Arick, she didn't even tell me before the announcement."

The soft snick of Solmir's knife against the wood stopped. "That's less than ideal."

"Quite." Neve snorted. "It was…embarrassing, to be honest. He was so clearly in love with Red."

"Hmm." The sound of knife against wood grain picked back up, but slowly. Giving her space to talk about the man he'd inadvertently murdered.

But Neve didn't think about that. Not right now. "I think that's when I realized how little it mattered," she said quietly. "The title, the power…you're just somewhere for it to rest. The wheel of the kingdom keeps turning, whether you sit on the throne or someone else does."

Solmir set down his knife and the piece of wood, looking out over the gray horizon. "For what it's worth," he said, "you would've been an excellent queen, in other circumstances."

"I doubt it, to be honest. Though it probably would've been easier without you taking the form of my betrothed and twisting my desire to save my sister to your own ends." It could've come out poisonous. Instead, Neve just sounded tired. Anger was a hard thing to sustain, even righteous as it was.

"Can't argue there." Solmir rubbed at his scars again.

She gnawed on her lip, pulling her knees tighter, a physical rendering of the anxious knot her stomach had become. When she finally managed to ask the question, it was quiet. "Why did you act like you cared, when you were him?"

He froze. Stared down at his hands as if they were alien things. Solmir's brows knit, then his eyes closed, then the bitter line of his mouth pressed thin and tight. "At first, it was because I thought that was the part I needed to play."

It ached to hear, even though she'd known it. Part of her was glad that at least he wasn't lying. At least they'd arrived somewhere near honesty.

"He was your betrothed, and I didn't know what kind of relationship you had. Even though he'd bargained with me to save your sister. But then..." Another tightening of the mouth, his hands knotting self-consciously into fists, and the next words sounded like he had to force them out. "Then I acted like I cared because I fucking did."

She didn't know how to respond to that. So she didn't.

For a moment, it seemed like Solmir would leave it at that, leave the explanation bare and unadorned. But then he closed his eyes, opened them. Sighed. "You're easy to care for, unfortunately," he said. "You're strong. You're good."

"I'm not good." Neve nearly snarled it. "And I had to be strong. *You* made it so I had to be strong."

"I did," he said quietly. "So all your hatred is warranted."

Something certainly burned in her middle, an alchemy of emotion that made her want to hunch over. But she couldn't tell if it was hatred, warranted or not.

Solmir tugged all that long hair over one shoulder and started twisting it into a smoke-colored braid. When it was done, he let it drop onto his chest. "I didn't kill Arick, there at the end."

"Is that supposed to exonerate you?"

"Nothing can exonerate me. I know that."

All that not-quite-hatred in her middle coiled tighter.

"If my plan had worked—if I had been able to bring the others through, destroy them—I would've let Arick go," Solmir continued. "It was Red who killed him. To close the door."

She and Red, both with blood on their hands. It should've been a surprise, but instead it was just another thread in their tragedy. All Neve could manage to do was nod.

They sat there a moment in silence, neither looking at the other. "Tell me about being a King," Neve said finally. "When you were human." She didn't want to talk about herself anymore, whether she was good or strong. Better to hear about him, to learn what she could while she was trapped here with Solmir as her only way home.

Solmir tugged on his hasty braid, lips pressed together in thought. "Alpera wasn't much, back then. Centuries ago, I've stopped trying to count how many. Just a handful of people in the snow, surviving. Holding out against the Oracle."

The Old One they were going to next. The hair on the back of Neve's neck prickled as she thought of the Serpent's last confession, land laid to waste and water poisoned. "What did it do?"

"The Oracle isn't like the others." Solmir picked up the whittled wood he'd laid aside, twisted it in his hand. It was starting to take shape, though Neve couldn't quite tell what it was supposed to be yet. "Monstrous, but in a subtle way. The Old Ones weren't really the kinds of gods that garnered worship, but the Oracle did—peddling truth in exchange for sacrifice." He swallowed. "Worshipping the Oracle always ended in letting it devour you."

"Wonderful thing to find out right before we pay it a visit."

"Shouldn't be a problem." His voice was dark, not trying for any kind of levity. "In fact, I can't wait to kill the thing."

With that, he stood, pushing his carving knife and the piece of wood back into his boot. Neve swung his coat over her shoulders again, patting the pocket to make sure the god-bone was there. It was a comforting weight against her hip.

"How much farther is it?" she asked as she slid into her borrowed boots.

Squinting, Solmir raised his hand, pointer finger leveled at the bone-mountains in the distance. It wavered in the air for a moment before he settled it over one particular shape—more rounded, with a jutting promontory that extended level to the ground. "There," he said, letting his hand drop. "That's where we need to go to find the Oracle."

"Looks like quite the walk."

"Looks farther than it is." He started forward, long legs eating gray ground. "And it's not the walk you should be worried about. It's the climb."

Chapter Fourteen

Neve

H e was not being facetious.

The walk to the mountains was surprisingly easy. The ground was flat, making the distance look simultaneously closer and farther than it really was, and for once the earth stayed still. Being in the Shadowlands meant they didn't need food or water, so they didn't have to stop, and despite walking untold miles, Neve barely felt it in her muscles. It should've been disturbing, maybe—this reminder that, here, she wasn't necessarily *alive*, at least not in the sense she was used to—but mostly, it was convenient.

Until they got to the edge of the range.

What had seemed like the smooth side of a hill was ridged and spurred with bone up close. Had there been a sun, this would've blocked it out, a huge shelf of piled ivory that looked somehow precarious, despite its size and age. She couldn't shake the memory of what they'd seen on the way to the Serpent, the huge piece of mountain tumbling down to the ground in a cloud of bone dust.

And there was the matter of its height.

Solmir, apparently, had no such misgivings. One booted foot found purchase on what looked like a jutting tibia; his hand curled around the dome of a misshapen skull. "It's not that far. We're only going to the top of the first ridge." His head jerked up and to the side—a promontory speared out over the side of the bone-mountain, made of what looked like the massive knot of a vertebra. "And the way down the other side is easier than the way up."

But the shudders had already set into her shoulders; Neve's fingers were numb in the sleeves of his coat. "It's tall," she said in a small voice.

"Is that a problem?"

"Not a problem, no." But the lie was in her tone, and Solmir heard it.

He looked up, sighed. Jumped down from where he hung on the bones and turned to her, quirking an eyebrow. "Neverah Valedren, are you telling me that you—the Shadow Queen, stealer of sentinels, killer of gods—are afraid of heights?"

She scowled at him in answer.

Solmir laughed. He tipped his head back, scars darkly shadowed on his forehead, and he laughed at her.

Neve's scowl deepened. "Glad it entertains you."

"It doesn't entertain me so much as shock me." He shook his head, messy braid swinging. "You don't seem scared of much, Your Highness, and the fact that something so pedestrian as *heights* is what finally gives you pause is deliciously ironic."

Her arms crossed, tugging his coat tight around her. "I fell off a horse as a child. A tall horse."

"Yes, I'm sure it was very traumatic." He waved a dismissive hand. "But you don't really have an option here. We need the power of two gods to get to the Heart Tree. And the Oracle will be easier to kill than the Leviathan."

She knew she didn't have options, knew that she had no choice other than to climb up this massive pile of bones and kill the god at the top. Neve flexed her fingers back and forth, like the mountain was something she could fight.

Solmir watched her, hands hooked on his hips, face unreadable. "I won't let you fall, Neve."

Reassurance still sounded so odd, coming from him. She turned away from the mountain, looked at Solmir instead.

A moment, then he shrugged. "I need you."

Simple truth, uncolored by emotion. She nodded, one jerk of her head.

"This section is secure." Solmir kicked at the tibia he'd been using as a foothold. "The Oracle lives on top of it and can't leave. The mountain won't fall as long as the god is there." He inclined his head toward the bones, stepping aside. "You go first. I'll tell you where to put your hands and your feet."

Her insides were simultaneously tense and shivery. Neve mimicked what she'd seen him do—one foot on the tibia, then gripping the skull. Her hand trembled, slightly, but Solmir made no mention of it.

"Pull yourself up," he said, low and even. "Then, you see that piece of rib sticking out above your right hand? Grab that next..."

And so, directed by the former King at her back, Neve climbed the bone-mountain.

When they reached the top, her limbs felt like limp strings. Neve managed to walk over to a chunk of unidentifiable bone and sit down, breath coming heavy, all the fear she hadn't let herself feel as she climbed pouring into her nervous system at once. She buried her head in her hands and shuddered.

It was ridiculous, her consuming fear of heights. The fall from the horse started it, and it had only been nurtured the older she got—such a pedestrian fear, just like Solmir said. But being the First Daughter and then the Queen didn't give one much time to climb walls, so the fear remained, swelling and unconquered.

And it was refreshing, almost, to fear something so simple. Heights instead of forests, climbing instead of loss.

After a moment, she felt Solmir come sit beside her. She steeled her shoulders, waiting for him to make some cutting remark, but none came.

"Would you look at that," he said, stretching out his legs and propping his arms up behind him. "You did it."

"I did," she replied.

He sighed. "And now for the hard part."

"Could we take a minute first? Going right from mountain-climbing to god-killing might be a bit overwhelming."

Solmir snorted, reaching down to pull out his carving and small dagger from his boot. "Take five, even. The end of the world can spare that much."

Neve closed her eyes, took a few deep breaths. When she felt a bit steadier, she glanced at him from the corner of her eye. His knife dug at the wood in his hand, though the curve of his palm still kept her from seeing what exactly he was carving.

"What is that?"

A flinch; he hadn't seen her looking. Solmir's hand closed around the wood, as if he'd hide it from view, but then he opened his fingers on a sigh. "It's not finished," he hedged. "And it's not very good."

"Horseshit. Let me see."

"Such a mouth for a queen," he muttered, dropping the wood into her palm. Neve turned it over.

A night sky. He'd carved a night sky, a moon and scattered stars.

He shrugged again, looking out over the gray horizon instead of at her. "I didn't realize how much I missed the sky until I saw it again."

She rubbed her thumb over the whorls of stars, along the dip of the crescent moon. "I miss it, too," she murmured.

"Keep it."

"No." She turned to him, holding out the carving. "You said it wasn't finished." A smirk picked up her mouth. "An unfinished carving is hardly a gift fit for a queen. Give it to me when it's done."

"Assuming I have time to finish it before the Shadowlands collapse."

"You will." She said it like a command.

They looked at each other, half anxious and half confused and wholly trying to hide both feelings. Then Neve turned back to the horizon to see where all her climbing had taken her.

They sat on a shelf of bone, the vertebrae of some impossibly large thing, pockmarked and shining white in the gray-scale dimness. Behind them, a gigantic skull, the eye sockets big enough to drive a carriage through. It took her a moment to comprehend its shape, blown into such epic proportions, but there was the long snout, ending right before the vertebrae on which she stood, and the remnants of fang-like teeth below it.

A wolf. A giant wolf.

"Another dead Old One?" She sounded so polite, though her eyes felt as if they were going to fall out of her head.

"The Wolf." Solmir stood up, went to kick the toe of his boot against one of the oversize teeth. "The real one. Ciaran killed one of its whelps. That's how he got his evocative nickname."

Ciaran. The first Wolf of the Wilderwood. Even knowing that the monster of legend was technically her sister's father-in-law, hearing him spoken of like a peer still made her thoughts stutter.

Solmir looked at the wolf skull with only vague interest, but there was something in his eyes that said his mind was turned toward the same story hers was.

"You're the villain in that one, you know." She said it lightly. "The tale of Ciaran and Gaya."

Another kick against a giant tooth. "Every story needs one."

"Having become a villain myself, I assume there's more to that particular story."

One knife-slash brow raised as Solmir turned to face her. "Do you consider yourself a villain?"

It'd been a jibe, not an invitation for scrutiny. Neve shifted uncomfortably, tugged at the loose thread on the hem of her tattered sleeve. "I'm sure Red does."

"I think Redarys's feelings about you are a bit more complicated than that." His finger twisted at the silver ring on his thumb. "You were trying to save her, after all."

"When she didn't need to be saved," Neve murmured. "When she told me to let her go. If I'd just listened…"

She trailed off, not needing to finish the thought. If she'd just listened, she wouldn't be here. If she'd just listened, the cosmic question of the Kings and their souls and the Shadowlands and the Wilderwood could've been left for someone else to deal with.

"It takes more than not listening to make a villain," Solmir said. "With the caveat that I'm not an expert on the subject, having left most of my humanity behind long ago, that sounds mostly like human nature. We're rather predisposed to think we're always in the right."

Neve made a rueful sound. "What about you, then? Were you actually the villain?"

He crossed his arms, staring out into the gray sky. "It's a more complicated story than you've probably heard. But yes, I was undoubtedly Gaya's villain."

She didn't ask him to elaborate. But she did give him one arched brow, similar to the expression he turned on her when he wanted an explanation.

Solmir took the hint. He pulled in his knees, rested his forearms on them. Making himself smaller, almost subconsciously, before starting the tale that she'd heard so many times before.

"Gaya and I had been betrothed since we were children. I didn't ever imagine a life that didn't have us together. I assumed she didn't, either." A rueful noise. "I was wrong.

"She used to sneak out," he continued. "Pretend at being common. Valchior didn't really mind—he didn't give much thought to his family, anyway, and Tiernan, as his oldest daughter, was his heir. Valleyda wasn't strictly matrilineal then, but the oldest child inherited, regardless of sex or gender." He picked at his thumbnail; nerves always sat strangely on Solmir, built for arrogance and cold. "That's where Gaya met Ciaran, out in one of the villages. And I didn't know anything was happening between them until they ran off to the Wilderwood, after we'd created the Shadowlands." A pause. "It was my fault, I think. Assuming she was happy in the role she'd been given. Assuming she didn't want more."

Neve shrugged but didn't refute him. He was right. "Were you angry, when she fell for Ciaran?"

"I wasn't *thrilled*," he said, "but I wasn't the scorned, furious wretch I'm sure the story paints me to be. I wanted Gaya happy. And if that was with Ciaran, I would make myself fine with it. My anger was reserved for the Wilderwood. For trapping her."

"Is that why you wanted to kill Eammon?" His name still felt strange on her tongue, this monster her sister loved. "Because he...he *is* the Wilderwood?"

"Eammon needed to die for my plan to work," he said simply. "The fact that he's the Wilderwood—that he's Gaya's child—has no bearing on it."

But there was enough of an edge in his voice to make that explanation too simple. Neve narrowed her eyes. "But you'd feel guilty. If it had worked, you would feel guilty."

She expected him to scoff at that, but Solmir only went on picking at a thumbnail. "Maybe," he said finally. "But I have so much to feel guilty for already. What's one thing more?"

"I don't believe you really think that."

"Don't try to dupe yourself into believing I'm remorseful, Neverah." He snapped out her name, rising to stand, looming over her and blocking out gray light. "All of this is means to an end. Remember that. It will go better for you if you do."

Neve stood, too, glaring up at him. "Don't mistake understanding for forgiveness."

"As you say, Shadow Queen."

They stood there, the air tension-thick between them. She was the one to break, to turn away. He wasn't worth her anger. He kept trying to tell her that.

Neve turned to look out over the emptiness of the Shadowlands, over the remains of the gods they stood on, searching for a subject change. "There must've been a great many Old Ones, to make a whole mountain range from their bones."

"Not really." Solmir seemed as grateful to change the course of the conversation as she was. "This is the remains of three, I think, plus some of their lesser beasts. The Wolf, the Rat, the Hawk. They all had territories near here."

Three Old Ones, making false mountains that would put the Alperan Range to shame. Neve tried to imagine the sheer size of them, but it made an ache begin in her temples. "So they didn't get pulled to the Kings' Sanctum to die?"

He shook his head. "These three died early," he said. "When the Kings could still leave the Sanctum, before they mired themselves in so much power they were stuck there. They stabbed these Old Ones for their power and left their bones here after they absorbed it. The Oracle took up residence soon after." A feral smile twisted his mouth. "And I made sure it couldn't leave."

"Why didn't you kill it then?"

"Believe it or not, god-killing is only something I've taken up recently. Each Old One that dies makes this world a little more unstable."

"Then why were the Kings doing it?"

"Because they want out," Solmir said, turning away from the horizon and toward the mounds of bones beyond. "When the Shadowlands are gone, their souls are free. The Kings welcome the Shadowlands' dissolving."

We welcome it. Valchior's voice, whispering in the dark.

To Neve's right, stark against the gray sky, something jutted out from the side of one of the bone-peaks. Its dimensions made it difficult at first for her to realize it was another skull, as large as the Valleydan palace. The Hawk, apparently. It looked vaguely avian, with a short beak thrust out and pointed down toward the ground, like the Old One was screaming across the cracked landscape.

With a shudder, Neve turned to follow Solmir farther into the mountain made of corpses.

Chapter Fifteen

Neve

After scaling one smaller bone-shard rise behind them—Neve was afraid the pieces might slip, but they held fast—a small cave appeared, the path to it marked by another mound of fused-together bones. The cave was a dark pit, stark against the ivory.

Solmir stopped on the curve of a giant pelvis, gestured toward the cave's mouth. "Welcome to the Kingdom of the Oracle."

"Some kingdom," Neve muttered, balancing on an oddly shaped leg joint thrusting out of the mountain.

"Cold and small and barren, just like yours."

She made a rude gesture at his back.

It was a steep climb up splintered bones to reach the cave entrance. At the top of the rise, Solmir turned, offered a hand to pull her up. He tugged too hard when she accepted, and Neve crashed into his chest.

His skin was chilled where it pressed against hers, his hair feathered across her cheek, smelling of pine. The scars on his brow were deep punctures, ragged edges with angry welts in the centers. They'd be deep crimson, if there was color here, but in the Shadowlands they were only charcoal. There were six marks, deepest on either temple, the size gradually decreasing to be smallest in the center of his forehead.

"What are they from?" Neve asked quietly, eyes fixed on the scars.

"Some crowns are hard to take off," he answered. Then he stepped away from her, putting distance between them.

Neve stood there a moment, fists closed tight at her sides. Something like guilt churned in her stomach, something like shame. She'd told him that understanding wasn't forgiveness, and that was true. But Neve was starting to feel like forgiveness might be something she wanted to give him, and what kind of traitor did that make her?

Forcefully, she turned her thoughts to Raffe. A good man, a gentle man, someone who always strove to do right. He loved her, even though she didn't deserve it, and shouldn't that be the kind of connection she wanted? Love unconditional, love she couldn't tarnish, even with her hands so bloodstained?

But she could still hear Solmir's voice, calling down that corridor into the cairn. Coming to save her, even if it was just because they needed each other.

Solmir wasn't good, but he was... something. And that something made her have to fight to keep thinking of him as an enemy. Fight to keep her thoughts in simple dichotomies of right and wrong and good and bad, because the places between were treacherous.

The opening to the Oracle's cave was on another jut of bone, this one made of what appeared to be a giant femur, rounded ends spearing into open space. Smaller bones cluttered the entrance, creating a low wall. At first, the bones puzzled Neve, ridiculously small against the vastness of the Old Ones' remains. She took a step closer to the cave mouth to peer at them, wrinkling her nose against the fetid smell wafting from the opening.

The remains of lesser beasts, wings and claws, strangely shaped skulls, so many other bones that bore no resemblance to anything she could name. All of them were scored with teeth marks.

She backed up so quickly, she nearly tripped over her ripped hem.

Solmir stood near the rounded edge of the giant femur, like he didn't want to be near the cave, either. "Don't let its looks fool you," he cautioned, voice pitched low. "The Oracle was one of the most dangerous Old Ones even before most of them died."

"So how do we kill it?"

He didn't answer at first. When Neve glanced at him, Solmir was twisting that silver ring around and around his thumb again, jaw held tight. The tension of it made the scars on his brow darken.

"You don't worry about it," he said finally. "You stay as far away from the Oracle as possible."

No humor in his voice, just the flat tone of an order. Neve bristled against it—she resoundingly hated taking orders—but now, about to face a god he knew, didn't seem like the time to argue. She could always bring it up as a point of contention later.

And it was bolstering, to think there would definitely be a later.

The piece of god-bone lay heavy against her hip. Wordlessly, Neve dug it out, held it in Solmir's direction.

He shook his head. "You hold on to it for now."

"Are you sure?"

"Just trust me."

Their eyes met, dual realizations—both that the statement should have been totally ludicrous, and that, somehow, it no longer felt that way.

Neve slid the bone back into her pocket. Then she and Solmir walked into the cave.

It took a moment for her eyes to adjust, but not because of darkness—her pupils contracted against unexpected light, a soft glow from somewhere deeper in the cavern. On the floor, more rings of bones, stratified and grown higher than the one right at the cave's opening, as if whatever had made the piles once had a greater range of movement than it did now.

Solmir nudged one of the bones with his toe, turning it over to reveal more teeth marks. "It kept loosening its restraints," he said quietly. "I finally had to use god-bone to keep it lashed to the floor."

"*You* imprisoned it?" He'd said as much before, but now, faced with concrete proof of the Oracle's violence, the feat seemed nearly impossible. "How? And why?"

"Luck, mostly." Gingerly, Solmir stepped over the first ring of bones. "As for the why, it's a long story, and this timing is less than ideal."

She couldn't argue there. "But you'll tell me after."

He made a noise that wasn't assent or disagreement. Circumstances being what they were, Neve didn't push.

As they moved forward, the glow at the back of the cavern gradually grew brighter. It was soft, diffuse, like shafts of sunlight seen through morning mist. The gentleness of it sat strangely against the carnage of gnawed-on skulls.

The last ring of bones was high enough to obscure Neve's view of whatever lay on the other side, though she could tell whatever it was emanated that glow. Solmir paused, twisting his ring again. Blue eyes slanted her way, then down to her pocket.

Neve read his meaning: Keep the bone hidden. She nodded.

Solmir went first, climbing over the bone-pile with more grace that the shifting shards should've allowed. Neve followed, her torn nightgown making the ascent fairly easy. The chill of the Shadowlands might make it less than ideal, but at least she could run with her skirt tattered to strips, and that seemed more prudent.

Then she topped the rise.

A circular stone dais sat beyond the wall, its color bleached white in the glow from the figure that stood on it.

A beautiful, almost human figure.

The god was dainty and feminine, delicately boned. White hair fell shimmering to the floor, almost indistinguishable from the long white robe that covered the figure from neck to ankle, leaving its arms bare. Its forehead and eyes were covered by a silver wire mask, attached to a crown of rotting roses. Chains bound thin wrists, stained dark and crusted with what might've been ink or dried blood, anchored to the stone floor in front of it with shards of ivory. More chains around its waist, similarly anchored, a bound deity in a palace of chewed bones.

The Oracle.

Solmir stood at the foot of the dais, glaring up at the Old One with undisguised hatred. The god didn't acknowledge him at all, didn't so much as twitch when Neve slid down the bone-pile, though a clatter of stirred vertebrae fell to the floor in her wake.

Solmir didn't look at Neve when she stepped up next to him, but he did shoulder in front of her slightly, like he wanted to stay between her and the god he'd imprisoned.

Neve let him. Out of all the things she'd seen since coming to this strange, upside-down world, this slight, girlish figure in the decaying flower crown was the most unsettling.

For a handful of heartbeats, they stood in silence.

Then the Oracle: "Aren't you going to cede your power, Solmir? That's the polite thing to do. Or are you just going to stare at me all day?"

"I'd rather eat glass than cede power to you." He didn't snarl it. He said it measured and matter-of-fact, and the words were sharper for it.

The Oracle angled its head to look at them through its wire mask. Darkness stained the skin beneath it, as if the god's eyes had rotted and dripped from the sockets like egg yolks. More black stains marred its gown, the remains of some bloody feast.

Neve thought of all those teeth marks and swallowed.

"I see," the Oracle said slowly, voice gentle and smooth. "Still upset over centuries-old hurts. Not surprising, I suppose. Our kind have long memories, and the ages melt together eventually."

"You and I are not remotely the same thing," Solmir replied.

A slow smile spread over the Oracle's face, revealing double rows of tiny, pointed teeth. "It'd be easier for you if that were true, wouldn't it? But the only thing separating you from me is a soul, Solmir, and yours seems worse for wear lately. Well, a soul and belief. Believing yourself to be a god is the most important aspect of divinity, and you lost your belief in yourself long ago. In every way."

Solmir's expression didn't change, but his hands clenched by his sides, tight enough to blanch the skin around his rings.

"All that magic, swelling you like a tick on a vein," the Oracle murmured. "Truly, it's astonishing you've managed to hold on to your soul at all." With a burst of unnatural speed, the Oracle bent its head to the side at an angle that should've snapped its neck, exaggerated curiosity. "Does she know why you take the magic from her? Why you keep it, so she stays empty?"

"Yes," Solmir said, but there was a pause, and his eyes darted to Neve as if he wanted to gauge her reaction.

Neve was having a hard time coming up with any reaction other than cold dread.

The Oracle's fingers twitched through the air, arms held out to its sides by the chains. "You're still so angry," it said to Solmir, Neve apparently forgotten. "I can taste it, coming off you in waves. Anger and guilt, though the guilt is more complicated. You just can't stop pulling women into your underworld, can you? Or trying to, at least. This one seems to have worked out better than the other."

That, finally, was enough to get a reaction; Solmir lurched forward like he might lunge at the god, mouth bent into a snarl. Neve's hand shackled around his arm, holding him back, though she had to grind her heels into the stone ground to do it.

The Oracle laughed, a high, almost screeching sound. "Or has it?" the god asked, fingers still twitching. "The last one you wanted to open the Shadowlands for only because you loved her and wanted to escape, but this one...this one has a purpose. This one has strings attached, strings from stars, and you want to play them like a harp." A delicate shrug. "Better strings than roots."

Roots. Gaya. Neve's eyes cut to Solmir, her fingers tightening around his arm.

The muscles beneath her hand went the consistency of stone, but Solmir didn't lunge at the god again. "Don't talk about her," he said, voice low and poisonous. "You aren't allowed to talk about her."

"Fine with me," the Oracle replied. "Especially when you've brought someone much more interesting." Its head bent again, this time to the other side, wire-covered eyes fixed on Neve. "Hello, Shadow Queen. You want something from me."

Neve's eyes shifted from the horrible-beautiful god to Solmir, fear making her spine straight and her muscles weak. It knew. Somehow, the Oracle knew they were here to kill it, and it would—

"Don't look so shocked. No one comes here for any reason other than wanting something. Especially not Solmir, who hates me so." Another of those wide smiles, showing rows of teeth. "But you can't get something for nothing. I always get my due."

The gnawed bones around their feet gave the words unsettling weight. Neve tightened her hand around Solmir's arm, though she didn't think he would try to go for the god again. At least, not until he was ready to kill it.

And when was that supposed to happen?

What you want and what he wants are not the same thing, Shadow Queen.

The Oracle's voice was smoother than the Serpent's had been, a caress around her mind rather than a scrabble against it. Neve swallowed and clenched her jaw, not allowing the Oracle in, not allowing it to read her thoughts.

The laugh that echoed in her skull was just as screeching and unpleasant as the one that had echoed through the cave. *Your desires twine and tangle, but come apart at the most important seams.* A thoughtful pause. *He can count the number of people he has ever cared about on one hand. Do you think you're among their number, Shadow Queen?*

Her teeth ground together, but Neve's hand dropped from Solmir's arm. He glanced at her, brows drawn low.

The Oracle pouted, sticking out a lush lower lip. "The Shadow Queen doesn't want to talk to me," it said, straightening. A toss of its head, resettling the rotting rose crown. "But someone will have to. That's the price for what you want."

"What do you think we want?" Solmir asked. His hand kept flexing back toward Neve, toward the piece of god-bone in her pocket.

"To open the Heart Tree," the Oracle answered. "To do so, you need the power of a god." It preened at that, fingers twitching, shaking out its long white hair. "I knew you'd have to free me eventually, Solmir. This punishment couldn't be forever."

Punishment? Confusion twisted Neve's mouth.

The Oracle chuckled. Neve hadn't allowed it to read her thoughts, but it seemed to see the question in her expression. "I didn't tell Solmir that trying to open the Heart Tree with his former lover would kill her." A graceful shrug. "He didn't take it well."

Solmir's shoulders were tense ridges beneath his thorn-ripped shirt, but he didn't rise to the Oracle's bait. He looked to Neve, something fierce and half hopeful in his eyes.

It hit her then. The Oracle didn't know they were here to kill it.

The pieces came together quickly—the god thought they were here to break its chains, to make it guide them to the Heart Tree. The Oracle knew the Heart Tree could be opened only by the power of a god, and thought they meant to make it their prisoner, not their victim.

Which meant it would expect Solmir to get close enough to loosen its restraints. It wouldn't know the closeness was for killing until it was too late.

But only if they played this next part very, very carefully.

Moving so slowly her muscles shuddered, Neve slipped the bone from her pocket. She pressed her hand to Solmir's, the cool of his skin welcome against her fevered fear.

"But before you free me," the Oracle said, "I want a truth."

Her fingers went numb; Neve almost dropped the bone. She and Solmir both tried to catch it while also keeping as still as possible—her fingers closed around it just before it fell from their awkwardly clasped hands.

Neve pulled her arm tight to her side, hiding the bone in the tatters of her skirt. "A truth?" she asked, more to distract than to clarify.

"Oh look, she speaks." The Oracle's tone sounded exactly like the flippant cattiness of a seasoned court gossip. "Yes, Shadow Queen, I want a truth. There might be no food or drink here, but we all feed on something, unless we want to weaken enough to get reeled into the Sanctum."

Solmir stepped up on the dais, fists clenched at his sides. "Fine. Take one; I have truths enough to glut yourself on."

"But none of them are surprising, once-King, and when one has been in famine, they desire a feast to break it."

That only left one solution. Neve stepped forward. "Take one from me, then."

Another slow smile, all those pointed teeth. "Yes," the Oracle whispered. "You smell of secrets buried deep, of things left to age like wine. Your truths are sure to be delicious."

The word *delicious* made skitters of fear rattle down her spine, but Neve clenched her teeth, her fists. The point of the god-bone dug into her palm, held flush along the line of her forearm.

She shot a quick glance back at Solmir, read the inevitable and his fear of it in the flash of his eyes—she'd be the one close enough. She'd have to stab the Oracle.

Stab it, and hope that was enough.

The Serpent had wanted to die; it didn't fight back when Neve shoved the god-bone into its side. But she had no idea how the Oracle would react, what it would do as magic seeped out of its wound.

No time to think about that, no time for fear. Neve stepped forward, cautiously approaching the god in chains. "What kind of truth do you want?"

"Oh, Shadow Queen," the Oracle said, those twitching fingers stretching forward to brush lightly over her forehead. "You don't get to choose."

The finger didn't move. For a moment, Neve wondered if this would be easier than she'd thought, if the extraction of a truth was something simple—

Pain. Pain like a dagger slicing into her brain, paring to her heart even though the Oracle's finger still didn't move—so much worse than the pain she'd felt before, when she pulled magic from the Shadowlands and nearly drove her soul down into its foundations. Neve gasped, but she knew it only because she felt her mouth open. She heard nothing, nothing but an awful buzzing in her ears, like a horde of corpse-flies.

Down, down that sharpness traveled, down to the knot of emotion she'd kept so tightly tangled in her chest.

Her soul. Cold and small, wrapped in anger and guilt and all the things she didn't want to see, didn't want to feel.

But now they flashed before her, snatches of sight and sound, narration by the voice of the Oracle that she didn't hear in her head so much as in her very center, seething up and hissing against her bones.

You thought you loved him, but did you really? Was it more an idea of him, a clinging to who you thought you were, wished you could be? An image of Raffe, dark eyes warm, cupping her cheek in her cold bedroom. *You didn't avenge your mother, you would've held the knife yourself if you thought it was the only way.* Isla, distant across a dining table that felt miles long. *You knew Red was fine, you knew it the moment you saw her again, but you were in too deep to admit mistakes. You would've sacrificed her Wolf and killed whatever happiness she'd found because to do otherwise would mean admitting you were wrong, and you couldn't do that, not then and not ever.* Red, crouched in the Shrine, more wild than woman, and Neve knowing that was what she was always meant to be.

An image of Solmir leaning against the wall after Neve's coronation, arms crossed and mouth stoic. But that had been Arick, hadn't it? Or Solmir wearing Arick's face? It was all too knotted together for her to untangle, who he was, who he'd been.

Does it matter? the Oracle's voice asked, amusement twisting up the end of the question. *You knew something was wrong, and you did nothing. You never let yourself think deeply on what Arick was up to, because you knew you wouldn't stop him, no matter what it was. What kind of queen does that make you? What kind of friend? What kind of person? Not a good one, Shadow Queen. Never a good one.*

The bite of stone into her knees, her hands at her chest, as if she could reel all of this in and tie it back up. But once unspooled, her packed-down emotions kept coming, heightened and sharpened by the voice of the Oracle, slicing in and knowing all, an arterial pump of truth.

You never admit when you're wrong you'd rather die than let anyone

know you made a mistake all of this is your fault if you'd just listened to Red
and let her go you'd still be with Raffe even though you don't deserve him—

Neve wanted to pass out, to fade from consciousness, but the Oracle's onslaught kept her viciously, horrifically present, anchored in all the moments she'd done wrong, seeing the face of every person she'd let down.

It was terrible. It was deserved.

When she felt Solmir streak past her with a roar in his teeth, felt him wrench the god-bone from her hand, she barely noticed, crouched on the bone-strewn floor with her soul in tatters in her chest.

Solmir leapt at the Oracle, over the chains that bound it to the dais, and slashed the bone across the god's throat.

Immediately, the pounding of all Neve's failures through her head ceased, the endless parade of all the ways she'd fallen short. She looked up through swimming eyes.

The Oracle was shuddering. Though shuddering seemed like too gentle a word—the space the god occupied seemed scrambled, making its shape judder from side to side, edges unmatched as if Neve were seeing it through window slats. Shadows poured from it, writhing into the air with their chittering sound, louder and more violent than she'd ever heard before.

The bone dropped; Solmir thrust his hands out, calling the rogue magic to him as it drained from the gaping wound in the Oracle's throat. The shadows wound around his arms, filling him with darkness, and Neve saw the moment when his clenched jaw unhinged, when the pained scream became something he couldn't hold in anymore.

The ground rumbled, dust raining from the ceiling. The pile behind them shook, loose bones rattling, sliding down to the bloodstained stone floor.

The Oracle fell to its knees, knocking the rotting rose crown askew. Its mouth opened, letting loose a high laugh, chased by more gibbering shadows, a cacophony of madness and unraveling. It reverberated in the air and in Neve's skull; she clapped her hands over her ears.

Foolish of me, the Oracle whispered in her head. *Foolish to think he offered freedom instead of death, but I've grown so tired of shackles that one is nearly as welcome as the other. Though not quite as foolish as you are, Shadow Queen. Thinking there's something worth saving in him. Thinking there's something good.*

Pieces of rock fell from above now, chasing the dust. The bones behind them bucked and slid. Another quake, collapsing the cave, maybe collapsing the whole mountain. And still magic seeped from the dying god and poured into Solmir. Still he screamed, blue eyes flickering into black.

"You deserve each other," the Oracle said, aloud this time. "Two fools, damning themselves over and over again."

The Oracle's body twisted, jerked in painful angles, winnowing away into smoke and shadow. The drain of its magic ate it away to muscle, to bone, the skeleton oddly shaped. Then, in another plume of dark smoke, it was gone.

The shadow rushed into Solmir's hands, and he fell to the shaking ground. Darkness covered his skin, as if he'd dipped his arms in ink. His irises shuddered from blue to black, blue to black, his soul at a tipping point.

Neve had to get up. The cave collapsed around them, bones sliding and rocks falling; but she had to take some of that magic, too, siphon it out of him so he wasn't consumed. She lurched forward, ramming her knee against the broken end of a sharp tibia. It punctured skin, the warm weep of blood seeping down her leg and making her stagger. Between the wound and the weakness left over from the Oracle's assault on her mind, Neve could barely stumble across the floor.

When she made it to Solmir, he was pushing himself to stand, darkness seeping away from his veins, out of his eyes. "Don't." Loud and commanding against the screech of the falling mountain. "Don't take it, we'll need it all."

"But you—"

"I," he snarled, shoving the god-bone in his boot, "am perfectly suited to this."

Another shudder shook through the cave. A stone fell from the ceiling, careening directly toward Neve's head; Solmir grabbed her arm and pulled her to him, out of the rock's path, then immediately released her, unwilling to linger on her skin.

"Promise you won't take it," he said, shouting into her face to be heard over the crash and collapse around them. "Not until it's time!"

"Yes, fine, I promise!"

"Good!" Then he grabbed her waist and swung her up over his shoulders so her stomach pressed against the back of his head, her legs over one shoulder and her arms over the other, his silver-ringed hands wrapped around both to keep her in place. It was uncomfortable, and she barked a wordless protest even as he started forward, running toward the pile of sliding bones.

Solmir wiped a rough hand over her knee, held up his bloodstained palm. "Do you want to walk? Then stop complaining!"

A grunt punctuated the last word as he jumped up on the bones; they slipped under his feet, but Solmir moved quickly, stepping to the next before the one he stood on fell. Neve glanced back—the dais had sunk into the ground, the bloodstained stone crumbled. The bones slipped toward the ever-widening hole, like the mountain was eating itself.

The rasp of Solmir's breath was loud against her ear as he carried her out of the cave, onto the outcropping of giant femur that made the cliff outside it. Still not safe; the mountain trembled, all the bones fused over eons shuddering apart.

They turned in the opposite direction from where they'd come, Solmir running toward another short rise that crumbled even as they approached. Through the wild tangles of hair—hers and Solmir's, knotting together with wind and sweat—Neve could see where the mountain abruptly ended, gray horizon, beyond which looked like a sheer drop.

He swung her around to his front; it *hurt*, and Neve made another sound of protest as Solmir pressed her tight against his chest. "Apologies, Your Majesty. Hold on."

As the mountain of bones crumbled behind them, Solmir ran to the edge and tipped them over.

Chapter Sixteen

Red

T he trek to the Edge took much less time than it used to, now that
they didn't have to be on the lookout for pits of shadow or rotting
trees or escaped monsters. Under any other circumstances, it might've
even been pleasant.

But, circumstances as they were, everyone was tense and silent.
Especially Raffe.

Red watched him over her shoulder as she led their odd procession
with Eammon, crunching through the leaves of eternal autumn. The
other man's brows drew low over preoccupied eyes, his gaze barely rising
from his feet, deep in thought that drew his mouth tight. The only thing
he actually appeared to see when he looked at it was Kayu, who, though
quiet like the rest of them, took in the forest with wide-eyed delight. Even
then, the look on his face wasn't something Red could easily read.

This had to be awful for him. Raffe and Neve had never really been
together, as far as Red knew, but the way they'd felt about each other
was obvious. At least, it had been. Now things seemed more complicated. Layered in ways she no longer knew either of them well enough
to interpret.

Not that Neve's romantic entanglements were any of her business.
The last time one of them had tried to wade into the other's love life, it
had gone poorly.

For all his awareness of her, Raffe kept a careful distance from Kayu. Occasionally, she'd try to speak to him, or point something out that interested her, and he'd bend a slight smile before going back to brooding. Lyra and Fife indulged her a bit more, answering her questions about the healed Wilderwood when she voiced them. It appeared the third princess of Nioh had read quite a lot about the forest, about Valleyda, and was eager to have someone to discuss it with.

"I'm not sure about her," Eammon murmured, glancing back to follow Red's gaze.

"Neither am I." Red turned back around and leaned her head on Eammon's shoulder, half to further obscure their conversation, half because he had very nice shoulders. "But Raffe seems to trust her. And beggars can't be choosers—if we need to go to Kiri, we'll need a ship."

"I don't recall begging to sail to the Rylt," Eammon muttered.

Apprehension coiled in the muscle beneath her cheek.

"Maybe we won't have to," Red said. "If those key-branches are carved on the wall of the Edge, maybe Valdrek will know where the Heart Tree is. *What* it is." She sighed. "Anything about it at all would be welcome, really."

Eammon shrugged, jostling her head; when she frowned up at him, he dropped a kiss on her brow. "Maybe," he conceded, "but even if Valdrek can answer some questions, I feel like we'll have to deal with Kiri at some point. Call it Wilderwood intuition."

"That's what you call it?" She didn't have to elaborate—he meant the feeling of something running just alongside your mind, the golden thread winding through their bodies that was both wholly them and wholly *other.*

Eammon shrugged again, this time purposefully dramatic, to send her head popping up from his shoulder. He grinned when she swatted at him, though his eyes were contemplative. "Seems as good a term as any."

"*Wilderwood intuition* is a thorn in my side."

"You have thorns everywhere, Lady Wolf."

"Such a romantic," she replied. But she sounded as preoccupied as she felt, and Eammon gave her an understanding look before reaching down and threading his fingers through hers.

"She's fine," he said quietly. "The mirror shattering yesterday means she's done something, right? That's what it told you?"

Red nodded grimly. The forest within her—her Wilderwood intuition—had imparted understanding after the mirror broke, in that voice she'd heard in her dreams. She no longer needed the mirror, because Neve had done…something. Taken in the dark the way Red took in the light.

That meant she was alive. But it still wasn't exactly comforting.

The mirror's breaking had broken something in her, too—she'd passed out in the tower, and not awoken until deep night seeped around the windows. It'd delayed their trip to the Edge until this morning, bright and early. Pale yellow sunlight filtered through the autumn colors of the leaves, dappling everything in crimson and ocher and gold, a precursor of the fall rapidly approaching outside the Wilderwood.

"How do you keep the forest from turning?" Kayu jogged up to them, slightly out of breath. Her black hair shone in the autumn light as she gestured to the trees. "Turning with the seasons, I mean. I asked Fife, and he said to ask you."

Red doubted he'd said it so politely. "It's not conscious. It just…" She trailed off, looked to Eammon, who gave an inexpressive shrug. "It follows our lead, I guess. Takes on our aspects. It was early autumn when we… when we did what we did." Even now, she didn't quite know how to articulate it. The nature of what she was—woman and Wolf and wood—eluded easy language. "So it's frozen there. We stopped changing, so it did, too."

Kayu nodded, her eyes tracking between them. "Because you *are* the Wilderwood."

"Exactly." Red tried to sound sure of herself. Eammon shifted uncomfortably on his feet, the movement sending black hair feathering over the tiny points of his antlers.

"And because you are the Wilderwood," Kayu said slowly, "it won't call any more Second Daughters."

Something about the question prickled Red's skin, that damn Wilderwood intuition sparking enough to make her wary, but not enough to give her its reason. She slid a look to Eammon as she nodded. "Right. No more Second Daughters."

Kayu looked thoughtful but didn't ask anything further. She drifted back toward Raffe and the others, picking up a fallen leaf from the ground and twirling it between her fingers.

"That was strange," Eammon muttered under his breath as she walked away. "We can both agree that was strange, right?"

"It makes sense for her to be curious." Tugging absently at one of the ivy tendrils growing in her hair, Red flipped him a wry smile. "We are a bit of an enigma, after all."

"Still." A slight shake of his head. Eammon rubbed at one of the bark-vambraces growing over the skin of his forearms. "I think we should be cautious."

"When are we not cautious?" A joke, but a weary one. "And it's not like we have much choice. She knows Neve is gone. Like Raffe said, it makes more sense to keep her close." Red glanced at Raffe again. Kayu was telling him a story, shaping it in the air with her hands. He smiled at her, small but genuine.

Eammon made a gruff noise, somewhere between challenge and agreement. He looked at the pair over his shoulder, then turned curious eyes to Red. He didn't give voice to his question, but she could read it there.

"I don't know," she said softly. "I don't know how he and Neve...left things."

He squeezed her hand. "We bring her back," he said decisively, "and then she can figure out her own damn love life."

Ahead, the forest thinned, the golden autumn trees giving way to green moss and unencumbered sunlight. Red could just glimpse the Edge's outer wall, though even squinting, she couldn't quite make out any shapes in the arabesques carved there, key-groves or otherwise. Her own key was in the pocket of her tunic, beneath her bridal cloak. She slid in her hand, brushed a finger over one of its teeth.

Eammon picked up his pace as soon as he crossed the tree line, his much longer stride making it so the others would have to jog to match. Red was the only one who did, though—Lyra and Fife kept to a leisurely walk, and Raffe and Kayu seemed content enough to stay with them. Eammon stalked quickly to the gate, rapped once on the wooden wall, then stepped back to peer through narrowed eyes at the carvings.

Red reached him and leaned against the wall, out of breath from trying to keep up. "Your legs," she panted, "are *entirely* too long."

"Blame the forest." Eammon put a hand on her shoulder, moved her gently aside to look at the carvings her back had hidden. The markings didn't seem to follow any sort of pattern Red could make out—some were curved and flowing, others spiky and nearly runic. None of them looked like keys.

The others reached them, squinting against bright sunlight after the shade of the Wilderwood. Raffe's eyes tracked over the marks, a frown turning down his mouth. "Where was this carving you spoke of again?"

"I don't remember." Barely leashed irritation in Eammon's voice— all of them lived on a shatterpoint. "We'll ask Valdrek. If I can describe it, he'll know where it is. He can read the wall."

"Read the wall?" A new concept to Red. Her brow arched.

Eammon cut his hand toward the wall in question. "The marks are a map, sort of. A history. When the explorers ran out of paper, before they figured out how to make their own, they started carving things they wanted to remember on the walls of the Edge instead. It's a complex pattern, a language all its own. I can make out parts of it, but I'm not fluent."

Red's eyes widened. She looked back to the strange carvings with renewed interest, trying to find meaning in all those waving lines. She'd only ever thought of the carvings as decorative, but it made sense that they'd be more than that—those in the Edge made do with what they had, and resources like paper were prohibitively expensive even on the rest of the continent.

Kayu traced one curving line with a manicured finger. "Doesn't look like anything but shapes to me." She shrugged at Eammon. "But you're the forest god, so I trust you. Though trusting gods seems to be a fraught thing, of late."

"Gods who show their true selves are fine by me," Raffe muttered. "It's the ones who try to hide you have to look out for. On all the *shadows*, it seems like I can't walk two feet without running into something out of a story anymore."

"I think I'm at least three feet away," Lyra said.

Raffe blanched, swallowed. "I mean...of course, it's not...I didn't..."

"Need a shovel?" Lyra jostled his shoulder playfully as she stepped forward, joining Fife by the door. "Don't worry, Raffe. Just because you prayed to me doesn't really make me a god."

"What *does* make one a god?" Kayu mused, like it was an intellectual exercise.

Lyra tapped a thoughtful finger against her collarbone. "You have to believe you're one, first," she said finally. "At least, that's what I think. Magic and prayers aren't enough if you don't decide your own divinity."

"When this is over," Raffe murmured, "I'm never discussing religion ever again."

Fife snorted. "I'd also prefer to avoid it."

"Sorry, dear," Lyra said, ruffling his reddish hair.

The gate swung open, revealing a pleasantly surprised Lear. "Wolves! And Fife! And the Plaguebreaker! And..." His eyes tracked from familiar faces to unfamiliar ones. "...friends?"

"We *do* have those, shockingly enough." Eammon stepped forward, he and Lear grasping elbows and clapping backs. "This is Raffe and Kayu." He didn't offer titles.

"Welcome." Lear dipped his head, satisfied with the bare-bones introduction. If the Wolves trusted someone, the Edge did, too. And though Red still wasn't sure how far that trust went in Kayu's case, it was clear they'd have to deal with it in order to find Neve. "Valdrek is in the tavern, since I assume that's who you're looking for."

"Imagine that." Red grinned. "How's Loreth? Congratulations, by the way. Marriage looks good on you."

The other man smiled back, running a hand over his hair. The thin line of a tattooed ring snaked around his finger. "Thank you kindly, Lady Wolf. She's wonderful."

"Has she come around to the idea of leaving?" Fife asked quietly.

Lear sighed. He wanted to go beyond the Wilderwood, to reenter the world after centuries of his ancestors being locked away from it. Loreth wanted to stay.

"She still isn't decided," Lear answered. "But we have time, it appears." His face twisted, realizing what he'd said. "Not that it's a *good* thing, what with your sister...I mean..."

"It's fine, Lear." Red kept up her smile, but the edges of it dimmed.

She didn't bear ill will, but it still took the shine out of the conversation. Lear waved the rest of them in without another word, inclining his head as he pulled the gate shut behind them. Eammon gripped Red's hand, ran his thumb over her knuckles.

"A tavern, he said?" Kayu perked up. "I could go for a drink."

"As long as you don't mind it watered," Lyra muttered.

They wound through the main thoroughfare of the Edge, nodding at passersby. Behind them, Fife and Lyra fielded questions from Raffe and Kayu, similar ones to what Red remembered asking when Eammon first brought her—what this city was, why there were so many people here, why they were dressed so out of fashion. Kayu seemed to take the answers in stride, but Raffe was slightly shocked, and when Red glanced back at him, his eyes were wide as saucers.

It was impossible to know all the corners of the world. There was always some wrinkle left unironed, something tripping you up in your understanding of how things went and your place in them. That was something she'd been learning ever since her twentieth birthday, and she still went back and forth on whether it was terrible or comforting.

They reached the tavern, made their way through the dancers to the back of the room, where Valdrek was predictably playing cards for outdated modes of currency. The man across the table from him looked slightly familiar, but the way he held his cards obscured most of his face. Red didn't have time to try to place him before Valdrek noticed them.

"Welcome to the Wolves!" Valdrek raised his tankard—clearly not his first. "And their entourage. Lyra, darling, it's been too long. You've somehow grown even more beautiful. I'll have to write you a song."

Lyra cocked a brow. "You say that to all the girls."

"Only my favorites." He turned to Eammon, clapping him on the shoulder. "What can I do you for, Eammon? Did any of those books help you at all?"

"Unfortunately not." Even in the din of a rowdy bar, Eammon's quiet, leaf-laced voice cut through the noise without him raising it. "But I do have a question I think you can help with."

He explained it in quick, broad strokes—the key, the sentinel shards in the Shrine, Red's odd dream and how Raffe's mirrored it.

"So the question," he said, "is if there's any mention of something called the Heart Tree on the wall. Or anything that looks like a grove of keys? I remember seeing something similar, somewhere."

To Valdrek's credit, he kept his face mostly nonchalant, other than the steady widening of his eyes. "Quite a tale," he murmured, draining the last of his beer. His tankard made a hollow noise when he put it back on the table, and he kept his eyes on it as he spoke, as if he could read it as easily as the wall. "The carvings are enigmatic," he said finally. "Up for interpretation. My father taught me how to read them, after his father taught him. But it's not a recorded language, only passed down orally, by knowledge of our history. Not exactly foolproof."

"No." Raffe's voice was hard and with no trace of nervousness, despite the fact that he'd only just learned this place existed. "Trusting history is never *foolproof.*"

Valdrek only inclined his head, an acquiescence. "There are pieces of the wall that we never quite knew the meaning of, and were told not to try," he said. "Our ancestors…they were desperate, there at the beginning. The Kings had only just disappeared when they arrived, the

Wilderwood closing to trap them here. Some of them tried unsavory things to attempt an escape."

"Like bargaining?" Red asked.

"Not quite that simple." A sigh as Valdrek sank a hip onto the table and crossed his arms, settling in for a tale. "They were wayfaring people. Always on the sea. And they worshipped the god of it, worshipped it in the way the Old Ones liked to be worshipped, with blood and with suffering."

"The Leviathan." Eammon nearly spit the title.

The other man nodded, silver rings glinting in his beard. "They bled into the sea to secure safe passage. And once they were here, bound to the shores by all that infernal fog that kept them from navigating back to the world, those offerings became more…involved. Full sacrifices. Bodies bled into the ocean and sunk with stones."

Red shifted uncomfortably on her feet. She'd known the worship of the monstrous old gods was violent, back before the Kings banished them, but the books she'd read on them in the Valleydan library kept it vague.

Fife sat down in the chair Valdrek had vacated and wearily signaled the barmaid for a drink. Kayu did the same, holding up two fingers when the maid looked her way. The somehow familiar man at the table had laid down his cards, but kept staring at them, fair hair falling forward to obscure his eyes. Red only glanced at him, too taken with Valdrek's story to try to puzzle out where she'd seen him before.

"The worship didn't give them a way out," Valdrek continued. "Not once the Leviathan was locked away with the rest, the lines of communication blurred and broken by the Shadowlands. But it did give them odd knowledge. Pieces of things that came in dreams, seemingly unconnected. They recorded them, anyway, carved them into the wall alongside everything else."

Red thought of those spiked, runic carvings alongside the fluid lines on the wall. Violent marks that didn't seem to fit.

"But the shorthand language they used to carve those things died out with the worship. And good riddance, too. It apparently drove those who knew it mad." Valdrek fingered one of the rings in his beard, thoughtful. "It was only the first generation who knew how to decode it. The rest of us have left it alone."

The barmaid came with drinks. Kayu passed one of hers to Raffe. Fife shared his with Lyra when she held out a hand.

Red could've used one herself, but it felt like whatever they were headed for would require her mind to be at full capacity.

Valdrek took a long drink, leaving foam in his beard when he lifted the tankard away. "So yes, Wolf, I know the carving you refer to. But no, I don't know what it means."

"I do."

The man across the table finally looked up from his cards. His expression wavered somewhere between clarity and confusion, like he hadn't meant to speak up. Pale hair fell across a white brow, eyes dark.

It took her a moment, but Red finally remembered where she'd seen him before. "Bormain."

Chapter Seventeen

Red

The last time Red had seen Bormain, he'd been raving with shadow-sickness and halfway rotted, chained up beneath Asheyla's shop across the square. Even after she and Eammon had healed him, he'd been pale and waxen, still looking half a corpse.

He'd recovered since then, and well. Now Bormain looked like a healthy young man, none the worse for wear after his brush with something far more awful than death.

"That's me." He nodded, almost sheepish. "Um, thank you. By the way. And I'm..." A swallow down a tight throat; he looked pained. "I'm sorry for anything I said while I was sick. I know I—I said some unkind things, according to others, and I didn't—"

"Don't worry about it." The poor man looked so ashamed, and Red knew what it was like to try stringing that into words. She gave him a slight, reassuring smile. "No need for apologies."

Eammon didn't seem as surprised by Bormain's transformation as Red was. Apparently, he'd known the man well enough before being shadow-sickened to recognize him now. The Wolf leaned forward, all business. "So you know what the carving means?"

Bormain shrugged, like Eammon's attention made him slightly nervous. "I think so," he said, picking at the edges of his playing cards. "Ever since I was shadow-sick, I've been able to read some of the... the stranger carvings, for lack of a better term. So if your key-grove is one of those, it stands to reason I should be able to read it, too."

Valdrek still sat with one hip propped up on the table, but every line of his body had gone stiff. He looked at Bormain with an odd mix of grief and wariness. "You didn't tell me that, boy."

Another stilted shrug from Bormain. "I've been enough of a burden," he murmured. "And it's nothing, really. They give me a headache sometimes, but I can mostly ignore them."

Silence. Eammon's eyes flickered to Red's, both of them making the tandem decision to stay out of this moment.

A decision Kayu did not take part in. "Makes sense. In my experience, hiding your weaknesses is the only way to survive. Someone will take advantage of them, if you don't." She drained her tankard, then signaled for another. Her cheeks were flushed, her eyes overbright—the alcohol already at work. "Kings and shadows, it's been ages since I had a good beer."

A frisson of unease raced over the back of Red's neck. The statement felt like one more piece in Kayu's puzzle, but she still didn't have enough to fit them into a cogent picture.

The next beer came. Kayu drained it. Across the table, Fife's eyebrows climbed toward his hairline.

Raffe leaned closer to Bormain, ignoring Kayu's drinking habits. "What kinds of things have you read in the other carvings?"

A reasonable enough question—if the runic marks were to record messages from the Old Ones in the Shadowlands, there could be helpful information there, no matter how obscure they might be—but Bormain paled. He glanced down at his cards again, as if they were easier to look at than Raffe's face.

"Nothing worth repeating," he said finally. Something that tried to be a rueful grin twitched at his mouth, but it looked more like a spasm. "It isn't anything helpful. At least, not that I can tell. But I spend most of the time trying to block them out." He shook his head. "They aren't...they don't seem like things that our minds are meant to follow, if that makes sense. It hurts to try to comprehend them, and even when I can, they're awful."

Red thought of godlike monsters, of things far from human in an upside-down prison world, and what something like that might try to communicate to those worshipping with suffering and blood. She swallowed.

"Are you sure you want to try reading the grove carvings, then?" This from Eammon, oddly gentle, though his face was still hard lines.

Bormain nodded. "I owe you." Then, gathering up his cards, "And I've seen the carving you speak of before. It's less…less jagged than the others. Doesn't seem like it's meant only to hurt." He stood. "I remember where it is."

Eammon looked again to Red, brows drawn into a question.

In any other circumstance, Red would've been apprehensive. Bormain might look healed, but he'd been ravaged by shadow-rot only a short while ago, and something about that experience had changed him irrevocably. This might be nothing more than feverish ravings from his time spent drowning in darkness. Even if he really could read the markings from the long-dead Old One worshippers, it was no guarantee it'd be anything about the Heart Tree.

But, as she'd told Eammon, beggars couldn't be choosers. And she'd do all the begging she had to for Neve.

Lyra was the linchpin. She looked from Bormain to Red, gave a tiny nod. "I can't sense any shadow on him," she said, matter-of-fact, not trying to hide her words from Bormain. A slight smile. "And I haven't quite lost the touch for it, even without a Bargainer's Mark."

Red swept her hand toward Bormain. "Lead the way, then."

They left the city, all of them trailing conspicuously behind Bormain— Valdrek up ahead, speaking in low, friendly tones with Lyra and Fife, Kayu and Raffe in the middle, and Red and Eammon bringing up the rear. The villagers watched them curiously, but none asked what they were doing. The Edge was used to Wilderwood strangeness.

Once Lear cranked the gate open for them again, Bormain swung left, toward the rolling hills in the north instead of toward the Wilderwood. Even knowing how things had changed, knowing that the forest's roots wouldn't hold them back, Red's hand still tightened on Eammon's as they turned behind the wall.

He relaxed into her touch, as if the tensing of her hand reminded him that things were different now. Eammon looked down at her. "Feel anything?"

Red shook her head. The forest woven through her didn't stir beyond a fluttering leaf, a blooming flower. "Seems like we really can go anywhere."

Thoughtfulness darkened Eammon's eyes. The same thing in both their heads—here was concrete proof they could leave the forest without any ill effect. They could travel to the Rylt.

Nerves knotted in Red's stomach.

She changed the subject, giving her husband a quizzical lift of her brow. "So how exactly did you see this marking before, if it's all the way on the northern side of the wall?"

"Back before it got so bad, I used to test the limits of the Wilderwood. See how far it would let me go." A stilted shrug, and Red wondered if she shouldn't have asked, after all. It was still hard for him to talk about all that time he was the Wolf alone. "Sometime between Kaldenore and Sayetha, I made myself walk all the way around the Edge. Just to prove I could. It took a day and a half, and I didn't stop to sleep, barely ate or drank anything." He snorted. "I think I passed out when I was done. At any rate, I regained consciousness in the tavern, with Valdrek pouring ale down my throat. Damn near drowned me."

In a quick, impulsive motion, Red tugged his arm, made him stoop down so she could press a fierce kiss to his mouth. Eammon returned it, a curious grin curling beneath her lips.

"What was that for?"

"Because I wanted to."

"Fair enough."

Ahead of them, Bormain had stopped, facing the wall with a strange, blank expression on his face. Kayu stood with her nose nearly pressed against the wood, Raffe close behind. But Lyra was at least two paces away, nostrils flared and hand gripping the hilt of her *tor* so tightly her knuckles blanched. Fife stood in front of her defensively, fists clenched and jaw set, expression as if they faced an oncoming army.

As they drew nearer, Red felt why. The air around this section of the wall felt strange, charged like the air before a thunderstorm. A familiar scent knifed at her nose—cold, ozone, emptiness.

Pain speared through her as she took another step forward, a shallow reflection of the pain she'd felt the night Solmir and Kiri raised the shadow grove. The Wilderwood shuddered around her spine, making her steps falter.

"Shadow-touched," Lyra hissed. "Doesn't look it, but it's as shadow-touched as any breach ever was."

"Kings on shitting horses," Eammon cursed through his teeth, one hand pressed against his middle. The other shot toward Red, clenching around her shoulder in case he might have to hold her up.

"Did it feel like this before?" Red asked, turning to her Wolf. "When you passed the carving, that time you walked around the whole Edge?"

He shook his head, dark hair brushing over his clenched jaw. "Something's changed."

Oblivious to the tableau playing out behind her, Kayu glanced over her shoulder. "Are you going to come look at this or what?"

A moment's hesitation, then Red swallowed, stepped forward. The Wilderwood within her rustled in discomfort, but it was bearable.

And there was something almost leading in that bright spark of consciousness that lived beside her own. Like the forest needed her to get closer to the carving, needed her to understand something. Like this was a necessary step.

Clearing his throat, Eammon followed her toward the wall. From the corner of her eye, Red saw him shake his head at Fife and Lyra—no need for them to come any closer than they had to.

When Eammon turned away, Lyra grabbed Fife's hand and pulled him backward, running worried fingers over his brow. Lyra still felt the vestiges of her long connection to the forest, but she was free of it, carried none of it within her. Fife still had it buried in him, in ways none of them quite understood. His face was pale, mouth pressed flat, a sheen of sweat on his forehead.

The piece of wall Bormain stared at hosted more than one carving. Upon closer inspection, they reminded Red of the constellations painted in the tower—she could make out the rough form of what she thought was the Sisters, another smaller carving that might've been the Far-Flung Queen near them. But it was the carving beneath them that she knew, instinctively, was the one they were looking for.

It was simple. A group of lines carved at a curve so they looked like rays from a sun, forming a circle. Each ray of the strange sun had a few smaller markings coming off it, primitive representations that could be key teeth. The line in the middle went all the way through the circle, extending farther than the others on either side. The ends of that line were clearly meant to be keys, carved in exacting detail, one pointing up, the other down.

Slowly, working against the low hum of pain vibrating through her body, Red pulled her key from her pocket, held it up to the wall. It perfectly matched the longer line at the top of the carving, right down to every curve of the teeth.

"I still don't understand what it's supposed to mean," she murmured. Her fingers tightened; she loosened them through conscious thought, afraid she might snap the key in half. "I still don't understand how this is supposed to bring us to Neve."

"She must come to you."

Bormain's voice sounded strange. Low, inflectionless. Red looked over her shoulder.

His face was blank, perfectly neutral. But for his open eyes fixed on the carving, he could've been asleep. "She has to find the door on her own. It's only once she goes through and makes her choice that her key will come to her. Then the way is open."

Raffe's hand closed around his dagger, clearly unsettled by the change in Bormain's demeanor. Eammon glanced at the other man, gave a slight shake of his head. Raffe didn't let the dagger go, but neither did he draw it, instead stepping back and pulling Kayu with him, putting distance between them and Bormain. Valdrek wavered in the space left, like he was caught between wanting to go closer to his son-in-law and wanting to escape him.

"Two keys," Bormain repeated. "Two halves of a whole, matched in power. A match in love is enough to open it, but not enough to make an end. Just because a door is open does not mean its threshold will be crossed, when there is shadow waiting."

Red stood statue-still, scarcely daring to breathe, afraid any sudden movement might break the spell that gave them these answers, cryptic as they were. She recognized this, remembered it from the day she and Eammon had healed Bormain. Channeling messages from the Shadowlands, language from the magic that had roosted in him when he fell through the breach. But his voice didn't sound malicious this time. It sounded almost weary.

"The door is you." Bormain swayed slightly on his feet, eyes fixed to the carving. "You are the door."

A beat of vast silence, all of them staring at this shadow-touched man and the shadow-touched carving.

The rumble under the ground was subtle. Welling up from the dirt like a buried heartbeat, reverberating in Red's heels, up through her legs, rattling her bones and the forest held within them.

A tiny earthquake, there and then gone. Barely enough to mark. But to Red it seemed significant. Like something cataclysmic happening somewhere else, though she felt only the echo.

Whatever had seized Bormain let him go as abruptly as it'd come, his eyes clearing, his face rearranging itself into that sheepish half smile. He ran a hand through his pale hair. "Sorry, got lost in the clouds for a minute there." His mouth slowly fell from half smile to confused line, brow furrowing as he took in their stares. "Did something happen?"

"You could say that," Fife murmured.

Kayu, true to form, recovered from the strangeness more quickly than the rest of them. She gestured to the carving and the two flanking it. "These other markings...are they astrological? They look like constellations."

"They are." Valdrek spoke with forced good nature, trying to dispel the tightly coiled tension in the air. He tapped a finger on the carving that looked like the Sisters, oblivious to the shadow-touched wood that repelled Red, Eammon, and Fife. "This one is the Sisters. And that one, on the other side, is the Far-Flung Queen."

"In Nioh, we call the first one the Sun-Handed and the Moon-Handed," Kayu said. "And the other one the Blood-Handed. The story is that two rival queens harnessed the power of the sun and the moon, but the two powers were so balanced, they canceled each other out, and neither one of them could conquer the other. The Blood-Handed was another queen of a smaller territory, and she took over the other two queens' countries without a fight after they both disappeared." Her lip curled as she lifted a delicate shoulder in a shrug. "I assume the title was meant to be ironic."

"Our ancestors had a similar story, but different names, though the direct translations don't necessarily trip off the tongue or make much sense." Valdrek moved his pointing finger to the carving on the right, the one Red had always known as the Far-Flung Queen. "This one is the Third Daughter," Valdrek said. The ring-scabbed finger moved to the Sisters. "And they called these two the Golden-Veined and the Shadow Queen."

Chapter Eighteen

Neve

Darkness was a thing she'd grown used to in recent months. Neve seemed to spend most of her time in it—in the gloom of the Shrine, bleeding on branches in an attempt to bring her sister home. Pacing in her room, unable to quiet her mind enough for sleep. And now, in the Shadowlands, not dark like she was used to but their own kind of flat, blank emptiness, all shades of gray.

She wasn't used to darkness feeling restful.

There was pain. Sharp in her knee, a dull ache everywhere else. With a distant sort of clarity, Neve knew she teetered on the edge of consciousness, and the circumstances that had brought her there filled themselves in slowly.

The Oracle, an awful god in an awful bone-filled cave. Solmir, slicing its throat, taking its power. The mountain collapsing, all those fused-together bones finally breaking apart without the god to hold them together.

The way the Oracle had cut right through to the careful knot Neve had made of her emotions and unraveled it in an instant. Unspooled her soul like so much ragged thread.

A soft moan escaped her mouth, not just from physical pain. It was enough to jerk her from that wavering precipice of unconsciousness, ground her fully in her bruised body. Neve curled around her middle, eyes squeezed tightly shut.

"Neve?"

Solmir. He didn't touch her, but she felt the way his hand hovered just above her shoulder, a slight disturbance in the cold, empty air. "Are you hurt?"

A ludicrous question, one she could've laughed at if her throat didn't feel scraped raw. She shook her head. Solmir wasn't asking about her feelings. He just wanted to know if she could move, if she could continue their journey to the Heart Tree. That's what he needed her for— her emotional state was secondary, if considered at all.

But when she opened her eyes, saw the way his shone with worry, she wondered if maybe that wasn't true.

Concern honed his already knife-sharp features even finer, made his mouth pull flat, his high forehead wrinkle. His long hair was streaked with blood; it fell over his shoulder, the ends brushing her cheek.

"Neve," he said again, and this time the tone was different. As if he knew she was lying when she indicated she wasn't hurt. As if he wanted her to talk to him.

And he was the only thing to talk to in this whole cold, dead world.

Gingerly, Neve sat up, wincing as she did. Rubble lay strewn around them, pieces of broken bone. She turned to look at what they'd escaped.

The mountain had flattened, but not all the way to the cracked ground. Some of the bones remained fused together, making a nearly smooth wall of ivory that still towered above her head. Rattling still echoed in the air, as if the mountain was caught in a slow-motion collapse, dismantling made graceful by lack of speed. She thought of the Oracle's cave, how the dais had fallen through the floor and pulled the other bones into the hole it made, and shuddered.

"We can rest a moment, but we shouldn't stay long," Solmir said. He nodded toward the bones. "The mountain isn't stable."

"Did it hurt you?" Neve remembered the fall, in bits and pieces. Wind on her face and the groan of destruction, his arms holding her tight enough to bruise. He'd kept the worst of it from her, kept her as safe as he could, knowing they couldn't die but wanting to save her from pain.

Because he needs you. She said it fiercely to herself, forming the words into daggers so she wouldn't forget them. *Only because he needs you.*

He shrugged in answer, though the proof was all over him—abrasions on his arms, a bloody slash at the corner of his lip. It was strange to see someone bleed here, where there was no crimson to mark the cut. Just charcoal-colored liquid that could be almost anything. "My wounds are superficial, and not the kind that need to be talked about."

A lead-in if there ever was one. He'd watched her crumple as the Oracle extracted its truth. He knew it left a wound.

"I understand that I'm not someone you would choose to speak to about such things," Solmir said, sitting next to her on the ground with his knees pulled up, arms resting atop them. "But I'm here. And I'm willing to listen."

She kept her arms protectively curled around her middle, as if all these shards of guilt and shame and anger were physical things she had to stop from pushing out through her skin, thorns of a different kind. They all swirled in her head now, unfettered by the ways she'd lashed them down, always saying she'd deal with them later later later. Later was now, and the way the Oracle had delved into her head made all of those buried feelings impossible to catch, like trying to cup a river in her hands, like lying at the bottom of a grave and trying to swallow all the dirt.

A slight rumble tremored through the ground, rattling the bones.

"I wish I hated you more," Neve said softly.

No reaction from Solmir, though he started twisting that ring on his finger again.

"I wish I hated you more," Neve continued, "because then I could talk myself into blaming you completely. For everything." She shifted on the ground, tugging his coat tight around her. "I can blame you for most of it. You may not have held the knife that killed Arick, but you were the reason he died. You would've killed Red and Eammon if you had to."

He didn't deny it. Didn't do anything but twist that ring around and around and around.

"But none of it would've happened if I let her go," Neve said. "If I had done what she asked. If I'd told Arick to stay, if I hadn't listened to Kiri, if I'd cared more when my mother died instead of seeing it as means to an end. If I'd just listened to Raffe." She didn't realize she'd started crying until she tasted salt—Neve wasn't one for crying, and the sensation was strange. She swiped roughly at her cheek. "If I hated you more, I might be able to convince myself it was all your fault anyway, find some loop in logic that allowed me to think it even if I knew, deep down, it wasn't true. But I don't. So I can't."

Silence from Solmir. Neve didn't look at him, staring out instead over the gray horizon. The desert seemed to end, somewhere out there, becoming a gray gleam that reflected the light instead of dry ground that ate it.

"Would you like me to give you more reasons to hate me?" Solmir asked.

He could do it, she knew. He had eons' worth of material.

But it wouldn't change anything.

Neve shook her head.

Solmir's mouth twisted wryly, though the look in his eyes was far from amused. "Give it time." He reached into his boot and pulled out something gleaming. The god-bone. He held it out but didn't look at her.

Neve took it. Slipped it into the pocket of her coat.

Another rumble. They both marked it—tightening shoulders, stiffened backs—but they didn't mention it, and neither of them made a motion to move.

"What about you?" Neve turned to look at him, tearing her eyes away from all that gray emptiness stretched out before them. "The Oracle got in your head. Something about the past. About Gaya."

She tried to keep the extent of her curiosity out of her tone.

Something in his face shuttered, closed off. He stopped twisting the ring around his thumb and instead sat perfectly still and perfectly silent.

A heartbeat. Two. Neve flushed, looked away. "If you don't—"

"Do you want to know the real story of me and the Second Daughter and the Wolf?" His voice was clipped, devoid of feeling. "Of how I found the Heart Tree the first time?"

"Yes," she said softly. "Tell me the true story."

He didn't move. But a breath shuddered out of him, long and slightly shaky. "When the other Kings and I had been here for centuries," he said, still in that expressionless tone, "we approached the Oracle to see if there was a way for us to get out, since we all still had souls back then. A way that wasn't open to the Old Ones. It said there was." A sharp sound, not a laugh. "A door that could be opened by matched love."

Neve pulled her knees toward her chest, a sudden chill raising goose-flesh on her arms.

"I was the only one of us who had any chance at that, slim though it was," Solmir spat. "The Oracle told me that if I walked along the edge of the mountains, I would find the Tree, hidden in a place I knew well. It said that by the time I got there, the one I loved would be reaching for me." He swallowed, like he was trying to drown the small measure of emotion that wanted to creep into his voice. "I was elated. The thought that Gaya would try to save me, that she might believe I'd been forced to come with the others when they came to tear the magic back out of the Wilderwood—it kept me from asking what kind of strings might be attached."

"What happened?" Neve breathed.

He shrugged, sharp and jerky. "I walked. I walked along the edge of the mountains, down where it meets the marshes. I walked for what felt like weeks, and then I arrived at the place I knew well." A derisive snort. "A castle. Upside down. It looked almost exactly like Valchior's on the surface, where Gaya and I had met. Something about all the magic he did there made a reflection of it form in the Shadowlands."

The idea of something known so well being inverted like that unsettled her. Neve pulled her knees in tighter.

"And the Oracle was right," he continued. "The Tree was there. Churning roots, shadows. And a hand, reaching through. Hers." His fingers twitched, as if even now they wanted to reach for that phantom, remembered hand. "I got there just in time to watch it spasm as she died. The Wilderwood she'd knotted herself into, for Ciaran, slaughtering her to save itself. The door closed before I could try to get through." He rubbed at the scars on his brow. "After that, I broke with the other Kings. Stopped pulling magic from the Shadowlands, mostly stopped using it at all. Went to the edges, where the tower is, the forest. Watched this underworld grow unstable and start to dissolve as Valchior and the others sank further and further into it, their souls miring in magic until they couldn't be extracted. I stayed at the end of the world, and I waited."

"Waited for Arick," Neve said. "Waited for someone to be foolish enough to try bargaining with a shadow-infected tree."

"I didn't really know what I was waiting for. I just took what I could get." Finally, his eyes turned to hers, vivid against the gray sky. "You know something about that."

Neve sank her teeth into her lip.

Solmir stood in one fluid motion, wincing. Another shake moved through the ground, clattering bones. "We need to go."

"What makes you think I can open the Tree?" Neve asked, still sitting. She looked up at him, worry in her furrowed brow. "What if Red isn't reaching at the same time?"

"We'll figure it out when we get there. There might be a way to communicate with her through it."

"And what if the same thing happens?" Now that her worries had been given a voice, they wouldn't leave her alone. "The same thing that happened to Gaya? What if Red—"

"It won't," he cut in quickly, keeping her from finishing the awful thought. She shouldn't be grateful for it.

"How do you know?"

"Because your love is matched." He grasped her elbow and pulled her up to stand. "Mine and Gaya's wasn't."

He kept talking about the love between her and Red as some foregone conclusion, a fixed and unchanging thing. But Neve thought of the betrayed look in her sister's eyes as the sentinels in the Shrine collapsed, the distance they'd held between them. What if she'd wrecked it? What if she'd become something unworthy of her sister's love, and Red had cut it loose?

She wouldn't blame her if she had. Neve's sins stacked up too high to climb over.

"How can you be sure?" she whispered.

The look on his face made it seem like Solmir could read her anxieties in her eyes. The line of his jaw softened beneath his beard, the furrow in his brow smoothed. His hand half raised to her, sparking with silver, then dropped by his side as he turned away and started to walk. "The two of you have overturned worlds for each other, Neverah. It's hard to get more matched than that."

———

They walked until they ran into another pile of bones.

A few heaps of rubble from the mountain's collapse had blocked their way already, but they were easy enough to climb or skirt around. This one, however, was not. Upon a closer look, it seemed like one massive bone rather than a pile of them, smooth and strangely jointed, stretching from the larger mound of shards that had made the mountain out toward the shining line of the horizon.

Solmir approached the bone and rubbed his hand over it, trying to find a foothold. Then he stepped back, crossing his arms. "Well," he said conversationally, "shit."

Neve had to squint to peer up to the top of the bone. "Can we go around?"

"Not without ending up in the marshes."

"Is that bad?"

"The marshes were the Rat's territory," Solmir said. "And the Roach. Their children are hard to kill."

So they were probably still around. Neve grimaced.

With a kick at the bone, like it had personally offended him, Solmir pivoted, stalking down its length. "But it looks like we don't have much choice. Stick close."

Chapter Nineteen

Neve

Maybe an hour of walking later—still next to the massive bone—the landscape finally started to change.

First, there were trees. Nothing like the white, inverted trunks at the edge of the Shadowlands, but small and needlelike, spearing upward and laced with thin leaves that looked more like thorns. Then the ground changed, going from cracked and dry to almost muddy, pocked with pools of shining black water.

It was just as desolate as the desert had been, with no places for anything to hide. Still, disquiet prickled over the back of Neve's neck.

"The Rat and the Roach," she muttered to herself, picking her boot up from the marshy ground. It took effort; the dark mud sucked at her soles. "Of course there would be a giant rat and a giant roach."

"It *is* the underworld," Solmir said quietly from up ahead. "And technically, it's only their lesser-beast children who are left." He turned her way, face stern. "But keep your voice down. We don't want anything to know we're here."

Sound advice. Neve pressed her lips shut.

"And from here on out, watch where you put your feet." He twisted on his heel and placed his boot very deliberately, a test before he stepped with his whole weight. "The ground here gives way easily, and the Rat's children like tunnels."

"Ew."

"Precisely."

The jagged end of the massive bone was finally in sight, thrust out into the air above their heads. The sight of it drew a relieved sag into Solmir's shoulders. "Once we get to the end, we turn around," he murmured. "We'll be safer near the mountains."

Neve breathed a faint, thankful sigh.

But then she heard a high clicking sound coming from somewhere behind them. Almost like huge chitinous legs moving closer.

She paused, boot in the air, head whirling to look behind her. "Did you hear that?"

"Keep moving," Solmir said, answer enough.

Neve turned back around, finally putting down her foot without checking to make sure it was going where Solmir's had. And that was enough to push her off-balance, into the muddy edge of a pool of black water.

At first, she thought it an easy misstep, simple to fix. But the mud at the edge of the pool sucked her down like a swallowing throat, devouring her to the knee before she could cry out, already to her waist by the time she did and Solmir came running.

Cursing, he grabbed her hands, tried to pull her backward out of the mud—at her shoulders now and still going, her hands slick with it, hard to grasp on to. Neve didn't have the energy to scream again, everything in her concentrated on finding a handhold and pulling herself out of the bog before it reached her mouth.

But then, down by her feet—air.

She froze, wild eyes going to Solmir's. "There's something down here. A cavern or something." Kings, she could *taste* the mud; she had to tilt her head up to talk, the lower half of her body breaking through to whatever was below the pool.

"Tunnels," Solmir said, swiping his hair back from his forehead and leaving a streak of dirt. He looked away, calculation in his eyes. "When you fall through, be quiet. I'll come for you."

"Are they still in the tunnels?" Panic made her voice high and jagged. That clicking sound reverberated across the marsh again, faster this time. "Solmir, if they're in the tunnels, what do I—"

The mud closed over her face before she could finish.

⚬⚬⚬⚬⚬⚬⚬⚬⚬⚬⚬⚬

It felt like being buried alive. Mud seeped into every available orifice—her mouth, her eyes—damp and bitter and incongruous with the way she could freely kick her legs, having already slipped through the bog barrier into whatever lay beneath it.

When the bog finally let her go, with a disgusting squelching sound, the drop was short. Neve fell to the ground, knocking the wind from her earth-laden lungs, pulling in deep, gasping breaths of sour air. Mud caked her hair, her face; she clawed it away from her eyes, willing them to adjust to the dim.

A cave. A cave with rooty walls and a damp floor, smelling of earth and something almost fecal, animalic. Above, the bog, held in suspension by the strange physics of the Shadowlands, the leftover magic of the Rat and the Roach.

The reminder of the two gods who'd lived in this territory and their children who still did made her pulse thunder. Neve stood, trying desperately to quiet her breathing.

And when she managed to hold air in her lungs instead of heaving it, she heard something else breathing.

Slowly, Neve turned, barely able to make out shapes in the dark. Furry bodies piled in the corner, a heaving mass of flesh that inhaled and exhaled in tandem. She saw tails and tusks, the pieces of creatures all jammed together. They looked attached, tangled rats that had become one being instead of many. Ridges of dried mud marked bristling fur, fusing the already huge beasts into something of monstrous proportions.

Neve pressed her mud-caked hand to her mouth. She quickly glanced at the rest of the cave, looking for roaches, afraid that if she saw them, there'd be no holding back the scream in her throat. But it seemed the only thing living in this cave was that awful jumble of rats.

Something above, pressing through the mud. She crouched, hands over her head, but when her eyes opened it was to a tall, spare figure with muddied hair, not some looming rat god.

"Well," Solmir whispered, "this is disgusting, isn't it?"

A grumble from the rat tangle in the corner, movement that made both of them crouch, Solmir pushing Neve behind him. When the creatures settled, she whispered, "So how do we get out?"

He jerked his head to the side—there, hardly visible, a tunnel. "Cave entrance." Barely any sound at all, mostly mouthed, and only seen because she stood so close. "They open up to the cliffs above the sea. We can still get to the Heart Tree that way, though it's a bit of a walk."

"I think we're past worrying about *a bit of a walk.*"

"Agreed."

Neve's eyes darted toward the beasts in the corner again. "Are there more? Or...the other kind?"

"I'm sure there are. So keep your mouth shut." With that less-than-reassuring pronouncement, Solmir grabbed her hand and led her into the tunnel.

They walked beneath the marshlands with just as much carefulness as they'd walked above. Solmir's hand was slick with mud in hers, but as they moved, the mud dried, solidified, fusing their palms together like the rats back in the cave. Neve didn't think of it. She tried not to think of anything but getting out of here, hopefully without running into any more lesser beasts.

After what felt like hours in the dark, small shards of light speared the gloom up ahead—exits, somewhere close. It illuminated just how much mud they were caked in, both of them covered head to toe.

"Almost there," Solmir murmured. "A mile, maybe, and—"

A rustle behind them. The sound of many feet all moving in the same direction, an attempt at sneaking that would've worked if she hadn't been so attuned to the silence.

One heartbeat, two, both of them frozen. Then a skittering sound and the gnash of teeth, a *thud* that made the tunnel shake and dirt rain from the ceiling.

Solmir didn't look back to see exactly what they'd awoken, what pursued them through the earth. He just pulled on the hand Neve held, sending her careening in front of him, slipping on mud. She stumbled; their hands were still stuck together.

Solmir grabbed her wrist and held it steady, then wrenched his sideways—she saw him grimace, saw the half second when his arm bent at a painful angle. Not enough to break or sprain, but enough to hurt.

But then she was free, and he was pushing her in front of him. "Go!"

They didn't try at stealth, not anymore. Their boots slid in the close earth of the tunnel, as behind them, something followed, something with too many mouths and too many eyes and too many teeth, something making a terrible trilling squeak that sounded like an abattoir of rats being crushed together and fused by that sucking, suffocating mud.

Neve pulled the bone from her pocket as she ran, brandishing it like a dagger. A god-bone was only required to kill an Old One, not a lesser beast, but it was the only weapon they had and it felt good in her hand. Stabbing was stabbing—it'd worked on the Seamstress's goat. She'd take what she could get.

The tunnel shook again, the high, screeching sounds running together into something that made her want to press her hands over her ears. She didn't have the courage to look back, instead keeping her gaze straight ahead, trying to listen only to the squelch of her boots in the mud and the scream of Solmir's ragged breath behind her.

Light, streaming in ahead of them, dim but seeming beacon-bright in the darkness of the underground. Neve put on a burst of speed, felt Solmir's hand at her back shoving her forward, and almost ran into the wall.

"Shit," Solmir swore.

Neither of their eyes had been adjusted enough to see it before it was right in front of them—the gray light that signaled open air was coming through cracks in a piled-rock wall, too small for either of them to fit through. A sob built in Neve's throat, drowned out by the awful noise of the rat-creature behind them.

Solmir grabbed the bone from her, spun on his heel with it held like a sword. "Pull the rocks down. I have your back."

"But if it collapses—"

"Would you rather die in a rockslide or be eaten by a giant rat-thing?"

No contest. Neve scrabbled at the rocks, pulling them down as fast as she could grip them, tearing her nails as the opening slowly widened.

The tunnel shook as their pursuer came into the light.

Rats. She couldn't tell how many in the one horrified glance she tossed over her shoulder, but there were at least ten mouths, ten sets of milky blind eyes, ten snouts streaked in dirt and shit and dried gore. Their bodies had fused through mud in their fur, and their knotted tails held them all together as well as any graft of bone might.

The lesser beast shrieked, rearing up on too many legs, more sticking out from its sides like spines. A misshapen thing, unable to live anywhere but here, charging forward when all they had to defend against it was a sharpened length of bone.

And magic.

Next to her, Solmir lifted his hands. Black flickered in the blue of his eyes as darkness edged down his veins, creeping out from his center, as if he packed all that magic somewhere behind his heart. Thorns pushed from the ends of his fingers, slow at first, then gaining speed, a rope of brambles like the net he'd cast over that worm-thing what felt like ages ago, when Neve was newly woken in a world made of shadows.

"You might want to move." His voice didn't sound like his own anymore. It was low, graveled, too deep to come out of his mostly human-shaped throat.

Neve obeyed.

He spun again, one hand held toward the rat-creature, the other pointed at the wall. A net of thorns fell over the rats, their myriad voices shrieking in harmony with the crash of stone as another thorny blast of power broke through the piled rocks. Neve crouched, covered her head as stones rained down around them, as light speared through the dark. The knotted rats' shrieking intensified, like the light hurt their eyes.

Neve ran forward, squinting; Solmir followed. There wasn't far to go—the cave opened out onto a gray cliff over a rocky beach. Beyond it, a stretch of flat, black water, as far as she could see.

Behind them, the rat-thing screamed, high and shivering and awful, ducking its many heads back into the shadows as the light seared across it. The thorns of Solmir's magic slowly sank into the lesser beast's mud-mottled flesh, making it twitch and shrink. Plumes of rogue power rolled off the bristling legs, the matted fur.

Grimacing, Solmir raised his hand again.

The magic seeped into him as the rat-creature died, growing smaller and smaller as the thorns he'd thrown over it tightened. The gibbering of the shadows it let loose was quiet, quickly silenced when Solmir took them in. Still, he sank to his knees as the magic kept coming, the hand that wasn't gathering power from the air braced on the ground, his chest heaving. He closed his eyes; Neve couldn't see what color they were.

Besides, the slow click of chiton, the twitching of what she'd thought were stones set into the sides of the cliff, was somewhat more distracting.

The last of the magic drained into Solmir as the cliff side—not stone, but a massive wing—fluttered, sending a gust of foul-smelling breeze to stir Neve's hair. Her hand fell to Solmir's shoulder, squeezed.

She echoed his demand from earlier. "You might want to move."

A rush of wind, the smell of it enough to make her gag, and the children of the Roach launched themselves from the cliff face next to the cave.

The rat-thing had, strangely, been easier for Neve's mind to deal with. Fused together, too many legs and eyes and mouths, clearly a monster. But the children of the Roach looked, simply, like giant roaches, and something about that was far more terrifying.

"That's enough to turn your stomach," Solmir said, still in that too-deep, too-rough voice. Neve didn't realize that she'd cowered on the ground and he'd stood until he braced his legs on either side of her body, hands lifted in the air. This close, she could feel the tremor in him, the vibration of something bearing so much weight it was near to collapse.

Neve didn't watch, but she felt the impact in the atmosphere as Solmir's thorns shackled the children of the Roach, a sick, low thrumming as their wings beat against the brambles. No thuds of massive bodies hitting the ground—they dissolved in midair, broken down to nothing but shadow.

Through it, Solmir's breath came harsh, and she felt the legs pressed against her side tremble, harder and harder, so close to buckling.

When she reached out and closed her hand around his ankle—not to take magic, just to offer a reassurance, an anchoring—it felt like practicality. She still needed him, after all.

But the jolt that went through him, the look in his eyes when she raised her head, felt more like shock.

The last of the Roach's children winnowed away into nothing in the air above them with a chittering screech that made her skin crawl. Then, finally, silence.

And she still had her hand around Solmir's ankle.

Neve stood, flexing her fingers out and in as she awkwardly scrambled from beneath him. A slight rumble shuddered through the ground. The Shadowlands, slowly breaking apart, counting the time they had left.

He offered her his hand, wordlessly, veins still tracked in darkness and mud still clinging to his palm. She took it, let him pull her up. They stood there a moment, breathing hard, eyes locked.

She was the first to turn away, to look out from the cliff and over all that black water. The air wasn't foul, not like it had been in the cave or when the Roach's children flew overhead, but neither did it smell like salt. It was just empty. Nothingness. "I assume this is the Endless Sea?"

"You assume correctly." Solmir propped a boot on a rock, vainly attempting to brush dried mud from his legs. "The Kingdom of the Leviathan."

Neve glanced down at her mud-soaked nightgown, her dirt-streaked arms. "Would the Leviathan mind if I used its kingdom to wash off some of this mud before we go to the Heart Tree?"

"Probably," Solmir said. He grasped the edge of his thorn-torn shirt and tugged it over his head, grimacing. "But the Leviathan is a selfish old bastard, so bathe away."

Chapter Twenty

Neve

They climbed down the outcroppings of stone lining the cliffs to the short strip of beach, rocky sand that bit into the soles of Neve's feet once she'd worked them free of her caked-up boots. She picked her way gingerly to the tide line, though there was no tide here to speak of. No waves, either—the Endless Sea was glass-like beneath the gray sky, flat and rippleless as a pool of spilled ink.

She glanced at Solmir lingering behind her. Shirtless and mud-caked and still, somehow, able to look arrogantly regal, his posture perfect and his chin held imperiously. The impression she'd had before, of him being built like a knife, was only intensified by the lack of a shirt—broad shoulders tapered to slim hips, all of it pale and muscled without being bulky.

Her cheeks flushed; Neve turned back to the strange ocean. "I can touch it, right? It won't make me go mad or start sprouting thorns?"

"You looked good with thorns, as I recall."

The flush in her cheeks flared hotter.

"But no, touching the water won't cause any undue effects." She heard him approaching, crunching over the rocky sand. When he reached her side, he dipped a hand into the water and rubbed it over his face, attempting to scrub mud out of his short beard. "You'll remain un-monstrous."

"Maybe I should be monstrous," she muttered, the words coming out before she could reel them back in. She still felt raw inside from where the Oracle had cut through to her soul, unraveled all her truths; they lived closer to the surface now and were harder to deny. Vulnerability, here in a place where she couldn't afford to be vulnerable.

With a person she couldn't afford to be vulnerable with.

A pause. Solmir turned to her, dark brows drawn together. His irises were still blue, she noticed, but there was a thin ring of black around their edges, and the veins at his throat seemed darker than before. "What do you mean?"

She shrugged, stepping out into the shallows. The water was strangely warm, closing over her feet, her ankles, dragging at her torn nightgown's hem. "After everything I've done," she said, speaking to her wavering reflection instead of him, "it should mark me somehow, shouldn't it? Everything you did marked you."

She could've said it like it was a barb, one of the sharp jabs they'd grown used to throwing at each other. But it didn't come out that way. It was just a truth, offered with no judgment.

He rubbed at the scars on his forehead, sighed. When he spoke, he didn't look at her, staring with narrowed eyes out at the empty horizon. "I know you're not going to believe me—you didn't before—and I know me saying it doesn't mean much, anyway. But you are *good*, Neve."

Her eyes pressed closed. He was wrong. Both in the statement and in his assumption that it wouldn't mean anything coming from him.

"Everything you did was because you loved your sister." His voice was prayer-low. "You love without restraint, without settling. And that's a good thing. Never let anyone tell you otherwise."

It faded into the air, floated across the water. It hummed between her ears.

You are good.

The air hung close and expectant, chill against her skin. She could feel his eyes on her like a touch, and she turned to meet his gaze.

Solmir's arms were crossed across his bare chest, his jaw rigid beneath his beard. An expression as hard and unforgiving as any she'd seen on him before, but something in his eyes had changed—softer, less guarded. "You are far better than me," he murmured. "I know that isn't a revelation. But it's why I need you for this. Why it has to be you."

Her brow furrowed. "What do you mean?"

He swallowed. Then he shook his head, turning back toward the horizon. "Nothing new," he said, and his voice was different, back to his normal just-shy-of-arrogant tone. "You know. Prophecies, First and Second Daughters, doorways. All that shit."

"Ah, yes. Perfectly normal shit." The air felt diffuse again, the charge of the atmosphere settled. Neve was left somewhere between disappointed and relieved.

If Solmir felt the same way, he didn't show it. He dipped his hand into the water again, ostensibly to wipe at his face, but he splashed some purposefully her way as he turned back toward the beach. "Wash up. I won't look."

Her cheeks burned anyway as she tugged off his coat, pulled her nightgown over her head. She grabbed a handful of sand and used it to scrub her clothing, one piece after the other, doing her best to loosen the packed mud ground into the weave. When the gown and coat were as clean as they were going to get, she ducked her head under, floating for a moment in the completely still waters as if she were suspended in a womb.

Scrubbed hair, scrubbed face, and she emerged mostly free of dirt, wringing out and shaking off before she pulled on her nightgown and Solmir's coat again. "Your turn."

Contrary to his nature, Solmir had been a perfect gentleman, facing the cliffs until he heard her call. He glanced over his shoulder, still caked in mud. "Are you implying that you want to watch me bathe?"

"Are you attempting to make me use that bone on you?"

He took the aforementioned god-bone from his boot and lightly tapped her on the forehead with it as he passed on the way to the water. "If you were going to stab me, Neverah, you would've already."

Flippant, but something about it tugged at her chest anyway as she took the bone from him and tucked it into her pocket. He was right. The god-bone was their only weapon, and he'd trusted her to carry it. And she'd trusted him to hold all the magic they harvested from dead lesser beasts, dead gods. It was the most she could ever recall trusting another person, and it was *him*.

Neve pressed her lips together.

Solmir pulled off his boots when he reached the shallows, waded in to his waist before following suit with the tight pants he wore, scrubbing at them and then tossing them back toward the beach with his shirt. The curve of the tattoo on his bicep caught the light as he stretched, then ducked under the water. A moment later, he resurfaced, hair streaming, and he combed it back with rough fingers.

Neve hurriedly turned around to face the cliff.

"Decent," he called moments later. She turned just in time to see him tug his shirt over his head, then gather his hair into his fist, wringing it out onto the rocky sand. "I should just cut it off," he muttered, grimacing.

"Don't."

His brow raised.

"Just tie it back," Neve said, with a quick shrug that she hoped looked nonchalant. "It'd look nice."

A pause, Solmir's expression unchanging. But he ripped a tiny piece of fabric from the hem of his shirt and reached up, doing as she said.

She thought again of the bone in her pocket, a tool for killing gods. She thought of secrets and whispers in the dark and of trust, the thing he'd tried to gain from her through slow seduction on the surface, what he insisted he wasn't worthy of here.

It was true. But she found herself trusting him anyway. And whether it was desperation or stupidity or simple loneliness, she wanted it to be in full. No more half measures.

Which meant it was time to stop keeping secrets.

"I saw Valchior in the Serpent's cairn," she murmured.

Silence. Then, emotionless: "Did you?"

"He said that . . . that the Kings knew why I was here." She swallowed, eyes on the black sea instead of him. "That they *welcomed* it. What in all the shadows does that mean, Solmir?"

He stayed quiet, long enough that she finally turned to face him again, if only to try to force an answer. Solmir's arms were tightly crossed, his head bowed over them, the hair he'd tied back hanging loosely over one shoulder. Finally, he looked up. "It means things are going according to plan."

Neve gaped at him.

"Think about it, Neverah. Our goal is to bring the Kings through the Heart Tree so they can be killed in the true world, where their souls will be destroyed as well as their bodies. Correct?"

He waited; Neve jerked a nod when it became clear he expected an answer.

"If they've somehow figured out our plan, they probably think they can outsmart us," Solmir continued. "Use the open door to escape and overpower us on the other side."

Her still-damp nightgown was cold; Neve mirrored his stance, arms crossed to hide a shiver. "Can they?"

Solmir was quiet for a moment, the long strands of his hair stirring against his shoulder. "I won't let them," he said finally. "Leave the killing to me, Neverah. You just concentrate on getting through the door."

Clipped, snapped out like an order. She narrowed her eyes. "I'm just as capable of killing as you are."

Something flashed across his gaze, too quick to puzzle out. Pain, almost. Regret. "But you don't have to be."

She had nothing to say to that.

Solmir looked at the open stretch of beach, the cliffs above. "This is probably the safest place we're going to find for a while," he said. "If you want to rest, we should do it here."

Her limbs suddenly felt heavy, as if his mention of rest made her body crave it. Neve nodded. "I suppose that's a good idea. Before we go to the Heart Tree."

"Yes." That same shade of pain and regret lurked in his tone; he wasn't quite able to mask it. "You'll need your strength."

Neve shrugged out of his coat, bunched it up into a makeshift pillow. "Don't let me sleep too long. And wake me up if there are more monsters."

"On my word, the only monster here you'll need to worry about is me."

She scoffed, turning her head back and forth to find a comfortable angle.

"What part of that strikes you as funny? That I'm a monster?" It wasn't joking, not really. There was a chord to his voice that begged earnestness.

"Not that part," Neve said, already half-asleep. "The part about me needing to worry about you."

He didn't respond. But his jaw tensed, and his arms tightened over his chest as he stared out over the dark water, a monster watching for other monsters.

Chapter Twenty-One

Neve

S he woke to Solmir's hand on her shoulder, though he took it away as soon as he saw the slits of her open eyes. "We need to move."

Neve sat up, rubbing sleep from her face; immediately, she sensed the cause of his urgency. The ground was rumbling, bits of rock shaking loose of the cliffs to clatter onto the beach below. Ripples spread across the black water from the shoreline. Not a full quake, not yet, but enough of a reason to get going, and a reminder that their time was short.

They didn't make a show of leaving. Solmir hurried across the beach, parallel to the cliffs and the edge of the sea, and Neve followed.

"How long will it take to get there?"

"Not long." He looked over his shoulder toward the flat black water, mouth pressed thin and a calculating look in his eye. "Not if we take the ship."

"The ship?"

But Solmir was already striding toward the shoreline, determination in his gait. "It takes magic to call," he said, almost to himself. "But there should be enough."

She remembered what they'd been told by the Seamstress, about needing the power of two gods to get to the Heart Tree. Solmir had used quite a bit of magic to kill the children of the Rat and the Roach, but he'd taken some in, too. And he still held all the power of the Serpent, of the Oracle.

Solmir waded purposefully into the shallows, bending to place his fingertips gently to the water's surface. Closed eyes, furrowed brow, then darkness seeped down his veins, spreading from chest to elbow to wrist before finally flowing outward, ribboning into the water like blood from a wound.

The shadows were a deeper black than the sea; Neve could see them race from Solmir's hand out toward the horizon.

"Will that let the Leviathan know we're here?" she asked quietly. Telling the most powerful Old One left that they were near its kingdom didn't seem like the best idea.

"The Leviathan might be powerful, but it's not *all*-powerful." Solmir straightened, taking his hands from the water. "It keeps to the deep, and the Bone Ship always makes itself from things on the surface."

"Makes itself?"

He gestured to the sea.

Something pale raced across the water toward the horizon line. Many somethings—ripples wavered from multiple directions as shapes Neve couldn't identify skimmed over the surface of the sea, called from far-away shorelines to the center of the black ocean. In the distance, the shapes came together, cobbling themselves into something large and gleaming.

Something like a ship.

It crept toward them, slow and stately across the water. The closer it got, the easier it was to make out.

A ship, yes. But a ship made entirely out of bones. Smaller and more delicate than the massive things that formed the mountain range where the Oracle had made its home, fused together in graceful shapes to make something at once beautiful and macabre. The only thing not made entirely of bone were the sails—those appeared to be pieces of huge, scaled hide, still glistening with water, as if the skin had been in the shallows on some farther shore.

The ship glided toward them on an unfelt wind, finally washing up on the rocky sand and coming to a stop. With a creak, a makeshift gangplank lowered to the ground, made of interlocking pieces of vertebrae.

Solmir stepped up onto the gangplank, shoulders set like a soldier marching into a doomed battle. "You coming, Your Majesty?"

⟡⟡⟡⟡⟡⟡⟡⟡⟡⟡⟡⟡⟡⟡⟡

Of all the strange things she'd done since waking up in the Shadow-lands, sailing on a ship made of bones might have been the strangest.

Solmir had directed the ship to where they wanted to go—some complicated ritual involving pricking his finger and writing a series of symbols on the deck in blood—and now all they had to do was wait. Wait for the ship to bring them to the inverted castle that held the Heart Tree. Wait and see if the power they'd stolen from murdered gods would be enough to get them inside.

Wait and see if her and Red's love was matched enough to open a door between worlds.

It was oddly peaceful, sailing over the black ocean, the slight creak of bones beneath her boots and the groan of the scaled hide that made the sails the only sound. Solmir had gone to the prow as soon as he finished telling the ship where to go and loomed there still, elbows resting on a rail made from delicately fused ulnae and radii. He hadn't spoken since.

Neve sighed, leaning far enough over the side of the ship to watch her reflection in the black water. Maybe telling him about Valchior had been a mistake. Maybe trusting him—more than she absolutely had to—had been a mistake.

One more in her long line of them.

It'd be over soon. That's what she kept telling herself, watching her dark reflection slide by in an alien sea. When they reached the Heart Tree, when she opened it and its power pulled the Kings from their Sanctum, tugged them into the true world where Solmir could kill them, then it would be over. Then she'd return to her life and start making amends for all the things she'd done, the people she'd hurt. She'd never have to see the terrifying man at the prow again, never have to endure his mocking sense of humor, never have to see him rub at the scars on his forehead or twist his lips in amusement.

The thought didn't comfort her. She pushed it away before she had to look at it too closely.

On they sailed. The ship stayed parallel to the shoreline on one side and the horizon on the other, following the trajectory they would've taken had they not been detoured by the fallen bone, the children of the Rat and the Roach. Hours slipped by that way, or at least what Neve assumed were hours. It should concern her, probably, how used she was getting to the way time seemed to shrink and expand here, where there was no night or day to count it by.

"You should sleep again."

Solmir, at her elbow. She'd been so lost in her own thoughts that she hadn't heard him approach. He adopted the same stance next to her as he had at the prow, forearms resting on the railing, peering out over the water.

She glanced at him, just once, before returning her attention to her slow-drifting reflection. "Not tired."

"Opening the Heart Tree will take a lot out of you. You should try, at least."

"Fine." She wasn't in the mood to argue. Wasn't in the mood to do much of anything, really. The silence of the sea and the gentle creak of the ship had lulled her into a kind of stasis, calmed the low-level panic that had chewed at the bottom of her stomach ever since she entered the Shadowlands. Neve turned and slid down the wall, sitting with her chin tipped back. From this angle, she couldn't see Solmir's face—just the curve of his shoulder, the dip of his arm, the trailing length of his tied-back hair.

After a stretch of silence, she asked, "What's going to happen when we get there?"

A sigh, lifting his shoulders, then lowering them. "The Heart Tree is inside the inverted castle," he replied. "When I went there the first time, it took an immense amount of magic just to open the door and get inside."

The power of two gods, the Seamstress had said. Two gods for the two of them. But back then, when Solmir first went to the Heart Tree—first tried to open it with Gaya, unmatched in love—he'd been a god himself. She pressed her lips together.

"So we use the magic we've stored away to open that door," he said, "and then we approach the Tree." He angled his head so he could look down at her, one split second before his eyes went to the horizon again. "After that, it's up to you."

"You have no pointers for me?"

"I don't think you'd want my pointers, considering how utterly I failed."

It sent them into silence again. The ship rocked slowly beneath them, drawing down Neve's eyelids despite her pronouncement that she wasn't tired. She tried not to think about whether the gentle tip and sway was due to the water or another quake far beneath the surface, the Shadowlands slowly dissolving and breaking apart.

Above her, Solmir shifted, pulling the piece of carved wood and his knife out from his boot. The soft scrape of the blade across the grain made a gentle counterpoint to the rocking ship.

By the time he started humming—deep and sonorous, that same lullaby melody he'd hummed once before, in an abandoned cabin deep in the upside-down forest—Neve was already asleep.

⁕⁎⁜⁂⁕⁎⁜⁂⁕⁎⁜⁂⁕

She has her key already.

One of those dreams again. Fog and roots and that familiar disembodied voice. She pushed up from the oddly smooth ground, the gauzy fabric of that white, shroud-like gown shifting over her legs.

The tower of tree roots rose before her, stretching up into the mist. Tendrils of shadow seethed along the white bark, glowing dark against the white and gray.

"What do you mean?" Neve asked the voice. "What key?"

No need to ask what *she* the voice referred to. It could only be Red. Always her and Red.

She attempted to reach for the Tree already. Nearly lost herself, not knowing what she was doing. Same as it ever was. The voice sounded equal parts fond and frustrated. *But that's what it takes. Matched love. A willingness to lay down your life for another.*

"Is she all right?" Panic crawled up her throat, made her turn in a whirl, even though she knew she'd see nothing but more fog. "Is Red all right?"

Red is fine. Soothing, with a slight ache in it, like this voice had been worried for Red, too. *She has her pieces. Now you get yours.*

"And that will open the Tree? Draw the Kings, so we can kill them in the real world?"

The voice was silent, long enough that her teeth ground together. "Answer me. Isn't that why you're here?"

Yes. Begrudging. *Yes, the Tree will open. And then you make your choice. Both of you.*

"What do you mean?"

There are two paths here, and while others will make choices that affect which you take, in the end the decision is yours alone. Both paths will lead you home, but only one will offer healing. Penance.

"Penance?" Her voice came out quiet, small.

A pause. *Someone pays for the mistakes we make, Neve. Either we do, or we leave it to those who come after us.*

A jolt snapped her out of the dream, made her eyes open to ivory ship and black water and gray horizon. Solmir stood straight next to her, no longer leaning on the railing, blue eyes narrowed.

"We're here," he murmured.

Neve stood in a hurry, nearly tripping over her hem. The ship had taken them into a bay, a semicircle of black ocean lapping against a stony beach. Here, the last slopes of the bone-built mountain range slumped into the sea, leaving just enough shoreline to hold an upside-down castle.

It was an impossibility, a conundrum of architecture that her mind wouldn't let her fully take in all at once. Instead, pieces: the massive, wrong-turned doors against the outcropping of a cliff made from bone, the turrets pointing downward into the ground, holding up the entire structure like a body balanced on extended fingers. What should be the castle's foundation was instead in the air, a shelf of stone pockmarked with the honeycomb walls of dungeons, their openings letting through slices of gray light.

And in the center of that upturned foundation, a seething mass of roots.

"Where's the rest of it?" Neve breathed. The roots looked just like the ones in her dream, white bark traced through with glowing black lines. She couldn't tear her eyes away.

"I assume that's Redarys's part." A creak as the gangplank grew from the side of the ship again. Solmir didn't look at her as he walked toward it. "I never saw anything but the roots, the last time I was here."

"You mean there wasn't a trunk, when Gaya—"

"No," he snapped. "As we've established, that time, I did it wrong."

Neve closed her mouth.

"Let's hope you have more luck than I did, Shadow Queen." Solmir strode down the beach, toward the inverted castle and the Heart Tree inside.

Pulse pounding in her wrists, Neve followed.

Chapter Twenty-Two

Red

Both their palms were slick, pressed together so tightly Red could feel the thrum of Eammon's pulse. She didn't know who the sweat came from. She assumed both of them.

Neither she nor the Wolf was entirely ready to leave their forest. But for Neve, she'd do it. Sail to the Rylt, confront Kiri, do whatever she had to in order to bring her sister home.

Even if the sight of the open plain beyond the trees made her breath come shallow and her pulse run quick. She'd had three days to prepare for this as Kayu arranged their voyage, but none of it amounted to any kind of calm.

The edge of the Wilderwood loomed up ahead, autumn leaves filtering the early light of a day that hadn't quite yet dawned in crimson and gold. When they'd healed the forest, taken it all into themselves, the border had repaired itself, too—it was no longer the broken, jagged line it'd been when Solmir and Kiri pulled out so many sentinels, like a smile with missing teeth. Now, once again, it was a firm demarcation, a wall of trees blocking them from Valleyda.

A wall neither of them had breached since that day.

She kept waiting for the Wilderwood within her to riot at the thought of leaving. For pain to spike through her, like it had the day Neve disappeared into the Shadowlands, warning her away from the border, warning her she couldn't cross.

But there was nothing. Just the gentle sway of leaves over her spine, the creep of ivy through her hipbones.

Behind them, Fife and Lyra stood waiting. Fife was nervous to go farther than Valleyda, but he refused to show it, standing as still as he could even as his feet shifted against the dirt. Lyra stood next to him, one hand placed gently on his forearm. The two of them had apparently come to some kind of resolution, through the whispered conversations Red had seen them having in the corners of the Keep. At any rate, they didn't seem upset with each other anymore.

The Keep was under the not-quite-watchful eyes of Lear and Loreth, who had been more enthusiastic about the prospect than Red had thought they'd be. Eammon had snorted when she said as much to him, and tilted up her chin for a kiss that left her breathless. "Newlyweds," he murmured against her lips, "will take any privacy they can."

There was nothing of that easy humor in him now. Eammon stared at the tree line like someone might look at a gallows.

Red jostled her shoulder against his. "The Wilderwood is being nice to me. How about you?"

He shrugged, stiff and stilted. "Can't feel anything."

There was a current of wariness running beneath his words, one that made her chew her lip. The Wilderwood had lived in him so much longer than it'd lived in her. Her own relationship to the forest they anchored was a mostly amiable one, wrongs forgiven. Eammon's was more complicated, and she still didn't quite know how to ask him about it. If he'd even have the words to answer if she did.

She squared her shoulders. Stepped forward. And though Eammon's hand reflexively spasmed around hers, like he'd try to haul her back, he didn't. His breath pulled in sharp, and he didn't let it out as Red approached the trees.

One more pause. Then she stepped between the trunks.

And nothing happened.

The wind teased her ivy-threaded hair, scented with distant smoke, the acrid tang of livestock and many people living in one place. A slight hitch in the Wilderwood within her, like the deep breath of someone slipping into icy water—but no pain, no consequences.

Instead, a feeling of satisfaction, almost. A step taken in the right direction.

She held out her hand to Eammon, still in the shadows of the trees.

A heartbeat, and Eammon laid his palm in hers. He stepped out of the forest, the gold of a new-dawning day burnishing his hair. His eyes widened, then closed as he tipped his head back up to the sky.

"Welcome to the world, Wolf," Red murmured.

Behind them, Fife and Lyra followed, Fife with a fractioned second of hesitation. The four of them stood on the edge of the world they'd known for so long and were silent.

Fife broke the quiet, crossing his arms. "It smells better in the Wilderwood, I'll give it that. It's a revelation every time."

"You'd better get used to that animal smell." Lyra gestured toward the road winding back to the village. A small carriage approached, pulled by nondescript horses, the driver with a telltale flick of long black hair. "Looks like our ride to the coast is here."

⊱⊰⊱⊰⊱⊰⊱⊰⊱⊰⊱⊰

Eammon's back heaved, rippling beneath his dark shirt as he hung over the side of the ship. Usually, the work of his shoulders was something Red enjoyed watching, but today her nose wrinkled and her hand on his neck was tentative.

"I take it back." He pushed up, scraping his wrist over his mouth. The green around his face wasn't due only to the Wilderwood in him. "I hate the ocean."

The trip to the Florish coast, while exceedingly strange, was uneventful. The carriage pulled up to the end of the road before the Wilderwood, Kayu grinning at them from the driver's seat, wearing a tunic and trousers, with a cap pulled down over the waterfall of her hair.

Red had arched a brow. "So you drive, too?"

"I'm a woman of many talents."

"Debatable." Raffe's voice, somewhat shaky from his seat next to Kayu, his head tipped back against the carriage. "*Reckless* doesn't begin to cover it."

"Hush," Kayu said. "I might be slightly out of practice, but we got here with no injury to beast or man, so I count that a success."

"Maybe wait to tally the injuries until we get there," Raffe muttered.

The nerves of passing the Wilderwood's border wore off slowly, replaced by nerves of a different kind. Red twitched at her dark cloak—her scarlet bridal one was packed into her bag, since she and Eammon had decided the more nondescript they could look, the better. "And the crew you hired? They'll be...discreet?"

"I told them you and Eammon were cousins of mine stricken with an odd strain of gangrene," Kayu replied. "I don't think they'll want to get close enough to see the veins or the eyes, but if they do, that will be our explanation."

"Delightful," Eammon muttered.

Kayu flicked the reins. "Come on, we want to make sure we get to the harbor before it gets busy."

Two hours' hard traveling after that, the four of them packed into the back of Kayu's coach like fruit in a market box. Lyra just watched the window, but Eammon gripped Red's hand, and Fife kept his eyes tightly closed.

"I didn't miss this," he said weakly, scrubbing a hand through his sandy-red curls. "I'd much rather travel on my own two feet."

But then they stopped. And then there was the sea.

When they first disembarked, they'd just stood there, blinking in the early-morning light. Kayu and Raffe went to the dock, where a small ship listed back and forth in the tide, a handful of rough-looking figures preparing it for departure. Lyra followed after a moment, Fife trailing behind her, though his eyes kept sweeping over the ocean like he couldn't quite fathom its size.

Red had never seen Eammon's eyes so wide. He stared out over the water as if he was looking for its end, trying to trace it all the way to the horizon line. "It's...huge," he murmured. "I mean, I knew it was, but... I've never seen anything..."

He didn't have to finish. Even in the brief years when he could leave it, before he was the Wolf, Eammon had never seen anything larger than his forest, never bothered to go so far as the coast.

"We'll see how much you like it once you're on a boat," she'd said, pulling him toward the harbor and Kayu's waiting galley. When they stepped on the gangplank, the sailors working over the ropes gave them a wide berth. Red bit back a bitter smile.

Now the coast was long gone behind them and the sun blazed noon-high, painting the ocean in shades of green and blue. The rocking of the ship proved not to settle well with someone who'd only ever known the solidness of forest floor.

The sailor working the sail at the stern glanced over their shoulder at Eammon. "Will he make it?"

"No," Eammon muttered.

"He'll be fine," Red called, waving a hand in the sailor's direction, hoping they wouldn't come any closer. She still had her hood up, but Eammon's was off. "Just not used to sailing."

"Water with a squeeze of lemon," the sailor said, turning back to the ropes. "Always helped me. Though it could be different with his... condition."

Eammon swiped his wrist over his mouth again. "You have no idea." Red grimaced and pushed his sweaty hair from his eyes.

He leaned briefly into her hand, then waved her off, sinking to sit with his back against the ship wall and his chin tipped up. "Let me know when we're close."

She glanced out at the open water. "It's a three-day voyage, remember?" Eammon groaned.

"Go below and try to sleep. I'll wake you for dinner."

"I don't think I can move, to be honest." He cracked one eye open. "And please don't mention food until we're off this shadow-damned thing."

Red tousled his hair before pulling up his hood, then walked to the prow, leaning on her elbows to look out across the water as the ship skipped over it. She'd never spent much time on boats and didn't feel a particular affinity for the sea, but there was a freedom in it, salt-soaked and coarse. The Wilderwood in her was quiet, far more settled than she'd anticipated it being, so far away from earth and growing things. Experimentally, she flexed her fingers. The veins along them blushed emerald.

She tilted her head back and closed her eyes, letting the briny wind whip at her hair.

"I'm sorry."

Her eyes opened. Fife stood next to her, staring down into the water, hiding his expression. He held his scarred hand close to his middle, the other gripping the railing. "I chose this, to save Lyra," he continued, like he was afraid he wouldn't start speaking again if he stopped now. "I chose to be bound to the Wilderwood. To you. And I shouldn't have taken it out on you the way I did."

Brief surprise chased itself into relief. Fife and Lyra had made up, but he hadn't made any such overtures to Red or Eammon—though they all behaved mostly normally, it'd been a cloud over them, a tension in the air that wouldn't dispel. Having Fife finally decide to speak to her about it felt like laying down a heavy pack she hadn't remembered picking up.

"I'm sorry, too," Red murmured. "I'm sorry we haven't figured out a way to let you out of your new bargain. I'm sorry that we don't understand much about it."

"Not your fault." Fife shrugged, but it was stilted. "Everything's changed now. None of us really know what the new parameters are. And I would've done it anyway, no matter the cost."

Red glanced over her shoulder. Lyra stood above them, on the platform that housed the ship's wheel, talking animatedly with Kayu and one of the hired sailors. The wind snatched their words away and covered Red and Fife's from being overheard.

"I understand," Red said softly. "I'd do the same thing."

"I know you would."

"When you were called, there in the clearing…" Red shook her head, looking back to the sea. "Fife, I promise it was an accident. Eammon didn't mean to do it."

"I know. He was just trying to protect you." A flicker of his eyes to Lyra above them. "Not one of us has ever been smart about the people we love, have we?"

Red snorted.

They lapsed into silence. Red knotted her fingers, lightly misted with salt spray. "Have you talked to Eammon about it?"

"I suppose I should, shouldn't I?"

"I'm honored to be the first stop on your apology tour, but yes, probably." Her lips quirked, half a smile, then pressed together. "The three of you…you're tied together in ways I can't even begin to understand. He loves you and Lyra, Fife. So much. It's killed him, thinking he hurt you, but he didn't know how to approach it. Wanted to give you space."

She'd pushed Eammon, at first, to find Fife and apologize, to make him talk it out. But Eammon had gently refused. "I told him I was sorry," he'd said, "and trying to make him forgive me is about my feelings, not his. We'll talk when he's ready."

Fife sighed. Pushed off from the railing. A moment later, she heard the soft rumblings of Eammon's voice behind her, a creak as Fife settled in beside him.

She smiled down at her hands.

"Is Eammon going to live?" Kayu moved gracefully down the stepladder from the crow's nest. She still wore a tunic and trousers, both soft and cut large, and a multicolored scarf that bound her dark hair back from her face. She smiled brightly, but something in her expression was faraway, preoccupied. She kept glancing westward, toward the Rylt, almost apprehensively.

"He's survived worse," Red answered.

"I suppose that's true." Kayu turned, elbows propped on the railing, back to the sea, and eyes canted toward Red. "So. You and the Wolf."

Red leaned back, stretching out her arms with her fingers still curled around the rail. A frisson of discomfort tightened her shoulders. "Me and the Wolf."

"You're immortal now, like him? Unable to die?"

Red's brow furrowed, sudden tension in her straightened arms.

Kayu shrugged, casual despite the baldness of the question. "He can't die, right?"

"No." Clipped and short and not entirely true. "He can't." Not of natural causes, anyway, not unless he was killed. That's how it had been when he was just the Warden. Now that he was the whole Wilderwood, that *both* of them were, Red didn't really know.

But she wasn't going to tell Kayu that.

"Quite a deal," the other woman said. A lock of black hair had escaped her scarf to dangle by her temple; she idly twirled it around her finger. "Getting all knotted up in a forest in exchange for immortality. Especially if you get a hulking tree husband in the bargain."

Red bit back a huff of laughter at that, though now that Kayu had mentioned the issue of immortality, her mind wouldn't let it go. Her concentration had been on other things for the past few weeks, but it was certainly something she'd thought about, the magic of the forest in her bones extending her life like it had Eammon's. There was joy in it— of course there was, spending an eternity with him—but trepidation, too. Everyone knew forever was a long time, but staring down into the pit of it was a special blend of awe and terror that her mind shied away from.

"I have no complaints on the tree husband front," she said.

"I bet not. He looks at you like you're personally responsible for the sunrise every morning." Kayu quirked a brow. "Or, usually he does. Right now, he looks like he's about to lose whatever is left in his stomach."

Red grimaced. "Hopefully he gets used to it."

"For all our sakes."

Kayu stared off into space, but when Red followed her gaze, space was Raffe. He stood at the opposite end of the ship, much like they did at the prow, leaning on his elbows and gazing at the receding horizon. At Valleyda.

Her eyes swung between them, her childhood friend and the far-flung princess, lips twisted.

"He loves your sister." A statement rather than a question, as if Kayu had seen the play of thoughts across Red's face. She shifted against the railing, face unreadable. "Always has."

A pause before speaking—it might not have been phrased as a question, but it still wanted an answer, one Red didn't quite feel qualified to give. "Raffe and Neve grew up together," she said carefully, eyes on her dry knuckles. "And yes, they love each other. But it's... it's complicated."

Kayu snorted. "I don't expect anything to be simple with you lot. All tangled up in forests and gods." She shook her head. "More fool me, I guess."

Red made a rueful nose of assent.

A moment, and Kayu pushed off from the railing. "I'm going below to see about some food. Dinner should be soon."

As she walked away, Red went back to Eammon. He and Fife sat beside the wall of the ship in comfortable silence, apologies having been made and accepted. She smiled to see it and felt a subtle rustling of leaves in her ribs, like the Wilderwood had wanted them to make up, too.

"I think I feel better," Eammon said as she came to stand in front of him. He looked up at her, squinting, half a tired smile picking up his mouth. "As long as I don't have to move."

She settled in next to him. "Do you plan to sit there for the entire voyage?"

"Yes."

"Noted."

Lyra climbed down from the steering platform and ambled over, clearly the one of them with the best-adjusted sea legs. "Food in ten minutes," she said. "Kayu is getting everything sorted."

A grimace spasmed on Eammon's face at the mention of food. "Perhaps I spoke too soon."

Fife arched a brow. "I'm not seasick, and yet I am still not excited by the prospect of hard tack and questionable dried beef."

"Come on, where's your sense of adventure?" Lyra teased, sitting next to Fife so the four of them were in a line. "Sea rations are part of the experience."

Three groans answered in chorus.

Chapter Twenty-Three

Neve

They climbed up the bony slope to get to the door, a feat that Neve managed to accomplish while barely thinking about heights. Petty fears seemed small and easily shoved away when faced with such a monumental and strange thing as an upside-down castle, faced with the prospect of home.

Home. She kept repeating the word in her head, trying to imbue it with more resonance. It should leave her elated. Instead, trepidation gathered weight in her chest.

Someone pays for the mistakes we make, the voice in her dream had said. And she'd made so many of them.

Solmir didn't touch her as they made their way up to the doors. Not necessarily a strange thing, though before when they'd had to scale the side of a bone-pile, he'd offered a hand to help. Now he stayed away from her skin with almost methodical precision, keeping measured distance.

Neve was out of breath by the time they reached the cliff, the sharp side of it jutting beneath the inverted doors, one more improbable anomaly holding the structure sound. The bones here seemed more brittle, parts of them almost transparent in the cold light, a soft ivory glow that was beautiful and brutal at once.

The castle felt even stranger up close, even more precarious. The curve that would normally mark the tops of the doors instead arced against the cliff, and looking at it too long was enough to make Neve's head feel light. Salt and bone-dust crusted the hinges, cementing the door half open. Inside, darkness.

"There's a drop." Solmir's voice was low, his arms crossed. He looked at the doors as if he expected them to crawl off their hinges and attack. "We'll have to climb down to the floor."

"The ceiling, you mean." It came out thin. She wasn't sure if she'd meant it as a joke or not.

Regardless, he didn't laugh, didn't crack the hint of a smile. Ever since the ship brought them to this strange shore, Solmir had been quiet and stoic, as if something weighed heavily on his mind. "Call it what you want. The point is, you'll have to be careful. The bricks stick out enough to make climbing simple, but you have to pay attention."

Neve nodded, swallowed.

He finally looked at her then, mouth a thin line and blue eyes narrowed. A faint streak of dirt still crossed his forehead right below his scars, mud from the marshes he hadn't quite managed to scrub off.

A rumble. Low, but here on these brittle bones, it was enough to make them both tense. Neve started toward the door; Solmir grabbed her arm, covered by the sleeve of his coat, and hauled her back as an unsettling cracking noise spread through the cliff beneath them. "What do you think you're doing?"

"You said a doorway was the safest place in an earthquake!"

"Not an *upside-down one*, Neverah!"

He crouched as he growled it, his arm bending over her back, bundling her into his side as if he could make them both smaller. The rumbling slowly stopped, the cracking noise fading. The bones held firm, the castle still stood, and Neve was still underneath Solmir's arm.

He straightened slowly. Didn't offer a hand to help her up. She thought of power, how she could steal it through a touch, and wondered if that was the reason he avoided her skin.

"When will we need the magic?" Neve shifted back and forth on her feet, shaking off the memory of his arm weighted over her. "Are you going to give it to me then?"

"You'll know when we need it, and you'll get what you need." His hands closed to fists, like he had to gather courage from the air. Then Solmir strode toward the rusted-open door, gripped the curved top of the lintel, and spun down into the shadows.

She stood for a moment just outside the castle, looking up at its looming wrongness. This had been Valchior's, built where the palace she'd grown up in stood now. Parts of it still existed, back in her world—the dungeons, pieces of the foundation. This was supposed to be a homecoming, yes, but this twisted reflection of her home made that thought all the more alien.

Mirroring Solmir's deep breath, Neve stepped up to the doorframe. She grasped the splintering wood. And she followed him into the dark.

The climb wasn't the difficult part, not really. The jutting stones that made the wall were slick, but Neve gingerly felt her way, probing out her foot to find a hold before putting her weight on it. She could hear Solmir's breath below her, the rasp of it as he lowered himself down, and she did her best to follow. The only light came through cracked windows below, the panels in varying shades of gray telling her that they were stained glass, robbed of color in a monochrome underworld.

But after the climb came making their way across what was meant to be the ceiling, and that was harder.

"Stay close," Solmir muttered when she finally dropped down beside him, the first thing he'd said to her since they'd entered the castle. Fissured light from the window cast him in shadow, made his eyes look like beacons. "And if I tell you to run, you do it."

"Are you anticipating there being something to run from?" Her voice echoed in the cavernous ruin, though she kept it close to a whisper. "What territory are we in?"

"None. No gods have made a home here, or lesser beasts." Solmir strode forward, ducking to avoid a crossbeam. "Just tell me you'll do as I say, Neverah."

He sounded worried. Worried and preoccupied, with that same reluctant look on his face he'd had since they called the Bone Ship. "What's wrong, Solmir?"

The sound of his name made him pause. It made her pause, too. She'd used it before, but there was something different in her tone now. Like she was speaking to a friend.

"Nothing is wrong." A slight shake of his head, sending his still-bloodied hair feathering over his back. "Everything is going to work out fine."

Unconvincing. But Neve didn't press. He was nervous—she was, too. It was an emotion that made sense.

But the look he shot her, the one she caught from the corner of her eye... it looked almost anguished, and that didn't.

The floor—ceiling—was flat here, the doors to branching corridors far above them. Wooden beams crossed the space, low enough to almost brush the top of Neve's head, the rectangles of cracked stained glass windows between them. Up ahead, though, the flat expanse ended, a steep drop indicating what would be a higher ceiling if the structure were right side up.

"Staircase is over there." Solmir gestured to the drop. "We'll have to climb up it."

"Or down it, as it were."

He didn't acknowledge her. "The Tree is in the hall on the first floor—or what would've been the first floor, were this damn thing facing the right way. The one with the dais."

Neve nodded, swallowing. She knew the one. The hall where Red had been blessed as a sacrifice to the Wolf. The hall where Isla had chosen Tealia as the High Priestess's successor and thus sealed her fate.

She slanted a glance at Solmir, unsure whether she was looking for guilt or simple recognition. His face was blank.

They reached the drop—Neve anticipated another climb, but the ceiling was sloped gently enough that they could walk, albeit very care-fully. Solmir went first, gracefully, but Neve slipped halfway down. She cursed, scrabbled for a handhold, got fingernails full of splinters instead—

Then Solmir's arms, wrapping around her waist. Solmir's middle absorbing the impact of her fall with a grunt. Her knees bracketed his hips, her hands splayed across his chest, palms on skin bared by his half-open shirt.

And they stared at each other, her confused, him with the stoic face of a man marching to a noose.

"Are you going to take it?" he asked.

Her brows knit. "Take what?"

"The power," he sneered. "The magic. You could, you know. Right now. You could take all of it."

The furrow in her brow went deeper. "But it would make me—"

"Monstrous?" he scoffed. "You want to be afraid of that, Neverah, but we both know you aren't."

Truth, and it made her scramble from him, put her feet on solid ground, and close her hands to fists so she didn't feel him beneath them. "What are you trying to do?"

"Give you all your options." His eyes glinted in the dark as he stood, raised his arms to either side, a stance that encouraged a fight. "You have to take in the power of a god to get through to the Tree anyway. And if you decide to take it all—the Serpent's power, the Oracle's, all the damn lesser beasts we've killed along the way—I won't stop you. I'll let you become the monster you were always meant to be."

Cruelty came as a surprise now. She'd stopped expecting it from him. And maybe that was the reason he offered it; as if he realized they'd grown past animosity, and it scared him. So he threw it out like a wild punch, not caring whether it hit, only that he'd tried.

It made her want to answer in kind, to strike with sharp words of her own. But Neve was still a queen, and her voice came even, her chin tilted upward, regal in his coat and her torn nightgown. "As I've said before," she stated coolly, "one of us is more prone to monstrousness."

His teeth shone, not a smile, though the fierce expression was tempered by a regretful glint in his eyes. "Are you so sure about that?"

Neve's teeth set hard against each other, fingers flexing into fists and back out again. All the warm thoughts she'd had of him—in the marshes, on the Bone Ship, on the beach where she'd watched him wash his hair and let her cheeks heat for it—felt like indictments now. This man played her like a harp string, over and over, and she kept looking for goodness in those discordant notes. Kept looking for something worth thinking of fondly.

Strange and humbling, what loneliness could do.

She strode past him, close enough for her shoulder to brush his arm. "You were right," she said. "It appears having a soul does little to make one good. Maybe they're mostly just nuisances, after all."

He didn't respond. But she saw a wince pull at his mouth as his arms dropped back to his sides, no longer inviting a brawl.

So preoccupied was she with the fallen King, she hadn't taken a moment to marvel at what lay before her until she moved beyond him. A familiar foyer, one she'd walked through countless times in that other life, the one where she was merely a sister and a daughter and a future queen. But inverted, like everything else was here.

The marble floor she knew so well hung far, far above, so distant she couldn't quite make out the individual pieces of interlocking stone. The huge spiral staircase started right at the level of her eyes, spinning upward at an angle that made her stomach hook.

And there, at the top—the bottom—a shimmer of darkness, like shadow had solidified into a wall.

"Is that where we'll need the magic?" she asked quietly.

"Yes." Neutral-voiced, like their argument of a moment before was forgotten. Solmir stepped up beside her, scrutinizing the staircase. "The first time I came, I climbed that. It was less than pleasant."

"I haven't expected any part of this to be pleasant," Neve muttered.

"I think I can spare enough to make it somewhat *less* unpleasant." Solmir raised his hands, shooting her a barbed grin. "All that murder put to work."

Thorns sprouted from his fingers and grew slowly up the staircase, winding around the railings. A lattice, easier to climb than the inverted stairs would be. Solmir stood straight and unyielding as the magic spiraled out of him, but she was close enough to see the sheen of sweat on his brow, the thud of his shadow-chased pulse as ice crystallized on his palms.

"That's enough," she said quietly.

But he shook his head. His fingers twitched, and the points of the thorns blunted—not entirely gone, but filed down enough so they wouldn't slice.

Solmir wrenched his hands down, grimacing. "That's all I can spare." He didn't look at her as he grasped one of the brambles and pulled himself up. "I would advise you not to look down."

Neve followed his advice, her heart migrating to somewhere in the vicinity of her tongue as she pulled herself up the thorns. Even blunted, they were still an uncomfortable thing to navigate around, and her skirt kept getting tangled. Finally, with a curse, Neve leaned her weight into the thorns and used her hands to tug her skirt up and tie it in a knot, leaving her legs mostly free.

She glanced up at Solmir just in time to see his head whip forward, away from her.

One handhold, one heave at a time. Her eyes wanted to track downward, to see just how high she'd climbed, but Neve wouldn't let them, peering resolutely forward, watching the floor draw nearer rather than the crossbeamed ceiling recede farther away. It was incredible, really, the fears you could master when you had no choice.

Neve could feel it as they drew closer to the wall of shadow. A hum in her bones, a subtle rattle in her teeth. It felt like one of the quakes but tuned to a minor key, less jarring but just as unsettling. She firmed her jaw against it and heaved herself up again.

Two corridors branched out from the sides of the staircase, one to the left and one to the right. The shadowy barrier only blocked the right—the way to the hall with the Tree. The thorns made a precarious bridge across the empty space between the landing and the beginning of the ceiling. Solmir stood just inside the curved lip that marked the start of the hallway, arms crossed.

"Don't look down," he repeated quietly.

Movements small and fear-precisioned, Neve slipped over the thorns toward the solid ground. She couldn't help seeing what lay below as she worked her way across, and it made every nerve in the back of her neck tighten.

The brambles covering the stairs behind her slowly dissolved, fading into gray and silent smoke that drifted through the inverted castle like a ghost. The roof yawned below, what looked like miles of empty air, and her breath came shallow in her throat, a strangled gasp she couldn't hold back.

She felt his hands on her arms, guiding her from the thorns and down to the solid stone slope of the hall's ceiling. "Breathe, Neve. You're fine."

Solmir sat her down by the wall, and Neve pulled up her knees, pressed her forehead against them. She tugged in deep breath after deep breath until her heart no longer felt as if it were trying to break free of her ribs.

He crouched before her, face unreadable, hands with all their silver rings hanging between his knees. "Can you go on?"

One more deep breath, scented with pine and snow. She nodded.

He nodded back. Then he stood and turned to face the churning wall of shadow blocking them from the Heart Tree.

When Neve and Red were ten, a huge storm had rolled in from the Florish coast. Such things were fairly common in the summer months there, but this was the first and last time she could remember one coming close enough to see from Valleyda. They'd stood on the roof, necks craned upward, watching a mass of black cloud spread slowly over the sky, spangled with lightning. It'd raised the hair on her arms, made the very air feel charged.

That's what this looked like. What it felt like. A storm of shadow, though not shot through with any light. Only churning darkness, covering the corridor, making it impossible to pass.

Neve stood, tried to step closer. But her bones buzzed against it, as if she and the shadow were the same polarity, repelling each other. "So what do we do?"

"I give you the power of one of the gods. I keep the other." Solmir's mouth was a grim line. "And then it will let us through."

She thought of how they passed power, through a kiss, through a touch. She knew instinctively which it would have to be. Time was short, and the magic they exchanged was strong.

Solmir turned to her, jaw a pained ridge beneath his short beard, blue eyes alight. His shoulders tensed, making the sharp line of his collarbone stand out under moon-pale skin, casting a smoky shadow she could trace to his heart.

They didn't speak. There wasn't a need to, not now, and Neve didn't think she could fit words to what she felt, anyway. Warmth he didn't deserve and that she didn't want to feel, magic-required closeness. A homecoming, an ending.

It made no sense, that she should feel this...this *regret*. Like she was leaving something undone.

Wordlessly, Solmir held out his hand. She placed hers in it. Magic sparked between them, cold and stinging, the prick of brambles in her veins.

He pulled her forward, slowly. He tucked her hair behind her ear, his hand fit to the side of her face. Intimacy beyond what the magic needed, but she didn't stop him.

When his mouth lowered to only a breath away from hers, he was already changed, the power rushing forward and making itself known—teeth sharpened and elongated, eyes black around the blue of his irises, veins night-dark. He paused, looking down at her, monstrous.

"Remember what I said," he murmured. "If you decide to keep it, I won't stop you." Then his lips were on hers.

It was gentler than before, when he'd kissed her just minutes after she'd awoken in her glass coffin, taking the power that would twist her out of being human. And her mind fought against that, the knowledge that this was for more than one purpose, but what was the point? Loneliness wanted easing, and if things went according to plan, she'd never have to do this again. Never have to seek solace from a former god who was a breath away from being an enemy.

Neve had kissed for comfort before, purely physical, with no feeling behind it deeper than attraction and opportunity. The son of a visiting duke who kept pronouncing her name wrong, the daughter of a marquess with pretty eyes. It wasn't always an act that had to mean something important.

That's what she kept repeating to herself as her mouth pressed to Solmir's, as magic spilled down her throat and raised thorns in her veins. This didn't mean anything. It was the passing of power, and if she derived comfort from it, what did it matter?

Neve had always been good at lying.

When they broke apart, both of them were breathing hard. She backed up before he did, putting space between them. His hands dropped to his sides. Neither of them spoke. There weren't any words.

In tandem, they turned toward the shadows. Neve recovered her voice first. "What now?"

Casual, nonchalant. None of the churning emotion that both of them wanted to avoid.

"Now," Solmir said, "you let it go."

Deceptively simple, punishingly easy. Neve lifted her hands, she and Solmir acting as one, like the power was thread that strung them together and synced their movements. Palms out, bent fingers, thorns pouring from them both, the power of two gods spilled into the storm.

When it was all gone from her, all spun into smoke and thorn, Neve braced her hands on her knees, breathing hard. Next to her, Solmir shook out his arms. "It always gives me pins and needles," he muttered.

For a moment, nothing happened. Then a groan, like the air itself was tearing apart.

The shadowy storm split, slowly, the sides billowing away from each other with a grace that the shrieking sound it made belied. A path cut through the dark, leading into the hall beyond.

Solmir gestured toward the shadows. "After you, Your Majesty."

And she rose to the title, her head held high, even as fear made her wrists flutter with her pulse's tide.

Walking through the storm made every inch of her skin prickle. Neve felt her hair lift up from the back of her neck, wave around her head like a crown. Gooseflesh ran down her arms, over her shoulders, making each step forward a push through a thick current.

Reaching the other side felt like being released from a giant fist; Neve nearly stumbled. She caught herself on the curved side of the ceiling where they walked, as her hair settled back around her shoulders, unpleasant sparks itching at her nerves and slowly fading away. Solmir lurched out behind her, swiping a hand over his own hair, turning back to scowl at the shadows as they billowed back together, once again impenetrable dark.

Neve pushed up on shaky legs. "It closed again."

"Yes, it did." He strode forward, passing the upside-down stained glass windows, striped in light and shadow.

"Is that going to be a problem for you?"

Solmir paused, a muscle twitching in his back. "Don't worry about me. Just focus on opening the Heart Tree."

"And getting home."

"Yes," he said softly. "And getting home."

She knew the way now. The bottom floor of the castle hadn't changed much between her time and Valchior's, other than general upkeep and repairs, and she'd attended enough blessings and ceremonies and court hearings for her feet to take her without conscious thought to the hall.

Still, she wasn't prepared for what she saw when she passed through the last upside-down archway.

Tree roots. A huge mass of them, just like in her dream. She'd seen them from the ship, the way they spilled out of the castle's sky-facing foundation like the tentacles of some massive creature. But seeing them up close, the sheer size of them, was enough to make her mouth fall open.

Neve didn't realize she'd taken a step backward until Solmir made a soft sound of pain. She looked down—she'd stepped on his foot. "Sorry."

"I'll live," he muttered, moving away from her.

The roots moved. They swirled over each other in a slow, sinuous dance, almost serpentine, pale bark and dark veins in a continuous spiral that made her dizzy if she watched it too long. The roots pushed up through the dais above, the one that would be on the floor in the true world. The place where Red's sacrifice had been cemented. The place where her and Kiri's and Arick's—Solmir's—true plans had been put into motion.

"Will it take me to the palace?" she asked quietly, transfixed by the twisting roots. "When I go through?"

Solmir shook his head. If Neve watched the roots with awe, he watched them with barely checked wariness. "The geography of the true world and the Shadowlands isn't exact. Places that had high concentrations of magic were duplicated here, but not in the same place as their counterparts. I have no idea where it will take you." He made a rueful noise. "I would assume anywhere is an improvement."

Neve didn't answer. After another moment of staring at the shifting roots, she turned to Solmir. His blue eyes were narrowed, watching her every move like he expected each one to be the start of a fight. Arms crossed, tight enough to make the tendons in his muscles stand out, hair falling from where he'd tied it back to feather around his face. She couldn't read his expression.

"What do I do?" Neve asked.

But even as the words left her mouth, the Tree was what answered.

This wasn't a groan, not like when the shadowed storm that guarded the way wrenched itself apart. This was a softer sound, a sigh, a shift in the air.

Neve turned around.

The roots twisted down, extending toward the stone where Neve stood, slow and graceful. As they did, they parted, revealing darkness beyond.

Darkness, and the pale glow of gray fog.

She looked back at Solmir, filled with a host of feelings that were too sharp-edged to grasp fully. "Are the Kings on their way?"

"Not until you step inside," he answered. "That's the true opening. That's when its power awakens and calls them forward."

She turned to face the massive roots, the path between them. "And when they do," she said, "you'll follow them."

"Yes."

"And how will you kill them?"

His eyes were cold, his expression impassive. But his hands curled into fists by his sides, like he was trying to hold on to something that was swiftly slipping away. "Don't worry about it, Neve," he said finally. "It will be easier than you think."

Another nod, this one short and decisive. But one more quiet question forced itself up her throat. "And you think Red loves me enough, even now?" She swallowed past sudden roughness. "You think she'll reach down into the dark for me?"

She already has.

The voice. The one from the dream. It seeped out from between the roots, barely a shade above silence. When she glanced back at Solmir, he didn't seem to have heard it at all, as if the words were only for her.

She's reached and found her key, the voice continued as Neve turned back to the Tree. *Now it comes down to you and your choices, Neverah. Shadow Queen.*

"Of course I think so." Solmir, answering her question a breath after the disembodied voice did. She whirled around; he stood right behind her, closer than she'd anticipated. Close enough for her to feel the brush of his hair against her cheek and see the determination in his eyes, like a decision recently made.

"You're worth reaching into the dark for." Then he grabbed her chin and kissed her.

It was real, even more real than the one outside the shadow. Real, and pouring dark magic down her throat, every bit of it he still held, draining all of it out of himself and into her. Real, and she should want to pull back, but she didn't.

Before she could process any of it, Solmir broke their kiss and pushed her forward, into the mist-seething darkness between the roots.

Instinctively, Neve closed her eyes. Her breath came shallow, her heart pumping. It felt, almost, like her heart's rhythm echoed elsewhere, something else responding to the beat of her pulse.

And when she opened her eyes, she saw the Tree.

Chapter Twenty-Four

Red

Sleeping on a ship should be easy, Red thought. The slow creak of ropes, the gentle rocking—by rights, she should fall effortlessly into rest. Eammon certainly had. He lay next to her, large and warm and snoring, on a bunk that was far too small for the two of them, his seasickness banished by sleep.

But for Red, it wouldn't come.

After dinner—jerky and some kind of bread, yes, but well spiced, and far more appetizing than anticipated—the sailors had gone to smoke on the deck, and Kayu had taught them all a Niohni board game that involved dropping smooth stones into a simple grid and seeing who could collect the most in multiples of four. Red wasn't quick enough with numbers to be much good, but Raffe, Eammon, and Lyra all won nearly as many rounds as Kayu did. Raffe had pretended to be annoyed, but the smile he flashed at Kayu when she poked him hard in the shoulder was genuine, and the two of them had stared at each other for a moment after as if the rest of them didn't exist.

But when Raffe saw Red looking, the smile had dropped. He'd gone to the other side of the table and didn't speak to Kayu again. After a few more rounds, everyone but him had gone to bed. Raffe's excuse was he wasn't tired yet, though the shadows beneath his eyes showed it for a lie.

Now, in bed next to Eammon, Red stared up at the dark beams above

her and sighed. Gently, she extracted herself from Eammon's arms and
crept to the ladder leading to the deck.

When she emerged under the dark sky, it seemed she was alone. One
of the sailors would be up at the wheel, she knew, making sure they
stayed on course toward the Rylt, but they paid her no attention.

Red went toward the back of the small galley, the wooden boards
rough beneath her bare feet. When she reached the railing, she pulled
off her hood, tipping back her head and letting the wind pull at her ivy-
threaded hair. It was too dark for anyone to see, unless they were standing right next to her.

"So you couldn't sleep, either?"

She jumped back, hands raised defensively. "Shadows *damn* me,
Raffe!"

Raffe just quirked a brow and drank from the chipped ceramic cup
in his hand. "No wonder, if you're this jumpy."

The trajectory of her raised hands went from defensive to deprecat-
ing. Red snorted, settling her elbows on the rail. "I think I'm entitled to
a little jumpiness, all things considered."

"You'll hear no arguments from me." The sound of liquid swirling—
Raffe took a sip of wine, then held out the cup to Red. She accepted,
took a swallow. Made a face.

"Not Meducian," Raffe said, taking the cup back.

"Not Meducian," Red agreed.

They lapsed into comfortable silence, listening to the rhythm of the
tide against the hull.

"Do you think she'll come back different?" Raffe asked finally. "I
mean, it'd be impossible to not be…changed by all this, somehow. But
do you think…" He trailed off, like he didn't quite have the words for
what he wanted to ask.

Red knit her fingers together. Even in the color-stealing dark, the green
tint of her veins was evident, incongruous in the grays and blues of the sea
at night. "You're wondering if she'll come back as changed as I was."

No response from Raffe, but that told her she was right.

The Wilderwood rustled down her spine, spread new leaves toward her shoulders. Almost like an offered answer.

"She made a choice," she said quietly. "There in the grove. You saw it. She pulled all that shadow in, made it part of her."

"But it *wasn't* a choice, not really." Raffe's voice was harsh in the quiet. "Not like yours was. You fell in love and took the roots, she...she had to close the door, and she did it the most obvious way she could. It wasn't the same."

"No, not exactly the same," Red conceded. "But it was still her decision."

Silence, again, but she felt the way he tensed, the way that this quiet was no longer the comfortable kind between friends. It was something waiting for a shattering.

Red sighed and started braiding her hair, for something to do with her hands as much as to keep it out of her face. "Neve's taken the first step to becoming my mirror. That's why the mirror in the tower shattered. She's taking in the Shadowlands like I took in the Wilderwood."

Another bloom along her rib cage, flowers opening wide in the gaps between organs. The forest agreeing.

"Then what will it make her?" Raffe's whisper was agonized. "Red, if she has to do for the Shadowlands what you did for the Wilderwood, what will she be when she comes back?"

"She'll be Neve. She'll be who she always was," Red answered automatically, and waited for the stretch and sprout within her, the Wilderwood's sign that she was right.

None came.

Her teeth set on edge, animosity for the forest she carried rising for the first time since it'd given her Eammon back. "Whatever she is, she will still be my sister. And I will do whatever she needs."

She held her breath. One twitch of branches, curling around her hip.

Next to her, Raffe took a deep breath. Nodded. "I trust you."

Red turned away from him, looking out at the water instead. "Speaking of trusting," she said lightly, "bringing Kayu in seems to have worked out well."

He said nothing, but his hands tightened on his cup of wine. A moment, then he tossed the rest of it back, grimacing as he swallowed.

She drummed her fingers on the rail. "You never told me *how* she figured out Neve was gone."

"She intercepted a letter from Kiri," Raffe answered, looking at his cup as if its emptiness was a personal offense.

"How'd she manage that?"

Raffe shrugged. "She saw someone delivering it to my chambers late one night and told them she was coming to see me. They gave it to her."

"That's odd," Red murmured. "I never had a letter delivered at night. Granted, I never received many letters." She paused, frowned, unease the plucking of hair on the back of her neck, a subtle twist in her gut. "You should probably—"

"Spare me your advice, Redarys."

Her teeth snapped closed.

Raffe didn't look at her, staring instead out over the water, his jaw clenched tight and his fingers blanched around his empty cup. He closed his eyes, took a breath. When he spoke, it was calm and even, though fire lurked just beneath. "You don't understand how difficult it's been, trying to keep people from prying, trying to pretend like everything is fine when the fucking Queen is missing." He shook his head. "So please don't presume to give me advice. I am doing all I can."

"I get it," she said quietly. "I understand that it's been hard."

"Do you?" His eyes glinted at her in the dark. "You've been living a fairy tale in the woods, busy being some kind of forest god, while I try to hold things together in a country that isn't mine, for a woman who never told me if she loves me back, and now I don't know exactly how I feel about her, either."

The middle of the night had always been an opportune time for confessions.

Red sighed. "You're right. I can't understand, and I shouldn't tell you how to deal with things." She paused. "I'm sorry, Raffe. For all of it."

"Me too." A stretch of quiet where she could tell that he had more to say but wasn't quite sure how to say it. There weren't easy words for things like this.

"Have you had more dreams?" he asked finally. "With a tree, like the one you told me about?"

"One or two," Red answered. "Why?"

"Because I haven't." He sounded almost ashamed by it, like the lack of dreams was some cosmic allegation. "Just the one."

She picked at the skin around her nails. "Is that…bad?"

"It feels like it is," Raffe murmured. He ran a weary hand over his face. "I stopped having them when…when I realized I didn't know how I felt about her anymore."

Ah. "Raffe," she said gently, "it's fine. Really."

"It doesn't feel fine. It feels like I'm failing her somehow."

"Being honest about how you feel isn't failing." The voice in the dreams told her the Heart Tree could only open with matched love. And Raffe didn't know what kind of love he had for Neve anymore. That had something to do with who had the dreams, she figured.

The Wilderwood bloomed along her vertebrae. Another reassurance she was right.

"You are an excellent friend, Raffe," Red continued quietly. "And that's what Neve will need, when she comes back."

When. Not if.

The other man took a breath. Nodded. But his jaw was still held as tight as a prison lock.

"For what it's worth, I'm glad we brought Kayu on board." She gestured to the ship with a snort. "It got us a way to Kiri. Surely, if anyone has answers, it will be her."

"Let's hope," Raffe murmured.

They stood there a moment, rocked by the swaying ship. Raffe yawned into his hand. "I'm going to actually attempt sleeping."

"If Eammon can manage it, anyone can."

"He seemed to recover well enough to beat me at three rounds of that game Kayu taught us," Raffe muttered as he turned away from the railing. "You try to sleep, too."

"At some point," Red reassured him.

With a nod, Raffe disappeared down the ladder into the hold.

Her key weighed in her pocket, heavy against her hip. Red pulled it out, tracing the familiar contour with her fingers.

Though she'd kept it on her since it appeared, Red hadn't looked at it since they left the Wilderwood. Part of her had almost been afraid it would change, warp, one more dead end. But the key looked exactly the same, gilded in the moonlight and touched with threads of gold.

When it pulsed in her hand, harder than it ever had before, Red nearly dropped it.

Cursing through her teeth, Red clenched her hand around the key and stepped away from the railing, determined to keep it in her grip. The key continued to beat, as if there were a heart concealed somewhere in the wood, a counterpoint rhythm to her own. Before, she'd thought it was half a hallucination, a phantom of her own pulse, but this was too strong to ignore or reason away.

Eammon. She should tell Eammon, should—

But then there was a rush of darkness, and a roar of sound, and the feeling of falling.

And when Red opened her eyes, it wasn't to a ship. It wasn't to a moonlit sky scattered in stars.

It was to fog.

And to the Tree.

Chapter Twenty-Five

Neve

It was different than the dreams.

There, Neve had been at the bottom of the Tree, next to the massive tower of roots that directly mirrored the ones she'd just walked into. This time, she stood on...well. She wasn't quite sure what she stood on. Fog snaked around her feet in an obscuring billow and spill.

But whatever it was, it placed her directly in the middle of the Tree.

Roots far below, the white bark churned with threads of shadow. And branches above, those tendrils of darkness fading gradually to gold. Though she'd seen it before, something like awe still spiked in her chest.

It was real. Mythic and impossible, but real.

And that meant she could go home.

The thought was forced, what she felt should be the logical next step in the pattern of relief her mind followed. But it sat heavy, didn't quite fit.

"Neve?"

Quiet, shaken. But she would know that voice anywhere.

A tremble started in her hands, worked all the way up her arms as she turned to face her sister.

Red looked feral. Dressed in a worn tunic and leggings beneath a dark cloak, hair loosely braided and threaded through with ivy. The veins in her hands blushed a faint green, had a slight pulse to them that perfectly echoed the gold in the branches above. A green halo surrounded the warm brown of her irises, and delicate bracelets of bark encircled her wrists.

More wood than woman. More wild, more Wolf. But the first thing Neve said to her twin was "You look beautiful."

And Red straightened from her crouch, and her green-and-brown eyes widened, and she replied, "So do you."

Suddenly, the lack of a solid floor in all this fog, the gold above and the black below and the massive Tree they stood beside seemed utterly inconsequential. The First and Second Daughters of Valleyda ran through the mist, across whatever substituted for the ground, and fell into each other's arms.

Neve felt something, as she rushed to Red. The ghost of fingers across her skin, like someone else was here, someone else wanting to fall together with them, too. A sound like a sigh, echoing through the endless fog, and then it was gone.

And Neve saw, as her arms wrapped around her twin, that the veins in them were blackened, her wrists wreathed in thorns. Solmir's parting gift. Was it because she needed it? Had he just grown tired of holding all that power?

There was an itch beneath her skin, a subtle hook in her middle. It felt like something abandoned, something left undone.

Red scraped in a breath against Neve's shoulder. "I thought I lost you." The breath shuddered, became a sob. "I let you go, I chose him over you, and then you were gone—"

"But I made you." Neve put a hand on her sister's hair. The leaves of the ivy twitched against her fingers. "I made you choose, because I wouldn't listen." Her own tears started, burning in her eyes, slipping down cheeks blushed with shadow. "I wanted to make your choices for you."

"Neve," Red started, reassurance in her tone, but Neve took a step back and held up her thorn-studded hand. The Oracle had given her a gift, when it rent through that knot she kept her emotions tied up in, brutal though it was. There were things she needed to say.

"I didn't want to admit I was wrong. Even though I knew it." There it was, her most damning confession. "I knew it was wrong, and I did it anyway, because I wanted some kind of control." Her breath hitched on the last word, her fingers shaking. "I was willing to do anything to feel like I had some kind of control."

A heartbeat, both of them standing there tearstained. Then Red's green-veined hand closed around Neve's thorns. "You had your reasons."

Neve pulled in a shaking sigh.

Red dropped their hands, but kept her fingers laced with Neve's. "I should've told you why I had to go. I was so...so scared, and ashamed, and I thought..." She trailed off, like whatever she'd thought didn't lend itself easily to words. Her eyes closed. When she spoke again, it was measured and unwavering, as if she was reciting something she'd rehearsed over and over in her mind. "Neve, do you remember what happened that night?"

There was only one night they ever referred to with that kind of weight. Four years ago, turning sixteen, running under endless, star-strewn sky toward the dark trees. Toward the Wilderwood and its Shad-owlands beneath, the place that would swallow them both.

"Parts of it," Neve murmured. "But not...not whatever made you think you had to leave." She had to force them up her closing throat, those words. How often had this sliced at her, cut her so deep she grew almost numb to it? That night had started their splintering, and there were such huge swaths Neve didn't remember.

And the biggest question, the one that sliced deepest—was it something she'd done, that made Red feel like she could only belong to the forest? Was it somehow her fault?

This was all so much bigger than they were, but in the end, it narrowed down to her and her sister and all the things that had grown up between them, surely as roots, surely as thorns.

Red's eyes stayed closed. "I almost killed you."

Whatever Neve had expected, it wasn't that. "What?"

"The power of the Wilderwood, its magic…it came into me, partly, when I bled within the forest's border. And I didn't know how to control it, and when the thieves came, I…I killed them…but the power wasn't under my control, not fully. I didn't know how to rein it in, and it almost killed you." Her eyes opened, green glowing around the brown. "That's why I wanted to go to the Wilderwood, Neve. Not to get away from you. To protect you."

Even in that, they were mirrors.

"I thought the only way to keep all of you safe, from me, from the monsters"—Red snorted, a quick acknowledgment that they both now knew the monsters were real, that they'd *become* them—"was to leave." She sighed, flicked her eyes up to Neve. "But then I met Eammon."

Not so long ago, that name—one she didn't even know existed until she heard it on Red's lips—had sparked visceral rage in her. Anger that the monster's name made Red light up, proof that he'd made her care. Made her think that she belonged to him, to the Wilderwood.

Now it just sounded like a name. She knew monsters, and he wasn't one.

And it wasn't like she really had a leg to stand on anymore where that was concerned.

"So all we ever wanted to do was save each other," Neve said.

The corner of a smile on Red's mouth, as fierce and wild as the rest of her. "And we've done such an *excellent* job."

A moment of silence. Then, improbably, they both started laughing. Shouts of it rang through the mist and off the massive trunk next to them as they fell together, tears streaming from their eyes, caught in paroxysms somewhere between joy and sobbing.

"Kings." Red mopped at her streaming eyes. "*Kings*, Neve, what did we *do*?"

Neve shook her head, banishing tears with a swipe of her wrist. "If what every Old One in the Shadowlands has told me is true, nothing the stars didn't lay out for us."

"Old Ones?"

"The monsters. The gods the Kings imprisoned." Neve waved a thorny hand. "Long story, and you already know the important parts."

"I'll take your word for it." Red shook her head, crossing her legs beneath her with a thoughtful look in her eyes. "Stars, though...when we went to the Edge, to see the carving of the key grove, there were carvings of constellations, too."

"The Edge?"

"Another long story. There's a country behind the Wilderwood. The people there are our friends."

A click as Neve's mouth closed. There was so much about her sister's life she didn't know. So much she had no reference for. For all that they'd grown up together, and shared a womb prior to that, sometimes it seemed like they barely knew each other.

Red dug her hand into her pocket, then cursed softly. "The key. I had it when I..." Her brows drew together. "How did you get here?"

Neve's cheeks heated, the name she'd been trying to avoid creeping closer to being inevitable. She took in a deep breath, blew it out. "Solmir brought me."

Silence. Red stared at her, face expressionless, though the hand hanging by her side curled slowly into a fist. "Did he hurt you?"

"No." At least, not in the way Red was thinking, not in any way that lent itself to easy explanation. "Red, he's on our side. Well, he's on his own side, but his side is our side. Mostly. He's against the Kings. When he was trying to bring them through—"

"When he almost killed my husband, you mean?"

"I'm not making excuses for him." *That* would be a useless endeavor. "But we have a common enemy. He was trying to bring the Kings through to kill them. Their souls are mired in the Shadowlands, and the Shadowlands are breaking apart. If they dissolve while the Kings are still here, they'll be freed—not their bodies, maybe, but their souls. They'd find a way to come back, and they'd be even worse than the Old Ones were."

Red's jaw worked, her eyes bright and fierce. Her fist still clenched by her side, nearly shaking with the force of her grip. But when she spoke, it was even. "Fine." She loosened her fingers with marked effort. "If you trust him, I will...not kill him."

That was the best Neve could expect.

"But if he ever hurts Eammon again," Red said, "I will pull each one of his organs out of his mouth. Individually."

"Noted," Neve replied. She would tell Solmir that exactly.

If she saw him again. Was she going to see him again?

Red was here, and she was here, and clearly something had happened to the Heart Tree—the door open, the way cleared. She could go home now, leave the Shadowlands behind, let Solmir do what he needed to do and call it all as out of her hands.

But it didn't feel...right. There was something more for her to do here, and the shadowy magic Solmir had passed to her right before she entered the Tree nearly *hummed* with it.

"So how did *you* get here?" Neve asked, rubbing her thorn-laced arms to try to dispel the magic's itch.

"I had a key," Red said. "I got it...well, when I tried to reach you, the first time." She shifted uncomfortably, like the memory wasn't a pleasant one. "I tried to let loose a sentinel. From inside me. Make a tree, and then make that a doorway."

Neve cast a glance behind them, at the massive trunk of the Heart Tree. "I suppose you weren't that far off."

Red snorted. "Anyway, it clearly didn't work. But it gave me a key, one made from white bark with golden veins. I was holding it, and it started to pulse, and then I was here."

Neve's brows drew together. "I don't have a key. Am I supposed to?"

Only if you choose to see this through.

The voice. The one from her dream, the one she'd heard whispering right before she stepped into the Tree. She and Red turned, back to back, facing down all the fog.

"You've heard it before?" she murmured to Red.

"Yes," Red replied. "You?"

"Me too. In dreams, and other places."

Red shook her head. "I don't know whether I'm excited or terrified to hear about everything you've done in the Shadowlands."

She said it lightly, but Neve chewed her lip.

The key is the Tree, the voice continued. It seemed closer somehow. The timbre of it easier to pick out, still just at the edge of being recognized. *The key is the Tree, but you are not yet the mirror, though you draw close.*

"Does she need a key?" Red's voice cut through the fog, sharp and demanding. "Or are you spouting cryptic nonsense? Just tell us if I can bring her home!"

A pause, hanging heavy.

She can go, the voice finally answered. *If it is her choice. Finding a key and becoming the mirror are pieces of a larger story, but they are not required for Neverah's return. Only for the Shadow Queen's.*

The title reverberated in Neve's bones, made all the magic wrapped up in her sing. Shadow Queen. What she'd been called since she entered the Shadowlands, words that were both terror and touchstone. She hadn't thought that it was something that could be separated from her, but the voice's phrasing made it clear: the Shadow Queen was Neve, but Neve wasn't just the Shadow Queen. That mantle was one she'd have to choose.

And if she did, it meant this wasn't over. Neve had made mistakes— they all had—and sooner or later, someone would have to pay for them.

She could go home now, pass the torch. Or she could become what she was meant to be. Whatever that was. Whatever that entailed.

Slowly, Neve turned, facing her sister. The person she loved most, the person she'd tear worlds down for without a second thought. She reached up, cupped her cheek in a thorny hand. "I love you, Red."

The realization was a slow bloom in her twin's eyes, widening, tearing up. "Neve, you can't."

"I have to."

"But what does it *mean*? What do you have to do?"

"I'm not sure yet." Already the fog was thickening, covering the Tree, clouding the space around them so all Neve could see was her sister. "But this has to end. Solmir thought he could do it without me, but that isn't true—he needs me still, for more than just opening the Heart Tree."

"Neve, you can come *home*." Red put her hand over Neve's on her face, pressed in as if she could hold it there.

Her sister didn't care about her thorns, her sharpness, and something about that made Neve want to start crying all over again.

"Forget Solmir," Red said. "Forget the damn Kings. Just come home."

Neve shook her head. "I choose to see it through," she murmured. "I choose to be the Shadow Queen."

And with those words, the fog closed over Red's face, silencing her panicked shout. Neve's eyes closed, peaceful with her decision.

But her eyes opened on anything but peace.

The room was half flooded. Black, briny seawater covered Neve's ankles, steadily rising, as if the whole inverted castle were slowly falling into the ocean. The structure shook.

Solmir stood in front of the Heart Tree, arms stretched to either side and legs braced, like he was waiting for an onslaught. He saw Neve, looked away, did a double take. "Neverah, what are you doing here?"

"What I'm supposed to." Something was in her hand, rough edges cutting into her palm. Neve looked down—a key, white wood threaded with black veins.

He snarled in response, moved toward her as if he'd throw her back into the Heart Tree himself. But another shake tossed him off-balance, sent him splashing into the rising seawater. "Something's coming," he said through gritted teeth. "But I don't think it's the Kings."

"It's not."

The voice was everywhere and nowhere at once, almost more like two voices that had been sloppily soldered together. The room darkened.

At one of the upside-down windows, a massive eye pressed up against the cracked glass.

Chapter Twenty-Six

Neve

The eye looked at her.

Neve had never felt so small. Not in the presence of the Serpent, its huge bulk unknown but felt in the dark, and not before the Oracle, an inhuman thing in a humanoid shape. Not even next to the Heart Tree, the nexus between this world and the real one.

That huge, dark eye seemed to see all the way through her, and though Neve had spent quite a lot of time in the company of gods in the past weeks she'd been in the Shadowlands, this was the first time she felt like it.

The paralysis that held her didn't extend to Solmir. He cursed and splashed through the rising water to her side, grabbing her still-thorny arm and spinning her to face him, his other hand cupping the back of her head to press her face against his chest. "Don't look, Neve."

A laugh echoed through the shaking castle, worse even than the words had been. Neve clapped her hands to her ears, mindless of their thorns, and made a low, pained sound.

"Apologies," the Leviathan said. "I thought she could take my true form. *You* can, after all, and you're no god anymore."

"I'm not enjoying it," Solmir growled.

Another laugh, this one sounding truly amused. "You always were the rudest of them, Solmir."

The water was at their waists, too dark to see through and ice-cold.

Neve pushed herself as close to Solmir as she could, teeth beginning to chatter. He touched her carelessly now, with none of the distance he'd shown as they made their way to the Heart Tree. He'd given her all the magic and apparently didn't want any of it back.

What had changed?

No time to puzzle over it now, not while they were stared down by the most powerful Old One left, not while her mind felt as if it were starting to winnow away at the edges as she was scrutinized by something so massive, so unknowable.

Solmir's arms tightened around her. "Whatever you're planning to do," he snarled at the god, "do it."

"As you wish," the Leviathan said.

In an instant, the water rose, closing over their heads, drowning them in black and cold. The current rushed around them, trying to pull them away from each other; she clawed into Solmir's back, held on to his hair. His arms felt stone-hard from the strain of his muscles.

Neve held her breath until it felt like her lungs would burst. They couldn't die here, not ensouled as they were, but it still felt like death when her mouth inevitably opened, finally took in a drowning throatful of the dark, endless sea.

She choked on it, and knew nothing.

~~~~~~~~~~~~~~~~~~~~~

Neve came to with her head propped against Solmir's bare shoulder. His skin was wet, made sticky with drying salt, enough to make it hurt when Neve peeled herself off him. Though he'd lost his shirt in the maelstrom, she'd kept her nightgown, kept the dark coat. Her hand delved deep into the pocket, heart in her throat. It only migrated back down to her chest when her fingers closed around the god-bone and the branch-shard key. Neve let out a thankful breath, tipping back her head to see where they were.

A cavern. Huge and salt-pale, ridged with coral on the floor and the wavy lines of erosion on the walls, but mostly dry, and full of breathable air.

But whatever relief she might've felt was eclipsed by the sight of the Leviathan at the front of the cavern.

It had changed—partially, at least. Made itself something easier to comprehend, something that didn't tear at the border of her brain to contemplate. Before them, a figure on a throne, beautiful in the way a shark was beautiful, all paleness and sharp edges. Its black, flat eyes watched them with something like curiosity, though the emotion wasn't quite so human as that. Like an animal trying to feign interest, imitating things it didn't really understand or care about. The flesh, though pale, looked leathery, like it had been embalmed.

The Leviathan's lover, she realized in a rush, remembering what the Seamstress had said about how the Old One had made the corpse into a puppet. The knowledge made the creature on the driftwood throne even more awful to look at.

Though it was still better than looking directly at the massive being behind it—the thing she'd seen peering into the castle, the thing that had spoken with the terrible voice. Vaguely sharklike, but large enough that Neve could still see only pieces of it at a time, flickering in and out of view like something hidden behind a gauzy curtain.

She was thankful for that.

The entire cavern was bathed in a pale glow that made both shapes hazy, and if she focused on the man-figure, the monster behind it faded to nearly nothing but occasional flashes, shadow and light seen from fathoms below the surface.

Strings of seaweed, leached of color like everything else here, wound around the man-figure's ankles and wrists and neck, snaking backward into the haze. The leash by which the vast, sharklike thing manipulated the marionette it had made of its former penitent.

Neve fought down a shudder.

The stone of the cavern was damp; barnacles clung here and there, shells scattered, holding tiny pools in shining upturned centers. Spikes of glittering rock thrust up from floor and ceiling, still speckled with waterdrops. Neve glanced behind her—the back wall of the cavern was open, and beyond was the black ocean, glassy and endless. The water stopped right at the cavern's lip, held back by some invisible force.

She thought of drowning, swallowing cold water. The Leviathan could snap its hold so easily, let all that immense sea come rushing in on them.

Next to her, Solmir pushed up on shaky legs. He didn't look at her, blue eyes fixed on the man-monster-god, but when he held out his hand, she took it, let him pull her to standing beside him.

"Welcome." Still that reverberating, terrible voice, but softened somehow. Forced through a throat that had once been human, and thus made easier for her mind to comprehend. "So pleased to have the pleasure of your company."

"You didn't exactly extend an invitation we could refuse," Solmir said drily.

Strings of seaweed tipped the corpse-puppet's head back, unhinged its jaw. Laughter rolled out, a slithering tone that hurt Neve's ears. "Come now, once-King, you didn't think you could sail through my kingdom without my knowing? I may be diminished, but not so much as that." The thing rose from its seat, fluid as a current despite its seaweed articulation. "I assumed you knew I would call on you."

"You know what they say about assuming."

"Manners, manners." The Leviathan's tone was distracted, its shark-black eyes fixed on Neve rather than Solmir. With a subtle twitch of his shoulder, Solmir put himself between the two of them, chin tipped up, wet hair dripping down his back.

The Leviathan smiled, showing razor rows of teeth. "Step before her all you want, boy," it said quietly, "but you can't hide that kind of magic."

And for the first time since he'd given it to her, before she stepped into the Heart Tree, Neve truly looked at what magic had made her.

Before, it had only darkened the veins at her wrists, her neck, places where skin was thin and the nexus of blood showed through. But now, as she pushed up the sleeves of Solmir's coat, her arms were dark-laced all the way to her elbows. And when she shrugged the coat off her shoulder, all the veins there were black, too, coalescing in a knot of shadow right over her heart. Thorns made vambraces around her forearms, studded the jut of her collarbone.

She looked up at Solmir and saw the reflection of her own eyes in his. Black, the whites swallowed, with only a slight hint of brown at her irises. Her soul, still in there.

She thought of how Solmir's eyes had flickered in those moments when he took in so much magic, like his soul wanted to sink into it, become part of it. Neve didn't feel anything like that, didn't feel anything that might be a sinking soul, and she didn't know what that meant.

"You held all this?" she whispered. "But you didn't look…I didn't…"

A swallow worked down his throat. "I'm rather accustomed to holding shadow, Neverah."

Another chuckle from the Leviathan, standing before its driftwood throne. "And this isn't even the power of a god. You've only killed two, correct? The Serpent, the Oracle? And you had to use that up to get to the Heart Tree. So this is just all that magic from the lesser beasts you've slaughtered along the way." It shook its head, bones clicking. "It appears you had a practical reason for holding it all, once-King, if she changes so with such a small amount of power." Black eyes narrowed, and the seaweed tendrils attached to either side of its mouth pulled rubbery lips into a sinister, too-wide smile. "More than one practical reason, I mean."

Solmir's jaw clenched beneath his beard.

"You had a change of heart." The Leviathan's bony hand rose to rest over where its heart should be. "Or should I say a change of soul?"

Neve's brows drew together. "What is it talking about?"

"Yes, Solmir." The Leviathan steepled its fingers, smiling again. Behind it, the flash of a massive dark eye, there and then gone. "What am I talking about?"

Silence in the cavern, other than the drip of salt water from the ceiling.

Solmir's eyes closed. He pulled in a breath. He shifted forward in front of Neve, so no part of him touched any part of her.

"I changed my mind about sacrificing you," he said finally.

For a moment, Neve stood motionless, thoughtless, as much a

marionette as the corpse before the throne. When she found her voice, it wasn't articulate, wasn't anything but wounded. "What?"

He'd tensed as if he expected her fist, but the broken sound of her question seemed to wound him more. Solmir kept his eyes closed, reached up to rub at the puckered scars on his brow. "The easiest way to bring the Kings to the surface is with a vessel," he murmured, like he didn't want the Leviathan to hear, like he wanted this confession to be between them alone. "Something to hold their souls and take them to a place where they can be killed. And magic and souls…you know how that goes. It's hard to carry both."

"But you did. *I* am, currently."

"Hard, not impossible." He dropped his hand, finally looked at her. His expression…she'd seen Solmir look pained, but this was different. His eyes were almost beseeching, a shine in them that spoke of deep aches unable to be hidden, no matter how he wanted to. "I was going to let them use you as a vessel. When the Heart Tree opened and they were drawn to it, the one of us with no magic would've been the easiest for them to take."

He said it quick and harsh, almost like he thought it could hide that look on his face, the way his hand kept twitching toward her and falling.

Neve swallowed. She knew how to keep calm when receiving terrible news, knew how to remain poised even in the worst circumstances. So she tilted her chin and steeled her spine and hoped that was enough to hide the burn in her eyes. Foolish. She was so foolish, to have thought he…

She didn't let herself finish that. "And what changed your plan, once-King?"

The use of the term from her hit home. Solmir flinched, just slightly, just enough for her to see it. "What changed my mind," he said, "is that I realized I couldn't kill you. Not even to save the fucking world."

Neither one of them moved. Neither one of them spoke. They only stood there, the confession thrown between them like a gauntlet.

At the front of the cavern, the Leviathan clapped its hands. "Well," it said, "that *does* make things interesting."

Solmir turned away from her, the movement heavy, like something weighed him to the spot. "Happy?" he spat at the Old One. "Is this why you brought us here?"

"No," the Leviathan answered, its tone nearly giddy. "Just an added bonus."

"Then why?"

"Curiosity." The Leviathan tapped one bony finger against its jaw. "I felt the Heart Tree open. I felt someone enter. But then I felt them come back out."

There was something calculating in its tone, something that told Neve the god didn't speak the whole truth, only a piece of it. But maybe that was just how gods talked.

"Odd, that a quest to find the Heart Tree would be successful, only to fail right after," the Leviathan continued. Its fingers twitched. Around Neve and Solmir's feet, a ring of coral began, slowly, to grow. "Odd, that someone would enter the nexus between worlds, their only way home, and then decide to stay."

The coral grew faster now, nearly to Neve's knees. She tried to step over it; a thread of seaweed wound from between the stones and tangled around her foot, holding her in place. When she stumbled, Solmir grabbed her arm, and she shook it off. She couldn't take him touching her, not right now.

"The two of you fascinate me," the Leviathan mused as the coral grew taller, now at Solmir's neck. "The once-King and the Shadow Queen, tied together and yet separate, trying to bring things back into balance when you're both so riddled in darkness. The Shadow Queen, especially. You chose the mantle; now I want to see how you'll wear it."

"By keeping me here?" Panic clogged her throat, the tiny prison the coral built making her breath come too fast, like her lungs couldn't find enough air.

"For a time," the Leviathan replied. She couldn't see it anymore; the coral blocked everything but a circle of light above Solmir's head. "Besides, it seems like you two have things to discuss. Enjoy the privacy."

Then the circle of light closed, the coral prison complete, and they were plunged into total darkness.

Chapter Twenty-Seven

Neve

It reminded her of the Serpent's cairn, a solid dark that pressed against her skin, that robbed her of all her senses, even deeper than the black water when the Leviathan brought them under.

"Dammit." Solmir, snarling right next to her ear, the close quarters of their prison pressing them shoulder to shoulder. "*Shit.*"

The pound of something against stone—his fist, whistling past her cheek. He was so close that she caught his arm on her first try, stopping him from slamming a punch into the wall again.

"Solmir." His name a command as she caught his hand, his fingers slicked with blood against her own. Without sight, her sense of smell was heightened, the pine of him and the salt of the sea undercut with thick copper. Her other palm reached out to touch the wall. Jagged coral, bloodstained. She was glad she couldn't see the mess he'd undoubtedly made of his hand.

Stiffness, then he sagged, the motion of it felt rather than seen. "We're trapped," he said unnecessarily.

"Can we kill it?" Maybe it should alarm her that killing was now her first idea, but Neve didn't care to think about that right now. "When we get out of here, if we get the chance—"

"No." Solmir cut her off, firm. "If the Leviathan dies, the Shadowlands will be completely destabilized."

The wall was too rough to slide down—Neve sat gingerly, keeping only a breath away from Solmir's legs as she did so, the shape of him guiding her in the dark. When she met seashell-pocked floor, she leaned her head back against the jagged coral. "What is it going to do?"

"Fuck if I know." His sigh was so heavy it stirred her hair. "Not kill us, we know that much. And it won't hurt you."

"What about you?" It shouldn't kick up her heartbeat, the thought of the Old One hurting Solmir. Not after everything she'd just learned, everything still swimming in the space between them. And yet.

"The Leviathan has never been what I'd call a friend." Dry, but with an undercurrent of apprehension. "And you're the interesting one, Shadow Queen."

There was a question in it, harkening back to what the Leviathan said—that she'd chosen the mantle, chosen to stay. But that discussion could wait.

First, Neve had a score to settle.

No tears—they burned in her eyes, but she wouldn't let them fall, even if he couldn't see. "You were going to *sacrifice* me." She couldn't keep the waver from her voice—Neve wanted to be a thing beyond hurting, but he softened all her armor. "Up until a minute before the Heart Tree opened, you were going to let me be a vessel for the Kings. You *bastard*." Her voice fully broke then, and she pulled in a deep, shaky breath. "How could you do that?"

"I didn't." Barely a whisper, rough and hoarse. "I didn't do it, Neve. I couldn't."

"You want another medal?" Neve wiped at her streaming eyes, her nose. "One for keeping your soul, one for deciding at the last minute not to kill me?"

"We both know I don't deserve any medals." Solmir moved to sit beside her, the salt dried on his skin rasping against the sleeve of Neve's coat. *His* coat. A sudden urge filled her to rip it off, but she didn't.

"There's one thing we can agree on." She swiped at her eyes with the back of her wrist, streaking his blood across her cheekbone. "I *trusted* you, Solmir."

The emphasis on the past tense was intentional. Neve let it hang in the heavy air.

"I know," Solmir murmured. Paused, and the next question came soft and low as a prayer. "Is it something I can earn back?"

She clamped her lip between her teeth, pulled her knees up to her chest. *Yes* welled in her throat like a river dammed back, that loneliness tugging at her again, reminding her that he was the only thing in this whole underworld even close to human. He'd intended to betray her, even if he'd changed his mind. Even if he'd kissed her to pass on the magic that would save her, even if that kiss felt real.

I couldn't kill you, not even to save the fucking world.

"You can try to earn it back." The dark made it impossible to see anything, but she turned her head in his direction anyway. "It won't be easy."

A nod, felt rather than seen. "It shouldn't be."

They sat in silence, other than the rasp of their breathing. The heat of their bodies ovened the small space, turning dampness to thick humidity. Neve slipped her hand into the coat's pocket, closed it around the bone and the key. The bone she stuck in her boot. The key she weighed in her hand for a moment before reaching up and threading the open end through the fine hairs at the nape of her neck, further knotting her tangles to hold it in place.

Then she pulled off Solmir's coat. Set it next to her. The lack of a barrier between them pressed their shoulders together, skin on skin. The magic curled in her center spiraled lazily, a billow of smoke from a snuffed candle. But there was no pull from him, no tug like he was trying to take it back. He'd given her the power and intended to let her keep it.

That was a comfort, at least.

"Did they ever come?" she asked quietly. "The Kings?"

"No." Solmir shifted, his salt water–coarsened hair brushing her arm. "Maybe they were on their way. I don't know how all that works, the way power pulls."

"Or they figured us out. Knew they couldn't outsmart us."

Solmir snorted. "That might be giving ourselves too much credit. Maybe there's a reason they didn't come, resisting on purpose."

"What kind of reason?"

"I have no idea, Neverah." He sounded weary. She felt the brush of his hair as he tilted his head back against the coral.

But she wasn't one to wallow. Neve had never let seemingly impossible circumstances leave her languishing before, and she wouldn't start here. "You said giving the Kings a vessel was the easiest way to kill them. But is there another?"

A pause. "Yes," Solmir said finally.

She waited for him to elaborate. He didn't. His shoulder was tense against hers, rigid as stone.

Neve gave one nod, decisive, even though he couldn't see it. "We'll do that, then."

Some of the rigidity bled from his muscles, relaxing against her by a fraction. The close quarters made touching inevitable, and both of them accepted it. There was reassurance in the solid shape of another person, giving form to the dark.

Her thumbnail worked nervously against the thin fabric of her nightgown. "I saw Red, while I was in the Tree."

"You did?"

"She was there somehow. Called when I went into the Tree, I guess. She said something about a key..." Neve reached up, touched the one she'd secured in her hair. "The Heart Tree gave me one, too."

"It gave you a key?" Solmir sounded puzzled. "I'm not sure what that means, to be honest."

"That makes two of us." Neve shrugged. "It was in my hand when I came out."

"When you chose to come out," he murmured.

That question again, hanging above her head like an ax set to fall. The key the Tree had given her shifted against her neck as Neve adjusted her seat on the hard, shell-pocked ground, its cold a welcome

counterpoint to the heat inside their coral cell. She said nothing. If he
wanted an answer, he had to ask the question, with words instead of
tone and waiting.

"Why did you do that?" There was incredulity in his voice, but also
something like awe. "You could've gone home, Neve. Why didn't you?"

And she still didn't know, not really, not in a way that lent itself to
easy words. All she had was that feeling, that indelible sense that something here still needed to be done. That were she to go home now, there
would be consequences. Maybe not for her, maybe not ones she would
see. But someone would. Mistakes demanded payment, and they'd
come due eventually.

"Because until the Kings are gone, I'm not done," she said finally.
"*We're* not done."

That collective pronoun made him sit up straight next to her. She
felt the stir of air as he nodded, then another as he moved again, his arm
rasping against hers. "Neve, I'm—*Fuck*, that hurts."

She fumbled in the dark until her hand found his arm, traveled
down to his fingers. Her palm slicked with his blood when it met the
mess he'd made of his fist. Solmir cursed again, jerking away from her.
"Shadows damn me, woman, what part of *fuck, that hurts* made you
think grabbing it is a good idea?"

"Stop whining," Neve muttered. Gently, she felt along Solmir's fingers. One of them bent at a sickening angle. "You broke a finger when
you punched the wall."

"The wall deserved it."

"It needs to be set, if you don't want it to heal crooked."

"I feel like a crooked finger is the least of my— Shadows damn me to
the *deepest* pits of the earth and leave me there!"

Neve let go of his finger, the bones now set straight. He couldn't see
her self-satisfied smirk, but she gave him one anyway. "That will swell."

"Oh, will it?" he muttered mockingly. But she felt him bend his fingers against her knee, testing them. "I suppose I should take that ring
off, then."

"Probably."

He lifted his hand from her knee. A moment later, his fingers found hers, placed something in her palm.

A cold circle of silver.

"Keep it for me," Solmir said.

Neve weighed it in her fist. Then she slipped it over her thumb.

Chapter Twenty-Eight

Red

"A re you going to eat?"

Eammon's voice was quiet in the dim of the cabin. Red saw his shadow against the wall, the edges diffuse from the sunlight up on the deck.

"You know, that wasn't really a question." The edge of the bunk sank down as he settled his weight on it. "You're going to eat, it's just a question of how pleasant the experience will be for everyone involved."

She snorted weakly. Flipped over so she could curl around his knee instead of her pillow. "In that case, the answer is yes. I'd rather eat jerky of my own accord than have you nearly drown me in broth again."

"Good girl," Eammon rumbled.

Red forced herself to sit up, wincing against the pain in her head, and accepted the napkin-wrapped dinner and cup of lukewarm ale Eammon handed her.

It was the first time she'd managed to eat since the night before last, since the key in her pocket pulled her into a strange dream-space—the Heart Tree—and revealed her sister, only to take her away. The key was still under her pillow. She'd considered breaking it, more than once, in a fit of rage that it'd brought her so close only to fail. But she couldn't do it.

Her sister, wreathed in thorns, black-eyed and black-veined, changed by the Shadowlands in ways that echoed Red's changes from the Wilderwood. Wasn't that what the voice meant, when the mirror in the tower broke? That they had to mirror each other, match each other? But they'd done it, and here they still were, stuck in opposite worlds.

Red chewed methodically, took a swallow of ale to wash it down. She tasted none of it. "I don't understand."

"I know." A constant refrain, what they'd repeated to each other over and over again since Eammon found Red collapsed on the deck. "But we still have the key. Maybe Kiri can tell us how to make it bring you to Neve again."

She nodded listlessly. "If she'll come."

There was the hardest part, the one that cut deepest. It wasn't that Red had done something wrong, wasn't that the Heart Tree wouldn't let Neve go. Neve had *chosen* to stay.

And Red didn't know how to process that.

On some level, she recognized the irony—Red had chosen to enter the Wilderwood, and Neve had chosen to stay in the Shadowlands. Both of them refusing to be saved. One more reflection.

And there were the things she said, about Solmir being on their side, about killing the Kings. Clearly, Neve thought she had a part to play in it. But couldn't she do it from *here*, where Red could keep her safe?

Because there, sunk into the shadows, the only person to keep her safe was Solmir. And that thought made Red's hands curl into claws, made tiny vines peek from her nailbeds and her veins run springtime green.

Eammon didn't try to tell her everything would be fine. He didn't speak empty words of pointless comfort. Instead, he put one large, scarred hand on her thigh and used the other to push her ivy-threaded hair behind her ear. "If she'll come," he repeated. Then, "And whether she does or not is her decision, Red. You can't make her do something she doesn't want to do." His mouth tipped up at the corner. "It's never worked out well for the two of you."

She huffed a halfhearted laugh and drained the rest of the ale. "No, it certainly hasn't." Her lips pressed together, brows drawing down. "I just…I don't understand. I don't understand why she pulled all that darkness in at the grove, why she let herself get trapped in the Shadowlands in the first place. Surely there was another way."

His green-and-amber eyes glinted in the dim light, gaze level. "She probably thought the same thing when you insisted on going to the Wilderwood."

"It's *not* the same thing."

"It's close." He shrugged. "You both got tangled up in something beyond yourself. With people who don't deserve it."

"Don't you dare compare yourself to him." It came out low, nearly a snarl. "He tried to kill you, Eammon. He killed your parents."

"He had a part in it," Eammon agreed softly, "but their death was a complicated thing. We could just as well blame the Wilderwood." He paused, looked away. "Or blame Ciaran and Gaya themselves. Very rarely can the entirety of fault be held by one person."

Red gnawed on the corner of her lip. She'd told him and the others what Neve said about Solmir while they were in the Heart Tree. That they were on the same side. Eammon hadn't seemed as incredulous as she thought he should be. When they'd become the Wilderwood, some of the latent anger in Eammon had been tempered. Forests were old, slow-growing things, patient and even, and some of that had seeped into Eammon, too.

Red kept waiting for some of that patience and placidity to temper her. Thus far, it hadn't happened.

"I'm not saying we forgive him. You know that." He lifted a heavy brow. "If you already laid your claim on the first punch, I have the second."

"Raffe can have third," Red said.

"Working with Solmir doesn't mean we forget what he's done." Eammon tucked another strand of ivy behind Red's ear. "Once this is all taken care of—once the Kings are gone, completely—then we can talk about retribution. About fault and blame."

"And we can kill him," Red said brightly.

Eammon snorted. "We'll see."

She watched him, lip still between her teeth. A hulking shadow in dim light was her Wolf, his hair long, the bark on his forearms rough against her leg. "You," she said softly, "are far more compassionate than you have any right to be."

He leaned forward, lips brushing over hers. "Someone taught me that sometimes it's all right to feel sympathy for monsters."

One kiss, for comfort rather than heat. They'd broken away, foreheads tilted together, when someone darkened the doorway.

"Land on the horizon." Kayu didn't sound exactly enthused about it. "We'll be at the temple dock by this time tomorrow."

<hr />

The Rylt looked very different from Valleyda.

All the greenery in Valleyda was carefully cultivated—flowers bred to keep hardy in the cold, banks of tough grasses that would survive short summers and long, bitter winters. Other than the Wilderwood, most forests were all pine and fir, more blue and gray than green.

But the Rylt was green all over. Even the beach beyond the small dock that serviced the Temple was fringed with waving fronds of grass, hillocks of it sprouting from the sand, like the earth here was so abundant, it couldn't be held back. Flowers bloomed in the moors beyond, carpeted a deep and verdant green.

Red expected the Wilderwood within her to be pleased when they stepped off the gangplank, feet once again on solid ground, especially among all these growing things. But it stayed as it had throughout the voyage, still and close and on edge.

She shot a look at Eammon. He met her eyes, gave her a tiny nod. He felt it, too. This place might be abundant, but it wasn't home.

And what waited for them here wasn't welcoming.

Kayu strode past them, headed for the dunes. "Temple is just ahead." Her voice was quiet, preoccupied. Nothing like the funny, playful woman she'd been in Valleyda and on the ship. She'd grown quieter and quieter as they drew closer to the Rylt, drawing in on herself. Even Raffe couldn't get her to laugh there at the end, only give a wan smile.

The man in question walked up to Red and Eammon, all three of them watching Kayu climb the path cut into the dunes beyond the dock. "She doesn't seem all that happy to be here," Red said after a moment of quiet.

"No, she doesn't." Raffe frowned as he watched Kayu draw farther away. With a sigh, he started forward, tugging up his hood against the wind off the sea. "Though frankly, if anyone was enthused about visiting Kiri, I'd be concerned for their mental stability."

Fife and Lyra were the last to disembark. Lyra looked around curiously, always excited to see somewhere new, but Fife seemed as apprehensive as Red and Eammon felt. He rubbed at the Mark hidden beneath his sleeve. "Well. Let's get this over with."

"At least the food will improve," Red said, searching for a bright side as they started through the sand.

"If you like sheep's stomach," Lyra replied.

Red grimaced.

The Temple was immediately visible when they topped the dunes, gleaming marble amid all the green. A profuse garden of herbs and wildflowers grew around the plain driftwood fence and shallow stone steps that led to the Temple doors, ruffled by the ever-present breeze off the water.

Kayu stood by the door, shifting from foot to foot, not making eye contact with any of them. Raffe stood next to her, face drawn into uncomfortable lines.

When the rest of them reached the door, he was the one to turn and face it, drawing his spine straight and his shoulders back. His hand lifted to knock.

But the door swung in before he could.

A priestess with a white, freckled face and golden-red hair stood on the other side, smiling. "The party from Valleyda," she said brightly. "We've been expecting you."

All of them cast sidelong glances, shifted from foot to foot. All of them but Kayu. She brushed past the priestess without looking at her. "Come on. I'll take you to Kiri."

The priestess at the door stepped aside with another smile. "Yes, do come in."

Red gave Eammon one more quick, apprehensive glance. His fingers wrapped around hers as they crossed the threshold, and it felt like crossing into enemy territory.

The inside of the Ryltish Temple was just as simple as the outside, the stone walls unadorned with anything but a single tapestry of five crowns—four in quadrants, one in the center, a pattern Red recognized from the Temple in Valleyda. Three hallways branched from the circular foyer, stretching from side to side and directly in front of the door, with no sign to what might lay within them. Sconces adorned the walls, providing wavering light in the gloom.

All the candles were dark gray.

Eammon gave the candles a wary glance. "Say the word, and we're gone," he murmured, low enough that only she could hear. Leaves rustled in his voice. "I won't even complain about the seasickness."

"We have to see what she knows," Red whispered back. The key burned in her pocket. "We have to see if she knows how to get to Neve again."

His teeth ground in his jaw, but Eammon nodded.

Kayu headed toward the central hallway, not looking behind her to see if they followed. Lyra's brow furrowed. "How does she know where to go?"

"Maybe she's traveled here before?" But even Raffe didn't sound convinced. A curse hissed through his teeth as he hurried after Kayu.

Fife slid his eyes to Red and Eammon. "Do you feel as nervous about this as I do?"

"Absolutely," Eammon muttered.

Red sighed, releasing Eammon's arm to start after Kayu and Raffe. "You two are worse than my old nursemaids."

"They have been for centuries," Lyra said.

The hallway was silent, the quiet broken only by the sound of their feet over the stone. A few more priestesses passed by, but not many, and none of them spoke, barely acknowledging them at all. The corridor was lined with doors, some of them open, revealing empty cloister rooms with naked beds and empty wardrobes.

"Not many priestesses here," Fife said. "Did they turn out the ones who didn't agree with them, or have them killed, do you think?"

Lyra scowled at him. "Do you *have* to make this more morbid than it is?"

Nerves were a ball in Red's throat, difficult to swallow past. Eammon rubbed his thumb over her knuckles.

Up ahead, Kayu stopped at a closed door, one that didn't look any different from the others lining the hall. "These are the High Priestess's quarters."

"How do you know that?" Red asked quietly.

The other woman's expression didn't waver, but her dark eyes widened, just momentarily, before she flicked them away. "I've been here before," she said airily. "I studied here before I went to Valleyda."

Red wasn't sure she bought that. The tightening of Eammon's fingers said he didn't, either. But what was there to do about it now? They needed to talk to Kiri, and Kayu had brought them here to do it. The rest they could figure out later.

After Neve was home.

A moment, then Raffe stepped up beside Kayu, put his hand on the door handle. "Here we go," he breathed, and pushed the door open.

Chapter Twenty-Nine

Red

The first thing Red noticed was how small Kiri looked.

In her memories of the woman—all of them dark and bloodied—the High Priestess *towered*, crimson and white and vengeful, eyes ablaze with unholy, unsound light. But the figure on the bed before her was brittle, frail. Bruises marred the thin skin beneath her eyes, and the rise and fall of her chest seemed labored, like it was an effort to lift the sheets that covered her.

The room was small. The six of them crowded it, especially with Eammon and Raffe's height. Nothing cut the blank white of the walls other than another tapestry like the one in the circular foyer, stitched with crowns.

Lyra broke the silence, though it was with a whisper. "What's the matter with her?"

"The High Priestess is ill." A new voice from behind them; another priestess, dark-haired and white-skinned, bustled around their group with a cloth thrown over her shoulder and a bowl of steaming water in her hands. She cast a glance at Kayu, but other than that focused only on Kiri. "She has been since she arrived. Knowing the Kings' will is heavy business and isn't easy on a body."

The priestess dipped the cloth in the water and gently patted Kiri's brow. The High Priestess's eyes rolled back and forth beneath her lids, chapped lips forming the beginnings of words but never quite managing to free a sound.

"She wakes occasionally," the priestess continued, as if they were family by a sickbed. "To impart what the Kings have told her to pass on. Good news." She turned a smile on them, apparently not noticing how her words made every other spine in the room draw up in worry. "Perhaps she will wake for you soon. Are you faithful?"

"Hardly." Eammon stepped forward, his voice graveled and near a growl. As he did, he pulled down his hood, revealing the green-haloed eyes, the small points that were left of his antlers, the ring of bark around his neck.

Red stepped up next to him, pulling off her own hood and shaking out her ivy and gold hair. Her crimson cloak was in her bag, but the signs of the Wilderwood within her branded her the Lady Wolf even without it.

Eammon held out his hand, eyes not leaving the priestess. Red grasped it, and bent her mouth in a sharp, feral grin.

The Wolves at the door.

But the priestess didn't seem taken aback. Instead, her slight, pleasant smile widened. "Ah," she said. "The Wardens."

There wasn't time for Red's confusion to show itself on her face. Because as soon as their title left the priestess's lips, Kiri's eyes flew open.

Piercing blue, the High Priestess's fevered gaze darted directly to Red, the rest of her staying preternaturally still. She gave the unsettling impression of a waking corpse.

"Redarys." Her name a rasp, the *s* held too long. "You've finally come."

Eammon's grip on her hand was tight enough to hurt. Red squeezed back, leaving her anxiety there instead of in her expression.

"Have you been waiting?" she asked.

The smile started at one side of Kiri's mouth, moved slowly to the other. "Oh, we have."

Beside her, Eammon waited like a bow poised to fire, all tense lines. Fife stood just behind him, hand on his dagger hilt and body positioned between the priestess on the bed and Lyra, whose fawn-brown eyes were wide. On Red's other side, Raffe had maneuvered himself between Kayu and Kiri, so subtly that she wondered if he even realized he'd done it. Only Kayu didn't look surprised. She just looked worried.

Kiri's eyes narrowed, unfocused. "You've seen her already," she murmured, like she was reading it out of the air. "You've been to the space between. The Heart Tree. You took it in, carry it with you."

The key in Red's pocket burned, almost hot to the touch. She reached in and pulled it out—the pulse in it was faint again, but the golden lines tracing the bark flared, glowing bright against the white wood.

"And she has her key, too, now," Kiri said, watching the gentle golden light in Red's hand. "The way back, strung between you both, two points of a compass. Either one of you can enter now, you know."

Red's heartbeat kicked against her throat. "You mean I can go there again? I can bring her out?"

Kiri's mouth opened and a laugh rang out, though nothing else about her expression changed. Her blue eyes still looked vacant. "Stupid wolf-girl," she chuckled. "The Shadow Queen chose to stay. She chose to fulfill her destiny. To become the vessel."

"Shadow Queen?" The title itched at Red's shoulder blades. "What do you mean?"

"You're the Golden-Veined, she's the Shadow Queen. How it was always going to be." Kiri turned back to the ceiling, as if looking at Red bored her. "They've whispered of you to me since I was a girl, you know. Since I bled on that branch at the edge of the woods. It lodged them in my head, and then I spent all my days just waiting for you. Listening to them whisper."

Something like pity made the leaves between Red's ribs stir. Here was another reflection, warped and twisted. "You bled on a branch, too. Like Arick did. That's how they could talk to you."

Kiri didn't answer. Instead, she laughed again, but this time she closed her eyes, and the corners of her mouth twitched, like the laugh might become a sob at any moment.

"She's mad," Raffe whispered, coming up to Red's other side. On the opposite, Eammon stood silent and stoic. "Does any of this make sense to you?"

"Almost?" Eammon murmured. Behind him, Fife nodded, rubbing at his Mark.

Red took a breath, tried to make herself calm and even. If she spoke to the High Priestess as if all of this was clear, maybe it would start to be. "So I'm the Golden-Veined, and Neve is the Shadow Queen."

"As I *just* said," Kiri singsonged to the ceiling. "You never were the smart sister."

A low sound started in Eammon's throat, but Red knocked their clasped hands against his abdomen, a silent request for him to hold his tongue. "All right," Red said slowly. "So how does that help me bring Neve home?"

"Oh, she'll come home. One way or another." Kiri's eyes twitched beneath her closed eyelids, back and forth, as if she were watching something play out in her head. "Solmir thinks he saved her. He knows nothing."

The name made all Red's muscles tense, but she stayed silent, hoping the mad priestess would fill the quiet.

"He knows there must be a vessel, and he thinks it can be him. It could've been, once, but now that they know there's another option, they'll never settle for him. Stupid. All of you, made stupid by your caring, over and over." She shook her head, red hair scraping over the pillow. "There are two vessels, mirrors, reflections. That is how it has to be. It will be either an end or a beginning, and that is up to her."

"To me?" Red asked.

"To the Shadow Queen."

So it all came down to Neve. Neve in the dark with only a fallen god for company, Neve in the shadows she'd chosen.

"The Kings know the stakes are high." Another smile crossed Kiri's face, but this one was almost dreamy. "They know all of it rides on her shoulders, whether they will find salvation or annihilation. But they are confident. It came so naturally to her, drowning in the dark."

"Tell me how to save her." It sounded like begging. It was. In a rush of movement, Red stepped forward, letting go of Eammon's hand. She heard him start after her, heard the low murmur of Fife's voice, telling him to let her go. "Tell me how to bring Neve out of the Shadowlands. Please, Kiri."

"You can do nothing. Even with your key, your way between worlds. She will not leave until her path reaches its end."

Tears blurred Red's eyes; she swiped them away with a savage slash of her hand. "Then what am I supposed to *do*?"

"Wait," the High Priestess said. "You are to wait." Her fingers twitched on the blanket, pale and thin. "You are a vessel, too. One for light, and one for dark. And what happens when they collide? Entropy. Emptiness." A soft laugh, made chilling by its gentleness. "You, Golden-Veined, Second Daughter, *Lady Wolf*, can do nothing but wait. Just like they did, all those centuries."

The last words faded, grew quiet. By the end, Kiri's chest rose and fell rhythmically, like her doomsday words had lulled her back to sleep.

They all stood still, silent. The key burned in Red's hand. Slowly, she closed her fist around it, the golden glow seeping through the gaps in her fingers.

"Well," the dark-haired priestess said brightly. "I hope that was enlightening. I'll show you to your rooms."

***

"We can't stay here."

The whisper came from Fife, low and anxiety-churned, only loud enough for the rest of them to hear. Paces ahead, the priestess who'd bathed Kiri's brow walked unhurriedly down the hall, apparently leading them to prepared quarters.

Red's mind couldn't catch up, still stuck back in the sickroom with Kiri. There was no way to bring Neve home. It reverberated, echoed, a constant tic at the back of her head. The key in her hand could bring her to the Heart Tree, but it couldn't make Neve come out.

She made a small, pained noise. Eammon's arm, wrapped around her shoulder, pulled her tighter.

"No, we can't stay," he agreed quietly. He glanced at Kayu. "The galley is still waiting, right?"

The Niohni princess had been silent since they reached Kiri's quarters, her dark eyes fixed straight ahead, her mouth a thin line. At Eammon's words, she seemed almost to rouse from sleep, shaking her head like her mind had been somewhere else entirely. "I think so," she said softly. "I mean, yes, it's been chartered for a week. They should still be at the dock."

"Then that's where we go," Eammon said. "We found what we came for."

Maybe, in the most stringent sense. They'd heard what Kiri had to say, learned that the key Red held would open the Heart Tree, learned that Neve had chosen to stay in the Shadowlands. But what they'd come here for was a way to get her *out*, and they still didn't have that.

Red's eyes pressed shut. Opened. Stung with tears she wouldn't let fall.

As if the thought came collectively, the six of them sped up their stride, hurrying toward the door that would take them out onto the moors, away from the Temple and its mad High Priestess.

But as they approached the freckled priestess still standing by the door, she said sweetly, "Where do you think you're going?"

The threatening words delivered in such a nonthreatening voice made Red's steps stutter. Her eyes narrowed, the veins in her arms already blushing green.

But it was Raffe who spoke, his tone low and courtly and more intimidating for it. "Excuse me?"

The priestess's expression was pleasant, her eyes blank. "We have rooms for you."

The other, dark-haired priestess nodded with a wide, guileless smile.

"We aren't taking them." Kayu spoke like a dagger strike, quick and sharp. "We're leaving."

The freckled priestess cocked her head like an inquisitive bird. "How?"

The question raised gooseflesh on the skin between Red's shoulder blades. She turned, rushed to the door, out into the fragrant garden with its bobbing blooms, out to the edge of the dune, where the sparkling band of the sea became visible.

The dock was empty.

Chapter Thirty

Neve

"Tell me a story," Neve said.

Time was a slippery thing at best in the Shadowlands, hard to hold on to, its passing difficult to mark. But in the utter darkness of their coral prison, it was completely impossible. They could've been there days, hours, and would have no way of knowing. There wasn't even hunger or thirst to go on. The only things that ever changed were the occasional rumbles through the ground, the echoes of larger quakes elsewhere.

The shudders of a world breaking apart.

Solmir tilted his head back against the wall. Her eyes hadn't adjusted enough to make out his facial expressions, but she knew one knife-slash brow was arched over one blue eye. "What kind of story?"

"Anything." Neve shifted on the floor. It was impossible to find a comfortable angle in here, but it didn't stop her from trying. "A fairy tale."

He snorted. "A fairy tale." A moment of thoughtful silence. "Did you ever hear the one about the musician's lover?"

"Doesn't sound familiar."

"It's old. Probably long fallen out of fashion." A sigh, the rasp of his boot heels over stone as he stretched out his legs as far as he could. "And it's sad. Just a warning."

"Most of them are, if you look at them hard enough."

A grunt of assent. "I'm no storyteller, but the tale goes like this: Once, there was a musician—I don't remember what instrument he was supposed to play, take your pick—who was deeply in love with his wife. But she got sick and died."

"Starting out strong with the *sad* part."

"Hush, Your Majesty. Anyway, she died, and he was very upset, moping about the village, as one does. Until he was approached by a wise woman who could harness the magic in the world."

Neve sat up a bit straighter. Tales about the time when magic was free—before it was bound up in the Wilderwood and the Shadowlands, when anyone who could sense it could bend it to their will—were fascinating to her. She couldn't quite wrap her head around the notion of power being free to everyone. The Order said that it had been a time of discord, people using magic for petty reprisals and selfish gain more often than not. But the stories and the historical accounts didn't paint it that way. More often, it seemed people had used magic for good, small amounts to make a crop grow strong or a child stop coughing.

"Anyway," Solmir continued, "this wise woman said that a person's essence never really died. It lingered on in the places they loved, in the elements that made up the world, the air and earth and fire and water."

"Their soul lingered, you mean?" Neve asked.

Solmir shook his head. "*Essence* doesn't translate to *soul* in the old languages. If you want to get technical, the closest translation would be *reflection*. The word used implies multiple parts of someone remaining after they pass—a faint impression of their emotions, their thoughts, the deepest parts of them. According to this story, at least, a soul isn't the only thing that can stick around."

Her lips pressed together. "Makes our plan to get rid of the Kings seem less than ironclad."

"It's different," Solmir said. "The Kings aren't whole people anymore. They've lost themselves in bits and pieces." A shrug, jostling her shoulder. "There isn't anything left of them to reflect, once the soul is gone. Everything else has already been subsumed into the Shadowlands."

"So if you keep your humanity," Neve murmured, "you're more than a soul."

A pause. She felt his arm tense against hers. "You're more than a soul," he agreed.

Silence, for a handful of heartbeats. Then Solmir picked up the thread of the story again. "So the musician gets an idea, and asks the wise woman if someone could manage to coax the essence back to life somehow. She told him it wasn't likely, but if he went to the place his wife loved most and played her favorite song—reminded her of all the things she loved in life—he might be able to call her back. There was one caveat, though. He had to start playing at sundown, and keep his eyes closed until sunup the next day. Otherwise, she'd fade."

He'd said he wasn't much of a storyteller, but the low cadence of his voice was soothing. Neve leaned her head against the coral as she listened, shifting it back and forth until she found some kind of comfort among the jagged edges.

"So the musician went all out. He made his wife's favorite foods and packed them in her favorite blanket and went to the hill outside the village where they'd always go to watch the stars. He picked up his—well, whatever instrument it is he was supposed to play—and as soon as the sun went down, he started playing, eyes closed. He played for hours and hours, played until his fingers ached. When he'd nearly lost track of time, he felt his wife. The barest brush of her hand across his shoulders, the whisper of her voice at his ear. He kept his eyes closed. He kept playing."

Why were her eyes burning? Neve blinked. The thought of someone calling after the person they loved, doing the impossible for just a chance at seeing them again, made her heart feel too big for her ribs to cage.

"When hours had passed and he was sure dawn had to be close, he saw a flash of light from behind his eyelids. And the musician, sure that he'd finally played through the night, opened his eyes, ready to see his wife." Solmir paused. "He did. For a moment. She stood before him as hale and whole as she had been before she got sick. But then she vanished, and he saw that it was still night. The sun was still down. The light he'd thought was dawn was the glow of a torch—the villagers had come to check on him." He shifted against the rock. "The end."

She swallowed past a throat that suddenly wanted to close. "That *was* sad."

"Told you," Solmir murmured.

His silver ring hung heavy on her thumb, just loose enough for her to twist. "So what's the moral?"

"Do all stories need morals?"

"They don't need them, no, but it seems like most have them." She frowned, spinning his ring. "And most of them aren't particularly good, now that I think about it."

He huffed a rueful laugh. "Then I'll make one up." Neve heard the slight thud of fingers drumming on his knees as he thought. "I guess 'make sure it's actually the sun and not a torch' is too on the nose?"

It was her turn to make a rueful noise. "A bit." The heavy ring turned around and around her thumb. "The moral," she said finally, "is to make the most of the time you have, because chances are it will be shorter than you think."

Silence, broken only by the soft sounds of their breathing. "Neve," Solmir said finally, a breath above silence, "I—"

Whatever he'd been about to say was swallowed in the sound of rending stone. Their coral prison cracked open, seeping hazy gray light that made them both throw hands over their eyes. A gash appeared in the ceiling, wide enough for a tentacle to snake through.

It wrapped around Neve's waist. Tugged.

Solmir was on his feet, teeth bared and eyes watering, lashing at the tentacle with the fist she'd just set back to rights. It did nothing—Neve felt her stomach flip as the tentacle pulled her through the crack in the coral ceiling, scraping her spine, the prison sealing itself closed again with a *boom.*

Her eyes stung and her vision blurred, unable to quickly recover from untold hours of utter darkness. The tentacle pulled her through the air and sat her down, her watering eyes unable to pick out anything but vague gray shapes.

Slowly, her eyes adjusted, feeling coming back into muscles made numb by close quarters. She sat on a finely upholstered chair, only slightly damp. Before her, a table.

Across from her, the Leviathan.

The god sat with long corpse-fingers folded beneath its rubbery chin, shark-black eyes avid. Thin ribbons of seaweed trailed off into the dark.

"Shadow Queen." A wide smile, sharp teeth, black eyes. "We should talk."

Gradually, her vision acclimated to light again, dim as it was. Gleaming place settings before her, surrounded by sumptuous foods the likes of which she hadn't seen since a court dinner. The Leviathan—its corpse-puppet—sat across from her, watching her with blank, dead eyes.

But the sense she got from the massive god that pulled its strings was one of hunger. Hunger and curiosity.

The food before her, wine and bread and cheese, all looked perfect. But none of it was real. Illusions crafted by the god across from her, made to look like idealized versions of themselves. It was meant to comfort, Neve thought, but it did the opposite. That perfect wine was the exact opacity of blood, and in the gray-scale gloom, it was easy to imagine it would taste of copper instead of alcohol.

The seaweed threads at the corners of the Leviathan's mouth pulled its lips back into a wide, sharp-toothed smile. "I know you're not hungry, but I thought you might miss wine."

Neve sat up straight, pulling the poise of a queen around her like a cloak, despite her tangled hair and bedraggled nightgown. "Good wine, yes." She tapped a finger against the glass. "Not...whatever this is."

"Thorny thing, you are. Both literally and figuratively."

Her fists closed. Thorns pressed out from her forearms, tracking up darkened veins, catching the threadbare fabric of her skirt. She'd grown nearly used to the roil of shadowy magic in her center, the chill of it crouching at the edges of her mind, but the changes it wrought in her were still a shock every time she saw them.

The Leviathan's sharklike eyes were hard to read, but she saw its head tilt toward her hand as if it noticed something. Solmir's silver ring, glinting on her thumb. "What a hold you have on each other," it murmured.

"I don't know what you mean." Not her strongest rebuttal, but Neve couldn't let something like that hang in the air unchallenged. It was too vulnerable, like an organ pulsing outside the boundaries of a body.

"Oh, but I think you do." One of the Leviathan's hands dropped to the table, the other propping up its tilted head. It was a posture one would adopt while speaking freely to a friend, and seeing it on the corpse of the Leviathan's once-human lover made her stomach knot. "You were there, Neverah Valedren. In the nexus between the worlds, with the sister who would do anything to bring you home, and you chose to stay." Its smile widened. "Strange, how you and she toss roles back and forth. Savior and saved, villain and victim. Though you're the only one who's ever truly been a villain, aren't you?"

Her jaw firmed. She didn't respond.

"So I suppose it's not that odd, after all, how you and the once-King are drawn together." The Leviathan lifted a piece of bread, bit into it with those rows of shark teeth. The glamour on it wavered just as it entered its mouth—a gray, spongy mass of seaweed, making Neve glad she hadn't tried the wine. "You both have experience being villains in complicated stories. Shouldering complicated mantles. Like that of the Shadow Queen."

The god fell quiet. For a moment, silence, then the *slam* of something colliding with stone.

Neve's head whipped around to follow the sound. The prison the god had built for them in an instant was a knot of spiking stone and coral, impenetrable and solid in the middle of the cavern. Another *slam* came from inside.

"Let him out." It seethed from behind her teeth, an order she hadn't meant to give. "It's cruel to keep him in there."

"You care enough for him to be treated kindly? After everything he's done?" The Leviathan sounded positively delighted. It took a sip of not-wine. "No, I believe I will leave our once-King where he is for now. Let him cool off."

A swallow worked down her dry throat. Neve almost reached for the wineglass by reflex, but then remembered the mess of seaweed the bread had turned into when the Leviathan ate it. Her hand curled back in on itself, empty.

"You've complicated things for him," the Leviathan said quietly, with an air of someone thrilled to be delivering bad news. "Made it all so much more layered. This was never going to be an easy thing for either of you, but you've made it positively *tragic*."

"I don't suppose you've brought me out here to tell me anything useful." Spine rigid, voice cold, a queen to her dark-wreathed bones. "I'd think gloating was below a god."

"And I'd think you'd have learned enough of gods in your time here to realize that nothing is below us." The Leviathan shrugged, the movement made jerky by the seaweed filaments attached to its shoulders. "Divinity is less complex than humans would like to think. Half magic, half belief. You don't become a god until you think of yourself as one." Another shark-sharp grin. "And I can't remember a time when I didn't think myself a god, worthy of worship."

"You haven't been worshipped in eons."

"You'd be surprised." The eyes of the puppet were blank, but they still managed to look almost sly. "And you'd be surprised how easy worship is to get back, under the right circumstances."

Neve looked away from the puppet's empty corpse-eyes, turning her attention instead to her surroundings. The table was in part of the cavern she hadn't seen before, a small alcove carved by years of saltwater currents, set up on a rocky platform. Gaps in the stone above their heads shone with watery light, the ocean suspended like a glass ceiling.

"To answer your question," the Leviathan said, as if annoyed that Neve's focus had wandered, "I didn't take you from your prison to impart any particular wisdom upon you, though if you have questions—good ones, clear ones—I might be moved to answer." It folded its hands on the table, almost demure. "No, Neverah, *Shadow Queen*, I took you from your prison to satisfy my own curiosity. To take the measure of your soul and see what I thought of it."

The answer took her aback, enough so that she couldn't hide it with an icy, poised exterior. Neve blinked, then trapped her questions behind her teeth. The Leviathan clearly wanted her to ask, simply so it could have the pleasure of saying *no*, and it was a game she had no intention of playing.

The massive shape of the true god in the back of the cavern shifted, a gray haze of huge eyes and the suggestion of a shining fin. The puppet it controlled stood, began a stuttering pacing back and forth across from her.

"When you arrived here," it said, all business, "you had the ability to pull magic directly from the Shadowlands. Correct?"

"So you get to ask questions, but I don't?"

"I'm still waiting for you to come up with a good one," the corpse answered. "And I'll take that as a yes. Did it hurt?"

Neve pressed her lips closed. Sat still, fighting the urge to cross her arms like a petulant child.

The god, apparently, had little patience for her anyway.

"*How much pain were you in, Neverah?*" It came out like a roar through all those teeth, and the Leviathan's skeletal hands slammed onto the table before her.

Neve jerked backward, hand raising—she didn't realize she'd grabbed the god-bone from her pocket until she saw it gleaming white in her fist.

The Leviathan looked at the bone. Smiled. "Good," it said softly. "You might need it."

Before she could process that, the Leviathan picked up its strange line of questioning again. "The pain, dear, tell me how bad it was."

"Bad." Neve didn't answer beyond that. She lowered her hand, nonsensically hiding the bone in the hem of Solmir's coat, even though the god had already seen it.

The Leviathan nodded, thoughtful. "And now?" The corpse didn't have eyebrows, but the seaweed-articulated muscles in its rubbery face still seemed to make one raise. "Now that Solmir has made you the vessel for the magic? Is there pain?"

"No." Her fingers flexed, cold seeping through her bloodstream.

"I see." The Leviathan's hands clasped behind its back as it continued to pace back and forth. "I can't read the future," it said finally, still not looking at her. "Not like the Oracle, or the Weaver's lover. But I can feel the currents of it, the ebb and flow." Its head tipped back, looking at the black, glassy expanse of the ocean suspended over their heads. "It will be you."

"What will be me?" That question she couldn't swallow, and the Leviathan grinned to hear it, clearly pleased it had finally drawn one out of her.

"The vessel," it said simply.

Talking in circles, giving answers that either cleared up nothing at all or told her things she already knew. Gods were a pain in the ass.

"So the things the Kings promised me in exchange for capturing you are, essentially, voided." The Leviathan shook its head, sounding as irritated as Neve felt. "Not that I expected much else, to be quite honest. One should always be on their guard when bargaining with once-enemies."

Something clicked in her mind, made her carefully curated stoicism fall away. "If the Kings sent you," she murmured, "that means they were never coming."

The Leviathan nodded, like a teacher encouraging a slow student. "They were strong enough to resist the pull of the Heart Tree. Not for long. But they didn't need long."

"They knew, then." A rasping whisper, fear making her throat rough. "They knew what we planned. So why didn't they try to stop us?"

"Because they didn't want to. They wanted you to reach the Tree.

And they counted on you to come back out. You've never been someone to leave a job half done."

Clammy sweat chilled her back. Neve knotted her hands in her nightgown's skirt, the bulky silver of Solmir's ring slipping on her thumb.

"They counted on you," the Leviathan repeated, "but that will backfire on them, I think. You took to shadow like a fish to water, pardon the saying. But I don't think you'll drown, Neverah Valedren."

It would've been comforting, were it not for the nearly sorrowful tone.

Suddenly, the cavern lurched, so violently that Neve nearly tumbled from her seat. The dishes holding the false feast shook, the glasses falling to the floor. They rolled across the ground, wine turning back to murky seawater.

Neve braced her hands on the table until the shuddering subsided. When it did, she shot an alarmed look at the Leviathan. "Another quake?"

"Would that it were so simple." The god righted its chair, jerky movements directed through the seaweed ropes leading back to the Leviathan's true shape. It sat down, then held out a hand across the table, palm up. "That wasn't a quake. That was a spasm."

Behind it, in the dim, the massive form of the Leviathan churned, gray fin and black eye.

"I'm dying," the Leviathan said simply. "We're being pulled to the Sanctum, all of us, by the magic of my death throes."

Matter-of-fact, precise. Neve's whole body felt numb. She thought of what Solmir had told her in the coral prison, how the Leviathan dying would destabilize the Shadowlands entirely, speed up its dissolving. Drastically shorten the time left on their ticking clock.

And she still didn't know what Solmir planned to *do*, how he planned to destroy the Kings now that he wasn't giving Neve over to them as a vessel.

Heedless of the maelstrom of panicked thought swirling in her head, the Leviathan reached across the table and took Neve's hand, the one still clutching the god-bone. "So here's what I need to happen: Kill me, Neverah. Absorb my power before the Kings can."

"Why?" It slipped from icy lips.

The look the god gave her was almost pitying. "Because your soul can take it."

Another lurch reverberated through the ground, shaking water from the stalactites pointing wickedly toward the floor, rattling the table and all the illusions of plenty piled on it. Neve grabbed the table's edge to stay steady, looking toward the coral prison that still held Solmir—a crack appeared at the very top, the same place the Leviathan's tentacle had snaked in to bring her out, spreading slowly down the side.

The Leviathan stayed still, her hand still cradled in its palm, the god-bone still snug in her grip. It stared at her with those dead eyes, and behind it, the true shape of the god shuddered, flashes of massive gray bulk showing through the haze.

"We'll be there soon, Neverah." Even and calm, not at all like something dying. "You chose your path when you chose not to follow your sister. When you chose instead to pull the Heart Tree into you, make it something you could carry."

The key woven into her hair was cold against the back of her neck. From the corner of her eye, Neve could see a strange, dark glow, like the shine of a star dipped in ink.

"Your way is set." Skeletal fingers squeezed around hers. "Now all that is left is to follow it."

The crack in Solmir's prison widened with a groan. A bloodied, silver-ringed hand thrust out, clawed at the rock. "Neverah!"

"He believes in you," the god murmured. Another crash, shaking the cavern. The death rattles of something divine, bringing it slowly to destruction, the gravity of rotten magic pulling them all toward doom. "And, for what it's worth, so do I."

The ocean held in stasis above their heads was changing. Neve couldn't look at it directly—something about it was blurred, like two thin pictures laid over each other so that the lines tangled. It was the dark sea, but it was also the inside of some huge cavern, almost pyramid-shaped, the hollow body of a mountain. Bones lined the walls, huge ones, twisted ones.

"Time grows short, Shadow Queen." The Leviathan still sounded calm, but the bite of its fingers into her skin tightened. "Either take my power, or they will."

Become more monstrous, or the Kings would.

Your soul can take it.

A repetition in her mind, the Leviathan speaking without sound for the first time. Its voice in her thoughts was as vast as its body, something that made her head ache to try to contain.

There was something bolstering about having a god believe in you.

Neve closed her fingers around the bone. She lifted her hand from the Leviathan's. The corpse-puppet sat back, waiting. Even the churn of the dying true god at the back of the cavern grew still, that one massive black eye fixed on her.

"How?" she murmured.

"A blade across the throat will suffice." The puppet's smile widened. "We are tied together by more than seaweed."

So Neve lunged across the table and swiped the sharp end of the god-bone across the Leviathan's neck.

Stillness. It was a profound thing, after spending so long with that ever-present rumble beneath her feet, the slight vibration of a breaking world.

Slowly, the corpse-puppet's head lolled back, the bloodless gash across its dead neck widening, widening as the weight of its head pulled at the wound, ripping the rubbered flesh. Behind it, the vast shape of the true Leviathan shuddered, that massive eye still fixed on her, lidless and staring.

The weight of the head tore through spongy skin and desiccated sinew, snapped brittle ossified bone. It fell to the ground.

And the cavern shook like the world was ending.

Power was a black rush, wilder than she'd ever seen it before. It rushed from the back of the cavern, where the true Leviathan rattled in death throes, ropes of shadow flowing straight toward Neve like she was the ocean to its river.

She raised her hands.

It slammed into her with the force of a hurricane, the Leviathan's power tangling in her fingers and slicing into her skin as if it were no barrier at all. It was cold, a chill deeper than she'd thought possible, ice poured over her head in a wave that just kept coming, a vein of darkness running congruent to her every limb, her every thought. Her mouth wrenched out a scream, but she couldn't hear it above the rush of magic, the power of the strongest Old One making a home in her instead.

When the last of the magic finally drained into her, Neve collapsed. She barked her knees against the shell-pocked floor, her hands sliced on coral shards. Above her, in that window made by a hole in the cavern ceiling, the sea and the wall of pyramid-stacked bones flipped back and forth, sometimes one and sometimes the other. The very stone of the cavern seemed to thin, growing nearly transparent, as the Kings pulled them to the Sanctum, power drawing power.

She curled up on the floor, flooded with dark divinity, and tried to remember how to breathe.

"Neve!"

Solmir, freed with a final shattering—the coral prison sundered in half, and he burst through, hands bloody messes and a snarl on his face, eyes gleaming impossibly blue. Stalactites shook free of the ceiling as he ran across the breaking floor toward her, gaze tracking from the headless puppet to the rapid interplay of rock and bone as the cavern faded away.

A jagged spear of rock broke away from the ceiling right above Neve. She heard the groan but couldn't make herself move—her limbs felt so heavy, so full of magic and darkness and cold.

Something landed on her first, softer than the stone, though not by much. Solmir stretched over her, wrapped his arms around her middle, and rolled, taking both of them out of the way of the falling stalactite seconds before it hit the ground where Neve had been. They landed with him atop her, hands on her shoulders, shock and fear and awe in his eyes.

"What did you do, Neve?" He asked it quietly. And the look on his face said he already knew the answer.

All her attention remained on him, on the blue of his eyes and the dagger-sharpness of his cheekbones, the line of puckered scars along his forehead. He was her still point as the world changed around them, rock fading away until it was gone, the sea merely a memory.

Power drew power, and they'd been pulled to the most powerful thing left in this dissolving underworld.

"You know what she did, boy."

It wasn't the voice she recognized, wasn't exactly the one she'd heard in the cairn with the Serpent. Deeper, more graveled, as if it came out of the earth instead of a throat. But the cadence was the same, the royal arrogance, the too-friendly tone.

Valchior laughed, low and rolling. "She did exactly what we thought she would."

Chapter Thirty-One

Raffe

Eammon looked like he hadn't slept in days. In the shadows of the cloister room, Raffe saw him drop a kiss to Red's forehead before heading to the door. He closed it softly behind him and ran a hand over his face. "This is the first deep sleep she's had since she saw Neve. I suppose I should be grateful for that, at least. She'll rest better on a land-bound bed."

"There's one good thing about being stuck here to add to the list," Raffe said, leaning against the wall across from the room.

"How many things are on the list?"

"So far, one."

The Wolf huffed a sound that was probably meant to be a laugh. "That sounds about right." He rubbed his magic-addled eyes with one heavily scarred hand. "Did Kayu say when we'd be able to get another ship?"

"We're headed to the main harbor now," Raffe said. "We'll have one by tomorrow morning. Maybe even tonight—at this point, I'm willing to sail back to Valleyda on a raft. Or someone's buoyant spare mattress."

"You and me both," Eammon muttered. But Raffe thought the tinge of green on his face at the thought wasn't only due to forest magic.

"Did she say anything else?" Raffe asked quietly. "About Neve?"

That night on the ship, when he left Red right before the key in her pocket pulled her to...somewhere else...had been chaotic, to say the least. Whatever force brought Red and Neve together had physically taken Red away, made her vanish from thin air in a wash of golden glow.

Raffe had been the only one to see it happen—the sailor at the prow hadn't been paying attention. And Raffe had seen only part of it, really. He'd been climbing back down the ladder when he saw a shower of what looked like sparks, heard something that sounded like a thunderclap, air rushing in to fill a space recently emptied. When he'd scrambled back up to the deck, Red was gone.

And, because Raffe had the *worst* luck, Eammon had chosen that moment to come up and check on her.

To say the Wolf had been frantic was an understatement. His eyes had blazed green, no whites in them at all, and vines had pushed from the ends of his fingers as he prowled around the deck, calling her name, half a second away from throwing himself overboard to see if she'd somehow fallen.

Thankfully, Red's absence was brief. She'd come back in the same gold-and-thunder crash she'd left in, dazed and teary-eyed, and sank to her knees, hands curled around her key. "I saw her," she whispered brokenly. "I saw her."

It could only be one *her*. "Is she all right?" Raffe started forward, the words crowding together on his tongue in their rush to get out. "How do we get her out? What do we—"

But then Red's face crumpled into a sob, and she buried her head in Eammon's shoulder. And Raffe had known that he wouldn't be getting any answers, and he didn't much have the heart for questions, anyway.

Now, outside Red's door in the Rylt, Eammon just sighed, hand dropping away from his face. "She said there was a tree," he said. "That the key took her somewhere with a massive tree, and Neve was there. The Heart Tree, I assume."

"And she can go back." Raffe tipped his head back against the wall as he tried to piece together sense from Kiri's words, the ramblings of a mad priestess whom they were supposed to follow into the shadows. "She can go back, but she can't make Neve come back with her."

Eammon nodded. His eyes slanted Raffe's way, thoughtful. "Red said that Neve chose to stay there, Raffe."

His spine stiffened. Kiri had said as much, in her circular and half-mad way, but to hear it from Red made it more real. Solid in a way he couldn't dismiss. "Why would she do that?"

The Wolf shrugged uncomfortably. "She said something about a job left undone. About how she couldn't leave until she finished what she started." A pause. "She and Solmir are trying to kill the Kings."

It made Raffe's stomach pit, but not with surprise. Of course that's what it was. Of *course.* He remembered Solmir's shouting as he was dragged into the churning storm of the dying grove, after Neve pulled all those darkened veins connecting her to the trees inward. About how they didn't understand. About how it would be so much worse.

This was always about the Kings. About monsters and gods and the worlds that either contained them or would be left to survive them.

Shadows damn him, he needed a drink.

"Why is that *her* responsibility?" His voice raised, though he didn't mean for it to. "You and Red are the forest gods—why is Neve being pulled into it?"

Eammon shot a meaningful look at the closed door, and Raffe took a deep breath, trying for calm. "I don't understand why she thinks she has to help him."

Him came out like a curse, and the look in Eammon's odd eyes was one of agreement. Neither of them had any love lost for Solmir.

"I don't know Neve well," the Wolf hedged. "Or at all, really, other than what I've heard of her from you and Red. But she seems like the type of person to make things her responsibility. She and her sister are similar that way."

"Damned savior complexes," Raffe muttered.

Eammon snorted. He crossed his arms, leaning against the wall next to Raffe. "I'm familiar with the need to take responsibility," he said quietly. "With feeling like you have to fix everything that came before you. Especially when you've made mistakes that ended up hurting other people."

Raffe tapped his foot, an outlet for nervous energy, and didn't respond. He thought of Second Daughters disappearing into the woods. He thought of bloody branches in a dark Shrine.

A moment, then Eammon turned, looking toward the door. "I thought I'd get her some water." Quiet, as if he thought he might wake Red even though solid oak stood between them. Maybe he could—the Wolves were tied together in ways Raffe didn't fully understand. "For when she wakes up."

It took Raffe a moment to figure out that he was waiting for a response. Asking slanted permission from someone else to leave. Otherwise, Eammon would just stay right here, staring at the door and straining his ears for any sign of wakefulness from within.

"I think that's a good idea." Raffe gestured down the hall. "Kitchen is that way, to the right. End of the short staircase."

"I'll find it." The Wolf turned to him, a considering look in eyes that seemed to be all the colors of the forest at once. "Neve's choice is about her, Raffe. Not anyone else."

Not you, hung the unspoken addendum.

"I know," Raffe replied. But it tasted thin and bitter.

Eammon nodded, giving one more look to the door before starting down the hallway toward the kitchen.

Raffe sighed, rubbing a hand over his short hair, and tapped the back of his head on the wall. Once, twice, three times, trying to gently knock away all the things he didn't want to dwell on. He'd managed to stop thinking of them—at least, he had since that night when he told Red about how he didn't dream of the Tree anymore—but they were hard to hold at arm's length here, like the Temple called thoughts of Neve forward, tied themselves together with his memories.

He cared for her. Deeply. And while lately he cursed himself for getting involved in all of this, it was more with exasperation than regret. He didn't regret being there for her, staying in Valleyda when he could've gone back to Meducia and avoided this entire situation. He didn't regret trying to get her back.

But *shit*, it would be nice if one thing could be simple.

The Ryltish Temple was a spare structure, with only the three hallways branching off the central room—one on the right for a Shrine that he had no desire to explore, one in the middle for cloister rooms, a bathing facility, and the kitchen, and one on the left leading to a domed amphitheater coated in dust, apparently little used. A sign that the world was moving on from the Order, that Kings who did nothing for them were falling further and further out of collective consciousness.

Good fucking riddance.

Raffe headed toward the front doors. Kayu was going to meet him there, and then they'd go to the harbor together to charter another ship with her seemingly endless supply of coin.

She was waiting just outside the door, arms crossed, body tense. Kayu had held herself scabbard-tight since they arrived here, like the oppressive atmosphere of the Temple weighed even heavier on her shoulders than it did on the rest of them. She turned as soon as Raffe pushed open the door, but her eyes didn't quite meet his. "Ready?"

"I suppose." They fell into step, both very determined not to look at the other. After they passed the flower-tangled gate, Raffe jerked a thumb back over his shoulder. "So when were you here last? You seem fairly familiar with the Temple."

Her steps stuttered, dark hair flicking behind her as she turned startled eyes on him. "What do you mean?"

"You said you studied here. Before you came to Valleyda."

"Oh." Kayu shook her head, grimaced. "Sorry. I've been distracted since we arrived. This place makes my skin crawl."

He snorted. "Mine too."

"I studied here for a month or so." Her lips twisted to the side, like she was thinking. "Languages. The Ryltish priestesses are some of the last to remember the old dialects the country spoke centuries ago."

"Seems an odd thing to want to learn."

"Not when you like learning." But she said it quietly, as if the distraction she'd spoken of was still in full effect.

Kayu loosened up the farther they got from the Temple. The dock they'd sailed to was down the shore from the main harbor, which grew busier as they approached. This harbor in particular was more for travel than trade, so most of the vessels were galleys like the one that brought them here, though a few larger ships idled in the water, too.

Raffe, lost in thought, let Kayu lead the way. He wasn't sure what to do now—now that everything rested on Neve, now that they knew it would have to be her own decision that brought her back. Just waiting didn't seem like an option, but what else could he do? What else could *any* of them do?

Even Kiri and the other priestesses seemed content to stagnate, to see what happened in the Shadowlands and how it reverberated here. They must expect Neve and Solmir to fail, the Kings to break through and rule the earth like they had once before; otherwise, wouldn't they be doing something about it? Kiri could speak to the Kings—at least, that was what Raffe gleaned from her ravings in the sickroom, talking to Red about choices and Shadow Queens—but she was just...lying there. Waiting. All of them, just waiting.

It made his palms itch. Such massive stakes, undercut by utter helplessness.

"Such is the way with gods, apparently," he muttered under his breath. He would truly kill for a glass of wine.

Kayu found her mark quickly, a grizzled older captain with a galley smaller than the one they'd sailed over on. Raffe hung back while she did the deal, falling into the role of brawn and letting her be the brains. He kept a hand on his dagger hilt—he'd left his *tor* back in Valleyda; his rudimentary skill with the thing was embarrassing when Lyra was around—and ambled up behind Kayu, trying to look like a hired guard rather than the son of a Meducian Councilor. His fine doublet had already earned him some looks, and he felt it was probably more prudent to stay beneath anyone's notice.

"Six of us," Kayu said emphatically. "As early tomorrow morning as you can."

"Only six will cost you extra," the captain said. He flashed a grin pocked with missing teeth. "I don't leave the harbor with less than ten, to go all the way to Floriane. Have to make the trip worth it."

That was a lie; the galley bobbing in the water behind him wouldn't carry ten passengers unless they slept on top of each other in the hold. Kayu knew that, Raffe saw it in the downward pull of her mouth, but she didn't argue. Instead, she tugged a purse from her waist and started counting out coins.

"Be ready when the sun rises," she said as she dropped the last coin in the captain's gnarled hand. "And remember the number of passengers."

"Aye." The captain, for all that he'd named the price, seemed taken aback at the amount of money he'd just been handed. With a surreptitious look at the bustling harbor, he shoved the coins into the pocket of his coat. "When the sun first licks the sky, I'll be waitin'. For six passengers." He held out his hand to shake.

Kayu gripped it. When she pulled, the captain gave a little grunt of surprise, tugged forward more by shock than any particular strength on Kayu's part.

"I have an eye for faces," she said, voice pitched low. "And friends in places that could make your life very uncomfortable, if you decide not to hold to our bargain. Just letting you know."

Raffe's eyes went wide, but when the captain shot a startled look his way, he tried to school his expression into nonchalance.

"You have my word," the captain said, fingers squirming to get out of Kayu's grip. "Sunrise, six passengers, at the Temple dock."

"See you then." Kayu turned on her heel. Raffe followed. When he looked over his shoulder, the captain was shaking out his hand, like Kayu's grip had squeezed off his circulation.

Once they'd left the harbor behind, Raffe sped up until they walked apace. "You drive a hard bargain."

"Had to." Kayu tried for a smile, but it fell flat. "Sailors will scam you cross-eyed if you aren't careful. You should've seen what I had to pay the ones that brought us here."

A sound enough answer; still, Raffe sped up again, overtaking her and then turning around so they were face-to-face, halting her forward stride. "Kayu."

Her full lips pressed together, dark eyes finally meeting his. "Raffe."

"Tell me what's wrong."

"Nothing is wrong." Something in her heart-shaped face went flinty. "Why, are you afraid I'm going to renege on your meal ticket if my mood goes sour? I know you don't think much of me, but I'm more trustworthy than that."

"Kayu," he said again, because her name was all he really knew to hold whatever feeling this was. Irritation, yes, but also worry, and not just for himself.

She didn't say anything, eyes wide on his. He didn't realize he'd put a hand on her shoulder until he felt her muscle tremor beneath his palm.

Raffe swallowed. Then he dropped his hand. "I'm not worried about the money," he said. "I'm worried about you."

Her mouth twisted; he couldn't tell what emotion caused it. Kayu took a breath, looked away from him. Thoughts raced behind her eyes.

"It's this place," she said finally, softly. "I don't have pleasant memories here."

"At the Temple?"

She nodded, making her waterfall of black hair ripple in the wind off the ocean. "I didn't come under the best circumstances." It was almost a whisper, like it was something she didn't want to admit. "My father... he wanted to marry me off. To a brute of a man who'd had four wives already, every one of them mysteriously dead within six months of matrimony. I'm the third daughter. My only value is in my marriage, how much money or power or strategic influence it can bring the Emperor."

He nodded, piecing together the narrative. "So you came here— started traveling, studying elsewhere—to escape."

A high, harsh laugh. "More or less." Kayu shrugged. "The night I refused the marriage, I stowed away on a ship. I didn't care where it was going. It brought me here, and things..." She stopped, swallowed.

Another flash of rapid thought behind her eyes, calculating, tallying up what she wanted to reveal. "I did what I had to do. Took shelter in the Temple. My memories of my time here are not kind."

His older sister, Amethya, had been married to a man his parents chose. But he'd been kind and funny and handsome in addition to being immensely wealthy, and Raffe knew his family wouldn't have consented to the marriage otherwise. He couldn't imagine sending someone he loved to marry a person he knew was dangerous. "And your father... he still doesn't know where you are?"

Her chin ducked; she tucked her hair nervously behind her ear. "Even if he does," she murmured, "it doesn't matter. He can't touch me."

The words could've been full of bravado, but the way she said them was almost regretful. Raffe nodded, arms crossed. "It's hard, being somewhere that holds bad memories," he said. "I understand."

"Do you?" Still so soft, so quiet. But Kayu brushed past him without a backward glance.

When they topped the dunes again, Fife and Lyra were standing by the fence, talking quietly. It seemed they were playing some kind of game—Lyra would point to a plant, and Fife would name it.

"Threader moss." Fife sipped from a steaming cup of tea in his hand—he'd found the kitchen, apparently. Lyra's finger moved, pointing to another variety of moss clinging to the fence. "Queenscarpet." Another, this one on the ground and dotted with blooms. "Mermaid hair."

"I hate it when they name real things after pretend things." The mask of a sunny smile and easy laughter had slipped back over Kayu at some point between the harbor and the dunes, the mask she'd been lacking since they stepped onto the shore of the Rylt. She rested her arms on the fence, leaned over to see the plant in question. "It seems inconsistent."

"Unless mermaids are real?" Raffe mimicked Kayu's stance, though he kept careful distance between them. "Honestly, at this point I wouldn't be surprised."

"If they are, I don't know about it." Lyra bent down and plucked one of the blooms she'd pointed to; small, pale blue petals drooped from a green stalk. "Maybe they're just too smart to leave the sea. Things seem much more complicated on land."

"What with the maidens to save and the plagues that need breaking," Fife muttered beside her. She bumped him with her hip and stuck the tiny flower behind his ear.

Kayu's eyes flickered between them, bright and full of questions. "Are you two…"

Raffe's brow lifted, his gaze slanting her way, then back to Fife and Lyra. The two Wilderwood denizens looked at each other, an unspoken conversation.

"Well," Fife said, putting down his tea and cocking a brow at Lyra. "I love you. But you know that."

"And I love you," Lyra replied. She reached up, adjusted the mermaid-hair flower so it brushed his temple. She looked back at Kayu, shrugged. "I'm not one for romance. Or sex, mostly. But we love each other. Always have." She gave Fife a wry smile. "Always will, at this point."

"To my great chagrin," Fife said. But he reached over and threaded his fingers through Lyra's, soft and easy.

That was the only mark of connection between them, solid friendship and clasped hands. No kisses, no signs of romantic love as Raffe knew it. But it seemed like Lyra and Fife ran deeper than that. A different sort of love, one perfectly tailored to them.

Raffe was feeling very out of his depth on love as a concept lately.

The four of them stood in silence. Down on the beach, a gull cawed.

Kayu straightened, dark-bright eyes turning from the moss to Raffe. An unreadable expression crossed her face, somewhere between hope and vulnerability and steel. "You coming?"

And even lost in a haze of thoughts about love and things he didn't understand, Raffe caught her meaning, the question behind the one she asked. A need for comfort, for something warm, for a place to not *think* for a moment.

So when Kayu started toward the Temple, a particular kind of determination in her gait, Raffe followed and knew what that meant.

Behind him, the murmur of Fife and Lyra's voices, gentle against the wind and the gulls and the crash of waves on the shore, a secret language only the two of them shared.

Raffe followed Kayu through the Temple door, down the hall, toward the small cloister rooms with their small cloister beds, toward the one she'd claimed for herself when it became clear they'd be staying at least one night. He didn't think of what was coming next, though his body knew it. He didn't let himself think at all.

It was nice, to let his mind settle. Let the rest of him take over for a while.

When the door closed behind them, Kayu turned. She was small, her nose nearly level with his sternum, and when her eyes tilted up to look at his face, her pupils were already wide. His breath went ragged in his chest as she shrugged out of the billowing shirt, the trousers, the boots, and stood before him pale and bare.

"It's been a while," she whispered.

"Same here," Raffe replied.

Kayu kissed him, and she tasted like spice and like flowers. His hands wove through her hair, impossibly silky, running over his skin like a black curtain.

"It doesn't have to mean anything." She pulled away, tugged his shirt over his head, ran her hands across the mahogany planes of his chest. "It doesn't have to mean anything you don't want it to."

Comfort. That's what they were both after. That's what he told himself as he kissed her again, as his hands came to her hips and lower. Comfort didn't mean anything, did it? He'd done this before, with other people who knew it wasn't anything deeper than solace, who knew his heart was elsewhere and didn't mind. This didn't mean anything beyond needing some respite. So few things Raffe knew about love, but this, he knew.

And if it did mean something more? If this was something beyond bodies doing what bodies did, what would that mean for him? For Neve?

In this moment, as Kayu backed up to that tiny cloister bed, all warmth and silk, and gulls cawed and waves crashed outside, Raffe found he didn't much care.

꠸꠸꠸꠸꠸꠸꠸꠸꠸꠸꠸꠸꠸꠸꠸꠸꠸꠸꠸

She fell asleep after. They curled toward each other like the two halves of a circle, space between them, the only point of contact Raffe's palm on the curve of her waist. Her hair feathered over her brow, caught in the current of her breath. He lifted his hand to push it away, and other than settling her head farther into her pillow, Kayu didn't stir.

Raffe sat up, ran a hand over his face. He felt better—it really had been a while—and now his mind was coming back to him, the endless churn of worry he'd become. It'd been nice to set that aside for an hour. It'd been nice to set it aside with her.

But reprieves didn't last long.

He was still for a moment, waiting for the guilt, waiting for Neve's face to paint itself on the backs of his eyelids. It didn't come. He felt warm and languid and, yes, still worried, but no part of him felt guilty.

It should've been a relief. An answer, finally, to the question of whether the love he and Neve had was something more than friendship. Instead, cruelly aware of the shape of the woman next to him, Raffe was afraid this realization would only make the whole situation even more complicated.

She'd said it didn't have to mean anything. He wished it hadn't.

Kayu shifted in her sleep, a slight smile curving her full lips. Kings, she was beautiful. Infuriating and meddling and too smart for her own good, but beautiful.

He stifled a groan in his palm.

A bag sat in the corner. Kayu's. Lavishly embroidered fabric spilled from the top to trail across the stone. Raffe pushed up, meaning to stuff it back in the bag—the dress looked expensive, it would get ruined lying on this dust-covered floor. It didn't seem as though the priestesses spent much time cleaning.

And he needed to get away from Kayu's warmth before he reached for her again.

He pulled the dress the rest of the way out of the bag, intending to fold it up and put it back. But as he did, something fluttered to the ground. Frowning, he picked it up.

Papers. Bound together with twine. He could catch one line written across the top: *For Her Holiness, the High Priestess.*

His pulse ratcheted up in his ears.

Raffe didn't waste time wondering about Kayu's right to privacy. He broke the twine with his teeth, sitting naked on the floor to read over the notes.

Notes on everything. All signed by Sister Okada Kayu, novitiate of the Order of the Five Shadows.

It was like a bone setting, the awful way it all came together in his head, the ragged pain of things snapping into place. Kayu's abrupt arrival in Valleyda right after the other priestesses left. Intercepting that letter from Kiri—except she hadn't really intercepted it, had she? It'd probably been written for her in the first place, a convenient thing to get into his circle of trust. To get into his bed.

Kings. That stung.

"I'm not going to give it to her."

The thin sheets puddled around Kayu's waist. She'd sat up while he was reading, probably watched him do it. Even now, though, she didn't look afraid. She knew he wouldn't hurt her.

Kings-damn and all the shadows, he was a *fool.*

"I only came here to get away from my father." The words came fast, now that she was finally giving a confession, as if they'd been waiting. "If I became a priestess, he couldn't compel me to return home. I thought the Rylt was far enough away from the continent to avoid its politics, but when I arrived, the priestesses here had already swapped their loyalties to Kiri's order, then Kiri arrived right after I did, and when she found out I was distantly in line for the Valleydan throne—"

"She sent you to spy on us." Raffe stood slowly, the pages of notes clenched in his fist. "To report back on any progress we were making to find Neve."

"I never sent any of them." She shook her head, black hair feathering over still-bare shoulders. "Raffe, I never sent any of those notes. I stopped taking them the day I snuck into your bedchamber. I never wanted to do any of this. I'm on your side."

"The only side you're on is your own, Kayu. I'm not an idiot."

"You don't know him." Near-panic in her voice, in the way she clutched the sheet to her chest. "You don't know how awful he is, Raffe. I wouldn't have lived out the year. I had to do *something*."

"Well, you certainly did." Raffe threw the papers to the ground, grabbing his discarded clothes and pulling them on without checking to make sure they weren't inside out. If he stayed here, if he listened, he might forgive her. And he'd done enough foolish things for one day.

"I want to help *you*, Raffe. I..." She trailed off, head dipping lower to obscure her face farther behind all that black hair. When she spoke, it was a whisper. "I have no love for the Kings. I want them dead. I want to help Neve however I can, and I want her to come back. Because *you* want her back, and you deserve to be happy."

She could've reached in his chest and pulled out his heart, beating and vital, and wrung it out in her hands. It would hurt less.

"I can't..." He didn't know how to finish the sentence. Not when she sat there, naked and gilded in the light of the sun setting in the window, golden skin covered in a white sheet and hair like a black river.

So he didn't finish. Raffe opened the door and strode aimlessly out into the hallway, wanting to be anywhere other than with the traitor he might've been falling for.

Chapter Thirty-Two

Neve

*F*oolish little queen.

She was only vaguely aware of her body as a physical thing, but still she flinched, trying to get away from this voice that battered her from every direction at once. The same voice she'd heard in the Serpent's cairn, warning her of Solmir's deceit, warning her of everything that was to come.

She hadn't listened then. And though she'd made every decision that led her here—though she'd known, when she didn't let Red lead her out of the Heart Tree, that the path might lead her here—Neve still wanted to curl up in a fetal ball, to hide away from Valchior's voice and everything it meant.

Too late for that, Neverah. A chuckle snaked through her skull, friendly and warm and all the more chilling for it. *You're truly in it now.*

She flinched.

Take heart, Shadow Queen. She hated how sincere he sounded. *The game draws to a close, one way or another.*

The power she'd taken from the Leviathan twisted and writhed through her veins, shadow like tentacles. More than anything she'd felt before, more than the power she'd used to open the way to the Heart Tree. It was right at the edge of overwhelming, balanced on the tipping point where she could either hold on to herself—hold on to her soul— or fall into the magic completely.

It had never been like this before. She'd seen Solmir struggle to hang on when shadowed magic threatened to overwhelm him, but she'd never housed enough to feel like she was slipping away, to feel like she had to latch onto herself with clawed fingers. Even when she'd first awoken and fear made her dredge magic up from the Shadowlands themselves, there'd been only pain. Not this...this sense of being lost. Of untethering.

Divinity is a hard thing to hold, Valchior murmured in her head.

"Shut up," Neve replied, and didn't realize she'd said it aloud until she felt the dried blood by her lips crack.

Awareness came slow. Her legs, first, tingling pins and needles, her middle, her arms. Neve kept her eyes closed, waiting to feel solid, to feel like her body was a fully knit-together thing. She kept her eyes closed, because she knew what she'd see when she opened them. Bones and Kings.

The Sanctum, where gods were pulled to die.

Neve took a deep breath. Then she opened her eyes.

Her mind could take in her surroundings only in fragments. First, the floor on which she lay—clean gray stone, perfectly circular. Then the walls—crafted from bones, colossal and misshapen, curved as if they'd been coiled into a hollow mountain. Closer, and it was clear the bones came from some kind of tail, starting small and growing larger as they traveled upward, fringed with sharp spikes.

Neve's head tilted, following the twirl of monstrous bone. There, at the top of the Sanctum, like the bell at the apex of a tower—a huge skull, a snout and empty holes for reptilian eyes, a carriage-sized jaw still lined with teeth. The expression on its dead face, as much as dead gods could have expressions, might've been a sneer or a scream.

"The Dragon." Not Valchior, not Calryes, but another a voice she didn't recognize. It came out loud instead of in her head, low and graveled, like stones rubbed together. "The first of the Old Ones to fall. Drinking down its power felt like fire and tasted like smoke."

Slowly, Neve looked away from the skull and faced the Kings in the flesh.

Or the stone, as it were.

At first, she wondered if she was hallucinating. There was no shadow, no handsome men flashing to decay in the blink of an eye, not like seeing the projections of Calryes and Valchior that they'd sent to the Serpent's cairn. Instead, four huge shapes on four huge thrones, with a fifth standing empty.

The figures on the thrones were as tall as three of Solmir, utterly different from the illusions their shadows spun. All of them were swathed from head to toe in white gauze, covering limbs and faces. Each wore a spiked crown that pushed through the fabric in a way that made it seem as though the shards grew directly from the heads beneath. None of them could be differentiated, all wrought in identical rock.

Everything that made them human was gone. All they had left were souls, tied down into the foundations of the Shadowlands, sunk there by the constant calling up of dark power. And to look at them now, as they truly were, Neve could barely imagine them ever having been flesh and blood, could barely imagine Solmir ever being among their number.

Solmir.

She whirled, searching for him—she stood in the center of the circle of Kings, hemmed in on all sides by these statues that looked dead but were terribly, monstrously living. But there was no sign of Solmir, no flash of blue in all this gray.

"Where is he?" The steel in her tone surprised her. Neve's voice seemed to echo and reverberate almost like the Kings' did.

"Even here, she asks after your wayward son, Calryes." Another voice she didn't recognize, one of the other kings. "He always was able to turn heads, wasn't he? A useful skill." A low *creak*—one of the statues leaned forward, slowly, painfully, the sound of it aching in her ears. "You know what his intentions were, and yet you care for him still? That's more than a death wish, Shadow Queen. That's a wish for pain."

"Leave her be, Malchrosite." Calryes. His voice seemed to come from behind her, but when Neve whirled again, she couldn't tell which of the stone monoliths was him. They all looked exactly the same. "Neverah deserves your respect, regardless of the foolish feelings she might harbor toward my disappointing son. She chose to return to us rather than go home, after all. Knowing what would happen."

"I didn't know." Neve didn't mean to say it aloud. She shook her head. "I didn't know what would happen."

"But you knew it would bring you here." A new voice this time. Old, with a quake in it that spoke of age or madness or maybe both. Byriand, must be, the oldest of the Kings, who'd been an elderly man when they ripped into the Shadowlands trying to steal back power. "You knew it would bring you to us. You and him both."

"No one answered my question." Neve turned in the center of the circle of Kings, addressing them all since she wasn't sure which was which. Her thorn-wreathed hands crooked, magic ready in her palms. She didn't know what she might do with it—faced with all of them, it was probably next to useless. But she kept the threat of it in her posture, in the snarl on her lips. "Where is Solmir?"

A low, rumbling sound, surrounding her so completely she didn't know which of the shrouded figures started it. A laugh, all of them together, the sound of a rockslide.

"The traitor is where all traitors go," Valchior said. "Even here, kingdoms have dungeons."

Her fists clenched, magic surging down her veins, painting them black and raising spikes. "If you hurt him, I'll kill you."

A groan behind her—another monolith, leaning down, the King's face level with hers. No eyes, but if they were lost in all that rock somewhere, they'd be looking directly at her.

"Neverah," Valchior murmured. "Isn't that precisely what you came here to do?" The stone head cocked to the side with a groan, obscenely slow. "Or, at least, what you think you came here to do?"

Dust from the Kings' movements peppered the air, made a cough claw up Neve's throat. How long had it been since they'd moved? She imagined centuries of sitting still, swallowing shadow and sinking deep into a rotten world, and suppressed a shudder.

She still held the shard of god-bone in her hand. The corpse of the Leviathan had no blood to stain it, so it gleamed white in the gray of the Sanctum, in the light filtering through the gaps of the massive skull above. All of them could see it, all of them knew she had it. And it didn't appear to bother them at all.

That, more than anything else, made a numbing terror prickle between her shoulder blades.

"Vessels," Valchior breathed. "You know a bit about them. When things changed at the Heart Tree—when Solmir gave you the magic—we felt it happen. We sent the Leviathan to collect you." The stone effigy wasn't capable of facial expression, but Neve sensed something like exasperation. "*That* didn't exactly work out how we planned, of course."

The Leviathan had decided to believe in her, instead of in the Kings. Neve's hands curled, darkness staining her palms.

"So now you are faced with another choice, Neverah." Valchior's inhuman voice was calibrated for comfort, but it still rang cold. "Give up what the Leviathan gave you and join with us instead. Become the vessel you were meant to be, and finally find some of that control you so desperately want."

The vessel she was meant to be. What Solmir had planned for her, before…before he decided he couldn't kill her, for whatever reason. Reasons she couldn't think of right now, didn't have the time to look at, because that would require her to look at her own.

Valchior was asking her to become a vessel for the Kings' souls. To be the vehicle that brought them to the surface.

To be part of the reign of terror they planned.

The key the Heart Tree had given her burned cold on the back of her neck. "And if I don't?"

"If you don't," Calryes said, his voice sharper and less warm than Valchior's, "Solmir will take your place. And we all know how poorly he copes with his own soul—I can't imagine he'll do well with four more."

More rumbles of awful laughter, the deep sounds of cliffs collapsing and continents splitting.

It took her a moment to put it all together, how this was an answer to two questions. What would happen if she refused to be the vessel, and what Solmir had meant in the coral prison when he said there was another way.

Here was why he'd tried so hard to make a different plan work. Why he'd come to the surface, tethered to Arick, why he'd led them to make the shadow grove. A desperate attempt to hang on to himself, to write a different destiny where he could be saved.

If Neve wasn't the vessel for the Kings' souls, Solmir would be.

And then what would he become?

She didn't realize she'd let go of the god-bone until she heard it clatter to the floor.

Another sound of groaning stone, a King leaning forward. "Perhaps this would be easier," Valchior muttered in a voice of gravel and shale, "if we were face-to-face."

He reached out, as slow-moving as the shift of a mountain. She could've run, but where would she go?

The giant stone hand touched Neve's brow. She clenched her jaw against expectant pain, but there was none. A moment of rough-hewn fingers, then the hand on her forehead felt only like flesh, an illusion spun straight into her mind.

Neve opened her eyes to the man she'd seen in the cairn, bright-eyed and handsome. The image of him was stronger this time, less wavering, and the vision he crafted covered everything she could see. Instead of billowing shadows, there was only the Sanctum, empty of everyone except the two of them.

Valchior gave her a small, sad smile, bittersweetness shaped by perfect teeth. "Oh, Neverah," he murmured. "What has our wayward brother done to you?"

She wished she had an answer. She wished she knew what exactly had woven itself between her and Solmir, a complicated kind of caring that wasn't quite friendship and wasn't quite something more, but lived somewhere outside both, heated and strange and volatile.

Her lips stayed shut. Valchior didn't deserve that explanation.

The King watched her through warm eyes, waiting. When it was clear she wouldn't talk, he clasped his hands behind his back, began a slow meander around the falsely empty room. Circling her like a predator, though he spoke like protection. "Solmir has always been more in touch with his humanity than the rest of us, I'll admit. Even before that whole debacle with my daughter, he didn't sink into this as readily as we did."

That whole debacle with his daughter. Valchior spoke of Gaya's death so flippantly.

"So when we felt the Shadowlands begin to dissolve—long before Gaya's whelp become the Wolf, long before he found your sister—we knew we would need a vessel, if we were to reenter our own world. If we were to escape the destruction of the prison we created." He flashed a smile, crooked and endearing. "That's why Solmir was so desperate for the Heart Tree to work with him and Gaya, why he tried to bring us through with the shadow grove when that failed. We would've been happy for either to work, but of course, they didn't. He's always been looking for an out, Neve."

Her shortened name was a murmur as he reached toward her, his fingers—solid, and though she knew that was illusion, too, she still shuddered—slipping into her hair. They brushed her temple, the back of her neck, came to rest against the cold shape of the key she'd hidden there, still faintly beating with a pulse that wasn't hers.

Neve's spine locked. She didn't breathe.

But the King didn't yank the key out of her tangles. Instead, his grin widened as he withdrew his hand. "Between you and me," he said, resuming his slow circling, "I don't think it's the loss of self that he's most afraid of. I think he's more afraid of becoming more like himself, with all of our souls subsumed into his. Solmir is not so far removed from monstrous godhood, and he knows it."

He'd told her she was good, once. Standing by black water and washing themselves free of mud and blood. *You are good*, he'd said. *That's why it has to be you.*

Because he was afraid of what would happen if it was him. He'd clawed his way free of the dark once and didn't know if he could do it again.

"And yet, he was willing to face that fear for you." Valchior chuckled. "Malchrosite said Solmir was always able to turn heads easily, but it means his head is also easily turned. He would make himself a monster for you, Neverah, but do you want that?"

She thought of him wreathed in dark and thorns, stalking toward her on that cracked desert plain. Fear had sparked in her, yes, but also recognition. The thorns in her seeing the thorns in him and knowing they were the same.

He'd made his decision at the Heart Tree, when he kissed her and passed power to her. Decided to become something terrible if it meant saving her life. But Neve had never been good at letting others' decisions stand if she thought they were the wrong ones.

Almost unconsciously, Neve looked down at her hands, the black veins, the studding thorns. She kept forgetting they were there, forgetting how the magic Solmir gave her and the power she took from the Leviathan had wrought her into something dark and inhuman, brutal and beautiful.

Valchior gingerly picked up her hand. "It wouldn't look much different than this," he mused. "*You* wouldn't become something terrible if you contained us, not like he would. You could use that power for good. Keep everyone you love safe." The corner of his mouth twitched. "Even him."

She snatched her hand from his grip but didn't speak. She didn't know what to say.

"You're so different from us, Neve, different in a way Solmir never could be." He didn't touch her again, but his eyes traced the angles of her face with such focus that it felt like he did. "Full of contradictions, full of love and anger in equal force, the two of them so tangled together, sometimes you can't tell one from the other. You were cast in shadows long before he was ever part of your story, darkened from your endless need for control."

Hot tears brimmed in her eyes, but Neve refused to let them fall. Refused to cry in front of a god.

"Think of this as a way to get all the control you've ever wanted," Valchior murmured. His thumb skimmed her jawline, tilted up her chin. "You swallow the apocalypse and use the power of it to reshape the world. Isn't that all you ever wanted to do, Neve? Make the world what you thought it should be?"

She didn't move. His thumb beneath her chin held her still, kept her gaze locked on his.

"You're stronger than him," Valchior murmured. "Your soul can take it."

You are good.

"Let me see him." A whisper, a way to sidestep the answer the King wanted.

His lips pulled up into that crooked smile again. "A tragedy until the end."

Slowly, his hand moved from her chin to her forehead. At the touch of his fingers to her brow, the illusion of his former self shattered. The pressure on her skin turned from warm flesh to rough, cold stone.

When Neve opened her eyes, Valchior's monolithic true form was leaning back, once again a giant covered in a shroud. The spike of his crown was close enough for her to see its sharp edges, honed like blades.

"I'll show you Solmir," he rumbled. "And then you can tell us your decision." A low laugh, like the earth cracking open. "You and your sister do have such tragic taste."

The other Kings took up the laugh, until the Sanctum echoed with it, the sound of breaking rock and grinding stone and a world slowly dissolving.

Chapter Thirty-Three

Red

Eammon was there when she awoke, walking a path into the dust, back and forth across the cloister room, anxiously holding a glass of water. Some of it had slopped over the side from his constant pacing, dripping from his scarred knuckle onto the stone floor.

"There's a perfectly serviceable table over here, you know."

It came out a barely audible croak, but he was by her side in an instant, spilling more water when he insisted on kissing her forehead before handing her the glass. "To be honest, I didn't notice the table."

"Too busy taking in the rest of the scenery?" She wagged her fingers at the room—dingy white and gray, all of it dusty—lips bent into a rueful smile. Eammon's worry had always been an all-consuming thing, especially where she was concerned.

He quirked the side of his mouth, though it fell quickly, his thoughts too churning to find any humor. His eyes flashed as he shook his head, sinking down next to her on the bed. "How do you feel?"

Red made a noncommittal noise. "About as well as one can, under the circumstances."

Now that she was awake, heaviness settled over her again, helplessness a weight on her shoulders. She had a key to the underworld, a key to getting Neve back, and it was completely useless unless her twin decided to leave.

The key lay against her side now, pulled out of her pocket by tosses and turns of sleep, glowing golden against the sheets. Red fluttered her fingers over it, just enough to reassure herself of its presence. She almost didn't want to touch it, now that she knew exactly what it was. Such a powerful thing, but it still couldn't bring her what she wanted. Setting her teeth, she gingerly picked it up and placed it on the bedside table.

Worry still sparked in Eammon's eyes, green-haloed and fixed on her. Red sighed, put her hands on his shoulders. "I promise you, I'm fine."

"You aren't," he rumbled. "But there's nothing I can do about it."

"At least that's true, this time." She gave him a tired smirk. "Not just something I tell you because I want to be a martyr. Unlike *someone* I could mention."

The Wolf rolled his eyes even as he tilted up her chin with his finger. "A *self-martyring bastard* was the term you used, I think."

He kissed her, quick and chaste, and Red leaned her forehead against his. "Did Raffe and Kayu get another ship?"

"They were headed to the harbor, last I heard." Eammon tucked her hair behind her ear. "We should hopefully be able to leave in the morning."

Morning would be soon, at least—night had already fallen, blackening the windows. "I'll probably stay up and let you sleep," Red muttered. "I don't much like the idea of all of us being vulnerable here with Kiri. We need to set a watch."

"Might not be a bad idea." Eammon scooted onto the bed until he sat next to her, leaning back against the spare headboard. "Though I don't think I'm going to be able to sleep, either. Plenty of time for that on the ship, with miles of water between us and the mad priestesses." He grimaced. "Maybe I can sleep the entire three days. That would be an improvement on my prior sailing experience."

"No more boats after this."

He nodded. "No more boats."

Red put her head on his shoulder, frowning as she thought back over

Kiri's ravings. "Kiri called Neve the Shadow Queen and me the Golden-Veined. Isn't that what Valdrek said the Sisters constellation was called, in some of the old languages?"

"I think so," Eammon murmured. "But what would that mean?"

"Maybe nothing." She burrowed farther into his shoulder, suddenly exhausted though she'd spent the last few hours asleep. "At the very least, it means this is bigger than us. This is something that was always going to happen."

He went quiet, thoughtful. "It's my fault, then."

"*No.*" She sat up, turned, crouched over him with his waist caged by her arms. "Don't you start that martyring shit again. I already warned you."

A slight smile, but the worry stayed in his eyes. "You've become far more wolflike than I ever was."

"And don't forget it." She sat back on her heels, still straddling his waist. After a moment, she picked up his hand, traced his scars with a light finger as she talked. "I think when I chose to become the Wilderwood, it...started something. Set something into motion. The roles were waiting, the pieces already set, and we just made the game begin. In that case, it's just as much my fault as it is yours. And Neve's, too." She sighed. "We all made the choices that led us here. They just had further-reaching consequences than we knew."

Silence, both of them sitting with the weight of the idea. "Well," Eammon said finally, "I should be sorry, probably. But I'm not."

"Sorry for what?"

"Making you fall in love with me and thus setting all this in motion." A mischievous smile twisted his mouth, made his eyes glimmer like autumn sunshine through leaves. "I should have tried to temper my raw appeal."

She tugged on his hair. "I feel like I was the one who had to make *you* fall in love with *me*. You were infuriatingly noble about the whole thing."

"I started falling in love with you the moment you crashed into my library," Eammon said, matter-of-fact. "I was just very good at hiding it."

They sat quietly for a few minutes that felt stolen. Red leaned forward and rested her cheek on his chest, listening to Eammon's heartbeat, the thud of it cushioned with leaf and branch. He loosely wrapped his arms around her waist, his breath warm against her neck.

The key lay on the table next to her half-drunk glass of water; she reached over and grabbed it, sitting back and holding it on her palm between them. It still glowed, still felt warm to the touch. She could still feel the faintest thud of a heartbeat.

Eammon eyed it warily. "You were right all along. What you did in the clearing, trying to get to Neve. That's what gave you the key, made the Heart Tree able to pull you to it when Neve arrived."

"I had to give up something for her," Red murmured, turning the key over in her hands. "She went into the underworld for me. I had to prove I was willing to do the same for her. That's how it works, I think. The same kinds of love, whether they're pretty or not."

Deep within her, the Wilderwood bloomed, pushing new shoots through her marrow. Agreement, acknowledgment that she was right.

Her Wolf's hands tightened on her thighs, his wary look at the key almost becoming a glare. "As long as it doesn't ask you for anything else," he said, low and fierce.

Red pulled her lip between her teeth. She didn't respond.

Finally, she clambered off him, stretching. "I need to wash my face and get out of this room."

He swung long legs over the side of the bed and stood. "Fife found a library while he was looking for the kitchen, said it was well stocked and had some volumes that weren't at the Keep or the Valleydan capital. Might be worth investigating."

"Somehow, you always find the books." Red gently pulled the ends of his hair until he bent far enough forward for her to drop a kiss on his forehead, right between the points of his nascent antlers. "Go leave me for reading, I'll be fine."

"You're sure?"

"I'm not above punching a priestess if the need arises."

Eammon nodded, kissed her one more time before heading toward the door. "The library is on the other side of the amphitheater, if you need me."

She nodded, and the door closed behind him.

Red splashed some water on her face from the ewer in the corner and rubbed the sleep from her eyes. Part of her thought of following Eammon to the library, seeing if there was anything they could find that mentioned the Shadow Queen or the Golden-Veined. But the thought made her stomach curl in on itself, her body signaling the need for a momentary reprieve, so she decided just to wander the halls for a bit first, work out some of her nervous energy.

The door closed quietly behind Red as she slipped into the hallway. The cloister room she'd ended up in wasn't far from the main foyer, the nexus of the entire Temple. When she came out of the mouth of the corridor, the door to the amphitheater was open to her right, revealing a sliver of dusty and little-used curving stone seats. It seemed the Ryltish Temple didn't see many worshippers.

She turned away from the amphitheater. On the opposite side of the foyer, a short stone hallway ended in a plain wooden door.

"Where are you going?"

Red's hands closed to fists as she whirled, a promise of what she'd told Eammon about punching a priestess. But it was just Kayu.

Her hair was mussed, the usual pin-straight strands tangled and frizzed behind her head. She wore the same clothes she'd worn earlier, but the way they hung seemed subtly different, as if they'd been removed and then replaced. She looked tired, and her eyes were glassy, like she'd either been crying or was about to start.

"Just wandering." The clear vulnerability on Kayu's face made Red want to reach out to the other woman, want to trust her. But there was still a small part of Red that regarded everyone warily, sharp and feral and unwilling to open her safe circle to new people.

Kayu shifted back and forth, eyes flickering down the hall before coming back to Red. "Can I come with you? I don't want to be alone. And you probably shouldn't be, either."

That made her brows draw down, but after a moment, Red nodded. Clearly, Kayu was dealing with something—she understood the desire not to be alone. And she was right; it might be safer for all of them to stick together.

"I was just going to see what this was," Red said, gesturing toward the tiny hallway with its small door. "You're welcome to come with me."

Kayu nodded, mouth still pressed into a thin line, eyes still shining.

Red wondered if she should ask what had happened, but decided against it—were she in Kayu's position, she wouldn't feel like sharing. Instead, she went down the hallway and grasped the door handle. At first she thought it might be locked, but then the handle turned, smooth and soundless, taken care of in a way that seemed odd compared with the rest of the Temple's obvious neglect.

The door opened into a small room lit only by flickering candles, all of them dark gray and dripping wax. In the center, a stone pedestal with a thick white twig, casting barred shadow on the wall.

A Shrine.

An instinct to flee flared from the woman Red had been before, the same one who pelted through a hungry forest with a bloody cheek, who'd knelt among the branch shards in the Valleydan Shrine and been prayed over by priestesses filled with piety for monsters. Lost and angry and helpless against powers she didn't understand.

"Are you all right?"

Kayu's voice shattered the memories, grounded her back into who and what she was. Not that woman anymore. Maybe scared, maybe out of her depth, but not someone who didn't know who she was, not someone who didn't understand the place she'd made for herself.

"I'm fine," Red said.

She stepped over the threshold.

This Shrine was tiny, barely large enough for her and Kayu to stand shoulder to shoulder without knocking into the table full of prayer candles in the corner. The walls were the same dark stone, but they seemed darker with the absence of any light but the flickering flames. The barely there hiss of wicks was the only sound.

Cautiously, Red approached the branch in the center of the room. Slight threads of darkness traced the bark, nowhere near as thick as true shadow-rot, but enough to make unease sink a hook in her middle.

The click of the latch behind her made her jump, her back to the branch and knees bent to a crouch, hands outstretched like claws. Next to the door, Kayu stood statue-still, her eyes wide and her jaw clenched.

The priestess who'd pushed open the door gasped, a pale hand with bandaged fingers pressed against an ample bosom. "King's mercy," she murmured, voice touched with a Ryltish accent that made everything sound musical. But something about the glint of her eyes seemed more eager than surprised. She turned and looked behind her, gave a tiny nod to someone just out of sight. Then the door closed.

Red straightened out of her battle-ready stance, the feral look on her face melting away to anxiety. Being this close to an Order priestess still made her nervous, even with the Wilderwood contained beneath her skin, somewhere they couldn't hurt it. "Sorry," she muttered, making herself as small as possible to try to edge around the priestess toward the door.

"Don't let me disturb you." Oblivious to her attempted escape, the priestess stayed square in the path to the door, a gentle smile on her face. The hand she hadn't pressed to her chest in surprise held an unlit gray taper. "Our Shrine is small, but more than one can pray here. Be welcome, Second Daughter."

"Lady Wolf." Not a growl, but close to it.

"Yes, yes, of course." The priestess lowered her unlit candle to the flame of another until the wick caught. Still, she didn't move away from the door, standing right before it like a sentry. "I'm Maera."

Maera. The Ryltish equivalent of Merra. Red had always thought the practice of naming children after Second Daughters was macabre, but it wasn't exactly uncommon. She crossed her arms over her chest, feeling suddenly protective of her own name, the possibility of it being given to someone else who had no idea the true legacy they called back to.

The wavering candlelight caught the shape of a pendant on Maera's chest. Pale bark on a thin cord.

"Pretty, isn't it?" Maera lightly touched the necklace. "It doesn't allow us to speak to the Kings, not like the High Priestess can. But with the right coaxing, it allows one to feel their will more keenly."

The bandages on her fingers left little mystery as to what the *right coaxing* would be. Red's stomach curled in on itself; the Wilderwood within her shuddered.

"It's a privilege to wear," Maera said softly. Her eyes flickered toward where Kayu stood in the shadows. "One must prove themselves worthy to receive their pendant. Worthy to remain within our sisterhood, to take advantage of the protections it provides."

Next to the door, Kayu's face was bone-pale.

Red didn't know what was going on here, but both the forest within her and what was left of her regular human intuition told her it was time to get out of this room.

"Thank you," she said, though she was unsure what exactly she was supposed to be thanking Maera for, "but I have to go."

She twitched her fingers, trying to call the Wilderwood to attention. There was nothing with roots in this room, nothing under her influence, but surely she could find *something*—

Her veins greened, but it was weak. So far from home, in this place made of shadows and rock, there was little forest to be called.

"You don't need to go," Maera murmured. "You should stay right where you are, Lady Wolf."

And the door behind her slammed open.

Kiri. Of course it was Kiri. The High Priestess still looked frail, still looked sickly, but she stood tall in the doorway, and her eyes blazed bright.

"Second Daughter." It was a sneer, emphasized, a clear choice to use this title and not the true one. "It's time we finished this, don't you think?"

The shadow grove was gone, there was no cold magic for Kiri to call. But she flew at Red with her hands outstretched, and in one was a dagger.

Red backed up, her spine knocking into the pedestal in the center of the room, the branch shard crashing to the floor. Her hands raised, fingers crooked and flushed verdant as the Wilderwood within her searched for something, anything—

Threading roots beneath the stone floor, grass and herbs snaking through the ground. Red grabbed on to them, directed them, the floor shattering with a crack of breaking rock as they shot up to follow her order. But Kiri was fast, and her knife was sharp, and even as the roots burst beneath her in a shower of shale, the shine of the blade kissed Red's neck.

Then—something wrapping around Kiri's throat, making her mad blue eyes go wide. A belt, a thin strip of leather that Red marked as familiar. Kiri still strained forward, veins bulging around the makeshift garrote.

Behind her, Kayu, teeth clenched as she twisted her belt around the High Priestess's neck. "Go, Red," she panted. "*Go.*"

"No!" Maera, her previously pleasant face alight with rage. She held no weapon except her gray prayer candle, and Red saw her intent the moment she decided it, moving to sweep the flame toward the loose fall of Kayu's hair.

A flex of Red's fingers.

The roots she'd called from the floor shot up through broken stone, twisted around Maera's arms, her legs, her neck. Just enough to keep her still, not to hurt her.

Maera's eyes flashed, her face scarlet and her mouth a grimace. "Unclean thing," she spat at Red. "Abomination. Your sister is lost, Second Daughter. She'll bow to the Kings' wishes, and there's nothing you can do."

The decision was made in that split second, that mention of Neve, a reminder that even with all this power, she was helpless.

The roots tightened. Maera's eyes bulged. And Red let them keep tightening until the life in them blinked out.

"Killing her won't make it less true." Kiri's voice, hoarse. She still moved forward, impossibly strong; behind her, Kayu struggled with the belt, but the magic that let Kiri hear the Kings somehow lent her unnatural strength. "You can't do anything to stop this. All of it rests on Neverah now, and I've seen her darkness. You're the only thing that could make her hold on to herself, and when you're gone, so is she. It's over."

"Yes, it is," growled a voice from the door.

Eammon. Veins green, eyes afire, striding across the broken floor. Eammon, wrapping one hand around Kiri's jaw and the other around the back of her neck. Eammon, twisting, a *crack* as the High Priestess's neck broke.

Green-haloed eyes checked over Red, made sure she was unharmed, then turned to Kayu. "I just spoke with Raffe," the Wolf said, his voice the sound of autumn chilling into winter as the body of the High Priestess crumpled to the floor. "You have some explaining to do."

Chapter Thirty-Four

Raffe

I only did it to escape my betrothal."

The six of them huddled around a tavern table, shrouded in cloaks, seated in the darkest corner they could find. They didn't attract much attention. Everyone here was very drunk or on their way to it.

Kayu stared into a tankard. Her third. Raffe wasn't one for beer, but they didn't have any wine here and a drink was a drink, so he'd downed two of his own. He stopped there, though—the look on the Wolf's face was murderous, and Raffe had made a point of staying between him and Kayu.

He didn't interrogate himself on why.

During their madcap flight from the Temple, the Shrine with its scene of bloodless death shut and locked and hopefully still undiscovered, they hadn't spared time for discussion. It wasn't until they arrived at the tavern, needing somewhere to wait out the two hours left until dawn, that the questions—and the anger—had time to reveal themselves.

"So you joined the Order." Lyra had established herself as the go-between, the cool head that acted as a buffer between the Wolves and Kayu. "Because then you couldn't be married off."

"It was the only way to avoid it," Kayu said. "I couldn't run from my father forever. I chose the Rylt because it was far away, remote. I'd heard the Order was in some…turmoil…but I didn't expect the Ryltish Temple to be caught up in it."

Raffe grimaced. The same reasons Neve had packed the priestesses that didn't follow Kiri off to the Rylt—the same reasons Raffe had sent Kiri herself and the remains of her followers to join them, after the shadow grove. But, apparently, adherents to a dying religion were willing to latch onto just about anything to try to keep it alive. The three-day voyage had changed the defecting priestesses' minds about what was acceptable, and they'd spread the poison across the sea, making it the perfect place for Kiri to land. A ready-made cult, just waiting for their leader.

Shit. He really was starting to believe in destiny, in things you couldn't escape. And destiny seemed to be a bastard.

"By the time I got here, the only priestesses left in the Temple were loyal to Kiri. And once they heard my story, they knew I'd be useful to her. As soon as Kiri arrived and found out who I was, she gave me an ultimatum." Kayu spoke into her beer, the words kept low so they wouldn't carry farther than their table. "Either I could go to Valleyda, or she'd send me back to my father."

"Just go to Valleyda?" Red didn't look nearly as angry as Eammon did—even though she'd been the one who was almost murdered—but there was a fierceness on her face that Raffe certainly wouldn't want to cross. "Nothing else?"

The way she asked the question sounded like she knew the answer already.

"I was to go to Valleyda," Kayu answered slowly, "and find a way to bring Red to the Rylt."

Eammon was almost completely hidden in a heavy cloak, but his scarred hand was visible, wrapped around his tankard. Every vein went bright, blazing green, his grip tightening until Raffe thought he might break the thing.

Red's hand landed on his, and from across the table, Lyra gave the Wolf a look that wasn't quite reproachful, but cautioning.

"Why?" Lyra's voice stayed even, but her own grip on her cup had gone tense, the slim lines of her hands etched in tendons. Across from her, Fife glared at Kayu, palm rubbing at his Mark. "So Kiri could kill her?"

A brief nod from Kayu. No change in Eammon's stance, though Raffe saw Red's grip on his hand tighten, as if she might have to hold him back.

It took Kayu a moment to answer, which seemed reasonable when faced with the ire of the Wolves and those who counted them as family. "Yes." She sighed, spilling the rest without being asked. "Kiri thought that killing Red would solve two problems—make it so Neve wouldn't have a reason to hold out against the Kings, and take away Eammon's help, so he'd have to anchor the Wilderwood alone again."

"What do you mean, *hold out against the Kings*?" Nerves sharpened Red's voice. "What do they want Neve to do?"

Kayu shrugged helplessly. "I don't know. I don't know if Kiri did, either. To hear her tell it, she was taking orders from the Kings themselves."

Silence at the table. Raffe took a long draft of his beer, even though it tasted like warmed-over piss.

Red's face was thunderous, her eyes glinting brown and green from within the shadows of her hood. The nexus of her wrist flushed with emerald, one hand still atop Eammon's. "So Kiri thought the Kings breaking free from the Shadowlands was inevitable."

Kayu ducked a nod. "Not in the way it was going to be before. Kiri was clear on that. It was going to be different." She rubbed a hand over her face, pushing back loose strands of black hair. A sleepless night had carved dark circles beneath her eyes. "How different, I never got a clear answer on."

Down the table, Fife gnawed on his lip, one hand on his mug and another on his Mark. His sandy-red brows drew together, like he was thinking hard. Or listening hard. Maybe both—the forest lived in him, not in the same way it lived in Red and Eammon, but similar. It was probably telling him to get the fuck out of the Rylt.

Raffe would be happy to listen.

Lyra twisted her mouth, darting a glance at Red. "It doesn't neces-sarily mean anything," she said soothingly. "We've well established that Kiri is mad."

"*Was*," Eammon grumbled. There was a note of satisfaction in the past tense that made the skin between Raffe's shoulder blades prickle with gooseflesh.

"*Was*," Lyra amended. She shrugged, the movement graceful, and took a sip from her tankard. "Maybe she just couldn't fathom her gods failing."

"She *spoke* to them." Red slumped in her seat. "If she couldn't fathom them failing, it's because *they* couldn't. What we don't know is what that means for Neve."

Nothing good. None of them said it, but it hung over their heads, storm clouds that hadn't yet erupted into rain.

"We need to get back to the Wilderwood." This from Fife, the first words he'd spoken since they flew from the Temple, trying to outrun the discovery of the priestesses' bodies in the Shrine. "As soon as possible."

"Dawn is coming." Lyra gestured to the windows. The first fingers of pink light seeped slowly into the sky above the ocean. "But we can't make the voyage go any faster."

As if to punctuate her words, the floor rumbled.

Cutlery clattered, the surfaces of foamy beer disturbed, sloshing onto tables. The quiet drunks populating the tavern at this hour looked up with bleary eyes, confusion on drawn, sleepless faces.

The quake wasn't enough to do any damage, and settled quickly, only a scant few heartbeats of shaking. When it calmed, the tavern patrons went back to their mugs, almost as if it had been a collective hallucination.

But Raffe knew it wasn't. And, somehow, he knew it had something to do with Neve.

"What was that?" Lyra voiced the question, though it was clear on all their faces that they'd come to same conclusion Raffe had.

"Neve told me the Shadowlands are breaking apart," Red said quietly. "I think that's what the quakes are. I felt another one back home, but it wasn't this strong."

The implications of *that* made Raffe drain the rest of his beer and consider ordering another. If they could feel a quake here, how bad was it back at the Wilderwood?

"There isn't much time." Fife's hand clamped over his forearm, like the Mark beneath his sleeve pained him. "We have to get back."

"And do *what*?"

Red nearly spat it, loud enough that more than a few heads turned in their direction. Her tone was all anger, but her lip wobbled, and there was a shine in her eyes that wasn't due to drink. Eammon's hand left the table, snaked into her lap, and she clung to it like ivy on a wall. "There's nothing I can do, Fife," she said, more quietly now. "It's all on Neve. Even if I go back into the Heart Tree, I can't make her come with me."

"This is about more than Neve." Fife's eyes glinted in the dim light, something almost distant about them, like he was listening to whispered words. "Red, this is about more than Neve, and you know it. You *are* the Wilderwood, both of you." His gaze went to Eammon. "When the Shadowlands break apart, when all that magic comes back, you have to be there to contain it. To do *something*, regardless of what comes out."

It was, Raffe thought, the most words he'd heard from Fife at once in the entire time he'd known the man.

Slowly, the distant look bled from Fife's eyes. He blinked, looked to Lyra, who was watching him with a confused look on her face.

"Did the Wilderwood tell you that?" Eammon, puzzled and low.

A pause, then Fife nodded, almost reluctantly.

Red frowned. "I didn't feel anything."

Fife's hand tightened over his Mark, eyes flicking away. "Maybe it knows you wouldn't listen," he said quietly. "I think it tells me the things that you two don't want to hear."

Eammon looked to Red, face unreadable. Red's lower lip clamped between her teeth, blanched nearly white.

Raffe ardently wished for another beer.

"What do you mean, 'regardless of what comes out'?" Red swallowed, her hand on her own Mark now, as if she could make the forest within her explain itself. "*Neve* is coming out."

"I'm just telling you what it told me," Fife said wearily.

"We aren't hurting Neve."

Raffe was almost surprised to hear the sound of his own voice; from the wide-eyed looks everyone else shot him, so were they. He hadn't spoken since they arrived at the tavern.

He straightened, looked Fife in the eye. "No matter what your forest told you, we aren't hurting Neve."

Next to him, Kayu's shoulders softened. Defeat or relief or a strange mixture of the two, he wasn't sure.

"No," Red agreed softly. "We're not."

Eammon said nothing, his lips pressing into a flat line beneath his hood.

Lyra broke the tension, one hand on Fife's arm and the other still curled around her cup. "Let's get back home," she said, "and then we can figure out what exactly we need to do to be prepared."

Not exactly a reassuring sentiment, but it was all they had.

Tension about Neve dispelled, replaced with one more pressing. Red gave Kayu a narrow-eyed look. "You saved me."

"Technically, Eammon did," Kayu said softly. "But I tried."

"I don't know how much that means, when you were the one to bring us into a trap in the first place," Eammon growled.

"Not a trap." A tendril of ivy trailed out of Red's hood; she tucked it behind her ear. "Even if it was meant that way, we learned valuable information. We have a better idea of what we're dealing with."

"Still." Kayu lifted one shoulder, let it drop. Her face was wan, carved out with exhaustion. "I understand if you want to leave me here."

"No." Again, Raffe was surprised by his own voice, doubly surprised by how strong it sounded. He leveled his gaze at Red. "We're not leaving her. It isn't safe."

The door to the tavern opened. A man stumbled in, clearly half drunk already, and took a seat at the bar. "You hear all that racket up at the Temple?" he asked the bartender. "Screamin' and carryin' on. You'd think someone died."

"Of course we're not leaving Kayu." Red looked over her shoulder, at the window above the bar. Sunrise stained the sky. "All of us are leaving. *Now.*"

Beer on an empty stomach had been a bad idea.

Raffe leaned his head back against the wooden hull, grateful for the dim light. His initial assessment of the ship had been correct—the cargo hold and what Captain Neils referred to as the "passenger bunks" were one and the same, with a few cots made from pushed-together crates and lumpy mattresses, divided three to one side and three to the other with a hastily hung curtain.

When they ducked out of the tavern's back door, the grizzled captain had been waiting, his tiny galley bobbing in the tide at the dock. His eyes looked bleary, and a yawn creased his sun-leathered face as they approached, all still swathed in hoods. If it took him aback, he didn't show it. Kayu had given him a *lot* of money.

"Welcome aboard." A large, blunt hand swept behind him, indicating the galley. "Ship don't have a name, but mine's Neils. Don't wear it out."

None of them were inclined to. The distant sound of shouts carried on the breeze from the Temple, echoed by the sound of voices rising in the tavern behind them. The six of them filed onto the gangplank, as fast as they could move without running.

"Let's go," Eammon said, bringing up the rear.

It was an order, and it was followed. Neils, apparently, was the type who allowed gold to outweigh his questions.

Now Eammon and Red were on the other side of the curtain, murmuring too low for Raffe to make out any words. Lyra was above, talking to Neils, and Fife was with her.

Maybe Kayu was, too. Raffe was trying very hard not to care where Kayu was.

Memories of that brief time in the cloister room kept rearing up in his brain, embers from a fire he couldn't stamp out. It hadn't been simple, not at all, but it'd been *simpler*. He'd at least had the illusion of knowing who she was, though it'd been thin.

Disappointment tasted bitter, disappointment and shame. He should've known there was something wrong. Looking back, he couldn't believe he'd ever taken Kayu at her word, that he'd ever trusted her with something so huge as Neve's absence. Yes, he hadn't had much of a choice after she found that letter—which was the entire purpose of the letter, he knew now—but what kind of absolution was that, falling perfectly into the trap she'd set? The Order had written a script, and he'd acted his part impeccably.

She'd planted the idea that they needed to speak to Kiri, that they needed to go to the Rylt. And though they'd gotten valuable information, it still stood that the entire purpose of this trip had been, at its heart, to kill Red.

Yes, Kayu had saved her in the end. And yes, she'd felt like she had no choice but to dance to Kiri's tune. But all Raffe could think of was what Neve would say if the plan had worked and Red had died.

If the worst had happened, Neve would've never, ever forgiven him. He would've never forgiven himself. Though Kiri would've held the knife, the fault would lay on Raffe, and even though it hadn't happened, he could still *feel* what it would've been like if it had—a possibility that lay right beside him, barely a breath away, so close he could feel its phantom echoes.

And still, he'd spoken up for Kayu at the tavern.

He couldn't square it with himself, couldn't make the ends match up. So he didn't try. He rested his head against the wall, and he thought of nothing.

"Raffe?"

Shit.

Kayu had taken off her cloak but was still dressed in clothes similar to the ones she'd worn on their first voyage—loose pants, loose shirt, hair tied back in a colorful scarf. For a brief moment, he wondered what she looked like in Order white, then thrust the thought violently away.

Her lips were chapped. Shadows still purpled the skin beneath her eyes. She shifted back and forth from foot to foot, like she was torn between staying and running.

"I know *sorry* is a weak thing to say," she murmured finally, looking down at where she worked the hem of her shirt nervously between her thumbnails. "And I know telling you I had no choice is cowardly, even though it's true. Or felt true." She shrugged. "You always have a choice, I guess. But when it's death for you or death for someone you don't know, it seems so simple."

"When did it stop seeming simple?" His voice was hoarse.

She gave a weak snort. "Pretty much as soon as I arrived in Valleyda. Seeing you... how much you cared for Neve, how much you wanted her back...that made me care for her, in a way. Anyone you cared about that deeply must be someone good."

Raffe thought of bloody branches and shadowed veins and dead queens. He didn't respond. But he did scoot over a little, an invitation.

Kayu took it, sitting next to him. "And then I actually met Red, and I started to care about her, too," she said, not breaking the rhythm of her explanation. A sigh slumped her shoulders. "I never had any intention of letting her be killed, not after we went to the Edge and saw those carvings, not after I got a chance to know her and Eammon. But I didn't know how to stop the things already set in motion. That's all I did the entire time we were sailing here, the entire time in the Rylt—tried to find a way to get all of us out of there alive."

Six passengers, she'd told Neils when they chartered the galley. She'd intended for all of them to leave, even if she didn't know how.

"In the end, it wasn't anything graceful or smart." Kayu made a rueful noise, knuckling her hair out of her eyes. "It was just desperation and using what I had. And I was almost too late." A slight shudder rippled through her. "I keep playing it over and over in my mind, what might've happened if I *had* been too late, or if Eammon hadn't showed up to finish the job when I couldn't."

"We don't have to think about it." A lifeline for the both of them, something to pull them out of those echoes of things that hadn't happened but had been so damn close. "You weren't too late, and neither was Eammon, so we don't have to think about it."

Kayu took a deep breath, nodded. For a moment, they sat in silence, both trying very hard to follow that advice.

"I want you to know," Kayu murmured, "that from here on out, I'm on your side. Unequivocally. I don't deserve your trust, and I get that, but just...just know that whatever we need to do to get Neve back, to make sure the Kings end once and for all, I'm in."

"I believe you." And he did, even if it made him a fool twice over. "The others might be harder to convince."

"That's fair."

Raffe shifted against the wall. The movement brought their shoulders together. It made him think of other things coming together, but he didn't edge away. "It'd be easier if we knew what we needed to do."

"It seems like we can't do much but get back to the Wilderwood and wait." Kayu's eyes flashed in the gloom. "Which I don't think anyone is taking well."

"Sitting tight and waiting for the monster prison to rupture isn't my idea of a good time," Raffe muttered.

Suddenly, the boat rocked to one side, then the other, fast enough to make them crash together in a tangle of limbs and knocked skulls. Raffe heard Red yelp, Eammon's garbled shout. From above, a clatter of something falling over, more surprised yelling.

Raffe was first up the ladder, Eammon not far behind, though there was a hint of seasick glassiness in his eyes. Neils was whooping with rough laughter, pulling at a rope to adjust a sail. Fife and Lyra stood near the railing, both soaked in seawater and wearing similar expressions of alarm.

"Rogue wave!" Neils waved his hand at the sea like it was a horse that had jumped a steep hurdle. "Like there was an earthquake under the surface or somethin'! I've never seen 'em come like that!" Another whoop rang out rough over the water. "Kings' kneecaps, the look on your faces! I don't think we'll be runnin' into another one, not to worry, lads."

Lots of worry, lads, Raffe thought wryly.

It seemed like the wait for the monster prison to rupture was growing shorter by the minute.

Chapter Thirty-Five

Neve

Neve kept her eyes closed as the Kings laughed. She kept them closed, and thought of her sister, thought of home, thought of Raffe and of Solmir. All the small things that she could draw around her like armor.

She felt the displacement of air as Valchior reached for her, the groan of rock on rock as he bent closer. His finger touched her forehead, collapsing the true world into an illusion of bone and whole flesh once again. "You still want to see your traitor?" Merry as a joke. It must be one, to him.

Neve nodded, chin held high, as queenly as she could be.

Valchior smiled, the skin of his jaw flickering out of existence, revealing skeletal teeth. "Come on, then."

The projection of the King turned toward the coiled bones that made the Sanctum's wall, headed for a gap in the dead Dragon's tail. He ducked through it, slipping easily into the ivory lattice. With a bladed swallow, Neve followed.

She'd thought the walls were made only of the Dragon's skeleton, but it seemed that assumption was incorrect. If the center of the Old One's coiled tail made the Sanctum, the rest of its jagged bones and those of other beasts formed the corridors, madcap halls and rooms built of tilted-together ribs, the broken plates of massive skulls. There was no pattern to it that Neve could discern, but Valchior moved confidently, the illusion of the man he'd been, stepping over broken bones like they were cobblestones.

They lived in a palace made of the things they'd killed.

The King looked back over his shoulder, the space around his eye becoming desiccated skin and empty orbital socket. A sly smile bent his mouth.

"So many bones," he said quietly. He inspected the ground at his feet, thoughtfully clicking his tongue. Then he bent, picked up the bone with the sharpest end.

"Outside of the Sanctum, we can't touch anything when we're like this. Projecting, showing ourselves as we used to be rather than as we are." He hefted the bone in his hand. "But here, where our power is greatest, there are certain perks. Our projections are more closely tied to our physical bodies. To hurt one is to hurt the other."

It happened too fast for Neve to react. Valchior lifted the bone and shoved it through his neck.

She didn't know what to make of it, that her first instinct was to step back, to raise a cool brow. Surely, someone compassionate, someone *good*, would step forward, body driven with the intent to help before their mind caught up and told them it wouldn't make a difference.

But Neve didn't.

And when Valchior realized it, his grotesquely wide eyes finding hers with a false look of alarm, he *cackled*.

He gripped the bone, pulled it from his neck. Open skin and ivory spinal cord shuddered back and forth as the superficial wound closed. "You take your lessons well," he chuckled, testing the point of the bone again before letting it clatter to the floor. "Just wanted to let you know it was pointless, before you got any ideas. It takes more than the bone of just any god to unravel us, Neve. And even if you did manage to start that unraveling, all you'd do is release our magic. Release our souls. And then they'd need somewhere to go, either into you or into Solmir."

"Shouldn't you tell me how to do it, then?" It was too easy an opening, deliberately leading her to a question she sensed he wouldn't answer, but she couldn't stop herself from asking. "Isn't that what you want?"

"Clever Shadow Queen." He reached out, cupped her cheek. His hand was ragged skin and gleaming bone, and Neve jerked away. Valchior caught her chin in an iron grip she couldn't pull out of, dragged her closer to his face. One eye was whole and green and fringed in auburn lashes; the other an empty hole in a bare skull. "Only the bones of a god can kill a god, but it must be a god made in the same way. And we made *ourselves* gods."

The last word was a sneer, his mouth barely a breath away from hers, lush lips blinking to overgrown skeletal teeth.

Neve snarled right before his mouth reached hers, arm coming up to knock his grip away with such force that she stumbled backward in a racket of bones.

Valchior laughed again, bright and jovial. "Kisses are only for Solmir, I see," he said. "Noted, noted."

The King's projection turned away from her, moved farther into the bone labyrinth. Neve followed, with the god-bone the Seamstress had given her still clutched in her hand, regardless of how useless it'd just been proven.

They wound through the rubble some more—Neve couldn't tell how long; her body had lost the ability to count time passing—until Valchior came to a stop, the dark space before him cavernous and too dim for details.

"Here he is," he said, waving a dismissive hand. "Your traitor."

And Neve rushed forward, nothing timid or queenly about it.

A rib cage. At least, Neve assumed it was a rib cage. Curved bones arced overhead, attached to a central piece that looked segmented. More bones crowded the spaces between the larger ribs, fused together by time, like the mountain where the Oracle had lived. A small fire burned in the center of the stone floor, spitting gray flame and acrid smoke.

And among all the bones, Solmir, bloodied and bruised. He'd been sitting, but on her approach he stood, a long chain rattling as he did. One wrist was wrapped in a gleaming ivory manacle—bone-built, too, then. Even the chain that secured him to the floor looked made of tiny interlocking pieces, wrong-shaped vertebrae with enough give to let him walk around the room but not beyond the threshold. Dust swirled around his feet, marked with skids and bootprints, like he'd tried pulling the chain free from the floor and failed.

"Take some time to think," Valchior said. "Though do remember that you don't have much. The Shadowlands grow more unstable by the minute." He grinned, eyes glittering. "Have fun deciding who gets to be the martyr. We'll even give you some privacy."

The feeling of a weight leaving her head, a presence lifting and pulling the illusion with it. The shape of Valchior winked out, leaving only her and Solmir and a weak fire in a prison made from a carcass.

She stared at him. He stared at her. Firelight glinted over the planes of his bloodied chest, the dips and hollows of lithe, fine-honed muscle. She'd thought him built like a dagger, once, and the comparison had only grown more apt. Long and slender and sharp, made for harming, dangerous to hold carelessly.

He swallowed, the work of it evident down his throat. She hadn't really had a chance to look at him closely, not since he gave her all the magic, became nothing but a man. His eyes were more brightly blue, the angles of his face less brutal, somehow softened.

"Neve..." Her name came out hoarse. His hand twitched toward her, then away with a conscious flex of his fingers and a rattle of his chain. He didn't try to say anything else.

"I know what the other way is." Tension broke in an explosion of movement—Neve turned and hurled the god-bone in her hand as hard as she could. It clattered against one of the massive ribs forming the wall, fell to the floor. When Neve whirled back around to face him, Solmir's expression hadn't changed, still drawn and unreadable. "You were going to make me your *murderer*, Solmir."

A martyr or a murderer. This could only end with one of them climbing on the altar and the other holding the knife.

"It's not that simple," Solmir said, low and nearly pleading.

"Of course it is. You gave me the magic so I couldn't be the Kings' vessel. So that *you* would have to be, even though you've been running from that for centuries." Years upon years of trying to save himself, and he'd given it up for her. Neve's mind shied away from that. Shied away from the memories of a conversation in a cobweb-strung cabin about something else that was supposed to be *simple*. "And if you did that, I would have to kill you."

"Or you could let Redarys and her Wolf do it for you," Solmir murmured.

"No," Neve said, sharp and immediate. "I kill my own monsters."

His eyes darted to her own. She'd called him a monster so many times, but this was the first time she'd called him hers.

Solmir lowered himself to the floor, leaning his head back against a rib, closing his burn-blue eyes. "And that makes you so angry? The thought of me dying?"

Angry. Hurt. Terrified. But Neve just nodded.

The silver ring in his earlobe glinted as he shook his head, lip lifted in half a sneer. "And here I thought you'd be jumping at the chance to get rid of me."

She stalked across the floor like she might slap him, fingers flattening in readiness. But to touch him would be to unleash something, her skin on his an ember sparking flame, and it scared her enough to stay her hand. Instead, she stood over him, teeth clenched, every muscle in her body held tense and tight.

It was a moment primed for something—her standing like an avenging god, him kneeling like a penitent to her wrath. But neither one of them took whatever volatile thing the moment offered. It would only make this harder.

"You're an asshole." Weak words, too brittle to hold up everything Neve needed to say.

He opened his eyes, reflecting firelight. "I'm far worse than that."

Holding back from him was too hard. She was too tired for it. So Neve sat next to him, head tilted against the bones the same way his was.

"Your eyes are still brown."

She turned to look at him, brows knit.

Solmir shrugged. "All that magic you're carrying—all that power—and your eyes are still brown. Your soul is still intact." He paused. "That means something, Neve. It means you're good enough to carry it all."

Too close to Valchior's words. Neve pressed her chapped lips together. "I'm not," she murmured. "I'm not, Solmir."

"Tell me why you think that."

He sounded almost angry. Neve snorted, mind spinning out spades of things she could tell him, a curated list of sins. But she narrowed it down to one word.

"Arick," Neve breathed.

That name snagged in her thoughts, a burr she couldn't pick out. The man next to her—the once-King, the fallen god, the villain of the piece—had caused the death of one of her best friends. And still she sat here and tried to think of ways to save him. Still she knew the distance between their bodies down to the inch.

Solmir's eyes slid her way, lit with confusion. "What about him?"

Shadows damn her, he was going to make her say it. Neve pulled up her knees and rested her bent arms on them, muffling her mouth. "Even if Red held the knife, you were the cause of his death. And I'm still here, trying to save you."

He didn't move, didn't speak for a moment. When he did, it was quiet. "Isn't that the mark of goodness? Wanting to help people who don't deserve it?" A pause. "Compassion for the monsters?"

She wished she could think of it in stark, black-and-white terms. Being able to point to herself as *bad* would be easier than this muddled gray area, not knowing if justice was wanting to save a man who didn't deserve it or seeking revenge for an unrighteous death. Heroes and villains and the spaces between, a prism that changed reflections depending on the angle you turned it.

If she was truly good, maybe she could hold all the Kings' souls without being taken over. Control their power, keep them contained. If she was truly bad, all of this was a lost cause anyway.

But Neve was somewhere between. Somewhere human. And it carried no certainty.

"I don't know," she said, closing her eyes. "I don't know."

After a moment, he put his hand on the ground between them, palm up. Neve slid her fingers between his. Magic buzzed where their skin met, but she didn't let it go, and he didn't let it in. No decisions had been made, not yet.

A low rumble, rattling the walls of their rib-and-rock cage. The tiny bones on the floor jumped and skittered.

"Neve," Solmir murmured as the last of the shuddering faded, "let it be me."

Her grip on his hand was white-knuckled. "Can you take it?"

They both knew what she meant, what lurked around the edges. Could he take in all the souls of the Kings without losing himself to them? Without becoming something terrible, something in their control, and making all of this for nothing?

Solmir's fingers twitched in hers. "I can try," he said finally. "For you, I can try."

For her.

It should be a relief. But Neve's throat ached. "You think I can be part of your death so easily?"

Silence. Then Solmir swore, long and harsh. He dropped her hand and stood, pacing away, scrubbing a hand through all that long hair. Blood streaked at his temple, turned it dark.

"I'd hoped it would be hard for you." He turned, teeth bared, his eyes a cold blue glitter. "Damn me, Neverah, I hoped it wouldn't be easy, and that, more than anything else I've done, means I'm absolutely the villain here. I deserve to be the vessel, and I deserve for you to kill me."

She said nothing. There was nothing to say. Neve just sat there, knees clasped to her chest, heart a gaping maw.

Then she stood with a curse almost as impressive as his had been, reaching for him. He grabbed her arm, the sleeve of his coat a barrier between their skin, like he knew what she was thinking. "You're not giving the power to me, Neverah, don't you even think of it."

"I'm not, you bastard." It was a burning thing to admit, and it came out almost like a snarl. "Not every kiss has to be about magic."

And his mouth was open with surprise when Neve's crashed into it.

It was nowhere near gentle, nowhere near soft, this collision that felt as ordained as stars on the same path, combining into a sun or a burnt-out void. It was need, ravenous, distilled *want* that knew this was the only moment it would have.

His surprise lasted only a moment. "Damn me," he muttered against her mouth, then his hands were in her hair, tugging her as close as he could.

She dragged her teeth against his lips, tasted copper; he growled deep in his throat and pressed closer, until her back collided with the rib bones that made the wall, his knee between her legs, running hot lightning to her core.

Solmir tasted like cold. Neve wasn't sure how that was possible, but he tasted like cold, like the space between winter pine trees. It was fresh air; she wanted to gulp it down. One of his hands gripped the jut of her hip, raked her up his thigh so their chests pressed together; the other shoved his coat off her shoulders. He bared his teeth as he did it, even through their rough kiss, his hands rising to tangle in her hair and tilt back her head, mouth on her neck, tongue on her collarbone. Everything between them was sharp angles, even this.

Clothes were easy to discard, tattered and bloodied as they were. Solmir kicked away bones before he laid her back, lips on throat, clavicle, lower. Quick and desperate as this was, his arm beneath her head was gentle, muscle tensed to make her comfortable.

He broke away long enough to look up at her, blue eyes on brown in a gray void. The signs of souls. Neve had nothing to pray to, but she sent out an anguished hope anyway that he'd be strong enough to keep his right until the end. An end she still couldn't think about.

"I love you." Solmir said it like it made him angry, like he was throwing down a gauntlet, harsh against her throat. "Don't you dare say it back."

So she didn't.

Chapter Thirty-Six

Red

The voyage was supposed to take three days. But with the strange waves and the whipping wind, they made it in barely two.

Neils didn't know what to make of the rogue waves, which came up with enough force to push the ship but never threatened to capsize it. "I've never seen something like that," he said, shaking his head as he hauled on ropes. "And never once has it knocked us off course."

"Thankfully," Eammon muttered. He and the grizzled captain had fallen into a quick, unlikely friendship, since Eammon's seasickness—still present, though not as forcefully—kept him up on the deck more often than not. Red couldn't tell if Neils bought the story Kayu hurriedly told him as the galley left the harbor about a strange strain of gangrene, but he didn't question Eammon's bark-covered forearms or the green along his veins, both of which were more vibrant than they'd been before.

The changes were evident in Red, too—the ivy in her hair grew lush, the ring of emerald around her irises almost eclipsing the whites the closer they drew to Valleyda. The Wilderwood flourishing as it neared home, she'd think, if it weren't for the sting of it, the pull deep in her gut that told her something was *happening*, something that golden thread of consciousness beside her own didn't know how to tell her.

The waves, the quakes they'd felt—all of it tied back to the Wilderwood and the Shadowlands. To Red and Neve.

It was night when they reached the Florish shore, a full moon floating in an indigo sky. The harbor was somewhat busier in the very late hours than the very early, but there still weren't many people on the docks other than a few sleepy fishermen. The cold of autumn chilled even worse at the coastline, and no one was eager to sail when the wind blew over the water like a cracking whip.

Neils steered them to an empty dock, slapping a calloused hand on the wheel before dropping anchor. He turned to Red with the look of someone who had a lot of questions but wasn't sure if he would ask them or not.

In the end, he decided not to. "Whatever trouble you ran into back in the Rylt," he said, "I hope you're far enough away from it now."

"Unfortunately," Red murmured, "it's the kind of trouble you can't really run from."

He snorted. "Been there." A moment's hesitation, then he clapped her quickly on the shoulder. "In that case, I hope it's a trouble that resolves."

It would. One way or another. Red gave Neils a wan smile and pushed away from the railing at the prow, going to get her bag from below. She passed Eammon on the way, who dropped a kiss to her forehead before heading toward the captain. He said something too low for her to make out, and Neils responded with a hearty laugh.

Kayu emerged from the hold, looking somewhat better than she had when they left the Rylt. She'd combed out her hair to its black, straight waterfall again, and the dark circles beneath her eyes had softened after a full night of sleep.

Yesterday, after Raffe left and Kayu was alone with her head tilted against the wall and her eyes closed, Red had gone to thank her. She'd stood there, unsure of how to start the conversation, the gentle roll of the ship making her legs unsteady.

"You can slap me with a vine or something." Kayu only opened her eyes enough to confirm it was Red before closing them again. "Whatever angry forest gods do to those who cross them."

"I'm not going to slap you with a vine." The idea was so ludicrous that it broke the tension. Red slumped next to Kayu, arms braced on her knees. She could rehash everything—the plot, Kayu foiling it, thanks given and denied—but the thought was exhausting.

"You did what you thought you had to do." Red shrugged. "I think we're all familiar with that."

A pause. Then Kayu turned to look at her, a quizzical twist to her mouth. "You're letting me off entirely too easily."

"Would you prefer to talk to Eammon about it?"

"No, I'm fine, thank you." Kayu sat up and rubbed a hand over her face. "Whatever you need to find your sister, I'm here to help. It's the least I can do."

"I wish there was something I knew to ask you to do," Red murmured. "All I can think of is to go back to the Keep and…and wait, I guess."

Wait to see if Neve would decide to come back. Wait to see what happened when the Shadowlands broke apart. Wait to see what was left of her sister when it did.

"Then I'll wait with you," Kayu said.

So now, that's what they were all headed to do. Wait.

As Red descended into the dark of the hold and grabbed her bag, she couldn't help but think of Neve, those long days after Red had disappeared into the Wilderwood, stretching into weeks and then months. Waiting to see if her sacrifices would bring Red back. Waiting to see what her blood on sentinel branches bought her.

She paused before going back up the ladder. Her scarlet cloak was stuffed into her bag; Red pulled it out, took off the gray one she wore, swirled the bridal cloak over her shoulders instead. Golden embroidery glinted in the gloom.

Better.

At the stern, Raffe was looping rope, doing some vital ship activity Red had no context for—two voyages in a week, and she still had no idea how boats worked. He'd been quiet. The most she'd heard him say was when she overheard him speaking with Kayu, his voice too muffled to make out specifics.

"Need help?" she asked.

"I've got it."

Kayu and Lyra helped Neils shove down the gangplank, ready to disembark. Kayu went first, walking up the shore to where the horses were stabled and the carriage parked, beyond where the sand turned to grass. Raffe watched her.

Red chewed her lip. "I know it's none of my business—"

"Here we go," Raffe muttered.

"—but you should know you don't have to feel guilty, Raffe."

He stopped in his endless looping of rope, tilting back his head so his breath plumed toward the sky. At first, she thought he would ignore her or brush it off. But then he shook his head and turned back to his rope. "I know I don't. And yet."

Red didn't push. She leaned against the railing.

Raffe spoke without her prompting, like this was something he'd been waiting for. Knowing him, it was. "The way we left things, Neve and I... well. That's the point, I guess. There wasn't a thing to leave. I told her I loved her, and she never said it back, even though she showed it, or at least that she cared, and I..." He ran a hand over his head. "Now I feel like I don't know who she is. I only know who she *was*."

"We change," Red murmured. Not an indictment or an absolution, just a statement of fact. "We grow in different directions sometimes."

"I still care about her," Raffe said.

Care about. Not *love*. "I know."

"And when she comes back, I..." He lost the words and couldn't find any more that fit. Raffe shook his head.

"When she comes back," Red said decisively, "you will be an excellent friend to her. You two will talk. You will figure out what kind of relationship you want to have." She gave him a tiny, reassuring half smile. "All of this is complicated, Raffe. It always has been. You don't have to know exactly what you're doing all the time."

He huffed a rueful laugh. "Even half the time would be welcome."

The coach clattered up the road that led to the docks, Kayu driving. As the horses stopped, a rumble moved over the ground, shaking the docks, the sparse trees, making the waves in the ocean grow taller.

At the wheel, Neils boomed another laugh. "This keeps up, and I'll be down to Karsecka in less than a week!"

Red gave him a tight smile, dread chewing at her spine. The Wilderwood sent a skitter of thorns across her ribs, a branch stretching over her collarbone, sharp and pinching.

⁂

Kayu drove fast, but the earthquakes were faster. They felt at least three in the two hours it took to travel from the Florish coast to the edge of the Wilderwood, growing in intensity the closer they got to Valleyda. By the time they crossed the border, only minutes from the Wilderwood, Kayu had to stop the carriage each time one started, the horses prancing nervously in place as the ground shook. It'd snowed while they were gone, white drifts of it lining the roadway, flakes spinning off to twirl in the air as the earth vibrated beneath them. Snow always started early this far north, barely giving summer time to fade to fall.

"The quakes are too close together." Lyra shook her head, fawn-colored eyes glassy with worry. "How do we know the Shadowlands haven't dissolved already?"

"We'll know." The forest within Red rustled, a bloom of a vine along her shoulder blades, the snaking of a root down her spine. Not for the first time, she half wished the Wilderwood could speak to her in words again, wither part of itself as a price for speech. "We'll know when they dissolve."

Across the carriage, Fife's face was pale, his hand clamped tight around his forearm. Red watched him with her lips pressed into a thin line, waiting to see if the Wilderwood spoke to him in ways it wasn't speaking to her.

It tells me the things you don't want to hear.

But Fife stayed silent.

Another painful twist of root in Red's sternum. Eammon's hand tightened on her knee—he felt it, too. Not the deep, piercing pain of the sentinels being ripped out, nothing like what they'd felt the night of the shadow grove when Neve disappeared, but the ache of the forest doing…*something*.

Something none of them were sure of yet.

"What then?" Lyra asked. "Will it be like a breach? A million shadow-creatures erupting at once?" Her hand flexed to the hilt of her *tor*, its scabbard on the floor by her feet. "Do we just fling blood at them again?"

"No."

Every head turned to Fife, all of them surprised that the answer had come from him. He kept his gaze on the floor, his jaw a ridge of discomfort, his Marked arm held close to his body. "No blood. The blood was always a bandage, it didn't truly fix anything."

Red slipped her hand over Eammon's scarred one, holding tight.

Another quake shook the carriage, snow sliding from the hills at the side of the road. The horses squealed, Kayu's soothing voice jagging up toward a shout as she sawed on the reins. The carriage lurched back and forth, tipping up onto two wheels.

"Bail out!" Raffe's voice sliced through the sounds of the horses. "The thing's about to flip!"

Fife shot up, levering open the door; he pushed Lyra out before jumping after her.

Eammon tugged Red with him out the door to tumble into the snow. One of the wheels broke, sending the whole structure leaning in their direction; teeth bared, he swept her up against his chest, rolling out of the way just as the entire carriage crashed to the ground exactly where they'd been.

The earth ceased its shaking as the horses galloped away, cut free by Raffe as he jumped down from the driver's seat. He and Kayu stood at the edge of the road, breathing hard; her palms were red and welted from trying to hold on to the reins.

"Well," Kayu said, voice surprisingly even, "I guess we're walking."

They were close, thankfully. The trees of the Wilderwood speared into the sky ahead of them after half an hour, more snow twirling in the air between the branches. Another low quake rumbled through the ground, calmer than the one that had crashed the carriage, but enough to make them all stop and brace against the road.

Raffe turned to look at Red after the third quake in fifteen minutes, the border of the Wilderwood visible up ahead. "What if the Shadow-lands dissolve while Neve's there?" His eyes sparked. "What if Solmir keeps her there, and she can't get away even if she wants to?"

She shook her head. Her voice came out hoarse. "I don't know what to tell you, Raffe. I can't make her leave."

He stared at her a moment, eyes glittering. When Neve first disappeared into the Shadowlands, he'd asked Red how they were going to save her. Then, too, she hadn't known. And he'd told her that wasn't good enough.

It still wasn't.

Red couldn't save Neve, any more than Neve could save her. She wondered if anyone could, really. Saving someone else was a wall you couldn't scale unless they threw you a rope.

As they reached the tree line, Red gave an involuntary sigh of relief. A tension she hadn't known she was carrying softened in her shoulders, the forest beneath her skin opening wider blooms, stretching out longer branches. Next to her, Eammon let out a deep breath, the sound like rustling leaves.

Fife rubbed at the Mark on his arm, flickering them a surreptitious look from beneath ginger brows.

"So we just go to the Keep?" Lyra asked. The bright light off the snow gilded her curls in silver. Even though she wasn't connected to the Wilderwood anymore, being close to it still seemed to soothe her. "Wait for the shadows to find us?"

Another quake, this one enough to knock Red off-balance. She slid in the snow, Eammon catching her arm. Down in the village, hidden beneath all the white, she heard the sounds of frightened animals, distant calls of alarm.

The key in her hand pulsed more quickly, its heartbeat speeding up. And something about that made the dread in her middle spike higher, a connection that, once made, seemed obvious.

It was Neve's heart. She could feel Neve's heart in her key.

Which meant she was still alive. Still alive, and still choosing to stay in the Shadowlands, to finish the Kings in whatever way she and Solmir could.

Red pulled the key from her pocket. The threads of gold in the bark had grown, were *still* growing, nearly eclipsing the white. It glowed as bright as a miniature sun in her palm, glinting off the snow. The heartbeat—Neve's heartbeat—sped and sped, nearly visible, pounding to a crescendo.

"That has to mean something," Raffe murmured.

"I think so." The Wilderwood in Red expanded, new leaves unfurling, flowers opening wide. "I think she's—"

She cut off with a yelp, the warmth of the key flaring suddenly to a bonfire-burn. Red dropped it, stumbling backward into Eammon, holding her hand to her chest.

The snow melted where the key dropped, hissing as it fell through the drifts, finally coming to rest on the earth.

Then an explosion threw all of them back in a burst of blinding light, as a white-and-gold trunk burst from the ground and reached glowing branches toward the sky.

Chapter Thirty-Seven

Neve

The stone floor inside the dead god's rib cage could never be called comfortable, but cushioned by Solmir and his tattered coat, it was perfectly fine. The languid aftereffects of a sated body lulled Neve into a deeper rest than she'd felt in years, for once free of massive white trees and in-between places. Just sleep, dark and silent.

But when she woke, she still knew exactly where she was, none of that fading in and out of consciousness that usually accompanied deep sleep. Bones creaked above her head; the gray embers spat in the fire pit. Solmir pressed close to her back, chest still bare, his tattooed arm twisted over her waist and the other under her head. He held it at an odd angle; his wrist was still encircled by a manacle, the long chain still tethering him to the stone floor.

She reached out and threaded her fingers with his, black-veined against his pale gray.

Valchior would be returning soon, more than likely. She couldn't find the energy to care. They'd come to a decision, she and Solmir, but Neve didn't want to think about it. Didn't want to look it in the eye until she absolutely had to.

First Red, then Arick and Isla, then Raffe when she entered the shadows, and now him. Neve was always losing someone.

Gooseflesh prickled over her skin, only warm where she pressed against Solmir. He breathed low and even in her ear, but she knew he wasn't asleep any more than she was. Every time he moved, she smelled cold pines. Thorns pressed through Neve's wrist, through the knuckles of her fingers. Lightly, he brushed a thumb over them. "Jagged thing," he murmured against her neck.

She turned, not speaking, hid in the hollow of his shoulder. He pulled her closer, face buried in her bloody and rock-dusted hair.

Before, they'd been rough, all sharp edges and desperation, but now things between them seemed to have settled into softness. It scared her a little. Softness was easy to wound.

"Are you..." He breathed the words against her ear, clearly as unable to find the right emotion as she was.

She kissed his jaw. Let that be an answer for a question neither of them knew how to ask.

The thrum of Solmir's heartbeat under her cheek had almost lulled her back to sleep when he spoke again. "When you go home and they ask what happened with you and me," he murmured into her hair, "don't feel like you have to tell them."

Her thorn-wreathed hands curled, digging into his skin. No need to define *they*. Red, her Wolf, and Raffe. "What if I want to?"

His arms tightened. "You don't have to explain yourself," he said. "You don't have to absolve me."

They lay in silence, wrapped up in each other, the only anchors either of them could find. The branch-shard key, still tangled in Neve's hair at the back of her neck, pulsed cold against her nape, raising goose-flesh. Distantly, she wondered how long they'd been here. Time moved strangely, with no sun and no moon and no real need for food or sleep.

However much time it'd been, she wished for more of it.

Solmir nudged her up, grabbed her tattered nightgown off the floor. He shook it out before pulling it over her head, brushing loose rock and bone from its length, the chain on his arm clicking delicately over the floor. Then his coat, settling over her shoulders. He reached into his pocket and pulled out a piece of wood.

The night sky carving.

"It's as done as it's going to be," he said, holding it out to her. "If you still want it."

Neve stretched out her hand. Let him drop it in her palm. Her fingers curled around it like a promise.

"I'll be the one to do it," she said, hand still hanging in the air between them. "When we...when we get to the surface. Not Red or Eammon."

"You kill your own monsters." A rueful smile picked up the corner of Solmir's mouth.

She dropped the carving into her coat pocket. And when she wound her fingers in his hair and pulled him back to her, he didn't protest.

They were still kissing, slow and languid and not leading to anything else, when she heard the chuckle.

There was no illusionary King to watch them, since Neve wasn't there for Valchior to lay his hand on her forehead and spin a lie of the man he used to be. But apparently the Kings could still see them, even without that. Their awareness seeped into every bone of their Sanctum.

"Don't worry, Shadow Queen." The voice reverberated in the floor, in her ears. "We didn't watch."

Solmir snarled, fingers arching like claws. "Fuck you," he whispered hoarsely into empty air.

The chuckles intensified.

Neve lay her hand on Solmir's cheek, turned his wide, scared eyes to hers. She was beyond shame now. Who cared if monsters knew she was a dark thing made all of want? "I know you told me not to say it," she began.

"Don't," he murmured, and kissed her instead, swallowing the confession.

They turned to the opening in the rib cage together, the arch of bones that served as an entrance. The long chain on Solmir's wrist snapped off, fell in a cloud of dust. The Kings, releasing him with a thought.

Hand in hand, Neve and Solmir wound their way through the bones, pulled back to the center of the Sanctum like planets on the curve of their orbit.

The Kings sat on their thrones. The Dragon's skull glared down from the apex of the ceiling, immense mouth eternally open in an endless, silent scream. Neve strode to the center of their circle with her jaw firm and her eyes narrowed, graceful, regal. Her hand trembled in Solmir's, but she didn't let the fear show on her face.

Solmir's expression was a mask to cover terror. A sneer, blue eyes cutting, lips twisted like he wanted to rip each stone effigy limb from limb.

"Well." It took Neve a moment to place the voice—Malchrosite, the most reserved of the four. "Did you have time to say goodbye?"

"Oh, she did." Byriand tittered, a strange sound in these voices of shale and stone. "She said a thorough goodbye."

Valchior said nothing. The King faced her, rock-still, face shrouded by gauze and stone fingers steepled. Waiting.

Damn him. He wasn't going to ask. He was going to make them say it.

"I'm through running," Solmir said, low and seething. "I'll be your damn vessel. But you have to let her go."

A moment of quiet, the calm before a thundercrack. Then a low laugh, coming from everywhere at once.

"Well, Valchior, you did your best." Calryes's voice was somehow mocking, even layered in rock. "But it seems we'll be stuck with a second-rate vessel after all. You always were a disappointment, son. Running for centuries, only to end up right back where you started. You tried so hard not to be a villain, and look at you now."

"He's better than you," Neve snarled. "Better than you could ever hope to be."

"I suppose we'll see, won't we?" Calryes was incapable of expression, and the shroud draped over him hid where his face should be. But it sounded to Neve like he grinned.

A frisson of disquiet curled in her middle, a splinter of doubt.

The King in front of them shifted with the squeal of rubbing rock. Valchior leaned down, the spikes of his awful crown glinting. Solmir stepped between them, like he could block the King, but Neve laid a gentle hand on his shoulder.

"Wait," she murmured. The magic in her center swirled and writhed.

He didn't want to. She could see it in the thin line of his mouth, the terrified glitter of his blue eyes. But when Neve stepped around him, toward that waiting stone finger, Solmir didn't stop her.

The stone finger touched her forehead, alchemized to flesh. She opened her eyes, and she and Valchior stood alone in the Sanctum, an illusion of privacy.

The King didn't take his hand from her once the illusion was complete. Instead, he slid it from her brow to her cheek, cupping her face, a worried light in his eyes.

"I will speak plainly," he said. "You are making a mistake, Neverah."

Her brows knit. The uneasy curl in her stomach coiled all the way up her spine.

"You want to think there is good in him," Valchior murmured. "I don't fault you for it—we want to think the best of those we care for. Even when there is no proof of it."

"There's proof." Her mouth barely moved, a whisper in this vast cavern made from a corpse. "He's willing to sacrifice himself to end you. To keep you from coming back ever again."

"Are you sure?" He raised a brow. "Are you sure he would let himself be killed, in the end? I think it more likely he would do whatever he could to live. Especially with all that new power. Power you are throwing away."

Her mouth opened to say of course she was sure. But that sinking hook of doubt in her stomach, that needling unease.

Valchior continued, sensing the bruise and pressing it hard. "We are a heavy burden, Neverah. Our darkness is so much to carry, and it weighs on a soul. Changes it. Even one that starts out pure and unblemished, and you and I both know his isn't."

"No one's is." But it didn't sound like the strong rebuttal she wanted it to be. It sounded like an excuse.

"True." The King inclined his head with an amused smile. "But some are in better shape than others, and one can't deny that yours is better off than his. It is far more dangerous for him to be our vessel than you. It's what you were made for. To be the dark to your sister's light."

Neve didn't realize she was crying until salt touched her lips, tears sliding soundlessly from her eyes. She wanted to wipe them away, but Valchior did before she could, thumbing gently at her cheek.

"That's not fair." She didn't know she'd spoken it aloud until she saw Valchior nod, and she pressed her eyes closed. "It's not fair."

"It's not," he agreed. "But we all have to pay for our mistakes, Neve. You pulled in the darkness in the shadow grove. You started all of this by not being willing to let Red go."

The linchpin, the axis. She and Red, over and over again. She'd conspired with Kiri, let Arick be the collateral, she'd changed everything with no thought for the consequences. To save Red, yes, but also for herself. To feel like she had some modicum of control in a life that allowed her so little of it, some ability to change what was wrong.

"But you can atone." Valchior lifted her chin with his thumb. "Think of all you can do, with our power inside you. All you can accomplish, with our magic turned to your use."

She took a shaky breath. Thought of wrongs to be righted. Thought of control.

"I knew you were what we'd been waiting for," Valchior said quietly. "When I first caught a glimpse of you, a *feel* of you through the grove you made. This is what you were meant to be."

"I can't." She turned her chin away from his touch. "Whoever goes through as the vessel will be—"

"The Wolves won't kill you." There was something scraping in his tone, something edging up toward irritation. "Redarys won't let Eammon do it, and even if it were only Eammon, he wouldn't kill his wife's twin. He would step aside."

Even if it were only Eammon, he said, like it was a possibility Valchior had thought about. Panic spiked in her stomach. "Red—"

"Is perfectly fine." The soothing note was back in his voice, face once again handsome and introspective, a mask made to be trusted. "Can't you feel your key?"

Her key. The one hidden in the tangles of her hair. It pulsed gently against the nape of her neck, cold and comforting. Almost like a heartbeat.

Red's heartbeat. Reassurance her sister was alive.

"They don't even have to know," Valchior said, smoothing her hair back from her face. "You can hide us, Neve. Tucked inside your soul, feeding you power like you've never known. Magic that will make what you bled for look like party tricks. You take in our souls, you ascend. You live your life and leave a rich legacy. Famines alleviated, seas calmed, sicknesses healed. You'll be a god in your own right. They'll worship you."

"And when I die?"

The King smiled, something glittering in his eyes. "Who says you have to?"

That was what made her decide, what snapped her out of her wavering and her confusion, the muddled feelings of pride and guilt. That split-second smile, that malevolent glimmer.

"No," Neve said.

His expression warped. Gone were the gentle hands and soft words; he gripped her shoulders and tugged her forward with fingers that were all bone and sinew and the clinging meat of muscle, the flesh rotted away. His face went concave on one side, cheekbone arcing the wrong direction, desiccation along his lips and decay between his teeth.

"You have no choice," he hissed, carrion breath enough to make her gag. Valchior wasted no magic on making himself handsome and whole, not anymore; he used only enough to stay in a nearly human shape, the better to batter her with. "We cannot be killed by discarded god-bones, Neverah, you can't wrench a femur off the wall and stab us with it. If we are going to relinquish our souls, we do it on our own terms. You cannot force us."

Her mind cast back to when he'd led her through the labyrinth of bones to Solmir—hours ago, or days, a blur of time that didn't apply in the underworld. Only god-bones could kill gods, and it had to be a god made in the same manner, forged in the same fire. *We made* ourselves *gods*, he'd snarled.

She thought of the Leviathan, speaking through the corpse of its dead lover across a table full of seaweed and salt water in wineglasses. Telling her that divinity was simple, half magic and half belief. *He believes in you. And, for what it's worth, so do I.*

How had the Kings made themselves gods? Magic, on the surface, using more than anyone else could, letting it make them powerful. And magic here, too, of a different and darker kind—absorbing the powers of the gods, killing them and draining them dry.

Just like Neve had done.

Half magic, half belief.

Neve closed her eyes and threw herself backward, physically but mentally, too—tugging herself from the grip of Valchior's illusion so hard she stumbled when it cracked away, leaving her once again in the circle of the stone Kings. Solmir caught her, held her steady. His hands shook on her shoulders, though he still wore that arrogant sneer on his face, and Neve wondered if it had been an act all this time, a scared boy playing at being cruel.

She stepped away from him. Soon enough, she'd find out.

"Oh, Neverah." Valchior leaned forward, just like she wanted him to. "You could've been a god."

The edges of the spikes that made his crown were dagger-sharp, with a wicked gleam that reflected the ivory of the skull above them. Sharp enough to cut through skin and muscle and tendon.

Sharp enough to cut through bone.

Reaching up, acting before she could change her mind, Neve rammed the edge of her right hand against the razor edge of Valchior's crown, bent over her like prison bars. A sharp, blinding pain burst behind her eyes, a scream pouring out of her mouth before she could stop it. But still she pushed until she felt the snap of bone, felt the give of her smallest finger detaching from her hand.

She caught it, slick with blood that geysered gray in the monochrome light of the Shadowlands.

"I already am," she snarled.

Then Neve pushed her severed finger into where Valchior's eye should be, god-bone cutting easily through stone.

Chapter Thirty-Eight

Neve

For a moment, stillness.

Solmir stood behind her, his hands still curled as if he wanted to touch her but couldn't make himself move. Around them, the stone effigies of the Kings, the churn of their thoughts nearly palpable in the air though their forms were frozen.

"This isn't how it was to go." Byriand, his voice aged and shaking. "This wasn't—"

Shadow, hissing, seeping from the hole in Valchior's shroud. His power, his soul, pulled out by the piece of bloody god-bone wedged in his empty eye socket.

Neve's bone.

Valchior's stone hand lifted, almost disbelieving. Neve's blood dripped from the razor-sharp spike of his crown.

Then the huge rock-hewn hand shot toward her, the storm-squeal of shifting shale like a collapsing mountain.

Neve read the movements, knew what was coming. She'd believed herself a god and that made it true, and the power in her center thrilled to it, darkness flashing along her veins, making her thorns grow longer, sharper. She felt like a veil had been lifted, her new divinity polishing everything to the bright shine of perfect clarity.

Moving quicker than she ever had before, she reached up, tugged her severed finger from Valchior's face. It was slippery with blood, but she kept her hold. "Solmir!"

She didn't look behind her to see if he caught the grisly weapon she threw him. Didn't make eye contact to make sure he knew what he had to do. She trusted him.

He might even deserve it now.

The heel of Valchior's hand collided with her forehead, so forcefully that it might've knocked her out if she wasn't a newly forged god. Still, it hurt, and she had to fight to keep her balance as the touch of the King wrenched her out of reality and into illusion.

Half an illusion, anyway. Valchior was caught somewhere between the man he'd been and the monster he'd become as his soul poured out of his eye. The half of his face she'd stabbed was immense, monstrous, bone and stone and tattered veil, the proportions dissonant and unable to fit together. The other half of him was the man he'd been, the same physicality as he'd shown her before, but somehow twisted. Fury gnarled his hands into knotted fists and his mouth into an inhuman snarl.

The backs of his knuckles cracked over Neve's cheekbone. It abraded her skin, rock instead of flesh despite the flickering illusion. She stumbled backward, trailing blood from her four-fingered hand.

"Bitch." It roared from the monstrous side of his mouth, hissed from the other, full lips and cracked teeth in a harmony of rage. "I was trying to help you, Neverah."

"You don't have to pretend anymore." Even in the depths of this illusion, she could hear shouts and rumbles, the clatter of bone and stone. The hoarse sound of Solmir's scream.

The illusion stuttered, showing her the Sanctum for half a heartbeat. She saw Solmir, scored with cuts and bruises, her severed finger clutched in his hand. Behind him, two shattered stone monoliths, the remnants of spiked crowns. Jittering shadow coursed up and down his veins, growing his nails into claws and his teeth into fangs. Blue flickered in and out in his eyes, at war with deep, void-like black.

He'd known what to do—used her bone to stab the Kings, to release their souls so he could pull them into his own. The others weren't as strong as Valchior, weren't putting up as much of a fight. They'd slipped right into Solmir like a second skin, making his body react the same way it had to the magic, but magnified. Sharp and cruel and hurting.

The illusion fell back into place as Valchior backhanded her again, and though it was weaker this time, it was still enough to almost send her to her knees.

"I'm not pretending," Valchior sneered, his tongue visible in his skeletal jaw as it curled behind his teeth. He loomed over her, monster and man. "I was trying to give you a way to keep him, Neve. You've never been good at keeping the people you care about, but I didn't expect you to cling so doggedly to a path that would kill them *all*."

Her heart was a ragged, too-quick thud in her chest, a speeding counterpoint to the steady beat of the key tangled in her hair. "It's just him," she said, because the whole thought was too heavy to speak. It's just Solmir who would die. He was the only person she cared about that she'd have to sacrifice, and for good this time, with no hope of bloody branches and altered religion to try to bring him back.

The afterimage of Valchior's shroud strobed in and out over his face. In his illusion, she couldn't see the black smoke of his soul pouring into the air, but she could see how it slowly ate away at the human guise he presented, leaving less flesh and more rock.

"What do you think will happen when Solmir takes us all in, Neve? You aren't stupid."

A blink, the illusion flickering again. Solmir, on hands and knees now before the empty throne that had once been his, veins running black, fingers elongated, too many joints and too-sharp ends. Fangs protruded from his gasping mouth. The blue in his eyes was only a ghost, a breath of fragile color.

"Come on then, boy." Calryes, the last King, creaking as he leaned over to put his massive spike-crowned head next to his son's. "Be useful for once."

Valchior, again, standing before her, Solmir and Calryes gone. "He can't hold us," he said. "Not without losing himself entirely. And if you think your sister and her Wolf or *you* will be enough to stop his power—our power—you're wrong. We will take hold of the world again. We will bend it into what we want. And we will wipe everyone who stands in the way off the face of our *earth*."

The word was another crack of his hand against her face. Her new god-bones creaked but didn't break—still, Neve gasped, pain making her vision feather.

"If it was you," Valchior murmured, "we'd have time to make the world into what we wanted. Gently, easily, in a way that everyone would accept, because they don't want to look up from their tiny little lives to see how things warp." His head tilted, a razor smile traveling from the side of his face that was man to the side that was monster. "It would have been far more elegant. But destruction, devastation—that works, too."

The feeling of stone wrenching away from her, the god's heavy hand finally falling from her brow and taking the half-made illusion with it. Neve collapsed onto the floor, curling in on herself as Valchior's statue fell from its throne.

Not broken, not yet. The seep of smoke from his eye socket was still slow. Like he was waiting for something.

A rumble shook the ground, enough to rattle her teeth. Bone dust clouded the air, tiny slivers of ivory shaking free of the walls to glitter on the ground. High above, the skull of the Dragon quaked, the massive jawbone near to coming loose.

The stump where her smallest finger had been still pumped sluggish blood, inky in the colorless light. It should make her weak, make her lightheaded, but all Neve felt was a faint pulse of pain. She was a god now, and gods didn't die of blood loss.

They only died when their souls were consumed, snuffed out.

"Afraid?" Calryes's laugh groaned like a tectonic shift, a sound that made her head ache. "Are you really going to falter right here at the end, Solmir? Leave a job undone, just because you're scared of holding my soul?" It was impossible to see his face, but Neve could tell he sneered.

"Shall I tell you all the ways I loathe you instead of letting them seep into your every thought? Once I'm in your head, those will be the only thoughts you have. How much we hate you. How *disappointing* you are to me, to your mother, to Gaya, to your little Shadow Queen—"

With a snarl, Solmir launched up from the ground, Neve's severed finger held in his hand, her blood gloving him to the elbow. He slammed the bone into Calryes's stone-veiled thigh.

The statue didn't move as black smoke began to pour from the improbable wound, the King's soul let free. But his laughter echoed around the room, mad and jagged.

The smoke of his soul rushed for Solmir, flowing into his mouth, his eyes, his nostrils. His roar was pained; he dropped to his knees as shadow pulsed into him, his veins blinking dark, the blue of his eyes dimming. His lips stretched around overlong teeth, thorns cutting longer through his skin, the places where they bloomed weeping charcoal-colored blood.

The last of Calryes's soul rushed out of the rock, and the statue burst apart like it'd been hit with some invisible hammer, spraying stone and dust. The ground shook, a nearly continuous quake now, rattling the skull far above them and the bones that made the walls. Solmir made a choking noise, like the souls of the Kings were something stuck in his throat.

"Neve." Her name was hoarse, and he said it as if it was something he had to work to remember. "Neve, I can't—"

His head wrenched to the side, an unnatural movement that might've snapped his neck were he only human. His eyes opened, fully black now, face warped in an expression that could've been anguish or terrible glee. "Stupid boy." The voice wasn't his. Too high, almost shaking. Byriand. "He thought so highly of his soul, thought it was something he could hold apart, but it is a wretched, shriveled thing—"

Solmir grunted, turned his head again with clear effort. His hands curled on the stone, the claws his nails had become screeching over the rock. When he looked up, a sheen of blue ringed his pupils again. "They're so loud." His voice now, those arrogant, clipped tones blunted in a haze of fear. "Neve, they're so loud, they're all I can hear, I can't *think*."

She rushed to him, hands on his shoulders, on his sharp-planed faced. The magic within her coiled and writhed, blinking shadow in her own veins. Before, when she'd touched Solmir, the power had reached for him, too, something easy to pass back and forth. But now it shied away from her hands, like it could hide in her, like it wouldn't let itself be given away again.

Because now she was a god, and only death would relinquish her power.

"They want..." His eyes flickered, black then blue. "They want awful things, a world burning, and they're so damn *loud*."

"Don't listen." She tasted salt; her cheeks were wet. "Solmir, don't listen, you are *good*, you can—"

A wrench of his neck, and he was black-eyed again. With a cruel grin, he pushed forward into Neve's hands, knocking her off-balance so she sprawled on her back. He crouched over her, caging her face between his clawed hands, his fanged mouth close enough to kiss.

"Is he good?" Calryes's booming voice, so loud and so close that she flinched. "Or is that just what you tell yourself so you don't feel like a whore for falling into his bed?"

She slapped him with her bleeding hand on instinct, half because of the words, half because hearing Calryes come out of Solmir's mouth was anathema. Her hand hit one of his razor teeth, opening a shallow cut to bleed anew, and he grinned. This close, she could see those puckered scars on his forehead. Something metallic glinted in them. His painful, razored crown, growing back.

His eyes changed, went faintly blue. He looked down at her with dawning horror, mouth working, no sound. "Neve," he said finally, scrambling backward, cutting himself on his own claws. "Neve..."

"You see now?"

Valchior. The statue of the King still lay on its side, still unbroken, still with his soul drifting from the wound in his eye, a delicate tendril of smoke that paused and collected in the air instead of rushing straight for Solmir like the others. His voice was weak, but there was a note of triumph in it.

Dread curled cold in Neve's stomach. The key tangled in her hair sped slightly in its pulse, as if in concert with her own racing heart. "He can take it." A lie, one proven by the monstrous thing Solmir was becoming before her eyes, but she said it anyway, like she could make it true.

"He's fading," Valchior continued, soft and pleased and ignoring her entirely. "That scrap of a soul he's so proud of can't stand up to all of ours. The weight is too much for him to carry. It wasn't so long ago he was as straightforward a villain as you think we are."

"Not so long at all," Solmir agreed. And there was blue in his eyes, but it was so faint, and she couldn't tell if his fanged grin was delighted or sorrowing or somehow both. She couldn't tell if the voice was his or one of the Kings he caged.

"He will lay waste." Fainter now, more of Valchior's soul twisting from his stone body to coalesce in the air, like a storm in waiting. "You think your Wolves can stop him? You think you can? He—*we*—will be the most terrible thing the world has ever seen. We will make all the gods you've killed seem like pets."

"No." Solmir shook his head, eyes closed tight, trying to drown out the voices in his head. He pressed his hands to his temples, his claws raking bleeding runnels into his face. "No no no, I won't, please stop—"

"He's fading," Valchior whispered. "All he needs is one more *push.*"

And the word was a rush, the storm of the last King's soul over-whelming Solmir in a torrent of shadow. The statue flew apart. Black smoke flowed into nostril and eye and open mouth, a scream tearing from Solmir's throat as Valchior poured into him.

The Sanctum shook. More bones tore free of the walls and clattered to the floor. Neve stood open-mouthed, filled with godhood and useless power that could do nothing for him, staring at Solmir's twitching and broken form on the floor.

But when he stood, it was worse.

He was too tall. There were too many joints in his legs. The claws at the ends of his fingers were needle-pointed; so were his teeth. His hair hung loose around a face made even sharper, the planes carved to knife-like precision.

There was no blue left in his eyes.

"Pretty little Neverah Valedren." It was all their voices now, a chorus of Kings issuing from one mouth. "Who's never been enough to save someone she loves."

Then Solmir—what had been Solmir—lunged.

Neve knew with some deep instinct that he was going for her key. His claws swept for her hair; she feinted to the side and turned to run, stumbling on broken rock and bone. He laughed, five voices knit into a single terrible cacophony as one of those unnaturally jointed legs reached out, hooked her ankle. Neve crashed to the floor, biting her lip bloody as her chin hit the stone, the breath knocked from her lungs.

Then he was on her, crouched over her back, balanced on claws that stood like prison bars on either side of her head. She tried to flip over, throw thorns around his neck like she'd done so long ago, but the power wouldn't solidify; he batted tendrils of her meager attempt away.

"Neverah, Neverah," the voices whispered. "Now to decide if we want to keep you alive, or—"

Something shifted. She couldn't see his face, but she felt it in the atmosphere, an intangible struggle so intense it imprinted on the air.

"Neve, you have to kill me." Solmir's voice, ragged and hoarse against her ear. "You have to open the door and kill me *right now*."

Her eyes pressed closed. She reached for the back of her neck.

And the skull of the Dragon finally broke loose.

It fell toward them, so much larger than she'd thought, and Neve wondered what would happen to her if she was crushed by a skull in the Shadowlands where she couldn't truly die. Solmir rolled them away, his eyes still blue, his claws wrapped around her in an embrace that brought blood.

The skull landed hard enough to cave in part of the stone floor. In the places where it broke, nothing but seething dark, swirling and shimmering like the inverse of a star.

The Shadowlands, dissolving.

Next to the hole it made, Neve and Solmir, positions switched. She straddled his hips in a parody of how they'd been in the prison made of ribs. He looked up at her as the last bit of blue died in his eyes.

"You will lose everything," Solmir snarled in the voices of the Kings.

And hadn't she already? She couldn't return to her life on the surface. She'd already proven herself a vicious queen; didn't Valleyda deserve more than someone who would twist the political power granted them by nothing but their birth to her own ends? Red was safe with her Wolf, but untouchable, unknowable. And Raffe...

She'd already let Raffe go.

So what was left for her? Nothing but this. Making sure the Kings died and stayed dead. Making sure those who'd been wounded by the life she'd led had a place to heal.

She'd been willing to doom the world for her sister. Was this so different?

"Not if I give it up first," Neve murmured.

And she leaned down and kissed him.

His fangs stung her lips. His clawed hands came up to her waist, and she couldn't tell whether it was to throw her off or bring her closer, but she kissed him through it, a real kiss, one that held everything Solmir didn't let her say and everything she didn't know how to, one that held everything they'd never have time to figure out.

She felt them flow into her. The Kings' souls felt like rancid oil poured down her throat, a sickness she could feel herself catching. Slithering voices laughing in her head, foreign things shackling around her heart.

It *hurt*. Tears streamed down her cheeks. Still, she pressed her mouth to Solmir's until she felt all that darkness, every scrap of monstrous soul that didn't belong to him empty out and enter her instead.

Then the only soul Solmir had was his own. Small and withered, maybe, but dearly fought for. Not enough to hold up against the evil of the Five Kings, not yet. But someday it would be.

And now he'd have the chance.

It was the last coherent thought Neve had.

Ringing and shouting and laughing, a clanging storm of terrible sound that she couldn't escape inside her skull. Neve screamed and clamped her thorn-wreathed hands over her ears, barely conscious of Solmir scrambling out from beneath her, Solmir's hands on her shoulders.

"Neve!" He screamed it in her face, trying to be heard over the awful din of the Kings in her head and the falling Sanctum, the world collapsing around them. "Neve, you can't do this, you have to give them back—"

"*No!*" It came from her and it came from all the souls trapped inside her, five different refusals that made him stumble backward.

Neve pressed her eyes shut. She couldn't hear herself speak, only knew the words came from her mouth because she could feel it move. "It has to be me. If they have you, they'll take the world. I can hold them."

Can you? Valchior's smooth voice asked in her head. It felt like a worm making its way along the inside of her skull, a sliding invasion she couldn't grab hold of. *Or will you be just as terrible as he would be, only craftier about it?*

There was a satisfaction to the words, something pleased. She tried not to listen, but it was impossible to drown out her own thoughts. Neve reached up and yanked the pulsing key out of her hair with clawed hands. Strands tangled around the thorns growing from her wrists and spangled out from the key like rays of a black sun.

The tendrils of shadow in the white bark had grown; they covered almost the whole of the key now, and they glowed, a strange not-light that hurt to look at. Solmir tried to grab it from her, but she held up a hand and thorns wrapped around him, held him back.

Walking was difficult with all the Kings in her head, like their souls threw her off-balance. But Neve did it anyway, following instinct and the pull of the key to the hole in the floor the Dragon's falling skull had made, the seething dark it uncovered.

You think your sister will be able to kill you?

Valchior. It made her stop, her steps stuttering on the shaking ground.

You tried to save her, she tried to save you. He sounded so pleased, so content. It made the tiny parts of her mind that were still her own recoil, dread a freezing stone in the pit of her stomach. *It doesn't matter how terrible you are. Matched love, Neverah. All she wants is you alive.*

The Kings clamored in her skull, so much horror packed into her frame, all the magic of the Shadowlands. The tendrils of it that curled up from the breaking floor flowed into her without her trying, her gravity enough to bring it in. A woman made a monster, made a home for shadows.

But she had a job to do. She'd chosen to stay here so it wouldn't be left undone. This was her atonement, and she had to see it through.

Neve took the cold key in her hand, its pulse now rabbit-rhythm, a match for her own. She dropped it into the hole in the floor, into all that hissing dark that made the firmament of the Shadowlands.

And as the Heart Tree began to grow—the doorway she and Red had compressed into keys by the force of their matched love, by their willingness to do whatever it took to save the other—she heard Valchior laughing and laughing and laughing.

You've played your part to the letter, Shadow Queen.

Roots boiled up from the place where she'd dropped the key, a white trunk stretching toward the broken-bone ceiling of the Sanctum. An opening in the gray-fogged sky, a gash of color as a doorway opened.

Neve grabbed Solmir's hand, dragging him behind her. If he protested, tried to jerk away, she couldn't tell.

She stepped toward the Tree, trying to ignore the voice, trying to hold on to herself amid all this writhing shadow. The trunk opened, the dark inside filled with a wheel and a glimmer that looked like stars, like a place between worlds, a corridor to walk from one to the other.

As she stepped in, Valchior whispered, singing it along her bones:

I told you we welcomed it.

Chapter Thirty-Nine

Red

The Wilderwood was gold.

It flowed back from where the Heart Tree grew at the fore of the forest, blazing like a branch-shaped sun, a burn of light that spread through the veins of every leaf, wound its way up every trunk. A shadow-pit in reverse, not rotting the woods, but...awakening them. Touching each piece of forest magic, pricking it into light that made the surrounding plane seem dusk-dim.

Red pushed up from the snow, shading her eyes with her hand. Still no sign of Neve.

Her heartbeat quickened, a punch of dread she could almost taste.

"Red." Eammon's voice, hoarse. He was beside her, grimacing as he sat up, snow dampening his hair. But he had eyes only for her hand, and he picked it up with a mix of wonder and fear.

She followed his gaze, and the thud of her heart hit harder. Red had grown used to seeing her veins a color other than blue, but this time they weren't green—they were gold, like she'd traced her vascular system in gilt. Her eyes darted to Eammon, expecting something similar, the two of them gleaming to match their forest.

But Eammon hadn't changed like she had. Faint glimmers shone along his wrists, his knuckles, but they were nothing compared to the lines of light that shot through Red.

The Golden-Veined. It snapped into place, all of it. The Shadow Queen, the Golden-Veined. Things written in stars, roles already made that she and Neve stepped neatly into.

As if seeing the change sparked it into action, a draw began deep in Red's center, that same place where she'd felt the Wilderwood's power long before she claimed it and made it part of her. A tug toward the Heart Tree, mitigated only by Eammon's presence at her side. She felt pulled in two different directions, suspended between Eammon and the Heart Tree like they owned two halves of her soul.

Eammon's eyes raised to hers. She hadn't seen fear like that since the day Neve disappeared.

The others pushed themselves out of the snow, in all the places the Heart Tree had flung them when it burst from the ground. Kayu shivered, her dark hair damp with snowmelt. Raffe helped her stand, then wrapped an arm around her shoulder.

"Are we supposed to do something?" This from Lyra, standing to brush snow off her legs. Her gaze flickered to Red, then to Eammon, noting the gold in their veins, the way Red's shone more brightly. "It's not doing anything on its own."

Eammon banished the fear from his face, firmed his mouth and tightened his grip on Red's hands. Within the two of them, the Wilderwood shifted and stirred, disturbed but not in pain. Restless, waiting, anticipating.

Still not speaking.

She looked to Fife. His hand was tight on his Mark, his eyes distant. Unease prickled at the back of her neck.

Red's spine twinged, the tightening of the roots around it reminding her of when the Wilderwood was newly sprouted and growing in that dungeon beneath the Valleydan palace. Of when it'd pulled her away from Neve and back into its borders.

Now it pulled her toward the Heart Tree. Toward her sister, instead of away.

But Eammon didn't feel the same pull. She could see it in his eyes, the way they kept flickering from her to the Tree behind her, in the half snarl of his mouth. He could feel *her* being pulled away but didn't feel the same tug himself. Red reeled toward the Tree, Eammon reeled toward Red. Her heart torn down the middle, always, her two homes never content to share.

This magic she'd braided into herself was a selfish kind. It didn't allow for all the different strands of love she ached with.

Fife's mouth drew into a tight, pained line. His eyes darted from Red to Eammon, someone who'd just been given an order he didn't know how to complete. He rubbed at the Mark on his arm again.

Something like understanding began to unfurl in Red's mind, along the blooming branches of the forest she held.

The ground rumbled again, shaking hard enough to disturb the snow, to make them all brace against falling. Down in the village, voices raised. Red half expected them to come up the hill with torches and pitchforks, but apparently whatever magic had kept them from seeing the shadow grove also guarded the Heart Tree. The Wilderwood took care of its own business and didn't desire an audience.

It *burned* within her, twisting along her bones, the forest's magic sun-bright and shining. Red felt like she housed embers, like if she opened her mouth she'd spill out light. She didn't realize she'd stepped closer to the Tree until Eammon's hand caught her wrist, the pattern of his scars against her skin like home.

"Red," he murmured, worry and fear and wariness all tangled in his throat. "Wait—"

Another *boom*, teeth-clattering, earth-shaking. The air around the Tree vibrated, made nearly visible in its force.

The center of the Tree opened, the trunk arcing gracefully away from itself to reveal the hollow within. Shimmering, endless light filled the space, like a telescope dialed in to focus solely on the sun. It was beautiful and terrible and it hurt her eyes and drew her closer at once, the light of the Tree singing to the light in her.

The hollow darkened, slowly, as if something rose up from the depths, from the giant Tree's roots. Something huge, something awful.

But all Red could think as that immense shadow rose was *Neve is coming home.*

Thin traceries of darkness climbed the Heart Tree, sinuous lines of shadow following the veins of gold as the hollow went dark. But the darkness didn't overtake the gold—instead, the two of them twined together, one the inverse of the other, light and shadow in a twirling dance that painted the trunk in arabesques, mimicked the carvings on the walls of the Edge. For one beacon-bright moment, the Heart Tree stood tall, patterned in gold and black, a perfect nexus of the Wilderwood and the Shadowlands and the space in between. Red felt like a beacon, too, a lighthouse on the edge of a coastline, glowing to call her sister home.

Beneath her, the ground shuddered and heaved, something about to erupt. Shadow fully filled the hollow space in the Tree's trunk, seeped in until it drowned out all the gold—

Then another *boom* as all that darkness in the center of the Tree shot out.

Red flew backward, landing on her back, the breath knocked out of her lungs. The burn of the Wilderwood in her body grew white-hot, though not necessarily painful—it begged movement, a wild, kinetic energy that bloomed flowers around her heart and grew vines around her ribs only for them to wither away and start the cycle anew, an endless circle of life and death.

Inverses and mirrors, walking gyres of grief and loss. Her losing Neve, losing Eammon, and now them losing her.

The certainty of it bloomed along with the flowers, and a branch stretched across her shoulder blades in agreement. Not speaking but finally telling her the thing she hadn't wanted to hear, finally letting her understand what this would take.

To save Neve would be to lose herself somehow. Maybe death. Maybe something different, something stranger, an afterlife wrought by the forest she'd made a home, the magic as suffused into her as roots into ground.

With the realization ringing in her ears, Red sat up and looked at the Tree.

She couldn't see it. The Heart Tree was blocked by a wall of writhing smoke. At first Red thought they were shadow-creatures, an amalgam of them formed to keep Neve from her, but these shadows weren't black—they were the charcoal of a snuffed candle, and silent. Weak, somehow, as if they'd been drained of power.

Next to her, Eammon crouched, a snarl on his mouth and green-amber eyes narrowed at the shadows. With a grunt, he ran at the wall, and was immediately knocked backward, repelled by twisting smoke.

But Red felt pulled toward it. Beckoned.

Lyra's eyes were wide, tracking from where Eammon was once again pushing up from the ground to the dark, writhing wall where the Tree had been. Her gaze flickered to Red's, went from concerned to very near alarmed. "Red…"

She looked down at her hands.

Her veins grew steadily brighter, a strengthening glow. At the same time, the forest behind the shadows lost its luster, the gleam of golden light seeping out of the magic-touched trees, flowing into Red instead. As if the gold had gone to gather up all the stray magic and now delivered it back to its proper vessel.

Eammon looked from the forest to her, jaw tight, hands clenched into fists. He moved to stand between Red and the Wilderwood, like he could shield her from it one last time.

Too late for that.

"It won't take you." Eammon murmured it like an echo from the past, a battle already fought that had come to their doorstep again. "We didn't do all this just for the fucking woods to take you, Red."

But she felt the knowledge that it *would* take her humming between her bones, all the places the Wilderwood had seeped in and made her something else—not really a god, not really a monster, not really human. Red had never felt the weight of staring down the well of possible eternity, like she knew Eammon had. She'd assumed it would come with time, that the countless years would come to rest on her the same way they rested on her Wolf as they walked hand in hand into the belly of forever.

Their forever had been so short.

Kings, it hurt. Tears sprang to her eyes at the idea of leaving Eammon, of sending him back to solitude. It felt like a hole punched in her chest, like floating in the dark without a tether.

Is that what it would be like? Endless dark, and no one to be lonely with?

"Red, *stop*!"

Arms around her waist, strong and familiar, anchoring her to the ground—Red hadn't even realized she was moving toward the wall of shadow until Eammon caught her.

"Stay with me," he murmured, low and hoarse and pleading. "Red, stay with me."

He understood now. He knew. The Wilderwood rustled in Red's chest, another bloom of recognition—she needed it all. All of the forest, all of the magic. Saving Neve would require becoming what Eammon had become to save *her*, a circle coming back around to the point where it began.

The Wilderwood, entire. Girl made god.

At the edge of her vision, across the snow, Fife stiffened.

It would be different this time, someone becoming the whole of the Wilderwood, taking in every bit of its magic. She'd have to gather it all up, then walk into the shadow that was its antithesis and face whatever Neve had become in the dark.

Eammon didn't care about the magic—he knew he could call her back, just like she'd called him, love a line they could always follow back to each other.

But that darkness. That shadow. Neve changed, Neve waiting.

That was where he didn't want her to go. That was where she had to.

And neither of them knew if she'd come back out.

"It's selfish of me to ask." Eammon's hand cradled her face, warm and rough; a tear broke from his green-haloed eye and ran down his cheek, bisecting the scar he'd taken from her in a library that smelled like coffee and leaves. Red had never seen Eammon cry. She'd seen him get close, but never *this* close, and that more than anything else made anguish chew at the bottom of her heart. "Shit, Red, I know it's so selfish, but..." He stopped, leaned his forehead against hers. "Please stay," he whispered. "I know you want to save her, and I want you to, but I can't...there has to be a different way."

A way that didn't make her walk into that churning dark, leaving him forestless and human and alone. A way that let the world have both of the Valedren daughters, the one meant for the throne and the one meant for the Wolf.

Such a way didn't exist. Hadn't since Gaya died, since the Kings broke the Wilderwood. The world had never been big enough to hold both the First and Second Daughters unbound and free.

It had to change. This was the only way.

"I love you," she said, murmuring it against his lips. They tasted like salt, and she didn't know which of them it came from. "I love you."

He didn't say it back. He didn't have to. The pained catch in his throat said enough.

Red kissed him. It wasn't heated, wasn't full of need the way so many of their kisses were. She refused to think of it as a goodbye, but it was a benediction, an ending of something. Her hand curled in his hair and tipped his head down to hers, and with a ragged sound, he wrapped both arms around her, crushed her to him so hard she nearly lost her breath.

Then Eammon went rigid. His spine stiffened, chin tilting up to the snow-filled sky.

Behind him, Fife, his hand on Eammon's back, his face twisted in concentration. The Mark on his arm blazed green and gold, bright enough that he had to look away, painful enough that his mouth was a rictus.

His new bargain, the one none of them had understood until moments ago. Until realization snapped into place for Red, the Wilderwood growing and budding to help her know what was required.

Fife's new bargain was to be a conduit. A vessel, however temporary.

The look Fife gave her was sorrow tinged with rage, but it was the Wolf he spoke to. "I'm sorry. Eammon, I'm so sorry, but I knew you wouldn't give it to her, and she has to have it."

The Wilderwood drained out of Eammon slowly, so many years of tangling taking time to unknot. Ivy wound out of his hair, the points of his tiny antlers sank back into his brow, the green surrounding his eyes leached to white.

The forest leaked away to leave only the human man in its wake, and shadows damn her, he was the most beautiful thing she'd ever seen.

Fife grimaced, the Bargainer's Mark on his arm growing as the Wilderwood went from Eammon to him. It stopped right at his elbow, glowing gold and green, a vessel for magic. A way to take it from one of them and give it to the other.

Like the forest had known that the love its Wolves shared could ruin worlds.

I'd let the world burn before I hurt you. Eammon had said it, a confession that he loved her before he ever dared use the words. The Wilderwood had heard him, the Wilderwood knew it was true. And it built in a failsafe.

Eammon slumped into the snow, eyes closed. His face looked peaceful, his chest rising and falling in a steady rhythm. For the first time, she saw him unencumbered by forest, just a young man with a crooked nose and dark hair and mysterious scars, and she could've wept at the sight.

She took off her cloak, crimson and gold. She wrapped it around him. She didn't want him to get too cold.

Lyra, Raffe, and Kayu stood a distance away, like none of them wanted to get too close to what was happening between the Wolves and the man who'd bargained with their forest. Kayu looked alarmed, Raffe confused. But Lyra's eyes were wide and wet, her hand pressed against her mouth as if she didn't want a cry to escape.

"Do you think he'll forgive us?" Red whispered.

Fife looked at the slumped figure of the Wolf—the former Wolf—instead of her. "He'll always forgive you."

They all knew that love made monstrous things necessary some-times. They all knew their own capacity to burn worlds down.

Finally, Lyra stepped closer, snow lighting her dark curls, making a halo. She didn't ask for clarification, didn't pepper them with questions. She'd read between the lines, both Red's gilded veins and the swirling magic held in the vessel of Fife's Mark. She swallowed, then reached out, the tremble in her hand only visible for the glow of the snow around her.

Red grasped it. Lyra wasn't one for embraces, so Red stayed her arms, though they wanted to wrap tight around the other woman and pull her close. "Thank you," she said. "Both of you."

"Don't act like it's goodbye." Lyra shook her head, expression stony to counteract the moisture in her eyes. "Don't."

Her lips pressed together. Red swallowed.

Fife's palm was a running mass of green and gold, Eammon's portion of the Wilderwood's magic trapped and held, waiting for Red to take it.

Before she could second-guess herself, Red slammed her palm into Fife's.

A pause. Then the Wilderwood rushed, seeping into her, blooming between her bones. It was quicker than the first time she'd taken the roots, and it hurt less—her body was used to this by now, used to hous-ing something inhuman. Gold washed over her vision, blinding her, and when it was gone, she was the forest, whole and entire.

The congruent line of consciousness next to her own was loud, the sound of cracking branches and wind through leaves. For a moment, it almost overwhelmed her, but then it quieted, leaving enough room for Red's mind to stay her own.

When Eammon had done this, the Wilderwood had no experience with such a thing, no knowledge of how to take a host without drown-ing the whole of them out. Now it folded itself up, made itself something that could be carried.

The stretch of branches and susurrus of leaves cobbled into words, brief and quiet. The Wilderwood speaking to her, finally. She knew it would be the last time.

Hello, Lady Wolf. We're ready.

Red opened her eyes. The ivy tendrils in her hair had coiled themselves into a crown. Antlers weighed heavy on her brow, grown from white bark that edged neatly through her skin. The veins around her wrists had sprouted autumn leaves, like she wore golden bracelets made of foliage.

Beside her, Eammon lay on the ground, cradled in snow and her crimson cloak. Slowly, Red bent, pressed her lips to his forehead.

Then Redarys Valedren—the Second Daughter, the Lady Wolf, the Wilderwood—turned toward the Heart Tree.

Red stepped forward, her tread on the snow heavier than she was used to, hands already outstretched in preparation for tearing through that wall of shadow. If the Heart Tree wouldn't give her Neve, she'd go drag her out. She'd go to the underworld for her sister.

Steps away from the smoky barrier, a rumble ran beneath her feet, almost knocking her off-balance. Behind her, a cry as the others scrambled to stay upright, sliding in the snow.

One more massive heave, like the earth itself was about to give birth.

The shadow dissipated all at once, smoke feathering away into the air, as if whatever had held it at attention had loosed its grip. Behind it, the Heart Tree, still covered in gold and black, twisted light and shadow.

A moment of relief, the heavy burden on Red's heart lifting. If the shadow was gone, maybe Neve was close behind—

Then the Heart Tree broke completely apart.

Bark shattered as if a gigantic hand had smashed down from above. Branches fell, crashed to the snowy ground; bits of charred wood raced past Red's head, past her ivy crown and heavy antlers.

The Heart Tree was gone.

And in the midst of its ruin, a dark shape stood.

Chapter Forty

Neve

She felt the Heart Tree break apart as she closed her eyes, as she directed all that new power she'd absorbed into one unifying thought: the surface. Escape. Her own world.

Valchior's harsh laughter clattered in her mind, too loud and sharp to fully ignore. *The world you are turning over to me.*

The deep and star-strewn dark around them turned to blazing gold at the same time that the final threads holding the Shadowlands together snapped. The remains of the prison world created so long ago spun into nothingness, drained of magic, drained of gods. Neve was all the gods now, all the Shadowlands, all the power, and she was both herself and nothing and everything as she moved through the endless expanse between the ended world and the real one.

Neve felt it, the crash and collapse, felt it as if it were her own bones shattering. She cried out, but the sound was lost in the wrap of black space around her, nothingness rushing in to take the place of the underworld that no longer existed.

All its power within her now. She was a woman made a world, and that world was dark and seething.

She couldn't see Solmir, couldn't hear him, but she felt when his nails dug into her, trying to keep her close. It was pointless; this strange new atmosphere knew only how to be alone, and it ripped him away from her. Godhood was lonely, lonely, lonely.

All the magic she'd swallowed, mingling with the Kings' voices in her head: *new world make it ours make it dark and shadowed overrun it death and blood and cold—*

Neve realized she'd landed somewhere outside all of that emptiness only because she finally could hear herself screaming.

Snow—she felt it seeping through her torn nightgown, the old boots the Seamstress had given her. The scent of chilled air and leaves.

She stood in the center of a ruined tree trunk, formed around her almost like a throne, charred edges sending smoke curling through the cold. She stayed there. It was oddly comforting, and clenching her hands around burning wood helped block out the Kings in her head.

Our world now she'll live and we'll live in her Wolves won't kill her this is all ours she can't hold out for long—

Solmir lay a few feet away from her. Still, but she could see the rise and fall of his chest. It was so strange to see him in color—the brown-gold of his long hair and close-cropped beard, the slight pink of the puckered scars on his brow. His jaw was bruised a mottled purple, silver rings glinting against reddened knuckles.

Her monster, just a man.

A wall of gray shadow writhed around them, like smoke trapped in glass. Drained of magic, drained of darkness, serving only as a barrier between them and the rest of the world. Her fingers bent on instinct, the claws at their ends carving through the air.

Red was here. She could feel it. And she needed Red in order to end this.

The smoke dissipated at her command. Three people stood too far away for her to see, smudges against the snow. But one of them was closer, and they drew her attention, as well as the attention of the Kings she'd imprisoned within her.

A man, lying limp, sleeping. Black hair, curling where Solmir's was straight, long but not quite as long. Scarred on his cheek, through his eyebrow, on his hands. Neve stared at him. She'd never seen the man before, but something about him seemed familiar, like she should know who he was.

Other sounds echoed in the dark, other voices, and she could hear shouts from far away. But all Neve's awareness was trapped in her own body, in navigating a vessel that seemed to barely belong to her anymore.

Crimson dripped into her eye—blood. Neve stretched up her hand to her forehead, wreathed in thorns and black-veined. The tiny spikes of an iron crown speared through her skin.

Just like us. Valchior's voice, quiet and hissing against the cacophony of the magic Neve held. *All that talk of being better—you very nearly fell for it, didn't you, Neverah? You aren't better. You aren't* good. *Just another monarch with a hunger for power and a willingness to do whatever it takes to get what you want. I'll show you.*

"Shut up!" She had no control over her mouth, her vocal cords—it came out a scream when she meant to mutter it. Neve knocked a thorn-laced hand against her brow, thinking of nothing but drowning him out. The end of her hand was still a bloody mess from the finger she'd cut off, the wound reopening when she hit it against the spikes of her growing crown. "Shut *up!*"

A laugh rumbled through her head, made her teeth rattle. Was she laughing, too, her mouth unhinged for Valchior's voice to roll out? Her body was a puppet she had only the barest control over, the outside the same size she'd lived in for twenty years, the inside swollen by magic and shadows. She felt like she might split at the seams.

Already, destruction itched at her fingers, pulled slow through her veins. A desire to take the world by the neck and shake it until it went limp. Those distant voices of the people in the snow prickled at her ears, an irritation that swelled in her chest until it made her want to scream, and her clawed hands curled in anticipation, knowing she could reach with her thorned magic and rip out the offending throat—

"No." A moan through lengthened teeth. Neve pulled her hands in toward her chest, like she could cage them. This had to end. She couldn't hold on.

She stumbled forward on numb feet.

"*Neve!*"

A voice she recognized, rising panicked from the haze.

Neve turned, swirling shadow in her wake. The figure charging toward her was Red, but Red changed—antlers made of white bark on her brow, green completely overtaking the whites of her eyes, ivy crowning her dark-gold hair. She'd been a wild and beautiful thing before, but it was nothing compared to now. Red was all golden light to Neve's endless dark.

A sob lodged in Neve's throat, knowing what she was about to ask. What she needed her sister to do.

Even in her otherworldly grace, Red almost stumbled in her haste to get to her, charging over snowbanks churned nearly to mud. They fell into each other's arms, light and dark.

For a moment, Neve let herself relax into her sister's hold, let herself pretend this was just a homecoming.

"You're here," Red murmured into her hair. "You chose to come back."

Neve didn't respond, other than the harsh sob she couldn't quite swallow. Red's arms tightened around her, the leaves braceleting her wrists rustling against Neve's thorns.

The howl of the Kings rose louder in Neve's ears, nearly deafening, drowning out the string of comforting words that fell from Red's lips. Something about home, about healing, *I can fix this I can fix this I can fix this.*

There was only one fix.

Her grip on herself was shaky, glass vibrating at the shatterpoint. Valchior and the others battered against her mind, against her bones, against her soul that held theirs. Her fingers were blackened as if by frostbite, wanting to bend, wanting to force this world to bow to the might of her shadows.

My world, Valchior hissed into her ear, slithering around her skull. *We'll have such fun, Neverah. There are other vessels you could pour me into, once you realize that we're all better off together, once you see all the incredible things we'll accomplish. You could find one to your liking, another body for me to stay in. Even Solmir—*

"Stop." It came through chattering teeth, slicing through whatever comfort Red had been trying to give. It was a directive to the King's soul she held, but also to her sister. She couldn't take comfort now. It was too late.

Red closed her mouth, held Neve out at arm's length, hands firm on her shoulders. Her green-brown eyes were filmed with tears. "Tell me what you need me to do, Neve."

A soft sound from the snow beyond them where the dark-haired man lay. He stirred, amber eyes opening. "Red…" The Wolf. It had to be.

Red's eyes squeezed shut, a single tear falling down her cheek. "Tell me what you need," her sister murmured, the tendons in her neck standing out with the effort of not turning to the Wolf on the snow. "Whatever I have to do, I'll do it."

"Do you promise?" Neve whispered.

And her sister's eyes opened wide, horror and understanding and a sorrow sharp enough to cut.

Inside Neve's head, in her hollow places, the souls of the Kings rattled her bones like prison bars. The power of the Old Ones they'd killed swirled and spun, darkness that eclipsed everything else. She held all the power of the Shadowlands, the perfect dark mirror to her sister's Wilderwood light.

You are ours, Neverah, Valchior said. *How did you ever think you could be something different? You've been ours since you bled on the branches in the Shrine. Ours since you decided you were always* right.

Neve closed her eyes, gasping like she'd run miles, blood still dripping down her forehead as the iron crown grew from her brow. She wanted to collapse into Red, wanted to tell her sister she was sorry, but her control was so tenuous. She was so close to breaking.

And when Red reached out, her golden-veined hand cupping her cheek, Neve did.

Her jaw opened to scream, but instead it was a rush of shadow, pluming from her like she'd held a mouthful of black smoke. The shadows whirled around them like a cyclone, like the force of her grief and her regret and her rage held them in perfect orbit, fast enough to whip their hair and tear at their clothes.

"Red!" The Wolf was fully awake now; through eyes that wept black-ink tears and a blur of shadows, Neve could see him staggering toward them, face twisted in horror. "*Redarys!*"

His shouting woke Solmir, outside the barrier of her shadowed wall. The former King pressed up from the ground, hair wet with melting snow, blue eyes dim and then brightening with fear and rage. He ran toward them with a snarl on his mouth, like he expected the darkness to part for him.

It didn't. Not for him, not for the Wolf, blocking both of them out, sending them sprawling when they tried to run forward again. The only ruler the darkness acknowledged was Neve, and she knew that she couldn't allow anyone to stop them now.

She didn't know if Red understood, or if Red merely acted at the behest of the Wilderwood. Either way, it was what had to happen. The Wilderwood and the Shadowlands, two halves of a whole, just as they were.

And if Neve had this right, there would be only one left in the end. Only the Wilderwood, golden and shining, all the dark snuffed out.

Red closed her hands around Neve's, golden veins against shadowed. Teeth bared, she held on tight, and let her magic go.

At first, it acted like a dam. The rushing of both powers stopped, golden and dark, each frozen at the onslaught of the other. Even the swirling shadows around them paused, arrested mid-motion.

Then the magic crashed.

It was a wave meeting a shoreline, lightning breaking against the ground. Two opposites, feeding endlessly into each other, making a void between them that neither could fill. Canceling each other out.

And when both of them simultaneously fell to their knees, each held up only by the other's death grip on their hands, Neve realized the truth of it.

One couldn't live without the other. Both of them were part of this magic, two points of the same arrow. Their souls were so steeped in it that neither could sustain being drowned in opposite power.

This would kill them both.

In Neve's head, Valchior raged, his calculations proven incorrect, his plan not accounting for all variables. He'd thought Red couldn't bear to kill her sister. And maybe that was true—Neve hoped it was—but Red was the Wilderwood now, all of it in its entirety, and the Wilderwood knew what had to be done.

Neve tried to pull away, animal instinct opting toward self-preservation, but it was too late. Her hands stayed in Red's like they'd been shackled there, this outpouring of magic too overwhelming for either of them to stand against. Around them, the very atmosphere roared with swirling streaks of golden light and deepest dark, the two of them the eye of their own hurricane.

Red's green-haloed gaze said she understood. Said she wasn't angry. She tipped her forehead against Neve's, ivy-threaded hair whipping. "I love you." It was so quiet, lost in the chaos, but Neve heard it bell-clear.

She swallowed. Her body felt brittle and weak, draining magic into her sister and life into the wind. "I love you."

Her vision was hazy. Her heart was a drumbeat thud in her chest, slowing, slowing. The howl of the Kings in her head faded to whispers, all of them realizing this was it, they were done, their host's soul fading and taking theirs with it, here in the true world where death couldn't be cheated.

Then she knew nothing.

Chapter Forty-One

Eammon

*N*o no no no no no no no no no no no no no no no no no no no no no no *no no no no no*

Everything hurt, his body different in ways he couldn't catalog. Lighter, like he carried less, but all that meant was that he could run toward her faster.

He'd awoken not quite knowing where he was. Only that Red wasn't there. He knew her absence like he'd know a missing bone.

The shadows, the storm. Eammon caught glimpses of her between the strands of darkness, his girl become a god—antlered and crowned in ivy.

She was beautiful. He was terrified.

The shadows wouldn't let him through. He didn't know what Red was doing, just that she was doing it without him, and every flicker of her he caught had her slumping, fading.

No no no no no no no no no

There was someone else here, someone else trying to batter their way through a wall of shadow. Long hair, silver rings on each finger, nearly as tall as he was.

But before he could get a good look, the shadows threw him back, sent him sprawling head over feet to land in a sprained heap. Eammon thrust out his hand at the maelstrom as soon as he landed, trying to call up forest magic that might stop the storm. But there was nothing.

Not just *nothing*, as in his magic wouldn't work. *Nothing*, as in it wasn't there.

No no no no no no no no no

The storm froze. A *boom*, and the shadows dissipated, leaving nothing but moonlight on snow.

Nothing but two bodies on the ground.

Chapter Forty-Two

Solmir

H e should've known.

That day in the grove, the day he pulled her into the Shadowlands—it was a precursor to this, a ghost of something that hadn't happened yet. She'd pulled the magic into herself instead of expelling it, and why had he ever expected that to change? He'd tried to hold the Kings' souls, and wasn't strong enough, so Neve shouldered the burden instead.

Even now, trying to pick himself up after being thrown back by a wall of shadow, he felt his own soul like a sentencing.

A terrible thought then, though terribleness from him should come as no surprise—at least she hadn't made him kill her. At least it had been her sister, one draining the other, mirrored love and mirrored lives and mirrored death.

He couldn't have killed her. Even if she asked, even if she begged, even if it meant the world fell into howling hell. He'd let it before he hurt Neve.

He'd always been weak.

When the storm of shadows stopped, Red and Neve lay head to head, blond hair mingling with black. All vestiges of magic had left them in death. Just two young women in the snow.

The Wolf howled. He reached them before Solmir did, knees on the ground, one scarred hand on Redarys's brow and the other curled over his face, his shoulders bowed forward like he could squeeze the life out of himself and into her. One racking sob, harsh enough to make his throat sound bloodied.

Solmir hadn't cried in eons. He didn't know if he even remembered how. But his own throat felt tight, his hands opening and closing into useless fists. He wanted to hit something. Wanted to fight something. Wanted to run and run until he collapsed and was back to not feeling anything, *damn* her for making him feel.

How dare she make him feel something other than rage or sorrow or guilt for the first time in centuries and then *die*?

So when Eammon lurched up from the ground, snarling and wild-eyed, and launched his scarred knuckles at Solmir's jaw, it was almost a relief.

Chapter Forty-Three

Neve

S he didn't know how she expected dying to feel, but it wasn't like this.
It took Neve a moment to be aware of her body—limbs, torso, head, all present and accounted for. No pain, which she didn't realize she'd anticipated until she was startled by its absence. It all felt... mostly normal.

Neve kept her eyes closed, because as normal as this all felt, she still wasn't quite brave enough to see what death looked like. Tentatively, she pressed a hand to her chest.

Well. There was a difference. No heartbeat.

One deep, shaking breath, into lungs that felt surprised to be used. Then Neve opened her eyes.

Death, it seemed, was a field.

Rolling and green, stretching as far as she could see in either direction. Tiny white flowers pressed up through the grass, but their scent was that of autumn leaves, biting and cinnamon-like. An incongruity of seasons that she supposed shouldn't startle her.

She didn't realize she'd backed up until her spine hit something solid. Neve turned around.

The Heart Tree.

It was huge, the trunk thick enough that it would take at least five grown men holding outstretched hands to encircle it fully. The white bark was riven with swirls and arabesques, gold outlined in black, light and shadow harmonizing across the entire surface. If Neve looked at it with eyes unfo-cused, the shapes nearly looked like…not letters, not really, but something she could read regardless. Scenes, maybe. Scenes of her own life, of Red's. A hungry forest and a sinking grave and hands outstretched to both.

Neve stepped back, and it came to her in a rush, the poem from that book she'd found in the library right before Red disappeared into the woods. One to be the vessel, two to make the doorway. She'd burned the book in a fit of rage, thinking it told her nothing. But it told her every-thing. She just didn't know how to read it yet.

Their story had already been written, and here it was, carved in the in-between. Roles she and Red had stepped into by virtue of their love and their folly and their fierceness.

And here was the story's end.

Her gaze traveled up to the Heart Tree's branches. No leaves, but nestled at the ends, weighing down the limbs so that she could touch them if she stretched, were apples. One black and swollen, one golden and glowing, and one crimson.

"Neve?"

Red's voice, quiet and tentative on the other side of the Tree. Her sis-ter climbed over roots grown large as bridges, dressed in a diaphanous white gown, and for the first time since she entered the Wilderwood, she looked just like the Red that Neve remembered—long, dark-honey hair that refused to hold a curl, deep brown eyes, a rounded face and softly curved body that held no vestiges of forest. Her veins were only blue; no ivy crown crossed her brow.

Neve looked down at her own hands, her own body, clad in the same white shroud as Red's. Thin and pale, veins bluish, not black. No thorns. No monstrousness, no magic. Whatever they'd done—spilled their respective power into each other, fed into their opposite until it all canceled out—had left them nothing but the humans they'd once been.

Was she supposed to be thankful for that? She decided she was.

"What did…We both…" Red's sentences half formed and fell away, no words sufficient, and the question was one she knew the answer to, anyway. She looked down at herself, one hand lightly feathering over her brow where her antlers had been. Her face crumpled.

What was one supposed to feel when they were dead? Rest, relief, anger? Neve didn't know, and her chest was hollow, ready for emotion that never quite came. Instead of trying to puzzle through it, she wrapped her arms around her sister and let herself cry.

They weren't racking sobs, didn't bend her in half or tear at her throat. This was a slow leak of salt, a gentle letting go of everything she'd carried for so long. Warmth in her hair; Red was crying, too. They both deserved it, she thought. The tears they'd shed were always wrenched from them, storms that came harsh and too swift to escape. This, gentle and consciously allowed, was different. Necessary.

Minutes or hours later—it seemed ridiculous to try to count time when you were dead, and nothing in the flower-strewn field changed— they parted, standing beneath the boughs of the Heart Tree with their hands on each other's shoulders. Red ran her sleeve across her nose and sniffed, peering upward. "Apples?"

"I don't think they're actually apples," Neve said, breaking away to turn around beneath the laden limb. The sky through the branches was light gray, edging on blue, an eternally overcast summer day. "That voice—the one we both heard—"

"Mine."

Both of them whirled. The voice sounded like it was right next to them, but the figure it came from strode over the distant hills, an ambling gait that ticked at the back of Neve's thoughts, achingly familiar.

The figure stopped just outside the ring of the Heart Tree's branches, the light from the summer sky illuminating only the ridges of their features. Aquiline nose, strong jaw. "Come on, Valedren twins," the voice said, striving for jocularity but arriving somewhere sadder. "You didn't think you could get rid of me that easily."

Red's eyes widened, her hands opening and closing on the skirt of her gown. Her mouth worked for a moment before one hoarse word left her throat. "Arick."

As if the name made the light grow brighter, Neve could finally see his face. Handsome as ever, in a white tunic and breeches, black hair curling over green eyes. "Red."

Their embrace was one of friendship, the other complications between them long since scrubbed away. Arick sank into Red, his eyes closing tight, then he held out an arm for Neve, lifting his green gaze in her direction. A small, sorrowful smile pricked at the corner of his mouth. "Solmir really did a number on both of us, didn't he?"

A sobbing laugh, and Neve crumpled into their arms, the three of them holding tight to one another in the endless field death had made for them.

Arick was the one to peel away this time. He kept a hand on each of their shoulders, then nodded toward the trunk of the Tree. "This was all supposed to happen, you know. It's been prophesied for centuries, the Golden-Veined and the Shadow Queen. Since the Shadowlands were made. Tiernan even wrote about it, though it was never widely circulated." His brow quirked. "It got overshadowed by that whole Second Daughter bit."

Neve thought of the book she'd burned, the letters she'd seen on the cover as it curled in the flames. *T, N, Y.* Tiernan Niryea Andraline. She'd burned the journal of Gaya's sister.

She sighed. Add it to her list of sins.

Red frowned. "The voice in our dreams," she said, expressions cycling over her face as she put something together carefully, then all at once. "That was you?"

"It was me." But the way Arick said it sounded like he wasn't really sure. "But not... the words weren't mine, not always. It was the magic speaking through me, I think."

"The Wilderwood?" Red's face brightened, just a fraction, at the prospect of one familiar thing.

"The *magic*," Arick repeated. "The Wilderwood, yes, but the Shadowlands, too. All of it." He shrugged. "It's really the same thing, you know. Two halves of a whole." He dropped his hands to tuck a wayward curl behind his ear. "It's hard to tell sometimes, though. Whether it's the magic or me. It bleeds together."

"We know how that goes," Neve said. All three of them, taken and changed.

Arick nodded. "It was never meant to last," he continued quietly. "The Wilderwood, the Shadowlands, the tying up of magic into knots to keep it contained. It wasn't sustainable—especially once the Kings started killing the Old Ones, speeding along the Shadowlands' dissolving. There was always going to be an end, but it had to be an equal one. Balanced."

"So it used us," Red murmured. She kept absently tracing a line through her palm, a faint white scar against her pale skin. "It couldn't end itself, so it used us to do it."

The words could've been blame, had her voice been harsher. Instead, it was just an explanation.

"The magic was divided into two halves, so it needed vessels that were the same." Arick's green gaze swung from Red to Neve. "Mirrored souls that could take in each half and hold it suspended. Keep it locked away."

"Why?" Red shook her head. "Why would all the magic need to be locked away? Can't it just...just be free, like it was before the Wilderwood made the Shadowlands?"

"It could be," Arick said patiently. "But isn't that how we ended up here in the first place? There might not be Old Ones to roam the earth and use magic to subjugate anymore, but there are always people who can access more power than others, and those people will always try to use it to evil ends. Magic corrupts; it goes rotten. You've seen it yourself."

Red pressed her lips together. She looked away.

"But after what we did, maybe it wouldn't anymore. Wouldn't be rotten or corrupt," Neve murmured. "It wouldn't be...*anything*. Just free."

"Free to be misused," Arick said.

"Or not."

He shrugged.

Tears brimmed in Red's eyes, her arms crossed tight over her chest. "Then why take Eammon to keep itself alive, if the Wilderwood knew all along it would have to die?" A swallow, then, quietly enough to try to disguise the break: "Why take me?"

"The Wilderwood had to hold on until this moment." It was strange to see Arick so composed, speaking so evenly. Neve still thought of him as the rumpled man under that arbor, desperate to find a way to save the woman he loved. Death had tempered him, death and all these things he'd learned as he wandered in it. "It needed you to hold it until the Shadowlands were gone, to be the counterweight. And that's what it needs now, too, just in a different way." He paused. "We do what we have to do."

An echo, winding back, reverberating from a time when someone else wore Arick's face to say the same thing.

An awful, huffing laugh burst from behind Red's teeth. "So it was just *stalling*. Eammon and I splitting the Wilderwood between us, keeping it together—there was always going to be just one of us left in the end. The Wilderwood needed two on the surface to hold it, but when the Shadowlands collapsed, it only needed one soul to lock its magic up." Her fingers curled against her sternum, like she could still feel the roots between her bones. "It was always going to be one of us."

"Not one of you," Arick said gently. "It was always going to be *you*, Red. You were the soul the Wilderwood needed, the one that could mirror Neve. It was always going to be the two of you."

Red's breath sounded bladed and harsh in her throat. Neve turned slightly away, closing her eyes.

Souls as anchors, scales balanced. One holding the other in place.

This is bigger than you and your sister. She'd heard it over and over again. A warning that something large and cosmic would come to rest on the two of them, a First and a Second Daughter who loved each other so fiercely that their souls could balance worlds.

"Your souls have to stay here," Arick said quietly. "Now that the Shadowlands and the Old Ones and the Kings are gone, the purpose this magic was given has run its course. Your souls have to hold it in stasis, so it doesn't leak out into the world again. So that there's no chance of the cycle repeating."

Almost absently, Neve's hand pressed against her chest. No heartbeat, still, but that seemed like merely a symptom of something larger, something more essential that was missing from her now-dead body.

Slowly, she looked up.

Those three apples, hanging from the Heart Tree's otherwise barren branches. The black one shone down at her, skin puckered by the points of thorns pressing out from the inside, the single black leaf extruding from the stem glossy in the strange light.

"Souls," she said simply. "That's what they are. Not apples. Souls, Red's and mine." Her eyes went from the black apple—hers—to the golden one she assumed was Red's. Then the simple crimson one, slightly smaller.

She looked from the souls hanging on the tree to Arick. "And yours."

A single nod. "And mine."

Red's brow furrowed, turning to look up at the apple-souls suspended in the Tree. "Why are you here? You should...you deserve to rest, Arick. This can't be what your ending was supposed to be."

"Maybe not, before." He waved a hand. "This place didn't really exist until the two of you got here. I was..." His lips pursed, searching for words. "I was elsewhere, out in the in-between. But now my soul is here, with the two of yours. I got just as tangled up in this as you did." There was no anger in it, a simple stating of fact. "So were the other Wolves, the other Second Daughters. But they truly died, their lives drained away, so their souls have moved on. I was different. I was..." He stopped, faltering as he tried to frame what had happened to him— becoming Solmir's shadow, a bargain that left him only partially alive. "I don't think I was ever dead. Not truly. Just...gone."

Neve's not-beating heart contracted behind her ribs. "I'm so sorry," she murmured, choked with guilt at what had been done to Arick and what she felt for the man who'd done it. "Arick, I am so sorry."

His green eyes flickered to hers, understanding in them—he knew, of course he knew. "It hasn't been so bad. It's nice to understand everything." That slight smile again, the one made sweeter for the sadness that tugged at its edge. "Well, everything as far as magic and forests and shadowy underworlds go. Not *everything* everything."

It was the first time he'd really sounded like himself, and it made her want to laugh and cry in equal measure.

The three of them stood in silence, clad in white and heartbeat-less. Neve looked up at their souls again.

Wasn't it supposed to feel…*bad*, being soulless? Wasn't a soul the culmination of all you are? But Neve still felt like herself. She still loved her sister, loved Arick. Loved Solmir, despite herself—the first time she'd thought the word, and it being here, in a liminal space that was neither good nor bad, felt right.

She'd been prepared to die. She'd known when she chose to take the Kings into herself, to become the vessel of the Shadowlands, that the only way this could end was in *her* ending. Divinity wasn't something she could carry, not something she *wanted* to carry.

But though she could make that choice for herself, she couldn't make it for Red.

Neve felt at peace. She felt like she could wander these fields and lose herself and be just fine. But Red…the tears leaking from her eyes hadn't stopped, and she kept tracing that scar in her palm. Neve knew she was thinking about her Wolf.

It wasn't fair for Red to be dead because of a choice Neve had made. She was through making decisions for her sister.

She turned to Arick. "Can someone live without a soul?"

His eyes widened, the first bit of true surprise he'd shown in all this bizarre time together. "I don't think anyone has ever tried."

That had never stopped her before.

Neve gestured up to the souls on the limb, black and red and gold. "Those are what holds us here, right? Our souls. So if we…"

Movement before she could talk herself out of it, reaching up to pluck the dark orb of her soul from the branch. It weighed heavy in her hand, warm as if picked fresh from an orchard, buzzing faintly against her palm.

Neve held up the apple, half expecting Arick to try to take it back from her. "If I destroy this," she said, using the placeholder word because she couldn't quite make herself say the words *destroy my soul*, "everything in it is destroyed, too. Instead of being just...just held here, locked away, it's gone." She swallowed. "And I'll be gone, too. Not here. Nowhere."

It shouldn't have sounded as comforting as it did. She was so tired.

"Neve." Red stepped up, hand tight on Neve's forearm. "No."

"If my soul is gone," Neve said, "then it takes all the Shadowlands magic with it. And that's why yours is here, right? To keep mine balanced? So once my soul is gone, you can go back." She didn't know *how* she knew it was true, but she did, deeply—the knowledge running like water downhill, death whispering its secrets to her like it had to Arick. "You can live, Red."

"Without you?" Her sister shook her head. "No. I won't. I did all this to save you, I won't live without you now."

"This wasn't your choice. It was mine."

"Maybe not...not *this*, specifically. I didn't choose to die. I didn't choose to trap the Wilderwood in my soul so it could be a counterbalance for the Shadowlands and keep all the magic in the world contained." Red stood up straight, hair tossed back, and even though the forest had left her body, the regal strength of it was still in her stance. "But I chose to take the roots. I chose Eammon. And I chose to find you, and save you. And if this is part of it..." She reached up, just as easily as Neve had, and plucked the golden apple from the bough. "If this is part of it, I choose it, too."

Neve wondered if her sister felt the same conflicting things she did—the emptiness of being soulless, the realization that the emptiness wasn't really so bad. They knew who they were, she and Red. After all this, they understood themselves.

What had their souls ever done for them, anyway?

"If we destroy them both," Red said slowly, the same creep of knowledge that Neve felt, "then things rebalance. The magic is set loose—both

sides of it. But there won't really *be* sides, not anymore. It's all the same."
She swallowed. "All the same, and all free."

"Free to be used," Neve said quietly. "For good or for ill."

She tightened her grip on the black apple in her hand. She thought
of Solmir, what she'd felt as she took the souls of the Kings from him—
someone desperately striving to be good, someone who wanted to be
better.

You are good. He'd told her that, once. She could almost believe it.

No one was wholly one or the other. Goodness was daily choice,
endless possibility, a decision at every crossroads.

But she'd seen a former dark god attempt to atone, and that meant
anyone could.

"You'd risk the world for another chance to live?" It was the first
time Arick had sounded reproachful. She didn't know if it was him, or
the magic, or some combination of the two.

"I'd risk the world for my sister," Neve replied. "I've already done it
once."

Red's fingers dug into the skin of the golden apple in her palm. "And
I'm not going without her."

Arick looked thoughtfully at them, two women with their souls in
their hands. After a moment, he reached up, plucked the crimson apple.
A slight, impish smile lifted the corner of his mouth, another glimmer
of the man he'd been when he was alive. He tossed the apple in the air,
caught it. "Your souls made this place," he said. "So it stands to reason
that if the two of you smash your souls, all of this is gone."

"What will that mean for you?" Neve breathed.

"I guess we'll find out." He nonchalantly polished the apple against
his white shirt. "But I think I should hold on to this, regardless."

One breath, pulled into three sets of dead lungs.

Then Red and Neve hurled their souls at the flower-strewn ground,
where they shattered like glass, and everything went black.

Chapter Forty-Four

Neve

Coming back to life hurt worse than dying did.

It happened like a slow reverse of what she'd felt when she woke up in the field—head, then torso, then limbs, all tingling as they shuddered out of death. Her heart thumped once, enough to rattle her rib cage, then gave a flutter of smaller beats before settling back into a regular rhythm.

When her eyes opened, it was snowing. Gentle drifts of white swirling from a velvet sky, blanketing the world and making it new. To someone else, the scene might've appeared stark black and white, but Neve's eyes were used to monotone, and she could pick out the subtle shades of indigo in the night.

It took a moment for her to hear the shouting.

More growling than shouting, really, and all of it coming from her right. Neve turned her head, the movement slow and syrupy.

A brawl, as vicious and common as any ever seen in a tavern yard. Two tall men grappled with each other, sweat and blood flying, both of them fighting like they had nothing left to lose.

"Of course," Red's voice, as slow and tired as Neve felt. Her sister's head was next to hers, the two of them laid out brow to brow in the snow, legs pointing in opposite directions. "We die, and they fistfight."

Three more figures watched the brawl, stark against the pale expanse of the ground. When Neve realized one of them was Raffe, she shrank back, a strange alchemy of guilt and shame and relief making her body feel like her own again in one agonizing sweep.

But there was still something missing. Some kind of…of emptiness, a piece of herself that she'd left in death. Neve's hand was halfway to her heart, ready to check again for its beat, before she realized what that emptiness was.

Her soul. A prison for magic, obliterated.

She swallowed. Her eyes turned to Red, still lying beside her, their gazes made level by the way they'd fallen in death. Long hair fanned out on either side of them, dark gold and black, two sides of a circle.

"I feel it, too," her sister murmured. Her dark eyes were clouded and thoughtful—and only brown, with no halo of green around the irises.

Neve nodded. "I don't…" She shifted, looked up to the falling snow. "I expected it to feel worse."

Red shrugged. "What's a soul but the most concentrated piece of yourself?" A tiny, tired smile lifted the side of her mouth. "We know who we are. Maybe that means we don't need them."

"I guess we'll find out," Neve said.

Red's arms made wing shapes in the snow as she stretched, shaking out pins and needles. "Well, it's not so—"

She stopped as abruptly as if she'd hit a wall. Red's head turned to the opposite side, where Neve couldn't see her face, staring at whatever her hand had hit when she stretched.

With a grimace, Neve pushed herself up on her elbows to peer over her sister.

Arick.

His body was curled on his side as if the snow were a feather bed, chest rising and falling in easy rhythm. Dark curls brushed his forehead, and a slight smile curved his mouth, like worry wasn't something he'd ever known.

"He came back with us." Neve's voice sounded thin and cracked, someone waking up from a long sleep. "When we…did what we did, it must have brought him back."

Red's eyes were wide and glassy. "He wasn't really dead, not in the normal way," she murmured. "Just...caught in between. Like us. That must be why."

The enormity of what they'd done was slow-settling, a leaf incrementally weighing down into a river. Soulless, yet still themselves. Bereft of magic, when they'd both been a home for it. Alive when they'd been dead.

Then Red gave her head a tiny shake and swung her eyes to Eammon and Solmir, still rolling over the ground with their teeth bared and fists flying. "What a way to introduce Arick to my husband."

Neve followed her gaze, raised a brow. "Should we let them work it out, you think?"

"No." Red pushed to sit up, shaking snow from her hair. Her face had gone stony. "Eammon might kill him, and I'd like to punch him at least once first."

Nerves twisted in Neve's middle, the pinch of it more pronounced from the fact she'd been dead until moments ago. They'd solved one problem—the cosmic, god-proportioned one—but she was somehow far more apprehensive about the personal ones on the horizon. Like making sure Red and Eammon didn't kill Solmir, even though he deserved it.

Like explaining why she didn't want them to.

Red stood, called across the snow, "If you're fighting about us, everything is fine now! If it's over something else, carry on!"

Everyone on the plain froze, a tableau in the churned snow as more poured from the sky. Then Eammon—looking worse for wear—staggered over the ground toward them. He wrapped Red in his arms, and she buried her face in his chest, heedless of the blood crusting his nose.

"You were dead," he murmured into her hair, his voice still breaking on the word. "I felt it, you were dead."

Red's hands tightened around him, white-knuckled. "Of everything that's happened to us, me coming back from the dead is the biggest surprise?"

The Wolf—but was he the Wolf anymore? He looked like a man, only a man—huffed a jagged laugh and pulled her closer.

Neve pressed her lips together, wrapped her arms around herself. In the distance, Solmir stood, chest still heaving. He didn't move any closer. Neither did she.

Eammon looked up, eyes meeting Neve's. There was a flash of anger there, and she supposed she deserved it. But the anger settled to wariness after a moment, and she understood that, too. Love could wrench the most undeserved compassion out of you.

"I'm Eammon," he said with a nod. "It's nice to meet you, Neve."

She managed to smile, though it was a shaky thing. But she didn't trust herself to speak, not yet.

His eyes lighted on Arick's body over her shoulder, then widened. "Is that…"

"Let him sleep," Red said quietly. "He'll wake up when he's ready."

The slowly falling snow lumped around Arick, nearly obscured him from view. Neve put a hand to his forehead, afraid he'd be cold; he felt pleasantly warm, and shifted in his sleep, frowning. She took her hand from him and moved away.

Confusion still knit Eammon's brow, but he acquiesced to his wife. He sighed, shaking his head. "What happened to us? I feel…I don't…"

Her sister pressed a finger against his lips. "You're human," she murmured. "And so am I. The rest of it we'll figure out."

A shudder went through the former Wolf, mingled horror and relief, a long-held burden finally relinquished. Eammon tilted his forehead against Red's and closed his eyes.

Behind them, Solmir's dim figure stood still in the snow, like he was waiting for Neve to tell him what to do.

She didn't know. She didn't know.

The other ragged figures drifted over, the ones she'd briefly seen when she was all shadow—Red's friends. A white man with reddish, curling hair, his arm around a beautiful woman with golden-brown skin and a halo of dark curls, both of them looking at her like…well, like someone risen from the dead. The woman's face was only wondering, but the man's looked like he hadn't decided if her rising was a good thing or not.

She guessed that was fair.

Lagging slightly behind them, another woman she'd never seen before. Short, with dark eyes in a pretty, heart-shaped face and a fall of straight black hair. Her expression cycled between guilt and awe and something that looked almost like jealousy. Dark eyes flickered to Neve, then away to the last person trooping over the snow toward them.

Raffe.

Neve didn't know where to let her eyes land, what to do with her hands. She wanted to rush him, to wrap her arms around him and hold him close. She wanted to run away before he could see her, see what she'd become.

Just a soulless woman who'd been a god. Who'd been a queen. Who never wanted to be either of those things ever again.

The air around them seemed to spark, just for a moment. Filaments of light spangling in the snow, and a tiny, prickling feeling at her fingertips. But it was gone when she blinked, so quickly she might've imagined it.

Raffe stopped a few feet from her, a tall, imposing shadow against the sky. She couldn't read the expression on his face, his dark eyes glued to hers, his mouth slightly parted.

The woman with the long black hair swung her gaze between them, then away.

"Neve." Raffe's mouth worked before it settled on her name, like he couldn't decide what other words he could feed into the silence.

"Raffe." Her fingers clenched on the scraps of her nightgown. The diaphanous thing she'd worn while she was dead was gone, leaving her in only her nightgown and boots and Solmir's torn coat, and the freezing cold sank teeth into her newly human body.

It seemed to spur Raffe out of inaction. He stepped forward, shrugging out of his own coat before noticing the one she already wore. A pause, his arms awkwardly half out of his sleeves. He shrugged back into them with a pensive expression.

From the corner of Neve's eye, she saw a tall, long-haired figure step backward, farther away from her, farther into the snow.

"Are you well?" But as soon as he said it, Raffe shook his head. "No, of course you aren't *well*, you spent weeks in the Shadowlands—"

"I'm fine," Neve said quietly. "I'm fine."

Raffe's lips pressed together, unsure of how to follow the tangling thread of this conversation, but before he could try, Red turned her face from Eammon's chest. "We took care of it," she said decisively. "The Kings, the Shadowlands, the Wilderwood. All of it. It's gone." She looked behind them, at the forest—still standing but empty, drained of all the magic it had held. Her lip went between her teeth, like she wasn't sure if she wanted to laugh or cry.

Behind her, Eammon's eyes widened, his shoulders sagging slightly even as his arms stayed wrapped around Red. He looked down at his hand on her waist as if he'd never seen it before.

"Gone?" This from the pretty woman next to the red-haired man, her delicate brows drawn together in confusion. Fawn-colored eyes flicked from Red to the man beside her, to his arm, like she was looking for something. "Fife, what you took...you mean *all* of it..."

"All of it." Neve's voice still sounded quiet, whispery. All that screaming followed by death had left her throat raw. "We..." But there was no easy way to explain what they'd done, souls turned to apples and dashed on the ground, people become reliquaries. "We took care of it," she said simply, echoing her sister.

The woman's brow creased, lips pursing. "I still feel..." She trailed off, her fingers twitching at her side. Again, that spangling of the air, like currents of light ran just behind a veil.

The man at her side looked at her with his mouth pressed flat. Neve couldn't tell whether he saw the light or not. "What do you feel, Lyra?"

But the woman—Lyra—just shook her head. Still, when her hand dropped, her brow remained furrowed.

Raffe stood up straight, regaining himself now that there was a problem to solve, something to concentrate on other than him and Neve and the unnavigable space between them. "So what does that mean for us? For...everything?"

Such a large thing, such a far-reaching question. Red glanced at Neve, inclined her head. *You're the oldest,* the look seemed to say. *You answer the questions.*

Neve didn't really know how to do that. But she took a deep breath and tried. "We don't know," she began. "But I think...I think magic is here again. In the world, like it was before."

The atmosphere glinted, an agreement. Could everyone else sense it, too? Or just a few of them, like it had been so long ago?

There will always be people who can access more power, and they will always use it to evil ends.

She clenched her teeth. How much of that had been Arick, feeling phantoms of guilt from the life he'd lived, and how much of it had been the magic speaking through him? Neve wanted to believe they'd done the right thing. She wanted to believe that people could be good, that atoning was possible.

You are good.

Her eyes lifted. Solmir was still there, just a smudge against the snow. Ignored for now, the shock of everything else smoothing over his arrival. She didn't know how long that would last, and once it wore off, it probably wouldn't be safe for him to be here. He knew that—the brawl with Eammon made it clear.

And yet he stayed. Making sure she was all right.

You are good.

"It will be like it was before the Shadowlands were made," Neve continued, keeping her eyes on Solmir. "Where it's free. Where anyone who can sense it can learn to use it."

Lyra nodded. Almost subconsciously, her fingers twitched by her side again.

The other woman with the long black hair stepped forward, her face set like she'd decided something. "I'm Okada Kayu." Then she stuck out her hand, lips in a firm line, as if she expected to be rebuffed.

Okada. Neve remembered the surname. She took Kayu's proffered hand, inclined her head in the way one royal did to another. "You're next in line," she said simply. Something was starting to fill in, the final blanks finding their answers.

Kayu nodded jerkily, then stopped, like the agreement had been premature. "Or, I would be. But I'm the Third Daughter of the Emperor, and an Order priestess—novice, I mean." Her brows drew together. "Though I don't think I'm that anymore, either. Since I helped kill the High Priestess."

Neve's eyes went wide. Kiri. Dead. Something both relieved and sorrowful plucked at her chest. "I see."

More pieces falling into place. She almost had it, almost knew what this final act would be. The poem in Tiernan's book she'd burned held the answer, if she could just remember it.

Snow lighted in Kayu's dark hair as she shifted uncomfortably. Raffe's eyes flickered from her to Neve before he reached out and clasped Kayu's hand. The other woman swallowed, then looked back at Neve, new resolve in her face. "I'm willing to face whatever consequences you deem appropriate for Kiri's death, Your Majesty. Though I think we can both agree she deserved it."

Neve snorted. "I wouldn't argue."

Kayu's brow lifted, some of her apprehension shaking free.

The Holy Traitor. Neve remembered it now, the third part of the poem. A novice who murdered the High Priestess certainly counted. But there was something else, another role she felt Kayu should fill.

Majesty had sat so strangely on her shoulders.

"You said you're the Third Daughter," Neve said slowly. "Are your older sisters married?"

Raffe's hand tightened on Kayu's as she nodded, worry crowding her face again.

And there it was, the final piece clicking into place. Neve being given the freedom to cast off one more thing that didn't fit, a burden she knew she could no longer hold up under.

She sank to her knees in the snow, quick and graceful. Kayu backed up with a surprised noise, Raffe stiff by her side.

"By the power given to me by lines upon lines of Valleydan queens," Neve said, getting the words out in a rush, "I hereby cede my title, my holdings, and my queenship to my successor." The next line was *take up this task in the name of the Kings*, but Neve refused to say that. She wondered how long their legend would hold, how many more years would go by of people clinging to a lie before it finally faded away. "Will you take up this task, Okada Kayu?"

The other woman's mouth opened and closed soundlessly. Eammon looked surprised, still holding Red close to his chest, and Fife and Lyra seemed mostly confused. But Red had a small smile on her face.

Heartbeats of silence, then Raffe turned to Kayu. "It will mean safety," he said quietly. "Your father won't be able to marry you off."

The word *safety* made Kayu's shoulders settle, a deep breath leave her mouth. She turned to Neve, nodded. "I'll take up this task," she said quietly. "But... why?"

And Neve couldn't stop her eyes from drifting toward where Solmir stood in the snow. "I'm tired of it, frankly."

"And I would rather cut off my foot with a spoon than be the Queen of Valleyda," Red said cheerfully.

"That's as good a reason as any," Kayu conceded.

"You'll be fine," Neve said as she rose. Queendom seemed to fall from her like a cloak, much easier to shed than godhood had been. She'd been for a different kind of throne, apparently, and now she had none.

A weight lifted.

Anxiety flickered in Kayu's eyes as she nodded, looking at Neve with slight wariness. She wondered how she appeared to the other woman, ragged and so recently dead, in a ripped nightgown and boots stolen from an underworld.

On the ground, Arick stirred.

Raffe's eyes went to him immediately, hidden against the snow in his white tunic and breeches. His gaze cycled from surprise to joy to horror as he ran forward, fell to his knees next to his friend. "Arick?" He looked between Red and Neve. "How—"

"You wouldn't believe us if we told you," Red said.

A moment, then Arick sat up, pushing snow-dampened hair from his eyes. He looked at Raffe, puzzled, then to the rest of them, brow furrowing further in confusion. When his gaze landed on Red, the confused look wavered, like it might change. It didn't.

"Hello," Arick said carefully, pushing himself up from the ground. He chuckled mirthlessly. "Forgive me, but I'm not quite sure what I'm doing here."

Neve pressed her lips together. One tear slid down Red's cheek. Neither of them spoke, knowing instinctually what had happened.

The two of them sacrificing their souls had somehow brought Arick back from the strange half death that had tied him to them, to the Heart Tree. But it'd come with a price.

Though Neve wondered if Arick forgetting the whole nightmare, forgetting *them*, was actually more of a blessing.

"What's the last thing you remember?" she asked quietly.

Arick pursed his lips, thinking. "Floriane," he said finally. "I live in Floriane, I think."

Horror shifted into sorrow as Raffe stared at his friend. He looked to Neve, as if asking her what to do, whether he should try to fill in the gaps in Arick's memory.

Neve gave one slight shake of her head. "Let him rest," she murmured. She glanced at Red—her sister should have some say, she thought.

Red nodded, mouth pressed into a tight line.

Raffe swallowed once, then again, and when he spoke his voice was thick. "You're right," he said, turning back to the man in the snow. "Your name is Arick. You live in Floriane. I can...I can help you get back there, if that's what you want."

"I'd like that." Despite not remembering anything other than where he was from, Arick didn't seem bothered. He tucked his hands into his pants pockets, looked down at the white ensemble he wore, somehow brought here from a place that no longer existed. "Didn't dress for the cold, did I?"

"Here." Eammon stepped forward, shrugging out of his coat. Arick accepted it with a guileless smile. The former Wolf watched him a moment, dark eyes unreadable. Then he clapped the other man on the shoulder and stepped back to Red again.

A ragged sound from Raffe, one he choked off. Kayu stepped up to him, put a tentative hand on his arm. Raffe covered it with his own, unselfconsciously.

Neve's gaze strayed once again to the figure on the snow, watching. This time, Raffe's eyes followed.

"Him," he said, and started marching over the field. "I'm going to—"

"Not before I do." Red moved forward with her hands bent to claws, amply prepared for mundane violence in place of anything magic. Eammon turned with her, his fists clenched, ready to dive back into the brawl they'd interrupted.

But they didn't have to go meet Solmir. The once-King came to them, striding purposefully over the ground until he stood close enough for Neve to see his face.

Gone was the arrogance that she'd assumed was ingrained in him, as much a part of his features as his straight nose and high cheekbones. Solmir looked nearly as tired as Neve felt, face mottled with bruises, one eye puffed and purpled.

He held his hands out to his sides, a posture of martyrdom. But his eyes stayed fixed to Neve's. "Go ahead." His voice was hoarse—another bruise bloomed on his throat. "I won't stop you."

Maybe it was the defeated look on his face that stalled Raffe, and Eammon had already worked out his frustration, evident in the black eye and the bruises.

But Red took the invitation. She walked up and punched Solmir in the chin, hard.

Chapter Forty-Five

Neve

R$^{ed!}$" Neve's shout was, predictably, ignored. Her sister shook out her fist while Solmir grunted, gingerly touching his jaw. The skin had split, and his fingers came away bloody.

"Look at that," he murmured. "It's been a while since I bled in color."

"There's more where that came from," Red growled, ready to swing again.

Neve reached out, but she wasn't the one to catch her twin's hand.

Raffe was.

His fingers curled around Red's fist, holding it gently. Red whirled to face him. "If you don't want me to hit him, you'd better do it, and quick."

Solmir clenched his teeth. Blue eyes burned beneath lowered knife-slash brows, staring at Raffe like one might glare down an approaching predator.

But Raffe didn't return the same fire, his face thoughtful and drawn. He looked from Solmir to Neve, to the torn coat Neve wore.

Neve didn't move. Didn't speak. Wasn't sure what she was supposed to do here, where her prince and her monster stood so close and all her fear was for the wrong one.

Slowly, Red dropped her fist and stepped back, coming level with

Eammon. Fife stood beside him, an angry look on his face, though he didn't make any move toward Solmir. Lyra looked more determined than angry, her fingers continuously twitching toward the hilt of the curved blade she wore on her back. Kayu mostly seemed confused, though her tense stance and almost-reaching hand betrayed the apprehension she felt at having Raffe stand so close to the once-King.

And Raffe and Neve just stared at each other, neither having the words to explain what had happened.

Though after a handful of heartbeats, it seemed Raffe understood.

He turned to Solmir, still with that thoughtful expression. "You protected her." A murmur, but in the silence of the snow, it was loud enough for all of them to hear.

Neve expected Solmir to cant up his chin, to give some sharp, pithy response. But when words came, they were low and nearly pained, chased with a nervous swallow. "Not at first."

She thought of that moment in the upside-down castle when they found the Shadowlands' half of the Heart Tree in its first form, before she chose to stay and made it a key. When he'd kissed her, a real kiss, and passed on all that magic, made himself the more suitable vessel in anticipation of the Kings' coming.

He'd told her he loved her. She supposed that was when he realized it.

"But then I did." Solmir's gaze went from Raffe to Neve. "As much as I could."

Raffe nodded. His fingers flexed by his side. "Just one punch, then."

He delivered it as soon as the words left his mouth. Solmir reeled back, but when he straightened, it was with a rueful grin. "Oh, come on, don't you want to make it worthwhile? You and the Wolf can both take a shot, I've got nothing to lose but time."

"Stop, Solmir."

Almost a whisper; still, it rang. Every eye turned to Neve.

All this time, she'd agonized over how she would explain this to Raffe, to Red, to everyone who cared about her and hated Solmir, as if the two were part and parcel, something that came together automatically.

But those two words—the way she delivered them, maybe—seemed to do all her explaining for her.

She looked to Red, hoping her sister would understand, her sister who'd married a monster and become one herself. Their paths mirrored even in this, both of them falling for someone inhuman and following in their footsteps, only to be thrust back into rude humanity.

Red swallowed. She took a shaky breath, then looked to Solmir, eyes narrow and fierce. "I want you to know," she said, "that the only thing saving you is her."

"Same as it ever was," Solmir murmured.

Raffe stepped back, the effort of it conscious. "I'm thankful for what you did," he said. "But I never want to see you again."

"Believe me, you won't." Solmir wiped the blood off his jaw. "I'm not sure exactly what I'm going to do with my newfound humanity, but it will be something far away from here."

It twisted Neve's gut. Red's eyes darted to her, like she could tell.

Solmir didn't look at her, but she could tell he wanted to. Instead, he raised a brow at Eammon, standing behind Red. "What do you say, Wolf? You want one more round before I go?"

There was something hopeful in it, like Solmir wanted Eammon to hit him. If Eammon heard it, he didn't let it sway him. Red's husband shook his head. "I'm with Raffe. We're done."

"We're done," Solmir repeated, hands raised, walking backward, a pained smirk on his mouth. Then his hands dropped, and he turned, headed into the snow.

"Solmir..." Damn her, Neve could barely get out any word but his name.

He glanced over his shoulder, a flash of blue. "It's done, Neve," he murmured. "Let it be done."

Then he trudged away. And she let him.

They all stood there a moment, still figures in snow. Neve took a deep breath. Closed her eyes.

Steeling her spine, she turned to Raffe. "I loved you."

He didn't miss the past tense, and he didn't seem upset by it. Raffe nodded, his hand on Kayu's at his side, the action absent and natural. "I loved you, too."

One decisive nod, the matter closed. The love she and Raffe had shared was real, but it was different now, changed into something warmer and more placid. Kayu would need someone by her side who knew the Valleydan court, who could help her navigate her new role.

Her lip lifted in a bittersweet smile. She'd always thought that Raffe would make an excellent consort.

"Let's go to the Keep." This from Red, and said with a forced cheerfulness that only made it clear none of them had any idea what to do now. "It's better than standing out here in the cold."

Haltingly, the others started moving toward the border of the woods, glad that someone had given them something to do other than stand there. Neve stood still for a moment, watching that figure dwindle smaller in the snow.

Then she turned and followed her sister.

Low voices, murmuring as they walked—Fife, saying something that Neve didn't catch but that made Eammon bark surprised laughter. Kayu, leaning in with a smile to whisper to Raffe. Lyra and Red walked together, and Neve heard Lyra mention something about the air feeling strange, about pins and needles in her fingers.

Good people who would do good things. Maybe not always—maybe those forks in the road would make them choose different paths sometimes, walk somewhere in the gray in-between—but good people nonetheless.

She thought of Solmir. Of trying for goodness.

So deep was she in her thoughts that she didn't realize Red was waiting for her at the edge of the forest until she almost ran into her.

Red grabbed her shoulders, held her steady. Her eyes were wet, and there was a small, sad smile on her face. "Go make him tell you goodbye."

Neve's brow furrowed. "What?"

"You deserve a proper goodbye, dammit." Red dashed at her eyes. "I won't stand for my sister to be cast off without one, even if I begrudge the air he breathes."

Neve huffed a laugh that sounded more like a sob.

"So go make him tell you goodbye," Red said, "or I will."

And that was all the motivation Neve needed to turn and run.

"Wait!" It ripped out of her, stronger than she felt it should sound as she fumbled through snowdrifts in her borrowed boots. "Stay *right there!*"

To her surprise, he did.

The former god in the snow stood still, letting her approach at her own pace. Wind teased at his long hair, sending tendrils of it out to almost touch her face. His eyes were the color of lake ice, blue and burning.

They just stood there a minute, the once-Queen and once-King. Neither was sure how to move. How to step forward from all they'd done.

"What do you want, Neve?" Apprehension in his voice, like he expected her to ask for more than he could give. He knew this was an ending, too.

She swallowed. "A real goodbye."

Relief on his face, and a thorn-sharp sorrow.

His rings were cold against her skin when she reached out, grabbed his hand. The one she still wore on her thumb clicked against the one on his smallest finger. He'd never asked for it back. "Does it feel as strange to you as it does to me?"

"You holding my hand," he murmured, "or the sudden onset of humanity?"

"Both," she answered. Turning their palms, lacing their fingers together.

"The first feels natural," Solmir said, looking down at their linked hands instead of her face. "The second...I don't know yet." A deep breath, those blue eyes pressing closed. "I feel...heavy."

She thought of the hollowness in her chest, the empty space where a soul had been. And she thought of his soul, the thing he'd so painstakingly disentangled from Shadowlands magic. "You know what you said about souls being mostly a nuisance?"

He nodded, one confused brow arched.

"I'll be able to tell you if I agree soon." She tried to smile, but it fell apart. "I've lost mine."

He didn't look surprised. Solmir cupped her cheek, those silver rings points of ice, lifted her face so he could see her tear-pricked eyes. Tentatively, like even now he thought she might push him away, he rested his forehead against hers. "If there's anything I've learned, it's that souls are malleable things," he murmured into the space between them. "Lost and found all the time."

She laughed, but it shattered on the end, became almost a sob. The former god held her close, frozen pine filling every breath.

"Can I even be human without a soul?" she asked, the plume of it rising between them in the cold. "Soullessness is what marked the Old Ones as different from us. What made them monstrous. How can I be anything but a monster without one?"

"Because you aren't." He said it so simply, so sure. "You won't be a monster, because you aren't a monster." Solmir gently pushed her out from him, hands on her shoulders. "You are *good*, Neve. How often do I have to tell you that before you'll believe it?"

"More than you'll get time for," she whispered. "Right?"

She could go with him. She'd considered it as she ran toward him in the snow, but only briefly. Both of them needed time. Space. There was a whole world Neve had never really explored, and she wanted to, desperately. And Solmir...he had his own darkness to wrestle with. More atoning.

Still, she wanted to know, so she asked.

"Would you let me go with you?" she murmured.

"Are you going to ask?"

"No."

He nodded. "That's for the best."

They stood bent toward each other, and for a moment she thought he would kiss her. But he didn't, and strangely, it was a relief. This already felt like it might rend her heart in half, and now that she was soulless, her heart was all she had.

One more burning moment, the two of them staring at each other. Then Solmir bowed deeply. "My Queen."

"Not a Queen anymore."

"Always will be to me." Then he turned, walked away over the snow. She watched until he faded into the drifting white.

Neve curled her hand against her chest, the thud of her heart, the rattle of her breath in and out of her lungs. Her mind swirled with thought and feeling, unchanged since she'd lost her soul, still fragile and heady and confusing. All the things that made her human.

Slowly, she turned back to the woods, to where the rest of them waited. Her equally soulless sister, held together by a knowledge of who she was and the deep love of the people she cared about, her newly human brother-in-law who could go through the world without being its Wolf. Raffe and Kayu and Fife and Lyra, all navigating how to live when magic might be at your fingertips, when you could be god or monster or human and still willing to burn it all down for those you loved.

Red waited at the border of what had been the Wilderwood. When Neve got close, she held out her hand.

Neve grasped it.

Epilogue

Raffe

He refilled Kayu's wineglass without being asked. She didn't look up from the papers crowding the desk—greetings in every language Raffe had ever seen written, all in calligraphy at varying levels of ornate—but she sighed in appreciation and took a long sip, nearly spilling some on the letter she was currently reading.

Raffe peered over her shoulder, taking his own sip from the neck of the bottle. "Who's that one from?"

"The First Duke of Alpera." Kayu pushed the letter away and sat back. A stack of blank paper sat next to her hand, along with a fresh pen and inkwell, but she didn't reach for them. "He sends deepest condolences for our loss, says he has the highest hopes for my reign, and that he looks forward to speaking candidly about renegotiating grain prices."

He took another drink, pulling a face. "I wouldn't look forward to that, personally, but to each their own."

"I do have one piece of good news." Kayu sifted through letters until she found the one she was looking for—the paper less fine, the writing more economical and less flourishing. "Valdrek wrote back. He thinks official sovereignty sounds like the best idea for everyone still above where the Wilderwood used to be, since they've been governing themselves for so long anyway. Valdrek agreed to be my emissary in exchange for shipbuilding supplies, now that the fog has lifted and they can sail from there." She beamed, then put the letter in one of her haphazard stacks that apparently signified concluded business. "One thing down! Approximately fourteen thousand to go!"

In the month since Neve came back—and then left again—Kayu had stepped almost seamlessly into her role as Valleyda's queen. There'd been minor pushback, mostly from nobles who didn't like the idea of their next queen being an outsider, but after a meeting of the council, all had agreed that the line of succession was clear. Since Neve died without an heir, the throne went to Kayu.

The funeral had been one of the strangest things Raffe had ever experienced, which was truly a feat. Funerals for Valleydan queens were strangely private affairs—the family prepared the body and stood vigil over the pyre alone. Nobles and subjects didn't see any of it until the ashes were presented. He'd burned a thorny branch and one of Neve's old gowns, attended by Kayu and Arick.

Usually, a priestess would attend the burning, too, but there were none in Valleyda. News of the High Priestess's death had spread, though, apparently, it was being spun by the Order as self-inflicted. The few rumors Raffe had heard made it sound as though the Order had put all their trust in Kiri, curved their dying religion in her direction. Now that she was gone, faith was quietly fading. The Order and the Kings had long been something that most paid the barest homage to, and Raffe expected even that would be gone sooner rather than later. The world moving on, finding new gods.

Kayu had already preemptively canceled the prayer-taxes, a move that vexed Belvedere beyond belief. But, she argued, canceling them now would put them in the other monarchs' favor, rather than having to wait for them to try to weasel out of the taxes on their own. She also made a point of telling Belvedere that she never had any intention of taking money under false pretenses, and they all knew the prayer-taxes were pointless.

So now she had to negotiate things like grain prices. Candidly, if the Duke of Alpera's letter was to be believed. But Raffe thought she could do it.

And he could help, as her Consort.

It'd been prudent. That's what he told himself, when he put the idea forward to the council. He'd wondered if they'd allow it—typically, a foreign-born inheriting queen would have to marry a Valleydan citizen—but the council agreed that Raffe would fulfill that role just fine. He'd lived in Valleyda for most of his life, and he was a convenient tie to Meducia, their greatest ally. A marriage between him and Kayu made sense, especially as they released Floriane from annexation.

He dropped a kiss on her forehead. She smiled.

"Here's another one, from Elkyrath." She tapped the letter on the table. "All they sent were condolences for Neve's death."

It still sounded so strange to say out loud. In the end, though, it'd been the easiest lie to tell. Neve *had* died, after all. And when she left the Keep, days after coming back to life, it's what she'd told them to tell the nobles.

Raffe had woken early, that morning. Two days after everything happened, and all of them were still at the Keep—some of them because they didn't know where else to go, some of them because they wanted to stay close to others.

That was why he'd stayed. To stay close to Neve. Things were different between them now, but he still wanted to make sure she was safe. That she was as well as she could be.

So when he was walking to the kitchen and heard her and Red talking quietly in the foyer, he'd followed their voices.

Neve was dressed for traveling. A long cloak, leggings, and a too-large tunic that she'd undoubtedly borrowed from Red, a pack slung over her shoulder.

"I need to," she'd said, murmuring as if she didn't want to wake anyone.

"I understand, really, I do." Red's tone and the look on her face made the statement a lie. "But why can't you stay here, just for a little bit? Or let someone go with you—"

"No." Neve shook her head. "I need to go alone, Red. I just... I just need some space. Away from here. Away from..."

"Everything?" Red's voice edged to a break.

Raffe stepped forward then, not caring that he was interrupting, his immediate need for coffee upon waking forgotten. "You're leaving?"

Neve sighed. Nodded, lips pressed to a thin line.

Clearly, she expected resistance, for Raffe to form a united front with Red. But instead, Raffe nodded. He'd probably do the same thing, if he'd been through what she had. The desire for space, for distance between herself and the place where her life had reached such a definitive closing point, made perfect sense to him.

He'd thought Red would rage at that, but instead she almost mirrored her sister's stance, arms crossed, mouth tightly closed. Her eyes shone, and Raffe thought fleetingly that the past two days was the most he'd ever seen the Valedren sisters cry. "Please be careful," she said quietly. "And please come back."

"I always will," Neve whispered.

"Good morning!"

Arick. He stood halfway down the stairs, dark hair tousled, sunny grin on his face, and still looked at them all as if he had no idea who they were. His green eyes went from bright to concerned when he saw Red. "Or not good?"

"Everything is fine, Arick." She waved a hand, wiped at her eyes.

He didn't look convinced—even without his memories, Arick still seemed uniquely attuned to Red's emotional state, a fact that bemused Eammon—but he nodded. "I'm going to get breakfast. I can't remember much, but I do seem to recall a recipe for pancakes." He looked closer at Neve. "Oh. You're leaving."

She bit her lip. Nodded.

Arick met them at the bottom of the stairs, and for a moment Raffe was stricken by the synchronicity of it—the four of them, together again, the bonds between them so altered they were nearly unrecognizable.

"What should I tell them?" Raffe asked. "I mean, the lie has been that you're sick."

"Tell them I died, then." Neve snorted. "It won't even be a lie, not really."

"There's something, at least." Raffe ran a hand over his close-shorn hair. "I was getting too good at lying for my own comfort."

Arick's lips twisted. "I look forward to recovering my memories. It seems you all have had quite an adventure."

"You could say that," Red murmured.

Another bout of silence. Then Arick moved toward the kitchen archway. "Goodbye, then."

"Goodbye," Neve whispered.

Then she slipped out the door, into the woods. Into the world she'd saved. Red and Raffe had stood there a long time, staring and silent.

"If you're willing to share, I'll take some wine. I don't even mind that you drank from the bottle."

Arick's voice startled Raffe from reverie as he strode into the queen's suite as if he owned it. He was dressed like his old self now, a doublet and breeches rather than the white, flowing garments he'd been wearing when he came back from the dead. Or almost the dead. Red had tried to explain it to Raffe, and he'd never quite grasped it. Certainly not enough to tell Arick about it.

In any case, Arick was here. His family estate was ready for him in Floriane—to the knowledge of everyone in court, he'd never left, and he would be taking over the small country's rule sooner rather than later—but he seemed to want to stay near Raffe, in Valleyda.

Raffe still wasn't sure what the best course of action was, as far as telling Arick about his old life. So far, he'd given it to him in snatches—he was the betrothed of the queen who'd just died, and been in an accident that caused his memory loss. He didn't tell him that Neve was the queen in question, didn't mention Red other than as the former queen's sister. He'd tell Arick eventually. Somehow.

There were worse things than a blank slate.

For now, he poured his old friend a glass of wine.

Red

She'd never thought it would be Eammon who'd initiate another trip to the sea.

The small house, in a strange turn of events, belonged to Kayu. It was a tiny, one-room structure built on stilts right at the waterline, the only thing for miles in either direction, with a large deck that set out over the water and a giant bed taking up most of the space inside. After a thorough use of said bed, Red was standing on the porch, leaning against the railing and letting the sea breeze dry the sweat into her hair.

"What's on your mind?" Eammon, still shirtless, came through the door with a bottle of wine—Meducian, provided by Raffe—and two chipped mugs. He poured healthy servings into both, handed one to Red.

She took it without looking away from the tide. "Same thing as always."

He didn't pry further. Eammon nodded, tousled her hair, and took a drink.

Red closed her eyes. Over the month since she and Neve destroyed the Wilderwood and the Shadowlands, she'd grown mostly used to the empty feeling in her chest, so much so that now she didn't notice it unless she went looking. But other than that hollowness, being soulless didn't seem much different.

It had taken her a week to fully explain to Eammon what she and Neve had done, what it had cost. She hadn't realized how afraid she was to tell him until she was in the thick of it, vainly attempting to keep her tears from halting the truth, terrified he might not love her anymore once he knew she no longer had a soul. That was what people fell in love with, right? Souls?

But he'd gathered her in his arms and pressed his forehead against hers. "I love *you*," he said simply, with the vehemence of a prayer. "I don't care about anything else."

And then he'd proven it, which she didn't mind at all. Red hoped Neve had someone who could reassure her in the same way, if she needed it.

But she thought the one person who could was long gone by now.

"Do you think I should've made her stay?" she murmured against the lip of her cup.

Beside her, Eammon sighed, though it wasn't in frustration so much as sympathy. She'd asked this question over and over again, never satisfied with any answer.

"I think," Eammon said carefully, "that you have to let Neve do what she feels is right." He took another long sip of wine, the wind teasing his tangled black hair around his scarred shoulders. "And if that's wandering all over the continent for reasons unknown, you have to let that be fine with you."

The reasons weren't really unknown, though. Maybe Neve thought she was just going traveling to soothe the itch in her center, but Red knew her sister, and Red knew that deep down in her soulless depths, Neve wanted to find Solmir.

What Red still didn't know was how she felt about that.

She turned, picked up Eammon's arm to drop it over her shoulders and burrow into his side. He made a surprised, pleased noise, dropping a kiss into her hair before drinking more wine.

The air around them shimmered, a quick effervescence that could've been a trick of the light were it not for the slight tingle in Red's fingertips. "Did you feel it that time?"

"Not in the slightest," Eammon answered, and didn't seem upset about it at all.

The way he moved was so different now. Before, Eammon had walked heavily, every motion seeming burdened even after he and Red split the Wilderwood between them. Now, though he still bore the scars he'd made for the forest through all those centuries, Eammon had left the weight of magic behind. All of it, seemingly. Red could sense the tiny frissons of it in the atmosphere, wild power waiting to be harnessed. Eammon sensed none of it, and he seemed perfectly fine. Unencumbered humanity.

She didn't begrudge him that. He'd been so tired for so long, and their lives were still an uncertainty—she didn't doubt they'd live an unnaturally long time, after being so suffused with magic, but immortality was no longer a foregone conclusion.

And where would she go once she died, soulless as she was? She had no real concept of an afterlife, but having a soul seemed to be a requirement for such a thing.

Red pressed harder into Eammon's side. She'd shared those fears with him, too, all her truths pouring out like they always seemed to do with her Wolf. And he'd caressed her hair and kissed her gently. "Wherever you go," he murmured, "I'll find you."

She maneuvered herself between Eammon's chest and the railing, still facing the ocean so her back pressed against his abdomen, and drained the rest of her wine. "I don't think I'll ever use magic again," she said quietly. "Even though I can feel it. Do you think Lyra will?"

"I think Lyra feels it too strongly to completely ignore, even if she wanted to." His muscles moved behind her as he shrugged. "But if anyone is worthy of magic, it's her. And Fife will help."

Fife felt the magic in the air, too, though he tried mostly to ignore it. The two of them were off traveling, Lyra finally towing Fife along as she explored the places they'd been left out of for so long.

All of them scattered, trying to make sense of the world they'd made. In Valleyda, Raffe and Kayu were embroiled in the intricacies of succession, the official story being that Neve had died of disease. And there was Arick, still without his memories, building a whole new life. One where he'd never been wrecked by Solmir and Kiri and the Kings, one where he'd never loved her and been ruined for it.

So much uncertainty, so much change. But the Wolf behind her was her constant.

She sighed, laid her head back against Eammon's shoulder. "Come down to the water with me."

He gave a long-suffering sigh—he'd made it extremely clear on the trip to Floriane in a hired coach that this journey was solely for Red, and he was still no great friend to the ocean—but followed her down the winding steps from the porch to the sand.

The water was warm. Sunset played along its edges, painting them in pink and gold. Red pulled off the shirt of his that she'd stolen, ran into the shallows, splashing at Eammon and teasing him when he sputtered. He followed her in, lifting her up, threatening to dunk her.

They settled, both breathing hard, her legs wrapped around his hips, his chin resting on her head as they floated in the warm salt of the sea. "It's been strange," Red murmured into the space between their slicked skin. "But I wouldn't change it."

"Not one thing," Eammon agreed, and pressed his mouth to hers.

Neve
One year later

She was surprised to discover how much she liked taverns.

There hadn't been many opportunities for her to spend time in them before. As the First Daughter, she'd been always guarded; as the Queen, she'd been too busy, too recognizable. Now that she was neither of those things—just Neve, wholly human Neve—she had plenty of opportunities to sneak in for a pint.

Another surprise—she vastly preferred ale to wine. Wine gave her a headache, ale just made her mind pleasantly fuzzy. This ale, in particular, was extremely good. The Alperans knew their way around a beer barrel.

The pretty woman behind the counter filled her cup again and tossed her an inviting wink. Neve just gave her a wan smile back, uninterested.

In her first months of wandering, she'd allowed herself occasional companions. Fleeting people to keep her warm, nothing lasting. All she saw when she closed her eyes was Solmir, anyway. But now she'd taken to keeping herself alone. She *liked* being alone, another surprising discovery about herself. In her former life, she'd had so few opportunities for solitude.

Neve smiled slightly, took a sip of her ale. Slowly, methodically, she was finding out who she was. Every day, the empty ache left by her absent soul lessened, and some days she really had to try to feel it at all.

Souls are mostly a nuisance, she told herself. Again.

Every time she heard it in her head, it was in his voice. Neve didn't want to think she was traveling only to try to find Solmir, but it would be foolish to pretend that wasn't part of it. She didn't know what they could have—if they could have anything—but she wanted to see him. To know he was as well as he could be.

She twisted the silver ring around her thumb.

"Did you hear about Freia?"

The man sitting next to her addressed a newly arrived companion, knocking snow from his boots as he took a place at the bar. He shook his head, cheeks reddened by wind. "Other than that her youngest was sick, no. He hasn't taken a turn for the worse, I hope?"

The first speaker smiled. "The opposite. He's better. Woke up this morning like he'd never been ill at all." He leaned closer to his friend. "But to hear Freia tell it, his healing wasn't just a turn of luck. She says she...did something."

"Did something?"

A nod. "Magic." He drained his beer. "I went by to visit, and she looked like she'd seen a ghost. Just sitting there, staring at her hands as if she'd never seen them before. Said last night she put her palm on the boy's forehead, wishing for a miracle, and saw all this gold around her fingers. Felt something happen." He shrugged. "Could be she was dreaming, but the boy woke up good as new today. She's convinced it was magic, like long ago. Slinking around in the air and waiting to be used."

"That was centuries ago."

The first man shrugged. "Stranger things have happened."

Didn't Neve know it. She quirked a tiny grin into her own tankard. The world had magic again, and sooner or later, someone would make up a story as to why. She wondered how close the myth would get to the truth. She wondered if someday, someone would tie the disappearance of the Wilderwood and the last Second Daughter to the rebirth of magic.

She wondered if she'd be part of the story at all. Neve couldn't decide whether she wanted to be or not. It seemed exhausting, being a myth.

A shiver worked through her shoulders as the door opened again. Alpera was just as cold as Valleyda, especially up here on the northern end, right before you crossed into the Wastes—wide expanses of nothing but rock and ice. But inside the tavern, the light was warm and the air warmer, heated by the dancers enthusiastically twirling to the sounds of a string band at the back of the main room. Neve didn't understand the language they sang in, but the lilts of it reminded her of Solmir. She tapped her foot in spite of herself.

"A dance, sweet one?"

The asker was a big man, with shoulders half as wide as Neve was tall and a ruddy, good-natured face. A refusal was poised on her tongue, but his eyes were kind and his smile genuine and he didn't strike her as the kind who might pressure for more if she gave in to a dance. She'd grown skilled at ferreting those out.

So, with a laugh, Neve relented, tossing back the rest of her ale and offering her hand. "Lead the way."

The steps to the folk dance were as foreign to her as the language the song was sung in, but her partner—Lieve, he informed her, making the introduction between twirls with a dramatic flutter of his hand—led her gallantly through them, gentle touches on her wrist or hip to guide her in the right direction. Neve caught on eventually, laughing hard enough to give herself a side stitch, and when the dance ended with everyone clapping both hands above their heads and stomping one foot, she was right on the beat.

After, the band meandered into a slower tune, one whose melody seemed vaguely familiar. A slight frown creased Neve's brow as she turned toward the instrumentalists, trying to think of where she'd heard it before.

Lieve smiled, a more reserved one now, and once again held out a somewhat tentative hand. "Slow dances are much easier to learn."

She could see in his face that he wanted to keep dancing with her, that though he'd never push for something she didn't want to give, he still wanted to ask. The kind thing to do would be to cut him loose now, let him down gently.

Neve smiled, patted his hand. "I'm afraid I—"

But then a lone voice rose to accompany the melody, and Neve remembered.

It was the lullaby, the same one Solmir had sung her in the crumbling cabin at the edge of the inverted forest. The one he'd sung as he carved the night sky she still kept in her pocket, a worry stone to run her fingers over.

She stood there stricken, until Lieve's face went from sheepish embarrassment to concern. "Sweet one, are you—"

"May I cut in?"

The voice reverberated from behind her, the one she'd heard in her head all these months. Neve whirled around.

He looked the same and wholly different. Solmir's hair was still long, worn pulled back in the front, bleached lighter by time in the sun, making his dark brows that much more severe. The scars on his forehead weren't quite as pronounced, their color blending into his pale skin. His blue eyes were only on her.

"You," she murmured.

"Me," he answered.

Behind her, Lieve excused himself with as much dignity as possible. Neve barely noticed. She and Solmir stood in the center of a sea of twisting dancers and neither was quite able to move.

There were too many words between them. Too many things to try to say. So they didn't. Solmir held out his hand, and Neve took it, and he pulled her in. Neither of them tried to follow the steps of the dance, just swayed against each other, listening to each other's heartbeat.

She wanted to ask him if he was staying. She wanted to ask what he'd been doing with his time, if he'd been wandering like her, set adrift in a world that slowly changed to be what they'd made it. She could feel magic itching at her fingertips sometimes; could he? Did he try to ignore it as vehemently as she did, unsure if he'd ever be able to stomach the thought of power again? Did he look into the faces of people he passed, wondering if they could feel it, too?

Wondering if they were good?

"Have you decided to believe me?" His lips brushed the shell of her ear, as if he'd read the thoughts in the pattern of her heartbeat.

Neve pressed farther into him. "Tell me again."

A deep breath, as if he could root her in his lungs. "You are good."

Her eyes closed. "So are you."

"Not yet," he said, close enough to her ear that she could feel his smirk. "But getting closer, I think."

And she wanted to ask if he'd be there to tell her in the morning, the day after that, if he was staying to make sure she believed it for the rest of whatever strange lives they'd lead. But she didn't, because she couldn't be sure of the answer, and if she closed her eyes and breathed him in, lived in this moment until she wrung it dry of everything it could give her, it could be enough. For right now, it could be enough.

That was something else she'd learned about herself.

But when the song ended, when Solmir stepped away from her, when he cocked his head at the staircase that led to her room like a question— she nearly ran up the stairs, grabbing his hand as she went, tugging him behind her.

Acknowledgments

Second books are strange beasts; they take both careful planning and a relinquishing of what you thought they were supposed to be. And if you're blessed with as incredible a publishing team as I have been, they're also a ton of fun.

First thanks goes to my husband, Caleb—I plan to read you the funny parts out loud from now until eternity. Thank you for always letting me play my book playlists in the car, even though you really hate Mayday Parade. You're wrong, but I love you anyway.

Thanks always to Whitney Ross, my agent and partner in crime, who was the first person to tell me Neve deserved her own book. In this, as in everything else, she was right.

And to my amazing editor, Brit Hvide—working with you has been an absolute dream, and I'm so excited that I get to keep doing it. Thanks for pushing me to make every book better than the last, and for always calling me on my bullshit. You are the best of the best.

The entire team at Orbit has been a dream come true, especially Ellen Wright, Angela Man, Angeline Rodriguez, and Emily Byron. I am so appreciative of all the hard work you do to get these books out to the readers who will love them. You are incredible.

To Erin Craig—insert Blair and Serena gif here. Thankful for you always.

To the Pod, Laura, Steph, Anna, Jen, and Joanna—I really can't tell you all how much you mean to me. Let's send each other *Buzzfeed* quizzes until the end of time.

To Saint, Kit, Bibi, Suzie, Emma, Rosie, MK, and Jenny—your support and friendship mean everything.

And to Sarah, Ashley, Chelsea, Stephanie, Nicole, Jensie, Liz, and Leah—you all have been my ride-or-dies for YEARS, and you're never getting rid of me. Thank you for letting me send you unhinged TikToks. Thank you for being there.

And to the readers—I'll never be able to express how thrilled I am that you've let this story that lived in my heart for so long live in yours, too. None of this happens without you.

extras

orbit

meet the author

Photo Credit: Caleb Whitten

HANNAH WHITTEN has been writing to amuse herself since she could hold a pen, and she figured out sometime in high school that what amused her might also amuse others. When she's not writing, she's reading, making music, or attempting to bake. She lives in a farmhouse in Tennessee with her husband, her children, a dog, two cats, and probably some ghosts. You can find her online at hannahfwhitten.com, and @hwhittenwrites on Twitter and Instagram.

Find out more about Hannah Whitten and other Orbit authors by registering for the free monthly newsletter at orbitbooks.net.

if you enjoyed
FOR THE THRONE

look out for

THE FOXGLOVE KING

Book One of
The Nightshade Crown

by

Hannah Whitten

From the instant **New York Times** *bestselling author of* **For the Wolf** *comes a brand-new adventure filled with dark secrets, twisted magic, glittering palaces, and forbidden romance.*

When Lore was thirteen, she escaped a cult in the catacombs beneath the city of Dellaire. And in the ten years since, she's lived by one rule: Don't let them find you. Easier said than done, when her death magic ties her to the city.

459

Mortem, the magic born from death, is a high-priced and illicit commodity in Dellaire, and Lore's job running poisons keeps her in food, shelter, and relative security. But when a run goes wrong and Lore's power is revealed, Lore fully expects a pyre, but King August has a different plan. Entire villages on the outskirts of the country have been dying overnight, seemingly at random. Lore can either use her magic to find out what's happening and who in the King's court is responsible, or die.

Lore is thrust into the Sainted King's glittering court, where no one can be believed and even fewer can be trusted.

It'd been three years since any of them had paid rent, but Nicolas still thought to send his most unfortunate son to ask at the end of every month. Lore assumed they drew straws, and assumed that someone cheated, because it was always the youngest and spottiest of the bunch. Pierre, his name was, and he carried it nearly as poorly as he carried his father's already overfull purse.

A dressing gown that had seen better days dripped off one shoulder as Lore leaned against the doorframe at an angle carefully calculated to appear nonchalant. Pierre's eyes kept drifting there, and she kept having to press her lips together not to laugh. Apparently, a crosshatch of silvery scars from back-alley knife fights didn't deter the man when presented with bare skin.

She had other, more interesting scars. But she kept her palm closed tight.

A cool breeze blew off the harbor, and Lore suppressed a shiver. Pierre didn't seem to spare any thought for wondering why she'd exited the house barely dressed, right at the edge of autumn. An easy mark in more ways than one.

"Pierre!" Lore shot him a dazzling grin, the same one that made Michal's eyes go heated and then narrow before asking what she wanted. Another twist against the doorframe, another seemingly casual pose, another bite of wind that made a curse bubble behind her teeth. "It's the end of the month already?"

"I—um—yes." Pierre managed to fix his eyes to her face, through obviously conscious effort. "My father...um, he said this time he means it, and..."

Lore let her face fall by careful degrees, first into confusion, then shock, then sorrow. "Oh," she murmured, wrapping her arms around herself and turning her face away to show a length of pale white neck. "This month, of all months."

She didn't elaborate. She didn't need to. If there was anything Lore had learned in twenty-three years alive, ten spent on the streets of Dellaire, it was that men generally preferred you to be a set piece in the story they made up, rather than trying to tell it yourself.

In that regard, Pierre didn't disappoint. From the corner of her eye, she saw his pale brows draw together, a deepening blush lighting the skin beneath his freckles. They were all moon-pale, Nicolas's boys. It made their blushes look like something viral.

His eyes went past her, to the depths of the dilapidated row house beyond. It was morning, though only just, and the shadows hid everything but the dust motes twisting in sun shards. Not that there was much to see back there, anyway. Michal was still asleep upstairs, and Elle was sprawled on the couch, a wine bottle in her hand and a slightly musical snore on her lips.

"Is there an illness?" Pierre kept his voice hushed, low. His face tried for sympathetic, but it looked more like he'd put bad milk in his coffee. "A child?"

Lore's brows shot up. In all the stories she'd let men spin about her, *that* was a first. But beggars couldn't be choosers. She gently laid a hand on her abdomen and let that be answer enough. It wasn't technically a lie if she let him draw his own conclusions.

She was past caring about lying, anyway. In the eyes of the Bleeding God, Lore was damned whether or not she kept her spiritual record spotless. Might as well lean into it.

"Oh, you poor girl." Pierre was probably younger than she was, and here he went clucking like a mother hen. Lore managed to keep her eyes from rolling, but only just. "Do you know who the father is?" He raised his hand, settled it on her bare shoulder.

And every nerve in Lore's body seized.

It was abrupt and unexpected enough for her to shudder, to shake off his hand in a motion that didn't fit the soft, vulnerable narrative she'd been building ever since she opened this damn door. She'd grown used to feeling this reaction to dead things—stone, metal, cloth. Corpses, when she couldn't avoid them. It was natural to sense Mortem in something dead, no matter how unpleasant, and at this point, she could hide her reaction, keep it contained.

She shouldn't feel Mortem in a living man, not one who wasn't at death's door. Her shock was quick and sharp, and chased with something else—the scent of foxglove.

Her fingers closed around his wrist, twisted, forced him to his knees at the edge of the doorframe. It happened quick, quick enough for him to slip on a stray pebble and send one leg out at an awkward angle, for a strangled "*Shit!*" to echo through the silent morning streets of Dellaire's Harbor District.

Lore crouched so they were level. Now that she knew what to look for, it was clear in his eyes. All poisons worked differently, and foxglove was one of the riskier ones. Pierre's gaze was bloodshot and glassy; his heartbeat under her hand, slow and irregular. He'd gone to one of the cheap deathdealers, then.

One who didn't know how to properly dose their patrons, one who only gave them enough to make them sick, not bring them to death's threshold. Stupid.

The Mortem under Pierre's skin throbbed against her grip, thumping and meaty, a second, diseased pulse. Mortem was in everyone—the essence of death, the darkness born of entropy—but the only way to use it, to bend it to your will, was to nearly die. To touch oblivion, and for oblivion to touch you back, then let you go.

Most died before they got there. More never got close enough, earning only a sour stomach or blindness or a scattered mind for their efforts. And some didn't actually want the power at all, just the euphoria, a poison high that skated you near death, but not near enough to wield it. It took a closer brush with eternity to use Mortem than most were willing to try.

The Bleeding God and Buried Goddess knew Lore wouldn't have, if she'd had the choice.

"Here's what's going to happen," she murmured to Pierre. "You are going to tell Nicolas that we've paid up for the next six months, or I am going to tell him you've been visiting deathdealers."

That was enough to make his eyes widen, glassy and poison-heavy or not. "How—"

"You stink of foxglove and your eyes look more like windows." Not exactly true, since she hadn't noticed until she'd sensed the Mortem, but by the time he could examine himself, the effect would've worn off anyway. "Anyone can take one look at you and know, Pierre, even though your deathdealer barely gave you enough to make you tingle." She cocked her head. "You weren't after it to *use* it, I hope, or you were completely swindled. Even if you only wanted the high, you didn't get your money's worth."

The boy gaped, the open mouth under his window-glass eyes making his face look fishlike. He'd undoubtedly paid a handsome sum for the pinch of foxglove he'd taken. If it wasn't so imperative that she lie low, Lore might've become a deathdealer. They made a whole lot of coin for doing a whole lot of jack shit.

Pierre's unfortunate blush spread down his neck. "I can't— He'll ask where the money is—"

"I'm confident an industrious young man like yourself can come up with it somewhere." A flick of her fingers, and Lore let him go. Pierre stumbled up on shaky legs—Buried Goddess and her plucked-out eyes, she should've *known* he was on something; he stood like a colt—and straightened his mussed shirt. "I'll try," he said, voice just as tremulous as the rest of him. "I can't promise he'll believe me."

Lore gave him a winning smile. Standing, she yanked up the shoulder of her dressing gown. "He better."

Eyes wide, the boy turned down the street. The Harbor District was slowly waking up—bundles of cloth stirred in dark corners, drunks coaxed awake by the sun and the cold sea breeze. In the row house across the street, Lore heard the telltale sighs of Madam Brochfort's girls starting their daily squabbles over who got the washtub first, and any minute now, at least two straggling patrons would be politely but firmly escorted outside.

Soothing, familiar. In all her years of rambling around Dellaire, here was the only place where it really felt like home.

"Pierre?" she called when he was halfway down the street. He turned, lips pressed together, clearly considering what other things she might blackmail him with.

"A word of advice." She turned toward Michal's row house in a flutter of threadbare dressing gown. "The real deathdealers have morgues in the back."

* * *

Elle was awake, but only just. She squinted from beneath a pile of gold curls through the light-laden dust, paint still smeared across her lips. "Whassat?"

"As if you don't know." There was barely enough coffee in the chipped ceramic pot for one cup. Lore poured all of it into the stained cloth she used as a strainer and balled it in her hand as she put the kettle over the fire. If there was only one cup of coffee in this house, she'd be the one drinking it. "End of the month, Elle-Flower."

"Don't call me that." Elle groaned as she shifted to sit. She'd fallen asleep in her dancer's tights, and a long run traced up each calf. It'd piss her off once she noticed, but the patrons of the Foghorn and Fiddle down the street wouldn't care. One squinting look into the wine bottle to make sure it was empty, and Elle shoved off the couch to stand. "Michal isn't awake, we don't have to pretend to like each other."

It was extremely obvious to anyone with the misfortune of being in the same room as the two of them that Lore and Elle didn't like each other, and Elle's older brother knew it better than most. But Lore just shrugged.

Elle pushed past her into the kitchen, the spiderweb cracks on the windows refracting veined light on the tattered edges of her tulle skirt. She peered into the pot. "No coffee?"

Lore tightened her hand around the cloth knotted in her fist. "Afraid not."

"Bleeding *God*." Elle flopped onto one of the chairs by the pockmarked kitchen table. For a dancer, she was surprisingly ungraceful when sober. "I'll take tea, then."

"*Surely* you don't expect me to get it for you."

A grumble and a roll of bright blue eyes as Elle slunk her way toward the cupboard. While her back was turned, Lore tucked the straining cloth into the lip of her mug and poured hot water over it.

Still grumbling, Elle scooped tea that was little more than dust into another mug. "Well?" She took the kettle from Lore without looking at her. "How'd it go?"

Lore kept her back turned as she tugged the straining cloth and the tiny knot of coffee grounds from her cup and stuffed it in the pocket of her dressing gown. "We're paid up for six months."

"Is that why you look so disheveled?" Elle's mouth pulled into a self-satisfied moue. "He could get it cheaper across the street."

"The dishevelment is the fault of your brother, actually." Lore turned and leaned against the counter with a cat's smile. "And barbs about Madam's girls don't suit you, Elle-Flower. It's work like any other. To think otherwise just proves you dull."

Another eye roll. Elle made a face when she sipped her weak tea, and sharp satisfaction hitched Lore's smile higher. She took a long, luxurious sip of coffee.

Another knock, shivering through the morning quiet and nearly shaking the thin boards of the row house.

Elle rose up on her tiptoes to look out the small window above the sink, head craned toward the door. She raised her eyebrows. "Your boss is here."

Swearing under her breath, Lore plunked her mug on the counter with a dangerous *clink* of porcelain and strode toward the door.

"Hey," Elle whined from the kitchen. "There was *too* coffee!"

For the second time that morning, Lore wrenched open the door, the squealing hinges echoing through the row house. "Val."

Green eyes glinted beneath a faded scarf, white-blond hair a corona around pale cheeks sunburned to ruddy. Val always wore the same scarf and the same braid, and she never wasted time with pleasantries. "You and Michal need to be headed for the Ward in fifteen minutes."

"Good morning to you, too."

"I'm not playing, mouse." Val gave a scrutinizing look to Lore's dressing gown, her mussed hair. "This could be a hard job. You need to be ready."

"I always am." In the ten years since Lore had been running poisons for Val, she'd never had the woman herself show up like this, right before a drop. A confused line carved between her brows. "Is something the matter, Val?"

The older woman shifted on her feet, her eyes flicking away for half a heartbeat before landing on Lore's again, steadied and sure. "It's fine," she said. "This is just a new client. I want to make sure everything goes off without a hitch."

"It will." Lore nodded, channeling confidence she didn't quite feel. "Don't worry."

Val stood there a moment longer, mouth twisted. Then, whip-quick, she leaned forward and pressed her dry lips to Lore's forehead. She was off the stoop and headed down the road before Lore's teeth clicked shut, chasing the shock off her face. The old poison runner might be the closest thing Lore had to a mother, but she still wasn't one for affection.

Lore's brows stayed furrowed as she went back to the kitchen and collected her coffee again—though the look on Elle's face said chances were high she'd spit in it—then drifted toward the stairs.

Could just be nerves. It'd been a while since Val picked up a new client. Most of the deathdealers they ran poison for were well established, dug into the underbelly of the city like rot in a tooth. Mari, Val's partner, was historically picky about who the team took on. The two of them had raised Lore on tough love and hard choices, and *be careful about who you let in* was high on their list of lessons.

Maybe the collective coffers were low, though Lore couldn't imagine why. It seemed to her like more and more people were gobbling down poison every day, stuffing their mouths with petals to chase power or death or a few hours of kaleidoscopic high.

Whatever. She'd never had a head for the business side of things. Just the running. Lore was good at running.

The stairs of the row house were rickety, like pretty much everything else, and the fourth one squeaked something awful. Lore made sure to grind her heel into it. Fifteen minutes weren't much, and Michal needed the job with Val's team. Even with rent taken care of, they could use all the coin they could get. She didn't want him in the boxing ring again.

Michal had apparently heard the squeak. He was sitting up when Lore pushed aside the ratty curtain closing off their room, sheets tangled around his waist and dripping off the side of the mattress to pool on the floor. The light through the cracked windows caught his gold hair, so like his sister's. He ran a hand through it and squinted at her. "Coffee?"

Lore leaned against the doorframe. "Last cup, but I'll share if you come get it."

"That's generous, since I assume you need it." He grumbled as he levered himself up from the floor-bound mattress, holding the sheet around his naked hips. "You had another nightmare last night."

Her cheeks colored, but Lore just shrugged. The nightmares were a recent development, and random—she could never remember anything about them, nothing but darkness and the feeling of being trapped. Usually she could trace her dreams back to a source, pick out a piece and see how something she'd thought about that day had alchemized as she slept, but since the nightmares were so vague, she couldn't figure them out. It made them more unsettling. "Sorry if I kept you up."

"At least you didn't scream this time. Just tossed and turned." Michal took a long drink from her proffered mug, though his face twisted up when he swallowed. "Damn, that's bitter."

She didn't tell him that the taste was probably not improved by his sister's spit. "Val came by. We need to leave in fifteen minutes."

Another squint. His eyes were blue, also like Elle's, but deeper and warmer. If Elle's eyes were morning sky, his were twilight. "Guess I'll be late, then." He leaned in and kissed her, mouth hungry and as warm as his eyes.

She kissed him back, just for a moment, before pushing him away. "If we don't make it to the rendezvous point in time, it'll be *crawling*."

Michal frowned, concern cutting through the haze of heat and sleep. "I wish Val didn't make you watch the drop point," he said quietly. "It isn't safe."

The solemnity in his voice made her stomach swoop, for more reasons than one. Lore poked his shoulder, and her lips bent the corner of a smile. "I can take care of myself."

"Doesn't mean you should have to."

Her wry smile flickered.

But Michal didn't notice, running a hand through his hair to tame it while he bent to pull clothes from the piles on the floor. The sheet dropped, and Lore allowed herself an ogle.

"I don't get why she always gives you the most dangerous jobs," he said, voice muffled by thin cotton as he pulled a shirt over his head. "Didn't she and Mari *raise* you? They act like your mothers, and then they send you to be the lookout. It doesn't make sense."

Lore just shrugged. She'd only given Michal her history in broad strokes, an outline she had no intention of ever filling in.

He knew it, too, though sometimes he prodded. "Yes, they raised me, but that just means I know my shit," she said, turning to slip her feet in her well-worn boots. "And we need to get a move on. Val won't tolerate lateness, even if the guilty party is my..."

She didn't finish the sentence. She wasn't quite sure how.

The mischievous curve to Michal's mouth said he noticed. Now dressed, he crossed the room, hooking his hands languidly on her hips as she turned away to hide an answering smirk. He leaned forward, chest against her back, brushing his lips over the shell of her ear. "Your what?"

Lore turned, flicking his collarbone, biting her lip to keep it from turning up. "*Mine*," she finished decisively, and let him kiss her again.

Still, cold clawed into her chest. She could feel Mortem everywhere, now, like her realization that it was somewhere it shouldn't be had sharpened her perception of all the places where it *should*—the cloth of Michal's trousers beneath her hands, the stones in the street outside, the chipped ceramic of the mug on the windowsill. Here on the outskirts of Dellaire she didn't feel it as intensely as she would near the catacombs, near the Citadel, but it was still enough to make her skin crawl.

The Harbor District, on the southern edge of Dellaire, was as far as Mortem would let her go. She could try to hop a ship, try to trek out on the winding roads that led into the rest of Auverraine, but it'd be pointless. She was tied into this damn city as surely as death was tied into life, as surely as the crescent moon carved into her palm.

All of it, reminders—she shouldn't linger too long. She shouldn't get too close. It wasn't safe.

Michal's mouth found her throat, and she arched into him, closing her eyes like it might shut out the cold in her chest and the itch of so much death. Her fingers clawed into his hair, and

470

his arm tightened around her waist like he might lift her up, carry her to their mattress on the floor, and forget all about running poison for Val. Forget about everything but safety found in skin.

She wanted to let him, and that was the decision-maker, in the end. Lore had to stop using people like fences, like moats, like things to wall herself in with.

Masking it as playful, she pushed Michal away. "*Go.* Val won't wait."

Blue eyes hazy, Michal pulled back. "Will you?"

He asked every day. Neither of them knew if it was a joke. But today, there was something newly apprehensive in his face, as if for the first time he knew the answer was *no.*

So Lore kissed him again instead of speaking.

He lingered at her lips a moment before stepping back. "I'll see you at the Northwest Ward, right?" He switched into reciting the plans for the drop-off instead of asking her anything further. Smart man, not to push. "Right at the bell, when the guard is changing. Leave the cart at the old storefront. And you'll stay with it until it gets picked up from the catacombs' entrance."

A tiny shiver slunk over Lore's skin at the mention of the cata-combs. "Shouldn't take long," she said, trying to sound reassuring. It wasn't so bad, the outer branches of the catacombs—outside of the city center, they were little more than tunnels, the dead were all kept under the Citadel—but being close to them still made her feel twitchy.

Lore knew the catacombs. Not just in the sense of some-one who remembered the twists and turns of a place—Lore felt them, a part of her, like if you turned her skin inside out, a map would be printed on the wet, bloody underside. And because of that uncanny *knowing*, she'd be able to tell if someone was coming through them.

Another handy side effect of a dark, strange childhood.

She'd been the watchdog for the crew since she was thirteen, when Mari first found her wandering the streets with blank eyes, and brought her back to Val's headquarters at the docks. Val, thankfully, didn't ask why or how Lore had acquired such an odd skill. She just put it to use.

And if Lore stayed with Michal, who was increasingly vocal about his objection to her dangerous position, things could get precarious for him.

She closed her eyes.

A calloused hand on her cheek made them open again. Michal kissed her, sweetly this time, without heat. "Be careful," he murmured. Then he slipped out.

Alone, Lore took a deep, ragged breath. Despite the chill outside, the sun through the cracked window was warm on her skin. She rested her forehead against the glass and counted her breaths, an old trick from childhood to calm her heart, calm her nerves.

They'd still be looking for her. Lore knew that. And the longer she stayed in one place, the easier she'd be to find.

She could move in with Val and Mari again, if she wanted. That door was always open. But having someone who tried to control her comings and goings never sat well with her, after...after what her life had been like before.

So not with Val, then. But staying here wasn't an option.

It'd be awkward to end things, with both her and Michal on Val's team. Val would intercede where she could once she knew the situation, but it would be impossible for them not to see each other at all. Val had warned her as much, when Lore first took up with Michal. Lore had thrown it back at her, saying that Val and Mari had obviously made it work, so why couldn't she? But both of them knew it wasn't the same, that it was an argument for the sake of arguing. Lore wasn't looking to be settled. Lore was always running, always moving. She just liked to rest sometimes.

She sighed, forehead still pressed to the glass. It'd be easiest if she could make Michal hate her, probably. And though the thought was an ice pick, she knew she could do it. She could make Michal glad she'd decided to leave, hurt him so badly that he'd never try to get close again.

That would be easiest.

Lore opened her eyes, straightened. She pushed aside the curtain that served as a door and walked down the stairs.

A flounce of tulle on the couch indicated that Elle had resumed her pre-breakfast position. Lore huffed a laugh. "Bye, Elle-Flower."

Elle groaned in response.

At the threshold, Lore paused, placing her hand along the weather-beaten wood of the lintel. She'd stayed here longer than any of the previous places—with Michal, with Elle. He was a good man, one of the first she'd encountered. He cared about her.

She'd miss him more than the house, more than the safety. *That* was new.

Another pat against the doorframe. "Goodbye," Lore murmured, then she slipped out to lose herself in Dellaire's streets again.

if you enjoyed
FOR THE THRONE
look out for

ONE DARK WINDOW

by

Rachel Gillig

Elspeth Spindle needs more than luck to stay safe in the eerie, mist-locked kingdom of Blunder—she needs a monster. She calls him the Nightmare, an ancient, mercurial spirit trapped in her head. He protects her. He keeps her secrets.

But nothing comes for free, especially magic.

When Elspeth meets a mysterious highwayman on the forest road, her life takes a drastic turn. Thrust into a world of shadow and deception, she joins a dangerous quest to cure Blunder of the dark magic infecting it. Except the highwayman just so happens to be the king's own nephew, captain of the most dangerous men in Blunder . . . and guilty of high treason.

He and Elspeth have until Solstice to gather twelve Providence Cards—the keys to the cure. But as the stakes heighten and their undeniable attraction intensifies, Elspeth is forced to face her darkest secret yet: The Nightmare is slowly, darkly taking over her mind. And she might not be able to stop him.

Nothing is free.

Nothing is safe.

Magic is love, but also, it's hate.

It comes at a cost.

You're found, and you're lost.

Magic is love, but also, it's hate.

It began the night of the great storm. The wind blew the shutters of my casement open, sharp flashes of lightning casting grotesque shadows across my bedroom floor. The stairs creaked as my father climbed on tiptoe, my handmaid's cries still ripping through the corridors as she fled. When he came to my door, I was unmoving, delirious, my veins dark as tree roots. He pulled me from the narrow frame of my childhood bed and cast me into a carriage.

I awoke two days later in a wood, in the care of my aunt Opal.

When the fever broke, I woke every day at dawn to inspect my body for any new signs of magic. But the magic did come. I slept each night praying it had all been a grave mistake and that soon my father would come to bring me home.

I felt their eyes on me, servants quick to scurry away, my uncle with a narrowed gaze, waiting. Even the horses shied away from me, somehow able to sense my infection—the sprouting persuasion of magic in my young blood.

In my fourth month in the wood, my uncle and six men rode through the gate, their horses slick with sweat, my uncle's sword bloodied. I cast my gangly body into the shadow of the stable and watched them, curious to see my reserved uncle with a triumphant smile on his mouth. He called for Jedha, the master-at-arms, and they spoke in low, swift voices before turning to the house.

I stayed in the shadows and trailed them through the hall into the mahogany library, the wooden doors left slightly ajar. I can't remember what they said to one another—how my uncle had gotten the Providence Card away from the highwaymen—only that they were consumed with excitement.

I waited for them to leave, my uncle fool enough not to lock the Card away, and I stole into the heart of the room.

Writ on the top of the Card were two words: *The Nightmare*. My mouth opened, my childish eyes round. I knew enough of *The Old Book of Alders* to know this particular Providence Card was one of only two of its kind, its magic formidable, fearsome. Use it, and one had the power to speak into the minds of others. Use it too long, and the Card would reveal one's darkest fears.

But it wasn't the Card's reputation that ensnared me—it was the monster. I stood over the desk, unable to tear my eyes away from the ghastly creature depicted on the Card's face. Its fur was coarse, traveling across its limbs and down its hunched spine to the top of its bristled tail. Its fingers were eerily long, hairless and grey, tipped by great, vicious claws. Its face was neither man nor beast, but something in-between. I leaned closer to the Card, drawn by the creature's snarl, its teeth jagged beneath a curled lip.

Its eyes captured me. Yellow, bright as a torch, slit by long, cat-like pupils. The creature stared up at me, unmoving, unblinking, and though it was made of ink and paper, I could not shake the feeling it was watching me as intently as I was watching it.

Trying to grasp what happened next was like mending a shattered mirror. Even if I could realign the pieces, cracks in my memory still remained. All I'm certain of was the feel of the burgundy velvet—the unbelievable softness along the ridges of the Nightmare Card as my finger slipped across it.

I remember the smell of salt, and the white-hot pain that followed. I must have fallen or fainted, because it was dark outside when I awoke on the library floor. The hair on the back of my neck bristled, and when I sat up, I was somehow aware I was no longer alone in the library.

That's when I first heard it, the sound of those long, vicious claws tapping together.

Click. Click. Click.

I jumped to my feet, searching the library for an intruder. But I was alone. It wasn't until it happened again—*click, click, click*—that I realized the library was empty.

The intruder was in my mind.

"Hello?" I called, my voice breaking.

Its tone was male, a hiss and a purr—oil and bile—sinister and sweet, echoing through the darkness of my mind. *Hello.*

I screamed and fled the library. But there was no fleeing what I had done.

Suddenly it became bitterly clear: The infection had not spared me. I had magic. Strange, awful magic. All it had taken was a touch. Just a touch of my finger on velvet, and I had absorbed something from within my uncle's Nightmare Card. Just a single touch, and its power stalked the corners of my mind, trapped.

At first, I thought I had absorbed the Card itself—its magic. But despite all my efforts, I could not speak into the minds of others. I could only speak to the voice—the monster, the Nightmare. I poured over *The Old Book of Alders* until I knew it by heart, searching for answers. In his description of the Nightmare Card, the Shepherd King wrote of one's deepest fears brought to light—of hauntings and terror. I waited to be frightened, for dreams, for nightmares. But they did not come. I clenched my jaw to keep from screaming every time I entered a dark room, certain he would rip through the silence with a terrifying screech, but he remained quiet. He did not haunt me.

He said nothing at all until the day the Physicians came, when he saved my life.

After that, the noises of his comings and goings became familiar. Enigmatic, his secrets were vast. Stranger still, the Nightmare carried his own magic. To his eyes, Providence Cards were as bright as a torch, their colors unique to the velvet trim they bore. With him trapped in my mind, I too saw the Cards. And when I asked for his help, I grew stronger—I could run faster, longer, my senses were keener.

At times, he remained dormant, as if asleep. Others, he seemed to take over my thoughts entirely. When he spoke, his smooth, eerie voice called in rhythmic riddles, sometimes to quote *The Old Book of Alders*, sometimes merely to taunt me.

But no matter how often I asked, he would not tell me who he was or how he had come to exist in the Nightmare Card.

Eleven years, we've been together.

Eleven years, and I've never told a soul.

I did not often walk the forest road at night, and never alone. I cast my gaze over my shoulder, once more hoping Ione would come up behind me, that we might brave the darkness together, arm in arm.

But the only thing to stir at the edge of the wood was a white owl. I watched it soar from the thicket, startled by its quick descent. Night crept over the trees and with it came animal noises—creatures emboldened by darkness. The Nightmare shifted in the back of my consciousness, sending shivers up my spine despite the tepid air.

I crossed my arms over my chest and quickened my step. Just a few more bends in the road and I would be able to see the torches from my uncle's gate, beckoning me home.

But I did not make it to the second bend before the highwaymen were upon me.

They came out of the mist like beasts of prey—two of them, garbed in long, dark cloaks and masks obscuring all but their eyes. The first caught me by my hood and slid his other hand around my mouth, smothering the scream that escaped my lips. The second drew a dagger with a pale ivory hilt off his belt and held the tip to my chest.

"Stay quiet and I will not use this," he said, his voice deep. "Understand?"

I said nothing, choking on fear. I'd walked these woods half my life. Not so much as a dog had given me pause—certainly not highwaymen, not this close to my uncle's estate. They were either brazen or desperate.

I reached into the darkness of my mind, grasping for the Nightmare. He slithered forward with a hiss, stirred by my fear, awake and present behind my eyes.

I nodded to the highwayman, careful not to stir his dagger.

He took a step back. "What's your name?"

Lie, the Nightmare whispered.

I drew a hitching breath, my hair still imprisoned in the first highwayman's clutch. "J-J-Jayne. Jayne Yarrow."

"Where are you going, Jayne?"

Tell him you have nothing of value.

So they might take their gain in flesh? I don't think so.

Rage began to boil behind my fear, the Nightmare's wrath a metallic taste on my tongue. "I—I work in the service of Sir Hawthorn," I managed, praying the weight of my uncle's name would frighten them.

But when the highwayman behind me gave a curt laugh, I knew I'd said the wrong thing.

"Then you know about his Cards," he said. "Tell us where he keeps them, and we'll let you go."

My spine straightened and my fingers curled into fists. The punishment for stealing Providence Cards was a slow, grisly, and public death.

Which meant these were no ordinary cutpurse highwaymen.

"I'm just a maid," I lied. "I don't know anything."

"Sure you do," he said, pulling my hood until the clasp was pressed against my throat. "Tell us."

Let me out, the Nightmare said again, his voice slithering out from behind his jagged teeth.

Shut up and let me think, I snapped, my eyes still on the dagger.

"Hello?" said the highwayman at my back, tugging my hood again. "Can you hear me? Are you daft?"

"Wait," cautioned the one with the dagger. I could not see his face behind the mask, but his gaze held me pinned. When he stepped closer I flinched, the scent of cedar smoke and cloves clinging to his cloak.

"Search her pockets," he said.

Trespassing fingers roved down my sides, across my waist and down my skirt. I clenched my jaw and held my nose high. The Nightmare remained quiet, his claws tapping a sharp rhythm.

Click. Click. Click.

"Nothing," said the highwayman.

But the other was not convinced. Whatever he saw in my eyes—whatever he suspected—was enough to keep his dagger stilled just above my heart. "Check her sleeves," he said.

Help me, I shouted into my mind. *Now!*

The Nightmare laughed—a cruel, snakelike hiss.

White-hot heat cut through my arms. I hunched over, my veins burning, and muffled a cry as the Nightmare's strength coursed through my blood.

The man behind me took a step back. "What's wrong with her?"

The highwayman with the dagger watched me with wide eyes and lowered his blade. He lowered it only a moment—but a moment was all the time I needed.

My muscles burned with the Nightmare's strength. I struck the highwayman's chest with brutal force, knocking the dagger out of his hand and propelling him backward onto the road. His head slammed heavily onto soil just as the highwayman behind me reached for his sword.

But the Nightmare's reflexes were faster. Before the highwayman could free his blade from its sheath, I caught him by the wrist, my grip so tight my nails dug into his skin. "Don't come here again," I said, my voice not entirely my own.

Then, with the full force of the Nightmare's strength, I pushed him off the road into the mist.

Branches snapped as he struck the forest floor, a curse echoing through the moist summer air. I did not wait to see him get back up. I was already running—running full speed for my uncle's house.

Faster, I called over the drumming of my own heart.

My legs strained with effort, my steps so quick and so sure my heels hardly touched the ground. When I reached the yellow torchlight, I threw myself against the brick wall near my uncle's gate and forced myself to take long, burning breaths.

I peered over my shoulder down the road, half expecting to see them chasing me. But the darkness was merely punctured by trees and mist.

The Nightmare and I were alone once more.

My arms continued to burn, even when my lungs grew steadier. I rolled up my sleeves, staring at the ink-black tributary of magic shooting down my veins, flowing from the crook of my elbow to my wrist. It looked just as it had that night eleven years ago when the fever took hold of me.

It looked just the same every time I asked the Nightmare for his help.

I waited for the ink to burn off, grinding my teeth against the stinging warmth. *Do you think they realized I'm infected?*

They're Card thieves. Report you, and they report themselves.

A few moments later, the warmth was gone, its ghost twitching up and down my arms. I leaned up against the brick wall and heaved a rattling sigh. *Why does it burn every time?* I asked.

But the Nightmare had already begun to vanish into the dark chasm of my mind. *My magic moves*, he said. *My magic bites. My magic soothes. My magic frights. You are young and not so bold. I am unflinching—five hundred years old.*

Follow us:

f **/orbitbooksUS**

𝕏 **/orbitbooks**

▶ **/orbitbooks**

Join our mailing list
to receive alerts on our
latest releases and deals.

orbitbooks.net

Enter our monthly
giveaway for the chance
to win some epic prizes.

orbitloot.com